Praise for
Ever Faithful

"If you haven't yet discovered Karen Barnett's Vintage National Parks novels, *Ever Faithful* is a great place to start. Vividly set amid the stunning beauty of Yellowstone's bubbling hot springs, forested mountains, and thundering waterfalls, *Ever Faithful* celebrates the history of one of the US's oldest national parks. It provides a fascinating glimpse into the workings of the Civilian Conservation Corps of the 1930s, giving a time of national crisis the immediacy of heart and hope. Elsie, Nate, and the whole cast of characters had me caring, cheering, and second-guessing as a suspenseful plot and engaging prose kept the pages turning. *Ever Faithful* will delight fans of Karen's other National Parks novels and new readers alike."

—LORI BENTON, author of *Burning Sky, The King's Mercy,* and other historical novels

"Karen Barnett captures the lively time and place of Yellowstone in the 1930s in this charming and wholesome love story. Firefighting CCC crews and hardworking pillow punchers (housekeepers in Yellowstone-speak) live, work, and play in the national park while learning to trust themselves and their faith to make life-changing decisions. This book made me want to go to a dance in the now-demolished Canyon Hotel, take a ride in a yellow bus driven by a 'jammer,' and wander around Mammoth hoping to run into Herma Baggley, Yellowstone's first female interpretive ranger."

—ALICIA MURPHY, park historian at Yellowstone National Park

"With just the right touch of mystery and romance, Karen Barnett brings 1930s historic Yellowstone National Park to life in her new novel, *Ever*

Faithful. You'll fall in love with her strong yet vulnerable hero, Nate Webber, who struggles to overcome his hidden challenges, and you'll want to cheer for her spunky heroine, Elsie Brookes. Karen's background as a park ranger and her skillful research bring richness and depth to this delightful and inspiring story. Highly recommended!"

—CARRIE TURANSKY, award-winning author of *No Ocean Too Wide* and *Across the Blue*

"I loved, loved, loved Karen Barnett's *Ever Faithful*! Set in iconic Yellowstone National Park during the Depression, this story offers high stakes, rugged romance, and a mystery with a twist. *Ever Faithful* is as wonderful as the wonderland it's set in. Thank you, Karen, for a fantastic read!"

—LESLIE GOULD, Christy Award–winning and best-selling author of over thirty novels, including *A Faithful Gathering*

Ever FAITHFUL

A VINTAGE
NATIONAL PARKS NOVEL

KAREN
BARNETT

WATERBROOK

EVER FAITHFUL

Scripture quotations are taken from the King James Version and the New King James Version®.
Copyright © 1982 by Thomas Nelson Inc. Used by permission. All rights reserved.

Trade Paperback ISBN 978-0-7352-8958-1
eBook ISBN 978-0-7352-8959-8

Copyright © 2019 by Karen Barnett

Cover design and illustration by Mark D. Ford

Published in the United States by WaterBrook, an imprint of the Crown Publishing Group, a division of Penguin Random House LLC, New York.

WATERBROOK® and its deer colophon are registered trademarks of Penguin Random House LLC.

Library of Congress Cataloging-in-Publication Data
Names: Barnett, Karen, 1969– author.
Title: Ever faithful : a vintage national parks novel / Karen Barnett.
Description: First edition. | Colorado Springs : WaterBrook, [2019]
Identifiers: LCCN 2018046955| ISBN 9780735289581 (paperback) | ISBN 9780735289598 (electronic)
Subjects: LCSH: Yellowstone National Park—Fiction. | Christian fiction.
Classification: LCC PS3602.A77584 E94 2019 | DDC 813/.6—dc23
LC record available at https://lccn.loc.gov/2018046955

Printed in the United States of America
2019—First Edition

10 9 8 7 6 5 4 3 2 1

*In memory of Billie Barnett, who
always had a teacher's heart.
And to all those who work to change lives
through education, including the teachers in
my own family: Patty, Janelle, and Jonnie.*

A thousand Yellowstone wonders are calling,
"Look up and down and round about you!"

—JOHN MUIR, *Our National Parks,* 1901

One

April 1933
Yellowstone National Park, Wyoming

Elsie closed her eyes for a moment and breathed in the steamy air, imagining she stood beside Grand Prismatic Spring instead of the massive laundry boiler in the back of the Mammoth Hot Springs Lodge. She tucked a damp curl behind her ear before loading another stack of folded bedsheets and towels onto the molly cart. After pushing it through the swinging doors, she rolled the cart down the wooden ramp, the outside air a welcome respite. Two more summers—three at most. That's all it would take.

Mary stood waiting, fiddling with the pink kerchief protecting her pale-blond hair. "There you are. If we get these last housekeeping cabins finished in time, we can meet Hal and Bernie at the cafeteria for lunch." She flashed a smile at Elsie. "You'll come, won't you?"

Elsie guided the cart's wheels through the icy slush on the sidewalk. "You've only been back in Yellowstone two days, and you're already angling for dates? I thought you told me you weren't seeing pack rats anymore."

Pack rats, pillow punchers, pearl divers—the concession staff had a language all its own, and it all sounded like more laughs than being boring old porters, maids, and dishwashers. The rangers lumped the lot of them together, calling them all *savages*. No one could remember how the ridiculous name was chosen, but it had stuck for close to fifty years already.

"Hal's been promoted to front desk at the hotel—hadn't you heard? And though he's hardly the man of my dreams, I don't see any better choices around here at the moment." Mary leaned in with a conspiratorial air. "I hear the new gear jammers are coming in a couple of weeks. They always hire the best-looking fellas to drive the tour buses."

"That's probably why the jammers are notorious for having a girl at every stop." Elsie veered left to avoid a puddle. "I'd like to join you for lunch, but I need to run home and check on Mama. I'll be back right after, and we can fold the rest of the sheets."

"I've been meaning to ask how she is. Your last two letters didn't sound promising."

A knot formed in Elsie's stomach. "She had a few bad spells this winter. The doctor says it's her heart. He wants her to rest more."

"Has she had heart problems before?"

"She had rheumatic fever as a child." Elsie tightened her grip on the cart handle. "But I've never seen her like this."

"I'm sorry to hear that. She's like a second mother, not just to me, but to all the pillow punchers." She unlocked the cabin door and pushed it open. "I suppose it was a good thing you were here to help and not off at college with the rest of us."

Elsie had told herself the same, though it did little to ease the sting of being left behind. "When does Rose arrive, do you know? I've missed her."

"Around the same time as the jammers, I believe." Mary grabbed Elsie's hand and squeezed. "I'm glad I came early. We'll be the three musketeers for at least one more summer. Who knows where Rose and I will go after graduation?" She heaved a sigh that stirred the dusty air in the room. "Oh my. This cabin looks worse than the last one. How is that possible? Ugh, the smell."

"That's what happens when you latch the door and leave it abandoned for months on end." She understood too well. Elsie reached for the bottle of vinegar and a handful of newspapers. "I'll start on the glass. You can knock down the cobwebs."

Mary wrinkled her nose and lifted the broom. "If I find any spiders, it'll be up to you to dispatch them."

As Elsie scrubbed the veil of dirt from the panes, sunlight filtered into the tiny space and revealed a fine layer of dust coating the room. Just as spring renewed the world each year, it was the maids' job to refresh the old cabins and prepare for the visitors to come.

She'd continue making beds and sweeping floors until she had enough money for the teacher program at the University of Montana. She'd dreamed of being a teacher since she was little, and spending her winters helping at the school in Gardiner, just outside the park's northern boundaries in Montana, had only deepened the desire. Every new student arrived with potential hidden inside, like the seeds sealed up in the cones from the lodgepole pine trees. It was her job to help them find it.

After sweeping and dusting, Mary tucked the crisp white sheets around the mattress and patted the top. "I think we're almost done here. Are you sure you can't join us for lunch? Hal's brother will be odd man out if you don't come."

"Bernie is an odd duck, no matter what I do." Elsie shoved the dresser back in place after cleaning behind it. "Of course, I'm no catch myself." Her hand went to her collar out of habit, her fingers checking that the blouse was buttoned all the way to the neck.

Mary straightened, her eyes darkening. "Bite your tongue, Elsie Brookes. Any man would count himself lucky to earn your affection. You just don't grant it easily." She leaned on the broom. "Maybe this summer we'll both find nice boys to take us away from all this."

"Take us away? Why would anyone want to leave?" Elsie glanced out the open door toward the distant springs, the late morning sunshine casting a golden glow over the rising steam. If she could secure a teaching position in Gardiner, she would stay forever.

"You've got a classic case of park fever. You should just marry a ranger and get it over with." Mary dropped her broom and dustpan into the cart. "What about the new fella? He's a little quiet, but he looks like a movie star. What was his name?"

"Teddy Vaughn." Elsie managed to speak his name without her voice wobbling. The first time she'd encountered the brown-eyed ranger, she'd somehow lost all ability to string words together or even swallow for a heady moment. But she couldn't let her heart go there. No one would ever want her in that way. "I'm dedicating my life to education; you know that. I'm not looking to get married."

"I'll never understand you." Her roommate wrinkled her nose. "Why waste time on other people's children when you can have ones of your own? You and Ranger Vaughn would make beautiful babies."

Elsie couldn't help giggling at Mary's silliness. Just having her friend back in the park made everything brighter. "Why don't you head off to meet the boys for lunch? I can finish the last cabin."

Mary brightened. "Really? But what about your mother?"

"I'll still have time to check in. Go have fun."

Her friend tore off her kerchief and fluffed her hair. "You're the best, Els. I'll give Bernie a peck on the cheek from you."

"Don't you dare."

Elsie made short work of the last cabin and then pointed the molly cart in the direction of the laundry. A small herd of elk grazed on the green lawn surrounding the lodge. A cow elk, heavy with her unborn calf, lifted her head to stare back, chewing leisurely. The animals had over three thousand square miles of park to wander but seemed to prefer it here. And the visitors enjoyed the close proximity to the wildlife.

"There's my girl. I was looking for you." Her father strode toward her, the broad-brimmed Stetson casting shadows over his face. "Are you finished for the morning?" He reached for the cart handles.

"You don't have to do that. I've got it."

"You think I'm too good to haul laundry?" He cast her his usual grin. "How do you think I won your mother's affections? It wasn't with my stamp collection. Or my dashing good looks."

"She said it was your servant's heart." Her mother's true words wrapped around her own heart.

"Yes, indeed. 'Therefore, all things whatsoever ye would that men should do to you, do ye even so to them.' It's not just the key to a happy home, Elsie—"

"I know. It's the key to a happy life." Only her parents could make the golden rule sound romantic. "And I'll remember that when I finally get all my pennies saved for college. Then I'll make you proud."

"I've always been proud. You were meant for bigger things than this place."

"Bigger than Yellowstone?" The idea rippled through her. "That's ridiculous."

"Bigger than being a simple ranger like your old man."

Her eyes slid over her father's frame, his long years dedicated to the park showing in his stooped shoulders. Too much work, too few staff. It was as much a part of the job as the uniform. "You look tired. What have you been doing today?"

"I went to the new campsite, making sure everything's ready."

"You're opening the campground already? It's only April."

They arrived at the laundry, and he slid the molly into the waiting spot. "Not the auto camp. The ECW camp."

She thought through the acronym. As the daughter of a federal employee, she was accustomed to negotiating alphabet soup, but this was a new one. "What's that?"

"Emergency Conservation Work. Part of the president's 'New Deal.' He's recruiting unemployed men from around the country to work on federal lands. A tree army, he's calling it, but with civilians—the Civilian Conservation Corps. I'm overseeing the groups coming here to Yellowstone."

"What will they be working on?" She grabbed the cleaning rags and tossed them into the waiting tubs.

"Whatever needs doing, I'm told. I'm hoping we can put some of the fellows on the bark beetle problem. That's the biggest conservation emergency we've got at present."

"Do they have forestry backgrounds?"

"I guess we'll find out. I hope so."

Her heart lifted as she followed him back outside. "Maybe you won't have to work so hard this summer."

"We'll see. There's always more to do. And actually—work is why I came looking for you." He scrubbed a hand over his mouth and chin, as if trying to hide the lines gathering there. "This came across my desk today." He took a folded sheet of paper from his breast pocket. "I'm afraid it's not good news."

Unease trickled through her. "What is it?"

He unfolded the memorandum and handed it to her. "After last year's low occupancy rates, the Yellowstone Park Hotel Company has decided to keep the Mammoth Hotel closed this season and use only the housekeeping cabins and campground."

Had she just complained about making beds? Elsie scanned the typed memo, zeroing in on the last few lines that hinted at staff cutbacks. "They can't do this. People are counting on this work." Including her.

Her father shook his head. "I know. But jobs are scarce everywhere. Hardly anyone has money to waste on visiting fancy hotels. Those who are still making the trip are keeping a tight grip on their pocketbooks. Why rent a room when you can pitch a tent?"

Elsie bit her lower lip, even as the selfish thoughts bubbled up like the park's gurgling mud pots. "Who will they keep on?"

"A few pillow punchers and porters here at Mammoth, probably. We still need some folks to take care of the campground and the day lodge. But they probably won't see very many work hours."

"And the rest of the park?"

"The Lake Hotel and Roosevelt Lodge will stay closed, but the Old Faithful Inn and the Canyon Hotel will open on schedule. They'll shuffle some of the best savages to those two."

Elsie lifted her eyes and gazed out over the lines of cabins to the stately hotel in the distance. Closed? Would Mary and Rose both have jobs? Hal, Bernie, and all the others? The past few summers had been filled with their adventures and laughter. A lump settled in her throat. "I guess school will have to wait." She hated to be selfish when so many people were living hand to mouth, but she'd postponed her dream several times already. Most students started college at eighteen, not twenty-two.

Father took the paper back and folded it. "Not necessarily. I know you don't like me interfering, but I've spoken to a few people. There might be one other option for you, if you're willing."

"Anything."

"Put in for a transfer to the Canyon Hotel."

The Grand Canyon of the Yellowstone, with its pine forests and roaring waterfalls, was several hours away from Mammoth. "But Mama needs me here."

"Hear me out." His blue eyes locked on her. "I can take care of your mother. And if you do this, you might actually have the money you need by the end of *this* summer."

The world began to spin. "How?"

"They're building a second CCC camp in Canyon. We'll have four in all. President Roosevelt wants the recruits to have every opportunity to better themselves—maybe even earn a high school diploma."

"I don't understand. What does that have to do with me?"

He laid a hand on her arm. "Elsie, those fellas are going to need a teacher."

Two

Brooklyn, New York

What have you done now?" Nate kept his voice low as he tightened his fingers around his kid brother's collar and glanced down the rain-darkened Brooklyn alley. A cop stood at the entrance, blocking their path to the street. At fourteen Charlie already had two instances of shoplifting on his record. One more and they might send the youngster off to the reformatory. "How many times have I told you to keep your hands in your own pockets and out of other people's?"

"I was hungry."

"You're always hungry." Nate gave him a quick shake and released him. The truth of the statement stewed in his own gut. If he'd been able to find work, maybe the boy wouldn't be forced to snitch a bite here and there to fill his empty gullet.

Their father wasn't much help. Staggering home once or twice a month, the former cop rarely met their eyes—just plunked a few coins on the table before disappearing again.

If only Sherman had lived.

His life had become a Sears and Roebuck catalog of *if onlys*. He glared at Charlie and reached for the boy's pockets. "What did you take?"

The kid twisted away from Nate's probing. "None of your business."

"You're making it my business—keeping you out of reform school." A jolt of pain burst through Nate's hand, as if he'd been bitten by a rat. He yanked his fingers from his brother's pocket, light from the lone streetlamp glinting off the shard of glass jammed in his skin. "What's this?"

"Had to go out a window."

"Looks more like you went through one." Blood slid down Nate's knuckle. The officer was moving toward them. "Give it to me. Whatever you took, give it to me."

The boy scowled and jammed a small, paper-wrapped package into Nate's hand.

Hopefully not worth much. He shoved Charlie back toward the garbage cans. "Get out of sight. If you get taken in again—"

"Ma'll kill me."

"No, she'll kill *me*. You're my responsibility." The words burned in his throat. How many times had Sherman said that to him in years past? It had been second nature to the eldest son. Nate had never expected the mantle to fall to him. He wasn't worthy of it, a fact his father reminded him of every chance he got.

Charlie crept back, disappearing into the shadows like an alley cat. Nate noted that his brother seemed a little too practiced at making himself scarce.

An icy wind swept the chilled rain against Nate's face as he stared at the package, his blood smeared on the brown wrapping. Words spilled across the paper. It didn't matter how much he squinted; the letters refused to take shape in his mind. Given a few minutes, maybe he could sort out a few of them. He considered dumping the parcel into one of the trash cans behind him, but what would that teach his baby brother? Nate stuffed the bundle into his pocket. The kid could return it tomorrow. Would that be enough of a lesson?

"Who's back there?" The policeman advanced, a baton in one hand, light in the other. "What are you doing?"

The light blinded Nate as he curled his bloody fingers and held them close to his chest. "Bird-watching." Glib responses slipped from his tongue a little too easily these days.

The man stepped closer. "Nate? Nate Webber?"

The familiar voice sent a wash of warmth through him. "Yeah." He tipped his flat cap to shield his eyes from the glare, trying to make out the face. "Murray?"

"Never thought I'd run into you here. I'm tailing a cat burglar. A break-in. Seen anyone?"

A break-in? Nate kept his focus steady, fighting the urge to glance behind him. "Out here?"

The circle of light trailed over his open jacket, lingering on his chest. "Is that blood?"

"A scrape." He pulled the jacket closed. Still needed to fix those buttons. "Nothing to worry about."

Murray walked closer, his face appearing out of the darkness. Sherm's friend had always been a baby face, even though he had a good five or six years on Nate. The low light highlighted his round cheeks. His gaze held Nate in place. "How are things at home? Your . . . ma?"

The emotion in the man's voice cut worse than the glass. "You know how it is."

The officer's gaze dropped. "I . . . I do."

A second policeman thundered into the alley. "Murray, you got 'em?"

Murray turned his attention to Nate, his eyes pleading. "Tell me you're not involved with this, Nate. I couldn't take it. Couldn't stand giving your mom more bad news."

Nate's skin turned cold, the package weighing his pocket. He took an involuntary step back. "I-I don't know what you're talking about."

Murray's partner sidled up to him, billy club drawn. "Empty your pockets."

"Why? You need a dime?" A lump grew in his throat. What had Charlie gotten into? "Come on, we've all got empty pockets these days."

The man gripped Nate's fraying lapel, shoving him back against the brick building. "Say another word and I'll drop you, genius."

"Hey, take it easy." Murray laid a hand on his colleague's arm. "He's Sherm's brother. Unlikely he'd be knocking over jewelry stores."

The world seemed to tilt under Nate's feet. "No. You've made a—" The sight of Charlie's wide eyes peering out from between the metal trash cans stole his breath. A jewelry store? His heart sank to his shoes. Charlie was their mother's last hope—the family's, really—because no one expected much from Nate. He'd left school at ten. The best he could hope for was menial jobs at the dockyards or slaughterhouses, but lately he couldn't even get that kind of work. *At least Charlie can read and write.* And he'd do so much more, if Nate had any say in the matter.

But Charlie would accomplish nothing if he got sent up the river.

Trying to ignore the wooden club wedged against his chest, Nate thrust his hand into his jacket and drew out the package. Directing his eyes back to the two men standing in front of him, he swallowed. "I think this might be what you're looking for."

Police Chief O'Sullivan tapped meaty fingers on his mahogany desk. "Webber, I don't buy what you're trying to sell me. I've known you since you were a babe in arms. You wouldn't take a peppermint out of the candy bowl at the department St. Patrick's Day party without asking your pa first."

Because I'd get smacked up the side of the head. Sherman or Charlie could get away with those sorts of antics, but not Nate. Probably his father's attempt to make something, *anything,* out of his hopeless middle son.

O'Sullivan tipped his head down to stare over his wire-edged glasses. "And now I'm supposed to believe you're doing smash-and-grabs at jewelry stores?"

Nate tucked his feet under the chair to hide the holes in the soles of his shoes. Shouldn't he be in lockup? His family's legacy was the only reason he sat here in comfort. Sherm—saving him again, from beyond the grave. The idea prickled like so many needles. "Yes sir. Times are . . . tough."

"Don't I know it. And your family got the short end of the nightstick—in more ways than one." O'Sullivan picked up the blood-stained package. "But if this isn't the definition of red handed, I don't know what is."

Nate thrust his fingers, wrapped in Murray's handkerchief, deeper into his lap. At least he'd worked the glass free. He scrambled for a lighthearted answer, only to realize the commissioner hadn't actually asked his opinion. Silence might be the best option.

The man dumped the contents of the package across the green desk blotter—two necklaces and a ring.

Bile surged up Nate's throat. His younger sibling was on a crash course with disaster and determined to take the family with him.

"Kirschbaum Jewelry." O'Sullivan read the label on the paper. "Jewish. Is that why?"

Mr. Kirschbaum. The sweet old gentleman on the next block? Nate's jaw dropped. "No! No sir." At least, he didn't *think* so. Charlie wouldn't be into such foolishness, would he? "Just an impulse. Needed the money."

The older man sighed, shoving the gold chain around with the nib of his pen. "I worked with your father for years; you know that."

"Yes sir."

"And your brother, when he first joined the station."

As if Sherm had served for eons, rather than four short months. Gunned down in the street his first year as a cop. Nate managed a nod, his throat thick.

"Tell me what's really going on, Nate. Was it your old man?" Deep bags drooped below O'Sullivan's eyes. Perhaps he'd never gotten over drumming his friend from the force. Not that he'd had much choice.

"No." His father was a hard man and a drunk, but he wouldn't break a toothpick if it was against the law.

"Things that bad at home? What were you planning to do—pawn the stuff? Or are you working for someone else?"

Working? The mockery of the word nearly made him laugh. He set his jaw. Best to keep his mouth shut. Isn't that what hardened criminals did?

The commissioner stood and paced in front of the window. "Do you think I'm stupid, Webber? That I don't know what's really going on here?" He turned, drilling Nate with the type of glare that could glue the most nefarious crook to his chair. "I didn't get where I am by being dumb."

"Never thought you were."

"Shut it. I'm talking." The man's voice barked, all familial camaraderie vanishing from his demeanor.

Nate turned his attention to the floor. He'd grown up with the bluster; police bravado wouldn't cower him. It had long since lost its power.

"You're here because Charlie's a coward." He jabbed a finger toward Nate's face. "Your family has been splintering since the day Sherm fell. I thought I lost one man that day. Didn't realize I was burying an entire family. Your old man turned to the bottle. Your mother never leaves the house. That younger brother of yours—"

"Charlie's not—"

"No talking." O'Sullivan pounded the desk with his closed fist, finally making Nate jump. "Charlie's a coward. At fourteen he's feeding his own foolish impulses. I will not let him take the last good man from this family."

Exactly what I'm trying to avoid. Charlie's the only one with a future.

"That's why I'm putting you on the first train out of here." O'Sullivan slammed into his seat and drew out a sheet of paper.

Nate sat forward, his heart thrumming. "You're—you're what?"

"You're volunteering for this new Civilian Conservation Corps. It'll give you a chance to make something of yourself. It's made to order for a man like you—eighteen to twenty-five, unemployed, no criminal record."

With the last bit, Commissioner O'Sullivan retrieved the stained brown paper from the jewelers and crumpled it into a ball. He lobbed it into the corner wastebasket.

Nate choked. "That's evidence."

"It's garbage, and we both know it. If you're so determined to lose your freedom, at least you're going to do it at the federal government's expense."

"I don't know what you're talking about. What is this Civilian—"

"Don't you read the papers?"

A flood of heat rushed through him. "Too busy with *War and Peace.* No time left for the daily rag."

The commissioner shot him a long look over his glasses. "You got nothing but time, Webber. But I'm not letting you do *hard* time for something stupid like this. The Civilian Conservation Corps is Roosevelt's answer to unemployment and idleness. He's hiring men to work on public lands for six-month stints—a year if you do well. You're applying. Hopefully it will bring some peace to your poor mother."

My mother. Charlie. Eva. Little Lucy. "I can't leave them. They need me."

"Maybe this will be the incentive Charlie needs to step up. Be the man of the house."

"He's fourteen."

"And how old were you?" His pen scratched on the paper as he began to write. "It's not about age; it's about doing what's right. You won't teach him that by going to prison. You'll teach him by being a man." O'Sullivan huffed. "And if I have to haul the boy in here and scare him a little, I'll do it. But I won't abide you taking the fall for him."

"I'm the only one who can."

O'Sullivan paused his writing. "If you think yourself so expendable, then you should have no problem with this. At the very least, you'll be earning a paycheck."

The statement stilled Nate's arguments. "How much?"

"Thirty a month is what they're saying. Twenty-five of it automatically goes to your family. I'll have a chat with Abe Kirschbaum. I don't think he'll object once the merchandise is returned and the window repaired at no cost to him."

Nate sat back in the chair, the air leaking from his lungs. A paycheck. He hadn't seen one in months. The money was minimal, but . . . "Where would I be working? Doing what?"

"Wherever they send you, and whatever they tell you. Like the army. I figure they'll throw a shovel at you. A little ditch digging never hurt anyone." O'Sullivan slapped the paper in front of Nate. "Unless you'd rather recant your confession and let me bring Charlie in to face his crimes. Because if you get sent off to the Welfare Penitentiary, who'll step in the next time he gets itchy fingers?"

Nate stared at the document on the desk, the words swimming on the page.

"I've filled out your application. I know you're a mite"—O'Sullivan paused and clucked his tongue—"slow."

Dumb. He might as well say it. Nate closed his fingers around the fountain pen. As dumb as this whole idea. Nate scanned the paper until he found the empty line at the bottom. He drew a long breath and let it out between his lips as he inked his name. He could do that much at least. But signing his life away when he couldn't even read the terms? Something about that seemed wrong.

Three

Elsie followed Mary through the small railroad depot in Gardiner, Montana, just outside the park's northern boundary, tucking her bag of canned goods under her elbow. "You said we were only going to the grocery. Why are we here?"

Her friend grabbed her hand and tugged her behind a stack of wooden crates. "Don't you want a peek? The CCC recruits are arriving in a few minutes. Tell me you're not curious."

Curious, yes. But probably not for the same reason Mary was. Her father's flash of inspiration still sent a quiver through her stomach. She tried to imagine a classroom filled with grown men rather than children—destitute young men from around the country with varying backgrounds and skill levels.

A hum of conversations grew louder, and Mary peeked around the boxes. "They're already here!"

"Good, this will be a short stop, then. I need to get back to record eruption statistics."

"You and your geyser watching." Mary sniffed. "Who cares what time they go off? This is so much more exciting."

"I care. You've had your fun, Mary. Let's go."

"But you haven't seen them yet." She kept her cheek glued to the coarse wooden crate but groped with her free arm until it encountered Elsie's elbow. "Come, look. They're in uniform."

"Uniform?" She stepped to Mary's side, trying to peer around her shoulder.

The old army uniforms hung from the men's frames as though they were mere boys dressed in their fathers' clothing. The gaunt cheeks and oversized clothing did little to imbue this crowd with promise, though there were many smiles and laughs being shared as the fellows jostled each other on the platform. They may have been dressed as soldiers, but they sure didn't act like them.

Elsie's heart raced. How was she supposed to teach these men? They'd never listen to her.

Her friend drew back. "Well, that's disappointing." She turned, placing her gloved hands on her hips. "I guess it's back to chasing gear jammers for us."

"Gear jammers? Hal's a desk clerk, or have you tossed him over for a bus driver already?" Hal Henderson was a nice man. Mary could do far worse, if marriage was her ultimate goal.

"I haven't made any decisions yet. There's a whole grand summer ahead of me. Besides, Hal's staying here at Mammoth, and I'm going with you to Canyon." She shrugged, touching one hand to her hair. "I heard the company's bringing in some new drivers. They've got to be a more hopeful lot than these ninety-pound nothings."

Elsie examined the milling crowd. "I'm guessing many of these fellows gave up hope a long time ago."

"Hel-lo, ladies!" A short redhead ducked in from the far side of the crates, several more grinning men crowding behind him. "Looking for someone? Me, perhaps?"

Elsie scooted back until she bumped into Mary. "No. We're just . . ."

Mary steadied the crates she'd just jostled, her pose not unlike a bored Hollywood starlet out for a stroll. "No, boys. I don't see anything here worth a second glance."

The men gathering behind the ringleader laughed.

He took a few more steps, careful to keep one hand on the suspenders hitching up his sagging trousers—riding breeches that ballooned around his thighs. "Don't let these stylish threads fool you, Miss. I'm a mighty fine dancer, and I know how to show a girl a good time. Especially when she's a dead ringer for Jean Harlow."

Elsie grabbed her friend's wrist and tugged her back. "We're not interested. We're just—"

"Leave 'em alone, Red." A tall fellow with broad shoulders stepped forward and jerked his chin at the other. "Don't listen to him, ladies. He's all talk. Red might be able to manage an Irish jig, but that's about it."

The man's voice tickled in Elsie's ears. Something about how he said "tawhk." Where were these boys from?

Mary yanked free of Elsie's grasp. "And what about you?"

He grinned, cocking his head to the side. "No ma'am. I'm here to work, not dance."

"I'm Mary Prosser. And your name is?" She flashed him one of her hundred-dollar smiles.

He looked toward the throng, lowering his voice. "Nate Webber, miss."

"I'm pleased to make your acquaintance, Mr. Webber. And for your information, the savages throw some pretty keen wingdings." Her focus wandered down his puttee-clad lower legs and settled on his work boots. "So I hope some of you boys brought your dancing shoes."

"Mary." Elsie yanked on her arm. "Don't."

Red chuckled and sauntered another step forward. "Savages? I think

I'm liking the sound of this Yellowstone country better all the time. We'd love to come to your little clambake, dollface. Name the day."

Mr. Webber hooked a hand around the strap of Red's rucksack. "Sounds a little too hot for you, friend." He tipped his hat to Elsie and Mary, then steered the group back toward the main assembly.

Elsie managed a steady breath, clasping the collar tight around her throat. "Now can we go?"

Mary turned back to her, a familiar glint in her eyes. "I like him."

"Which one?" Elsie studied the retreating forms. As the taller man glanced back over his shoulder, the light caught his unusual green eyes.

"The cute one. Red, was it? I suppose that's a nickname. I wonder if he really is a good dancer?"

Elsie sighed and turned to leave, hoping her friend would fall in behind. She and Mary had been roommates for three years, their tiny staff dormitory always either ringing with laughter or hushed with whispered secrets. Mary's lighthearted antics never failed to amuse, but her obsession with the male of the species had multiplied with each summer that passed. It seemed to have reached a nearly frantic level.

"He said I looked like Jean Harlow." Mary bumped Elsie's elbow as they walked. "Hey, isn't that your father over there?"

Elsie's dad and Ranger Vaughn stood among a group of army officers. Elsie's breath hitched in her chest at the sight of the younger ranger, but she forced air through her lungs anyway. She refused to be that sort of girl.

Her father spoke to one of the army captains. "We need to get these supplies loaded and transported. Can your men see to that before we start toward camp?"

The officer nodded before moving to assemble the ragtag band of recruits. "Follow me, men. Wonderland awaits."

Elsie's father caught sight of the girls and strode over to meet them. "I didn't expect to see you ladies here. Did you need something?"

Mary hoisted her bag. "Laying in some supplies at the store, Ranger Brookes." She glanced over at the CCC crowd. "And maybe getting a sneak peek at the newcomers."

Elsie clutched her own satchel to her midsection as Ranger Vaughn wandered over to join them. "An interesting group," she said. "Where are they from?"

"This sorry band of tenderfeet?" Her father shook his head. "I thought we were getting foresters from the upper Midwest or ranch hands from Wyoming."

Ranger Vaughn chuckled. "No, President Roosevelt sent us a passel of half-starved boys from Brooklyn."

"Brooklyn—New York?" Elsie glanced back at them. That explained the odd accent.

Her father took off his hat and ran a hand through his graying hair. "I've never seen a more pathetic lot of misfits. I have no idea what the president thinks we're supposed to do with these rascals."

"Maybe they just need some direction and leadership." She watched as her father lifted one of the smaller crates. "If anyone could inspire them toward success, it would be you."

"I think it's going to take a lot more than that, Els." Her father jammed his hat back into place. "But with three squares a day and a whole lot of work, we'll put some muscles on these boys by the end of the season. That much is certain."

Mary winked at Elsie. "Now we're talking."

He tapped the end of Elsie's nose as if she were still four years old. "And with you teaching them some reading and writing, maybe a few of them will have a future."

Ranger Vaughn folded his arms. "Teaching the three *R*s to the three *C*s? You've got your work cut out for you."

"I'll do my best." She ducked her head, afraid his smile would have her stammering again. "Come on, Mary. I've got geysers to monitor." Chasing data seemed a lot more worthwhile than chasing after men.

❧

Every muscle in Nate's back and arms ached, and the stiff army cot did little to help matters. He shifted over onto his right side, hoping to ease the pressure on his spine. The mingled smells of damp canvas and sweat permeated the tent, hanging over him like a shroud. Snores punctuated the darkness.

An empty hollow took up residence in his gut, but for once it wasn't a lack of food. He'd eaten better in the past two weeks at the army's conditioning base in New Jersey than he had his entire life. This felt more like a chunk of his soul had gone missing. Two years had passed since Sherm's death, but sometimes grief still sprang at Nate out of the shadows, like the old pit bull at Barone's junkyard—especially when he was alone. He'd never figured himself to be the type of sissy to moan over being away from his family, but then, he'd never been more than twenty miles from Brooklyn in his life.

Every time he closed his eyes, he saw his two little sisters dancing as they waved goodbye at the recruiting station, not really understanding that the day's excitement would mean he wasn't returning anytime soon. His mother's tears, on the other hand, had nearly knocked his legs out from under him. He'd seen her cry countless times, but he could only remember one other time he'd been the cause—the day he'd been kicked out of school.

Nate rolled off the cot. Since sleep refused to cooperate, he might as well use the meager facilities they'd dug during the daylight hours. He eased his way through the line of sleeping men, careful to avoid jarring any feet hanging in the aisle.

He ducked outside, the brisk air stealing his breath in an instant. Glancing up at the night sky, everything else inside him stilled as well. Stars scattered from one horizon to the next, spilling across the dark background like the lights of Manhattan. Nate closed his mouth, but he couldn't take his eyes away from the scene playing out above his head. The sky back home had never looked like this. He could almost touch it, brush his fingers against the glittering edges of the distant stars. "God." He breathed the word, more in reverence than in vain. What other response could a man have in the face of such wonder?

The chill cut through him, icy air curling around his neck and arms. He drew his elbows close and wrapped his hands around them to protect what body heat he had left and started toward the outhouse.

Although nearly two hundred men had arrived, it had still taken ages for them to erect the massive tents and dig the latrines, not calling off work until well past dusk. The division captain, a brusque man in his late thirties, had warned them that they'd answer to reveille at dawn, just like any of his other soldiers.

Only they weren't soldiers. The chaos of the haphazard work had proven as much. After a short couple of weeks at Camp Dix—filled with medical tests, shots for typhoid and smallpox, calisthenics, and hot meals— the men were still ill prepared for the type of work thrust upon them. Nate had done his best, but even he seemed to be tripping over his feet. Likely the oversized breeches and stiff boots they'd issued him were to blame. Why did the uniforms all seem so ungodly large? Most of the men were swimming in their new duds, which was probably why those two girls at the station looked at them with such pity. Or was it contempt? The quieter one seemed to practically jump from her skin when Red came around the corner. You'd think he was a bear on the prowl.

There had been plenty of jokes about Yellowstone's grizzlies and buffalo on the train ride in. The thought curdled in Nate's stomach. He knew how to handle a mugger, but a bear? He wouldn't have a clue.

He opened the door to the latrine.

A pair of beady eyes glared at him from within, a violent hiss cutting through the night air.

Nate jumped back and lost his balance before landing hard on the snow-crusted mud. His heart jumped to his throat. Had he conjured up a bear with his very thoughts?

A loud chittering emanated from the confined space as the creature jumped from a shelf and lumbered into the open. A mask covered its pointy face and rings decorated its tail. He'd seen raccoons in Brooklyn hanging out around the trash cans and dark alleys, but rarely ones this size.

He scooted backward, allowing the perturbed creature to make its escape. As Nate's pulse slowed, he rolled to his knees and got to his feet, brushing the snow from his trousers. "Sorry, fella," he called after the critter. "Didn't realize this one was occupied."

"It's usually a good idea to bang on the side first." A voice came out of the darkness. "This time it was a raccoon, but next time it might be a skunk." The camp captain strode up, an unlit cigarette dangling from the corner of his mouth.

"I'll keep that in mind—sir. I hope I didn't disturb you."

"Nah. Late meeting with the park service reps. We're planning the next month's movements. Got another two hundred men coming in three weeks."

Nate glanced around at the sleeping camp. They were already squeezed in like sardines in a half-sized tin. "I hope they're bringing more tents."

"We'll be moving this company out and setting up two more camps in other areas of the park. More remote."

More remote than this? "Whatever you say, sir."

The captain tipped his head, taking the cigarette from his lips. "You military? Most of these fellas don't seem to take the 'yes sir, no sir' tack."

"No—" Nate bit off his words before adding the *sir* out of habit. "But my father was a police sergeant."

"That discipline will serve you well here. Name?"

"Webber, sir. Nate Webber." *Discipline.* Yes, he'd had plenty of that drilled into him. The real trick had been gauging the old man's mood before daring to open his mouth. Over the years he'd gotten pretty good at reading people's faces even though he struggled to read words on a page.

"Webber." The captain looked him up and down, seemingly unaffected by the bitter cold of the night air. "Am I mistaken, or do you have a few extra years on most of the guys here? How old are you?"

"Twenty-four, sir. Not a spring chicken, you might say."

"Indeed." The army man snapped his head in another nod, as if confirming some inner thought he hadn't bothered to share. "Good to hear. I hope you'll be a voice of maturity and wisdom here."

Nate managed to stifle a chuckle. He'd never heard the word *wisdom* associated with himself. He must look different in the dark of night. Nate straightened his shoulders, trying his best to meet the man's standards. If only his bladder would cooperate.

The captain stepped back. "Don't let me interrupt. Carry on, son." He turned and stalked off toward the command tent. "We start on the plumbing tomorrow."

Nate ducked in the door and it closed behind him, sealing him in the dark space. A moment later he realized he'd forgotten to implement the captain's first piece of advice: *bang on the side of the latrine before entering.*

Scraping sounds from the rafters proved the bandit hadn't been alone. Nate swung the door open and lunged back out into the bitter cold. The last thing he needed in a latrine was an audience. After a few seconds went by, two raccoon kits appeared at the door and bumbled off in the direction of their mother.

Four

Steam drifted across the stark landscape at Norris Geyser Basin as Whirligig Geyser gurgled and belched water a few feet into the air, the sour smell wafting on the morning breeze. Elsie checked the watch dangling from the pin attached to her blouse. *Ten-sixteen.* Earlier than expected. She braced a notebook against her hip as she recorded the data, scribbling the time and estimating the small fountain's height. It had been a long and lonely drive here in her father's borrowed truck, but it was worth it to visit her old friends and record their greetings.

Even though snow still lingered on the nearby hillsides, the moist heat rising from the pools made pieces of Elsie's hair cling to her cheeks. She tucked the runaway strands underneath the knitted tam-o'-shanter as the quiet hissing and bubbling of the springs filled the day with a gentle music.

Closing the notebook, Elsie took a deep breath. The sulfurous air might send some tourists running, but to her it smelled of home. Not many people could count geyser watching as one of their favorite hobbies. She tucked the pencil over her ear. As she walked, her shoes made quiet thumps against the wooden boardwalk. She was glad the park service had built these paths, allowing visitors to get close to the pools while protecting the crusted-over soil. She could still see places where early visitors had carved their names into the mineralized outcroppings. The sight made her steam like the vents beneath her feet. Why must people destroy the very things they'd come to enjoy?

She stopped and gazed into the translucent pool of Blue Geyser, an aquamarine jewel in the midst of the bubbling masses. If only her heart could maintain that same placid response in the face of life's ups and downs. Instead she was more like Whirligig, churning and spouting off at unpredictable moments—even more so after learning she might start college this fall instead of next. School had been just beyond her grasp for so long, she didn't know what to do with her new reality. *Dreams always sound good until they show up on your doorstep. Then again, if they weren't a little scary, they wouldn't be worth dreaming about.*

Deep voices drew her attention from the pool. A large contingent of men appeared on the edge of the basin. Clothed in rolled-up dungarees, khaki-colored shirts, and neckties with the ends tucked between the second and third buttons, the CCC workers looked much more at ease today than they had in the ridiculous woolen uniforms they'd sported last week on the railroad platform.

Elsie turned her attention to the geyser. She wanted to catch its next eruption and note the time in her careful row of figures. The eruption cycle on this particular feature was a mystery, but if she collected enough data and kept careful track, maybe she could make sense of it. The group shouldn't prove too much of a distraction. After all, she didn't have Mary's roving eye.

The men plowed forward, laughing and talking loudly as they tromped down the wooden planks of the walkway in their heavy boots, occasionally stopping to stare and point at the various pools. One of them strayed off the path, bending over to examine a two-foot outcropping of calcified rock like some child's sandcastle frozen in stone. He dug in his pocket and took out a penknife.

"No! Don't you dare!" Elsie hurried toward him, her brown oxfords pattering on the pine boards.

Fifty sets of eyes turned her direction, stopping her cold. She reached for her collar with one hand and squeezed it closed at her throat. "Get back on the boardwalk—now!" She slapped the notebook against her leg for emphasis. "You shouldn't walk off the path out here. It's dangerous."

The man smirked, gripping the knife in his fist. "Looks like I just did."

Off to one side, Red, the smart-mouthed one they'd met the other day, snickered. "Sounds just like my third-grade teacher." He scrunched his nose. "Don't *do* that." He pitched his voice up in a mimicry of Elsie's, the sound carrying over the others' laughter.

Little did he know she might actually be his teacher soon. She gripped her notebook, trying to steady her rising temper. She hadn't expected a collection of grown men to act so childishly. "Do you only listen to teachers, then? Here's a study question for you. What's the boiling temperature of water?"

The two paused, as if at a loss for words—or more likely, for an answer.

A third angled through the group, coming to the front. The responsible one from the station—Nate Webber. "I believe the lady asked you a question, Mutt."

The man's face pinched. He folded the knife and jammed it into his shirt pocket. "Don't know. Why don't you tell us, Teach." He hurled the word toward Elsie.

A young fellow lifted his hand as if he were in class. "Two hundred and twelve degrees."

"That's right. And that's what's directly below your friend's feet right now. Boiling, highly acidic water." Elsie came several steps closer and gestured to the ground where Mutt stood. "By my calculations that crust is probably less than six inches thick. So I really think you might want to come back over here."

Mutt glanced at his boots, the laces hanging loose on one of them. His face blanched.

Mr. Webber walked to the edge of the platform and stretched out an arm. "Come on. I know you stink, but I don't think a scalding bath would improve you much."

The burly man grabbed Webber's wrist, allowing himself to be hauled back to safety. A snapping sound accompanied the swift motion. Several men surged to the edge of the walkway and gawked as a boot-sized hole appeared, cracks fanning out from the crevice. Water splashed up onto the edges, licking at the spot where Mutt's foot had been moments before.

Red jumped to the front of the line.

"Jeepers. He'd have been boiled like an egg."

Elsie stepped back as the men's eyes turned toward her again. The group fell silent.

Mutt wiped his hands on his shirt as if to dry his palms. "I-I'm sorry, Miss. I didn't . . ." He swallowed, his Adam's apple bouncing in his neck. "Thank you, ma'am."

She folded her arms across her chest, hugging her sides. "You should be more careful. This place is unforgiving."

"My ma always said *careless* shoulda' been my middle name." He smirked. "But I'll watch myself."

Webber gestured toward the path. "Why don't you and the fellas go find what else there is to see here."

Mutt touched the brim of his slouchy hat at Elsie before herding the group toward the Back Basin.

She watched them depart, uncomfortably aware of the one man

remaining behind. She turned to face him. "Mr. Webber, I'd appreciate you keeping an eye on your men."

"Oh, they aren't *my* men. I'm just one of the pack, I'm afraid. But I've got a few years on most of them, so it buys me a bit of respect."

She studied him, his eyes the color of the forest at dusk. "I doubt they would have obeyed me if you hadn't spoken up."

His brow furrowed. "He could have paid a heavy price for stubborn pride."

She tried not to think about what might have happened to the man. It wouldn't be the first time someone died from foolishness out here. "What brings you to this area of the park? Are you working on a project here?"

"The captain put us on a truck and ordered us to explore." A half smile crossed his face. "I don't think he wanted to be bothered this morning. He's meeting with the rangers to nail down some plans. Said something about building three more camps. I guess they're moving us on to the Grand Canyon." He looked at her quizzically. "Isn't that a different park?"

"He's referring to the Grand Canyon of the Yellowstone River, not the one in Arizona." She stopped herself before saying that she'd be moving that direction next month. Why should he care? "How are you finding Yellowstone so far? It must be quite an adjustment."

"You have no idea. Most of us have never been out of the city." He grinned. "The mountains? The critters? I saw those buffalo yesterday in the pen at Mammoth. I never dreamed such creatures existed outside western movies."

"The rangers keep some there to show the tourists, but there are wild ones in the park too." The wonder in the man's eyes sent a rush of warmth through her.

Mr. Webber folded his arms, apparently not in a hurry to rejoin his friends. "I noticed you back at the train station. Do you live here? At the park?"

"I work for the Yellowstone Park Hotel Company."

"Leading tours?"

"Oh no." She swallowed a laugh. "I'm just a pillow puncher—a maid."

"I didn't realize maids took notes." He glanced at her book.

"I'm going to the University of Montana in the fall to study education. I hope to take some geology classes too." She forced confidence into her words. After so many delays, nothing would stop her this time.

"Geology? That explains how you recognized Mutt's predicament."

The pool gurgled, its increasing steam a sign of action. Elsie dug in her pocket for something to write with. "That, and I've lived here most of my life. I grew up in Mammoth. My father's a ranger." Her pencil had gone missing. She scanned the boards at her feet. If she'd dropped it in her hurry to warn the careless fellow, it would have rolled through one of the gaps between the boards. "Oh no. Do you have a pen with you?" The spring had already started bubbling.

Webber tapped the side of his head and then pointed to her ear.

She felt a flush in her cheeks. "Oh." She grabbed the writing instrument, untucking more of her hair in the process. She checked her timepiece, then jotted down the time.

"What are you doing?" The sound of spurting water drew his attention. "Oh, that's remarkable." He fell silent, watching.

She stepped to the railing, bracing her elbows on the rough wood. "Your first geyser?"

He nodded, not taking his eyes from the action, the pulsing spray reaching about three feet into the air. "It's like the fountains in Central Park, except wilder."

She scratched a few more figures in her book. "Where's that?"

He finally dragged his attention back to her. "You've never heard of Central Park?"

"You've never seen a geyser?"

He chuckled at her quick response and turned back to watch the show. "I guess if you've lived here all your life, you've probably never been to New York."

The words stopped her. She'd been to New York, years ago. Before Yellowstone. She'd relegated that part of her life to the shadows of her memory. That was the only safe place to leave it. "I was born back East, but I-I don't remember much."

"Does the water always do that?"

The way he said "water" tickled her ears, and she wondered if her lips could form the sounds the same way. *Whah-teh. Watuh.* Something like that. What was it about this man's voice that intrigued her? "It erupts about every twenty minutes or so. But they're all different." She jabbed her pencil at the pages. "You can see here—this one went off at two minutes after ten this morning. Shortly before you arrived."

His smile faded as he glanced at her notes. He cleared his throat and took several steps back. "I . . . I should catch up to the guys."

"Of course." Elsie closed the book. Another man put off by a woman interested in science? The bubble of excitement that had been growing in her chest fizzled. She could almost hear Mary's voice. *"Always let the man do the talking."* Mary would probably have peppered him with questions about life in New York.

He touched his hat and hurried after the rest of his group.

No matter. She shouldn't have expected him to be interested. Elsie tugged her cuff over her scarred wrist.

The basin grew quiet. Elsie turned her attention back to the thermal feature, now little more than a bubbling pot. She checked her timepiece. She had time to wait for the next one. The more data in her book, the better. After all, facts didn't care that she was a woman.

Nate scrubbed a palm across his face as he hurried after his regiment. *College girl. Figures.* The eager look in her eye when she'd flashed him the records of eruption times had caught him off guard. How long had it been since anyone had treated him like someone with a brain? She'd never give him the time of day if she knew he couldn't make out the scratchings in her book. His heart sagged.

"Start using your head, you worthless . . ." His father's voice echoed over both the miles and the years.

The truth of the memory stung. For some incomprehensible reason, God had seen fit to make Nate Webber dumb. Maybe He only gave good brains to the people He loved. Once again, Nate didn't make the cut.

He paused on the wooden walkway and glanced back at the young woman tapping that yellow pencil against her chin as she stared at the steaming pools and bubbling geysers. He lifted his eyes to the grand landscape beyond, the sight filling his chest like oxygen to his soul. At least he had eyes and ears to enjoy the world laid out before him.

"Webber!"

Red hung back from the rest of the party, his hands cupped around his mouth. "Quit gaping at the girl and get up here."

A wave of heat prickled up Nate's neck as he hurried down the boardwalk. Gaping at the girl? Hopefully that wasn't what Miss . . . *Did she tell me her name?* He thought back to the encounter at the train depot with the woman and her friend. Red had gotten the sassy blonde's name, but what of this one? What sort of idiot talked with a girl but didn't think to ask her name?

He cast one last look at the attractive young woman. *The kind who doesn't expect her to bother with him.*

Five

Elsie gripped the mop handle with both hands, the lobby's gleaming floor a tiny compensation for her aching back. Mammoth Hotel might not be renting rooms for the summer, but the restaurant would still be doing business, and it was never too early to get things in shape. In a little over a week, she and Mary would pack up and move to Canyon where the work would begin anew. The Grand Canyon Hotel, the log Canyon Lodge, and the housekeeping cabins were all in need of a bit of sprucing up before their opening.

Mary's chatter in the background warmed her spirits more than the hard work. "Our whole crew has been mixed up like a tossed salad this summer. Sal and Millie will be at Canyon. Billy and Joe, Frank and Marcie—oh!—and Betty too—they're all moving to Old Faithful. But Frank's been promoted to front desk. Can you believe it? From busboy to clerk, that's quite a leap. But then, a handsome face like his shouldn't be hidden behind stacks of dirty plates." She rubbed the cloth on the wooden railing, then stopped to add a little extra polish. "And the new gear jammers come in today."

Elsie settled the mop back into the tin bucket, careful not to slosh the murky water. "Already?"

Her friend swiped the rag against the wood with an extra flourish. "Hal says they're doing extra training this year. Safety and all that." She cast a mischievous grin toward Elsie. "Want to go welcome them?"

"You mean spy on them? Like we did with the CCC boys?"

"Yes, but these are *our* boys. College students, like us."

"I spoke with some CCC men at Norris Geyser Basin. They seemed nice enough, though perhaps a little reckless."

"You didn't tell me that. Which ones?" Her eyes widened. "Did you see Red?"

"Yes, and the other fellow, Mr. Webber. And plenty more." She needed to steer this conversation back to safer ground. "Why don't you come over for dinner tonight? Mother would love to see you."

Her friend paused, biting her lip. "Is she well enough for company?"

"I think it might do her some good. She misses everyone when the park's all buttoned up for winter."

"She'll certainly miss you when we leave for Canyon." Mary leaned against the stair railing. "You do so much for her."

Elsie gripped the mop handle. "My father said he can manage without me."

"I'm looking forward to the change. Beds and floors are the same everywhere, but there will be plenty of new faces." Mary grinned. "And I hear Canyon's pillow punchers are the *best* punchers—"

"Don't start singing, please." Elsie groaned, but her admonishment came too late.

"The most punchy punchers there are . . ." Mary's lilting words carried through the Great Hall.

"Oh no, no, no," a disembodied voice hollered down the empty stairwell, picking up the song chant midstream. "Mammoth pillow punchers will welcome you home, and greet you with songs tonight . . ."

The familiar voice made Elsie's heart jump. "Rose? Is that you?"

The freckled face peered over the railing. "I do believe my eyes spy Elsie and Mary Contrary!"

The three of them met in the middle of the stairs, hugging and laughing together.

The petite brunette touched the scarf wrapped around her head, the look emphasizing her heart-shaped face. "And here I am, covered in dirt. This place is a disaster. We cleaned it from basement to rafters at the end of the season, and now look." She gestured to the old hotel. "Nothing but rodent droppings and dust. And I think a squirrel was holed up in my cabin all winter."

Elsie grabbed her friend's hand and led her to the landing. "How was school?"

"Top marks, even with everything that happened." Rose sighed, glancing down at the toes of her two-toned oxfords. "Now I have the summer to relax before my last term."

And this fall, Elsie would be heading off to school too. A rush of excitement swept through her. "What do you mean 'everything that happened'?"

Rose's eyes filled with tears. "I had plenty of time to study after Pete threw me over for a schoolteacher from Cody."

"What? You didn't say anything in your letters about this!" Mary's mouth dropped open. "You and Pete have been together forever. And longer!"

"I couldn't bring myself to write the words. It made it too real. He told me in December, just before Christmas. By March, he was engaged. Can you believe it?" Her lower lip trembled.

Elsie squeezed her arm. "Then it's good you're here, among friends. We'll help you shake those blues right away."

"You two are so good to me." She dabbed her eyes with a handkerchief. "Can you girls keep a secret?"

"Of course." Elsie stepped closer. After all, Rose and Mary had kept hers all these years.

"I met someone on the train ride. He's one of the new drivers. Said his"—she glanced at Elsie—"his uncle got him the job."

Mary pouted. "You met one of the jammers already? Unfair."

Rose's gentle smile softened her face. "He's really sweet. We talked the whole way here. You're going to love him. Poor fella had to listen to all my sob stories."

Elsie glanced around. "Where is this mystery man?"

"He's in the kitchen, helping Cook get the stoves running. He's handy that way, or so he told me." Rose trotted down the stairs, tugging Elsie along. "Come and meet him."

Elsie and Mary trailed after Rose, heading toward the kitchen in the rear of the building.

Sitting on the dirty floor with one arm deep in the large oven, a lanky fellow spoke quietly with the nearby cook. "It's the pilot light. It might need replacing."

When the cook glanced toward the girls, the young man on the floor jumped to his feet, knocking over a box and spilling matches across the floor. "I'm sorry; I didn't see you come in."

It couldn't be. A rush of memories triggered by the man's face and voice thrust Elsie backward against the door, her legs suddenly weighing more than lead.

Mary squeezed Rose's arm. "Rose, you didn't tell us your new fella's name."

"He's not my—it's not like that." Rose fidgeted, worrying the corner of her apron. "It's Elsie's cousin, Graham. He wanted to surprise her."

Graham. A wave of heat crawled up Elsie's chest, like the flames that haunted her nightmares.

Her cousin cleared his throat. "Elsie, I hardly recognized you, all grown up. It's good to see you."

Elsie tried to draw a decent breath, but it was as if the air had turned to molasses. Graham Brookes—here in Mammoth? She backed out of the room, retreating to the front hall, desperate for the freedom of the outside world.

Rose darted after her. "Elsie, what's wrong?"

"Why is he here?" She snatched the mop from its bucket, long forgotten, unlike other things she'd left behind. Water dripped across the parquet floor.

"Your father got him a job for the summer, driving one of the tour buses."

Graham, a gear jammer? "We don't need his help." Elsie bit the words. "I haven't seen him since I was nine. Not since we left Washington." She yanked at her cuffs as if covering her scars could protect her from what lay ahead.

Rose caught her hands, stilling the motion. "Then it will give you a chance to get reacquainted." Her brow wrinkled. "You've never spoken of him before. He seems nice enough. A little older than most of the jammers, but I think he'll fit in fine."

Graham appeared at the edge of the hall, his brow furrowed. "Elsie, I'm sorry. I didn't mean to shock you."

Elsie forced her feet to stay planted. It would do no good to run from him. If her father had gotten him a job, the problem wasn't going to vanish. "I-I wasn't expecting you."

Rose gave Elsie's hands a quick squeeze. "I'll go see what Mary is doing and let you two talk." She disappeared into the kitchen.

Elsie's stomach churned. The memories loomed large, but that's all they were—memories. They couldn't harm her.

Graham put on his jacket over his sweat-stained shirt. "Your father didn't tell you I was coming, then."

She shook her head, unable to put any words together.

He buried his hands in his pockets. "I've thought about you many times over the years, but you wouldn't return my letters." He took several steps toward her, then stopped short, his eyes filling with emotion. "Now that I'm here, I'm not sure what to say."

"Why did you come?"

His chest rose and fell with a deep breath. "After my father died last year, and then the business fell apart . . ." He lowered his head. "I wasn't sure where else to go. Your parents had always been kind to me. I hoped we could be a family again."

"Be a *family*?" The words tore at her throat. They hadn't been "a family" since the fire.

He closed his eyes. In that moment, he appeared every bit the boy he'd been when she'd last laid eyes on him. He must be nearing twenty-five now. "I was a kid, Elsie. It was a foolish mistake. One that cost me dearly."

"And cost my baby sister everything." Her mouth tasted like fireplace ashes.

He fell silent, shadows gathering around his eyes. He took his hands from his pockets and spread them in front of her, the scarred palms evidence of his own part in her memories. "I'm praying we can get past it. Start over." He dropped his arms to his sides. "I miss you, Elsie. You were the sister I never had. I'm hoping you can forgive me."

She stepped back. "I can't stop you from working here, Graham. But don't expect anything more from me."

❧

Nate pushed wet branches out of his way as they climbed the steep slope of Mount Washburn. The leather boots clung stiffly around his ankles, rubbing at the skin on his heels. Tomorrow he'd add a second pair of wool socks. Captain Dahl had said they'd be hiking in snow, but Nate hadn't envisioned waist-high drifts in late May. Thankfully, a sort of trail had been cut through the drifts by rangers on horseback. It had been difficult to imagine snow when the temperatures in Mammoth had been warm enough for shirtsleeves.

"A little farther, men." The ranger called back over his shoulder.

Nate fixed his eyes on the stiff brim of the man's hat, determined not to fall behind like so many of the others straggling along the path. He'd already heard the ranger and the captain talking about the crew's lack of skills. Could Nate and the others help the fact that they grew up in the city? But he'd prove himself, regardless. He needed this opportunity.

Val Kaminski, walking in front of him, let go of a branch as he passed. The wet evergreen bough swung through the air, catching Nate in the jaw with a sound *thwack,* nearly knocking him off his feet. "Hey, watch it." One bad step and he'd find himself rolling down the slope like a snowball.

The youngster glanced back and smirked. "Keep up, old man."

Old man. Nate dug his toe into the ice and surged forward in an attempt to match strides with the mouthy kid. He might be at the top of the age range for the CCCs, but it certainly didn't make him old. "Did you bother to shave this morning, Val? Or was that last week?"

The fellows behind him laughed, even as he bit back a second insult. He could talk circles around the eighteen-year-old, but he didn't need to make enemies. The captain suggested Nate might be leadership material—and such a position could earn his family an extra five or ten dollars a month. It seemed far-fetched that anyone would view him as command worthy, but if there was a chance, he didn't intend to botch it.

Val grinned, the remark not denting his good humor. "You seem on good terms with the ranger man. Any word as to what we'll be doing here?"

A bead of sweat traveled down Nate's spine, the exertion of the snowbound hike stoking his furnace from the inside regardless of his chilled feet. "We're looking for bugs."

"You're fooling me." The younger man squinted at him. "Bugs?"

"Didn't you listen when Ranger Brookes asked for volunteers this morning?"

"My *tata* . . ." He grimaced. The Polish word had slipped out. "My *father* taught me to always volunteer for extra work. Makes you look like a go-getter."

Sage advice. Nate squinted against the glare as the sun beat on the white snow. "Brookes said mountain pine beetles are attacking the trees at this elevation. We're doing a survey to see how far they've spread."

Val floundered in the deep drift. "But in the snow? Beetles wouldn't be out now, would they?"

The ranger had stopped and waited for them. "You boys doing all right?" He glanced back to where the rest of the group of eight struggled up the mountainside.

"Yes sir." Nate ran a gloved hand across his chin, hoping it would hide his panting for breath. "Lovely day."

"It is at that." The older man cocked an eyebrow. "Though I'm not sure your colleagues will agree. They look a little haggard."

Nate shrugged off the canteen he'd been issued and loosened the cap. "I'm sure we'll toughen up, sir."

"I'll make sure of it." The ranger shoved back his hat and glanced at the treetops before turning his blue eyes back to Nate. "What was your name?"

Nate choked on his mouthful of water. "Nate Webber, sir."

"What do you see, Webber?"

Nate glanced quickly at Val before turning to study the forest. *What am I supposed to be looking at?* "I see trees, snow. Birds?" He took a second swig from the canteen, his throat suddenly drier than sawdust.

Ranger Brookes folded his arms across his chest, his gold badge glinting in the light. "Look harder."

Nate stilled. He wanted to impress the man, but he had no idea what Brookes was asking. He lifted his head, searching the forest for something unusual. The snow lay thick on the ground but had melted off the tree limbs. The forest cloaked the mountainside in a sea of green as it stretched upward toward the crystalline blue sky. No, wait . . . "These pines, they're all evergreens, right?"

"Yes." The corner of the man's mouth twitched. "Go on."

"Then why are there patches of red?" Nate pointed to a stand of trees ahead of them, his eyes caught by swathes of fall-like red and orange colors—in May.

Val lifted his eyes, studying the area Nate had pointed out. "I'll be."

Ranger Brookes clapped a hand onto Nate's shoulder and squeezed. "Nice work, Webber. We might make foresters of you boys yet. If you learn to keep your eyes open, you can read the forest."

Read the forest? Nate stared up at the pines where the discolored needles called out to him. Anyone with eyes could see the trees were sick. It was letters and words on a page that made no sense to him. Trees were pretty basic.

Val cleared his throat. "Is that from the mountain beetle you were talking about?"

From the speech he hadn't bothered to listen to.

Brookes nodded. "Mountain *pine* beetle, yes. The larvae get under the bark and go to work on the trees. Most of our whitebark pines are already infested. I'm afraid in the next few years, we're going to see large sections of this higher elevation forest denuded." He shook his head. "And if it gets into the lodgepole pines, the whole park could be in trouble."

A chill swept over Nate as the heat from the hike dissipated. "How do you fight it?"

"That's where your crew comes in." He jutted his chin toward the trees. "You'll remove the diseased trees and see if it halts the progression. Otherwise the whole forest could die. And then a single spark could set the place ablaze."

Nate gazed at the steep mountainside. "You're talking about a lot of trees."

"And that's just this corner of the park." The ranger swept the back of his hand across his forehead and readjusted his hat. "But thankfully, we've got you boys."

"We're here to work, sir." *Work*. The word sent a charge through Nate's blood. How long had it been? He might not be a hero like his older brother, but he could learn to swing an ax. "We're ready and willing. Whatever you need."

Ranger Brookes smiled. "Then we're going to get along just fine."

Six

Elsie sat cross-legged on Rose's bed as she knitted another row of stitches on the half-finished sweater. Most of the employees preferred living in the dormitories, but Rose had requested one of the older staff cabins behind the hotel. Even with the window thrown open, the musty odor of rodent urine hung over the space. The three girls had wrapped themselves in blankets against the cold spring air flooding into the room— but better chilled than overcome. Elsie fixed her eyes on the interlocking strands of yarn, the clacking of her wooden needles creating order from the chaos of her mind.

Mary flitted around the room like a hummingbird. "Just one shindig before we head to Canyon? Come on. What could it hurt?"

Rose grabbed a shawl from her trunk and draped it over her shoulders. "There aren't very many of us here yet, Mary. How are we going to organize a party on such short notice? And where would we hold it?"

"But we really should welcome everyone back." Mary dabbed a tissue to her nose. "How about a bonfire?"

"The evenings are still so cold." Elsie shifted on the mattress, making the springs squeak. "How about a film night in the museum?"

"Too boring. We need to dance." Mary held the blanket around her like an imaginary ball gown and waltzed, her steps in perfect time to the music streaming from Rose's Victrola. "Maybe having the hotel closed is a blessing. We could use the Great Hall without having to worry about bothering guests. Do you think Mr. Nichols would allow a dance? It could be a reward for us getting the cabins all trim and tidy ahead of schedule."

Rose leaned against the windowsill, staring out at the night sky. Their sweet friend had grown melancholy since losing Pete. "How many people are you thinking? There are only a handful of pillow punchers and wranglers here."

Mary danced up behind Rose and nudged her. "There's the CCC crew. And the new jammers. We saw how you were staring all doe-eyed at Elsie's cousin."

"I wasn't. Why would you say such a thing?" Rose turned away from the glass as her voice pitched higher.

Elsie tried to ignore her distress. Rose was a bad liar. Of all the men she could pursue, why did it have to be Graham?

Mary rolled her eyes. "Don't get your stockings in a twist. I'm just teasing."

Rose hurried over to her trunk and grabbed more clothes to put away. "Well, don't. Elsie's not pleased to see him here, so that's good enough reason for me to be cautious." She held two garments against her chest, darting a glance at Elsie. "Right?"

Elsie released a long breath she hadn't realized she'd been holding. "I'd rather not talk about him."

"Of course, you don't have to tell us." Mary cleared her throat. "If you don't trust your best friends . . ."

Rose shot her a look. "Mary!"

"What?" She threw up her hands. "What did I say?"

Elsie slid forward until her feet hit the floor. "I'm going now." She knew her friends too well. They would keep digging until they pried the whole story from her.

Rose dropped the clothes on the bed. "Don't go, Els. We won't ask again. Right, Mary?"

Elsie shrugged on her coat. "I should get home anyway. I need to help my mother get ready for bed."

Rose looked surprised. "I'm sorry, Elsie. Are things that bad?"

Mary jumped up. "Should I come along?"

"Not tonight. But I know Mama would love to see you both. It always lifts her spirits. Maybe tomorrow?" She paused in the doorway, new resolve flooding her. "I think we *should* have that dance. We deserve some fun. But if you invite the jammers, wranglers, *and* the boys from the CCC camp, won't we have far more men than women?"

Mary swished her skirt about her knees and grinned. "Exactly! No shortage of partners for us."

Elsie headed out the door and let the starry night sky chase away her anxious thoughts. She wasn't much for dancing, but it might be fun. Mary would be the life of the party, and perhaps the merriment would lift Rose's spirits. Some of the other girls would be arriving tomorrow and the new crew of bus drivers would be a welcome addition. *Except for Graham.*

Maybe they should invite some of the park service staff too. The image of the newest ranger trailed through her thoughts. Her father mentioned that he'd had trouble making friends. Was that because he was so much younger than the other men? He might enjoy meeting Rose and the others.

She paused to gaze across the moonlit parade grounds as the rhythmic sound of water dripping off the hotel's roof added to the music of the night. Spring was in the air, and the damp smell was delicious. Elsie sighed. If only the memories Graham's arrival dredged up could melt away as easily.

Nate shivered, the heat from the morning calisthenics dissipating quickly as he stood in front of Captain Dahl. Nate fought the rising panic in his chest. Why had the captain singled him out?

Dahl drew a book from his pocket and passed it to Nate without a word.

Nate closed his hand over the book, its stiff green cover fitting neatly in his palm. "What's this?"

"CCC handbook." The man folded his arms, watching as the others dispersed and headed toward the showers. "As soon as we have enough, we're handing them out to the crew, but I thought you might like the first look."

Nate flipped through it. The tiny print might as well have crawled off the page and down his backbone. "Why, sir? I mean—why me?" Had Dahl realized he'd need extra time to decipher the pages? From the looks of the dense type, it would take a lifetime for him to piece together this many words.

"The men are already looking up to you." The captain reached out and tapped the manual's cover. "There's a chapter in there about leaders and advisers. Read it. See if it interests you."

Leaders? Nate could almost hear his father's laugh. "There are plenty of other fellows—"

"And you're not the only one I've got my eye on. But I observe, and I listen to what the boys say. Ranger Brookes also put in a good word for you. Told me you worked hard the other day and rallied the others to do so as well. That's the type of attitude that'll take you far in the three Cs."

Nate managed a nod, words failing him. Had anyone ever believed in him before? How long would it take before he disappointed the man? Probably as soon as he realized Nate couldn't read a page. He closed the small manual. "Thank you, sir."

"You might decide you don't want the extra work. And"—an easy grin softened his face—"it's easier being everyone's buddy than their boss. Take it from me; you can't be both." He turned and strode away toward headquarters.

The weight of the man's expectations pressed on Nate's shoulders until he was certain at least an inch had been stolen from his height. A few extra years of age and a good attitude—were those enough to make up for his many failings?

Nate pocketed the book and hurried back to the tent. Val and Red had already departed, but Mutt was still there, struggling to make his bed.

"If the captain makes me redo this one more time this week, I'm going home. Hospital corners are for . . . for nurses." Mutt snorted, then wiped his nose on his cuff. "I ain't got time for this."

Moretti, at the next bunk, sniggered. "Remember the nurse at Camp Dix? I'd let her fix my corners anytime."

Nate shoved the handbook into the small footlocker at the end of his cot, his stomach turning. Normally he'd join in with the raucous banter, if only to make a few more friends, but Captain Dahl's words rang in his ears. He made his own bed and reached for his shaving kit. A hot shower would wash away the crawly sensation he'd had since he'd tried to focus on those handbook pages.

"Hey, Webber, think they got a camp nurse here?" Moretti called to him.

Nate turned and eyed the younger men. "Like they'd trust you with a lady nurse? I have a feeling we won't be seeing anything but trees for months." He headed for the tent door and paused. "But you're in luck, Moretti . . ."

"How's that?"

"There are lots of mighty purty trees." Nate ducked through the door as the men laughed.

Panicked shouts from the direction of the new shower house made him double his pace. Men burst out of the long building in various states of dress and undress. Others lingered in the doorway, staring inside with mixed expressions of horror and amusement.

"What's going on?" Nate joined Red and Val, both standing in the cold morning air clad in nothing but damp towels.

Red kept a tight fist on his covering, red splotches and gooseflesh mottling his pasty skin. "There's some big, hissing . . . something in there. I nearly stepped on the monster."

Globs of shaving soap still hung from Val's jaw. "Raccoon. They hang out in the sewers back home. But boy, this one is big—and mad."

Nowak, a hotheaded young recruit, grabbed a pitchfork and ducked inside.

"Hey!" Nate lunged toward him, fighting his way through the growing crowd. "Don't hurt it."

The man gripped the tool in both hands as he stood there in damp trousers, every vertebrae and rib showing along his bare back. A smear of red on the tines suggested he'd already gotten in at least one jab.

The tubby raccoon growled and spat as it cowered under one of the metal sinks. Was it the same animal Nate had spotted the first night at the latrine?

"Knock it off, Nowak," Nate snapped. "Leave it alone."

The man swiveled his head toward Nate, eyes blazing. "It took a swipe at me."

The critter bared its teeth, hunching its spine like a fuzzy Quasimodo.

"The thing's probably rabid." Nowak hoisted the pitchfork, ready to drive it into the creature.

Nate stepped in front of him, arms spread. "You got it cornered; sure it's going to fight back."

"When I signed up, no one said I'd be showering with flea-bitten vermin."

"But you had no problem showering with Red and Val?" Nate got a hold on Nowak's arm and shoved him toward the door. "Go on, now. Get out."

Nowak glowered at him. "Fine. Let it tear you to shreds. I'm not coming to your rescue." He stalked out without a backward glance.

"Didn't ask you to." Nate kept one eye on the bristling ball of fur. It wouldn't do to get attacked while trying to save the critter's life. He turned and edged over to the far wall. "All right, now. No one's going to hurt you." He looked at the blood trail under the wary animal. "Not again, anyway."

It snarled, wedging itself behind a drain pipe.

"Yeah, it's nice to see you again too. We need to stop meeting like this." He glanced around the steamy room. "You got your babies in here now? Or are you alone this time?" He didn't spot any small bundles lurking in any of the corners. There weren't too many areas in which to hide.

A wooden closet had been erected near the showers. Nate backed toward it, careful not to let the angry critter out of his sight.

She crawled out from under the sinks and clambered up a set of shelves, dislodging shave kits and toothbrushes and sending them clattering to the wet floor.

Val poked his head in, still clutching the towel around his skinny waist. "You need a hand, Nate?"

Nate swung open the closet door, eyeing the cramped space. Maybe he could find a box or something to throw over the animal. A scurrying motion in a crate of cleaning supplies caught his attention. "What were you planning to do, Val—wave your towel at them?" He pushed aside the mop handle so he could get a better look.

The kid withdrew a few inches. "Them? You mean there's more than one?"

The mother raccoon hoisted herself up to the small window above the shelves and scrambled out, leaving a smear of blood along the edge of the windowsill.

"I'm afraid so." Nate used the toe of his boot to drag the wooden crate into the light. Two sets of eyes stared at him from tiny masked faces. "Congratulations. It's twins."

Seven

Morning sunshine warmed the room as Elsie brushed her mother's hair. It was hard not to notice how thin and silvery it had become in the past year. "Maybe I should stay here at Mammoth."

Mama shook her head, shadows deepening around her eyes. "We're not that far away, if you want to visit. You could always ride with Graham. He'll be making the rounds, you know."

The thought curdled in Elsie's stomach. "I wish you'd told me he was coming."

The touch of her mother's hand was soft as a wildflower's petals. "Your father and I forgave Graham years ago. It's time you did as well. Holding on to anger will only weaken you, like a tree rotting from the inside." She brushed fingers against Elsie's cheek. "Graham pulled you from the fire, remember? I hold on to that."

"The fire was his fault." Elsie gripped the edge of the quilt. "And he should have rescued Dottie—or let me do it."

Mama closed her eyes, as if the words struck too close to her weakened heart. After a long moment she opened them, looking into the distance. "If he hadn't found you that day, I could have lost *both* my girls." She shuddered and focused on Elsie. "We can't live in the ashes, Elsie."

"But why bring him here?"

"Graham lost both his father and the family business this year. What was he to do? There are already too many others dependent on the breadlines and soup kitchens. There was no need for him to join their ranks. Not when he has us." Mother swung her feet to the floor. "It's hard for men to be out of work. It wears at their souls, tears them down piece by piece like a crumbling brick wall."

"But surely he could have gotten work—"

Mama stopped her with an upraised hand. "There is so much heartache in our nation right now. We've been sheltered here at Yellowstone. We don't see the worst of it."

"That's what Papa said." Elsie swallowed against the lump of emotions in her throat. "Only not quite so eloquently."

"Your father is a man of action, not of words." She stood, swaying a little on her feet. "That's why he brought Graham here." She paused, lifting her eyes to Elsie's. "I don't know if you remember, but when we first arrived in this place, you were so frightened, so beaten down by everything that had happened. Yellowstone helped you grow strong. Let's hope it can do the same for Graham."

"What has he done to earn your forgiveness? How can you put aside your own feelings and think of his needs?"

"Forgiveness isn't earned, Elsie. It's bestowed." Mama shook her head. "Isn't that what God did for us?"

Her parents always made faith sound so easy. Would she ever reach a point in her life where she trusted God so completely? Elsie laid the brush on the table. "I should go. I told Herma I'd stop by the museum this morning."

"Oh good. Invite her and George for dinner Sunday evening, would you? Graham will be joining us." She wedged open the window to breathe in the spring air. "And bring the girls too. It'll be lively."

"Do you really want that many people over? The doctor said to rest."

"What I need is *life*. Life around me. Light inside me. Air to breathe. Laughter to lift my soul from the darkness. Especially on the Lord's day." Tiny wisps of hair floated about her face. "Don't take that from me."

"All right. But don't tire yourself with preparations. I'll come early and help get everything ready."

She leaned against the window frame. "Your father said the same. With the two of you in the kitchen, what do I have to fear?"

"Food poisoning?"

"Exactly."

Elsie pondered her mother's words about forgiveness as she made the short walk to the museum. Graham's actions had cost them all so much, and yet her parents were choosing to help him. It seemed too much to comprehend.

Two bull elk meandered along Fort Yellowstone's old parade grounds, a grassy lawn left over from when the army managed the park. Beyond the parade ground, the uniform rows of beige buildings with matching red roofs always seemed a little out of place in the otherwise natural beauty of the park. Elsie liked to imagine the army administrators ordering perfect blocks of sandstone cut from the nearby quarry in an attempt to put their stamp of military precision onto Yellowstone's messy wilderness. It was almost as if adding order to God's chaotic creation would somehow reduce it to something they could comprehend.

At the end of the row, the old bachelor officers' quarters now housed the park museum. Elsie trotted up the stone steps and let herself in, the door jingling as she pressed through it.

Ranger Herma Baggley stepped out from the back room. "Elsie! What a surprise."

"I wanted to see you before Mary and I head off to Canyon next week."

"I'm glad you did. Come on back." She returned to the cataloging room, glancing over her shoulder to make sure Elsie followed. "How is your mother? Your dad doesn't say much, and I haven't had time to stop by."

The concern in the woman's voice nearly undid Elsie. She took a moment to collect her words. "She's still weak and tired, but in good spirits."

The naturalist smiled, warmth in her brown eyes. "I'll bring some food over, if that would help. You know it's just George and me rattling around in our quarters. It would be a joy to cook for a larger group."

"She was hoping the two of you would join us for supper on Sunday."

"Done. Now what did you want to talk about?"

Elsie had admired the straight-talking woman since Herma first arrived in the park back in '29, determined to do what everyone thought of as man's work. "Did my father tell you I'm going to be teaching classes at one of the new CCC camps?"

"He did. And working at the hotel too? You'll be busy." Herma reached for a plant identification card sitting on the desk. Her passion for Yellowstone's flowers had made her an expert in the field. "I did my time as a pillow puncher." She wrinkled her nose. "Cleaning rooms just to earn my keep."

"How did you make the jump to park ranger?"

The naturalist rubbed a thumb over the pen-and-ink illustration on the card. "I volunteered the first summer and designed the nature trail at Old Faithful. The trail crew was never too happy with me. They didn't think my meandering pathways made much sense. But I wanted visitors to see all the little things they might miss if they didn't bother to look beyond their own noses."

"Did the male crew have trouble listening to you?"

"At first." Herma's brows drew together. "Why do you ask?"

Elsie rubbed her hands as though a sudden chill had swept over her.

"The CCC classes—they'll be filled with grown men. Not little children. How am I supposed to teach them?"

She smiled. "Well, that will be quite a picture. Tiny little you standing in front of a classroom of burly men."

"Exactly."

"You've seen me lead nature walks with both women and men. I find the little nuggets of information that catch the group's interest and then focus on those topics."

"But if I'm teaching subjects they're not interested in?"

"Children usually accept teaching without question. With adults, you have to look for things that provide value for their everyday lives." She tapped the illustrated card. "When I point out this flower along the trail, I don't focus on its life cycle and scientific name—at least not at first. I tell people how the natives in this area used it to make a healing tea for rheumatism. Or if they're interested in farming, how it enriches the soil. Once you catch their interest, you can delve into other details."

Elsie's heart sped up. "They'll spend their days working in the woods. Maybe I could teach science by concentrating on things they observe— forests, geology, wildlife."

"You've got it." Herma nodded. She leaned close. "Now, can I trust you with a secret? I might be giving up my post."

Elsie straightened. "Why?"

"You know how I've dreamed of writing guidebooks for the park. I'm working on *The Flowers of Yellowstone*. But with being here all day, I just don't have enough time." She stacked the cards and added them to the file. "I was thinking, when you're done with teacher's college, maybe you could find time to help me put together a geology guide. We could have a whole collection. Think of how many people you could reach through the written word!"

The thought buoyed Elsie's spirits. "Let's see if I survive my first teaching post. Then we can talk books."

❦

It was nearly dark by the time Elsie walked up the steps to her parents' house Sunday evening. The idea of entertaining sent a fresh wave of exhaustion through her. She did her best to shake off the selfish feelings as she let herself in. Whatever she could do to cheer up her mother was well worth the temporary discomfort.

Graham crouched at the fireplace, adding another log. Sparks spiraled upward, casting an eerie glow across his face.

Elsie froze. It had taken years for her to reach the stage where she could sit near a campfire, but seeing her cousin stoking the flames sent the familiar clutches of panic crushing into her chest. Her stomach roiled as she stepped back onto the front stoop, gulping air. *Just breathe.* Fighting back the dual urges to run or to be sick, Elsie turned to face the parade grounds and grabbed hold of the porch railing. She wasn't a child anymore. She needed to control these nagging fears.

The door creaked.

"I thought I saw you come in." Graham's voice sounded soft behind her, as if he was afraid his words would set her in motion. His fingers brushed her shoulder blade. "Are you all right?"

She stumbled off the cement step, the touch of his hand another thing she couldn't tolerate in this moment. "I will be. Just give me a minute." Elsie turned, keeping him within her sights.

How could it be that he looked so much like the cousin she remembered—his face awash with concern and warmth. And yet, he wasn't the gangly twelve-year-old boy anymore. Graham's shoulders had grown broad and filled out, and his wide-legged stance filled the doorway.

She swallowed the bile rising in her throat. She thought she'd put Graham out of her mind all these years, but she'd only frozen him in time, his terror-ridden face lit up by the fire's glow.

Her skin flushed again, this time the nausea refusing to be ignored. She clenched her fingers over her mouth and staggered a few more steps into the cold evening air and around the side of the house, her stomach rolling.

The spots dancing in front of her eyes finally slowed, and she drew a shaky breath. She'd spent so many years trying to forget, building walls around those memories to prevent them from seeping in. Now suddenly those barriers seemed tissue-paper thin and capable of being blown aside by the tiniest gust of wind. *"We can't live in the ashes." Isn't that what Mother said?*

If only Graham hadn't stepped into her present.

Elsie tucked the loose strands of hair behind her ear, retracing her steps to the front of the house. She had a dinner party to host.

Graham still hovered in the doorway. "I-I didn't know if I should follow you, or . . ." He glanced over his shoulder into the house and then turned back to meet her eyes. "Or just leave."

"You can't leave. My parents want you here."

His gaze faltered. "I suppose it was too much to hope that you might welcome me too." He expelled a quick breath, almost a laugh, but not quite. "I should have known better."

His sorrow cut through her, weakening the stiffness in her shoulders. "Graham, I wish . . . I wish I felt differently."

Graham nodded and opened the door for her, then flattened his back against it so she could pass. "I'll leave in the morning."

Elsie stepped into the small living room, careful to keep the fireplace in view. She ran fingers around her collar, her knuckles brushing against the ragged scars she kept hidden. "That's not necessary. I'm leaving Mammoth soon anyway."

"And Rose? Is . . . is she going with you?" The hesitation in his voice spoke volumes.

"She decided to stay on here when Mary and I transferred south. She took a post as a bubble queen—laundress—for the housekeeping cabins." *Graham and Rose.* Another thing she might have to get used to. She hung her coat in the hall closet and headed for the kitchen, leaving Graham in the front room.

Her mother stirred a large pot on the stovetop, the steam giving her cheeks a rosy appearance she hadn't sported in months. "Hello, darling. I'm glad you're home."

"Mama, you shouldn't be doing that."

"Stirring?" She lifted the spoon and tapped it on the pot rim. "Herma did all the hard work. And Rose sent over a big batch of rolls earlier. They're warming in the oven."

Herma appeared from behind the door to the tiny pantry. "I'm watching out for her, Elsie. Don't worry. But we're going to have far too much food unless you brought reinforcements."

Elsie retrieved an apron and tied it about her waist. "Graham is here. The girls should be along soon."

"My George is out back with your father and Teddy." Herma added another pot to the stove, dropping in some butter.

"Teddy Vaughn?" She caught herself before saying more. Thankfully she'd be heading south soon. A little distance would help her get over this silly crush.

Graham entered the room behind her, Rose and Mary on his heels. "It's the same everywhere. People gather in the kitchen."

Mother laughed. "That's because it's where love is cooked up. I'm so glad you could join us. I love it when the house is full."

Mary breathed in a deep whiff. "Thank you for having us, Mrs. Brookes. Dinner smells divine!"

Herma lifted a pan from the oven. "Chicken and dumplings, hot bread, steamed vegetables. Oh, and apple pie. That ought to fill you up."

"Sounds delicious." Graham patted his stomach. "I haven't had good home cooked meals like this in . . ." He thought for a second. "I'm not sure how long it's been, really."

Elsie studied him for a minute before turning to gather silverware and plates. Graham had lost both his father and his job in the past year. Her parents' compassion always put her to shame. "Maybe you can help me set the table."

His eyes widened. "Happy to." Olive branch accepted.

Mother wiped the spoon with a dishcloth. "I don't think we have enough space around our little table. Perhaps we'd best eat picnic-style wherever we can find a seat."

As often happened, the party divided into two comfortable groups. The rangers, including Elsie's parents, Teddy Vaughn, and Herma and her husband, Chief Ranger George Baggley, sat at the table, while everyone else took their food into the small sitting room. Elsie was the only one who seemed at ease in both worlds.

She perched on the small ottoman, letting the others claim the chair and tiny sofa. "This feels like the old days of being relegated to the children's table at holiday meals."

Graham grinned. "I remember. You and your parents would come for Thanksgiving, along with all the other aunts and uncles. I miss those days."

The picture hovered around the edges of Elsie's memory—one pleasant image scarred by the devastation that followed.

Rose took the seat next to him on the sofa. "I'm jealous. As an only child, I didn't have much family. It must have made for fun gatherings."

"Noisy." Graham chuckled.

"Speaking of noisy . . ." Mary shot Elsie a questioning glance.

Elsie swallowed her bite of food. Evidently the girls were waiting to see if she would invite Graham to the dance. Determined to follow her mother's advice, Elsie steeled herself. "Graham, the girls and I are throwing together a little party for all the savages. I hope you can come."

A shy smile brightened Rose's face. "Do you like to dance, Graham?"

His eyes settled on her. "You bet I do. And I'll be there. I can't wait to meet the rest of the crew." He glanced at the others. "Hey, I'm supposed to practice driving one of the buses tomorrow. Are any of you ladies interested in a private tour of the park?"

Elsie adjusted her seat. "I think we're going to be busy putting the Great Hall in order for the festivities on Saturday." She couldn't miss Rose's quick pout. Driving with Graham probably sounded like much more fun than scrubbing the hall, but she was too loyal to say as much.

"I guess I'll be tooling around on my own, then." Laughter spilled in from the other room. Graham smiled, then continued. "I'm looking forward to the dance. How many will be there?"

Mary gestured with her napkin. "We're inviting the usual—the wranglers, the pillow punchers, heavers, pearl divers, pack rats, and so on. Oh, and the CCC boys. Elsie, I spoke to your dad earlier about our concerns that there might be too many of them. He said they could put the invitation forward as a reward for a small selection of the boys. Those who show themselves worthy of such an honor."

"That might cut out some of the riffraff," Graham said.

Elsie felt a flush of indignation. "Just because they were unemployed doesn't mean they're bums."

"I didn't mean to imply that. I was out of work for a long time too. But I heard this program was designed to clear the streets of rabble-rousers and ne'er-do-wells. To quell civil discontent in the Hoovervilles."

This new bit of information didn't settle well with Elsie. These were the men she'd agreed to teach?

The three rangers walked in from the other room as Graham finished his statement. Her father balanced a coffee cup in his right hand. "No one with a police record was eligible. It seems to me most of these boys are pretty decent stock, though undernourished and sadly out of shape."

"I'm glad to hear it, sir—the 'decent stock' part, anyway." Graham corrected himself. "I'd hate to see these ladies led astray by any ruffians. Are you at all concerned about them consorting with the staff and visitors? At least the fellows working for the concessions are largely university students."

Elsie couldn't help but study Teddy Vaughn as he leaned against the doorframe, listening to the conversation. His brown-eyed gaze seemed to take in everything and everyone but gave up little of what he was thinking.

Her father cleared his throat. "Scripture tells us to show hospitality to strangers—'for thereby some have entertained angels unawares.'"

Elsie wasn't so sure about angels, but it did seem like there were a few gentlemen among the CCC crew. She'd already met one, at least. "I think the reward system sounds like a wonderful idea. We'd like to welcome them all, but it's such a large group. Assuming we stay with the idea of a dance, we wouldn't have enough ladies to partner with all those men."

Mary lifted one shoulder and smiled. "It sounds like a fun challenge to me."

Her father nodded, a twinkle in his eye. "It'll give the men something to work toward. A little carrot as incentive, you might say."

Graham cast a glance toward Rose. "But should Elsie and her friends be used as that carrot?"

"The social event is the carrot." Elsie folded her hands in her lap. "And we can take care of ourselves."

Her father chuckled. "That's my girl." He turned to Graham. "And there'll be plenty of other men there—the jammers, wranglers, porters, and such. I don't think we'll have any trouble. I'll be sure the New York boys are on their best behavior."

Mary bumped Elsie's arm. "And we'll welcome them to Yellowstone in style."

Eight

Nate followed the men into the tent, dropped his bag at the foot of the bed, and collapsed onto the cot. Every muscle in his arms and back protested the long day wielding a pick and shovel at the park's buffalo ranch. His hands were scraped and bleeding from removing old fencing. A few more weeks and he'd either be as tough as nails or shipped home in a box.

The massive, shaggy bison had taken his breath away. Who knew such incredible animals could exist in today's modern world—outside of cowboy shows, that is. The wrangler at the Lamar Buffalo Ranch said they'd started with around two dozen animals and now had over a thousand healthy head. Evidently the Wild West was making a comeback right here at Yellowstone as they tried to keep this impressive beast from going extinct.

In his exhaustion, Nate floated on the sounds of the conversations filling the tent, including Moretti and Ricci nearby laughing and joking in Italian. He still had things to do before dinner, but another minute on his bunk and he'd be out, if he wasn't careful.

Mutt kicked the foot of the bed as he sauntered past. "Webber, you smell like a buffalo's behind. Do us a favor and hit the showers."

"That's what good, honest work'll do for you," Nate jabbed back.

"What's your excuse?" A hot shower would be welcome now, if he could manage to peel himself off the mattress.

The raucous laughter was silenced by the sound of a clearing throat. The captain stood at the entrance, his hands clasped behind him.

Nate scrambled to his feet along with every other weary man in the company.

"Report outside, men. We've got a few items to discuss."

Nate buttoned his shirt, his stomach sinking. Did this mean the work hadn't pleased their superiors? A few of the men were slackers, but most had labored diligently.

The men fell into lines outside the tents, much like Nate pictured a military inspection, minus the discipline. He glanced about. Some of the men were shirtless, others slouched, most still bore the grime and sweat of the day on their skin and clothes. A pretty sorry-looking lot, overall. But it might be preferable to appearing neat and tidy after a long day's labor. They were grunts hired to work, after all, not soldiers on parade.

Captain Dahl stood at attention beside Ranger Brookes and Superintendent Toll. His face remained grim until the company's shuffling feet and hushed voices quieted. He cleared his throat for a second time as he surveyed the ragtag collection of men. "You worked hard today. Some more than others." He shot a glance down the row, his attention lighting on a few fellows in the rear of the group. "Ranger Brookes and Superintendent Toll have arranged for several large projects that we will be putting our backs into over the next few months, including trail repair, landscaping, and pine beetle control. I will be observing your work closely and watching for those who rise to the top. Leaders will be established, and we will find a variety of ways to reward hard work."

"Extra pay might be nice," Val whispered.

Red grunted. "Or time off."

Nate set his jaw, determined not to be drawn into the fellows' antics.

The captain folded his arms across his chest. "One mandate President Roosevelt has given us is that each man here should have an opportunity to educate himself. To that end, the government is restricting your labor to forty hours per week. That will allow you plenty of time for other activities including instruction and recreation. We are bringing in teachers and will be holding regular classes in basic subjects for those of you who have not had the opportunity to finish high school." His attention skimmed across the group. "I imagine that might be a large percentage of you."

Nate swallowed hard, careful not to move his gaze from the captain's face. So much for getting by completely on the strength of his back. Once again, his defective mind would be on display for the world to see. Perhaps he could manage to stay busy enough to avoid the classroom entirely. Could he volunteer for extra hours?

"We will also offer training in various professional fields including machine arts, truck driving, forestry, and electronics so that you might find yourself more employable when you leave the three Cs."

Red rocked up and down on his toes. "Hot dog. Red Walsh, machinist."

Dahl studied the lines of men before him. "I have already asked a few of you to begin organizing recreational and entertainment activities. I expect to see baseball games, boxing matches, Friday night talent shows, and a camp newspaper in short order."

A stitch of tension seemed to evaporate from the gathering as a few hoots and a smattering of applause met the captain's last statement. Nate relaxed. Sports and recreation would cut into any forced classroom time.

"Now, I'd like you to direct your attention to Ranger Brookes for a moment, lads. He has an announcement I think you'll welcome."

The ranger doffed his hat and clutched it to his side. "Men, I'm here to extend a special invitation."

A breeze swept through the camp with his words. Nate drew his eyes away from the snow-covered hills and jagged peaks in the distance and focused on the gray-haired man. He seemed so at home here that he was almost part of the landscape.

Brookes studied the ranks, a smile toying about his lips. "It has come to my attention that the young people working at the hotel and campground are planning a dance for Saturday night to welcome the new and returning seasonal staff to the Mammoth area. Several of the ladies approached me recently about possibly extending that welcome to you boys."

Whistles and whoops answered the man's announcement.

He lifted a hand to quiet the celebration. "Not so fast. Not *all* of you will be attending. Your captain will be hand-selecting the best and brightest—the hard-working, respectful, and well-mannered men only. We want to put our best foot forward, so to say."

Best and brightest? Nate's shoulders sank. He was about as bright as a burned-out bulb.

Mutt laughed under his breath. "Webber and Red are out, then. Can't have their ugly mugs representing us to the ladies."

Captain Dahl stepped forward. "You've heard it, men. We'll deliver the invitations at mail call on Thursday morning. That leaves you two days to impress the socks off your leaders. Now, I've heard that the mess tent has rustled up some—"

The captain's words were drowned out by a growling engine. A stake bed truck barreled into camp and pulled up short. A young ranger jumped to the ground.

Brookes rushed to his side. "Vaughn, what's wrong?"

"Fire." His breath came in short gasps. "We need you, sir."

The superintendent joined them beside the vehicle. "Where?"

"The western entrance, Madison River area. A roadside brush burn got out of control, sir."

"Fires already?" Toll frowned. "It's only May."

Brookes glanced across the company. "Dahl, any chance your boys can lend a hand? We're still short staffed until June. Vaughn could use some warm bodies—maybe twenty or so?"

Dahl snapped him a quick nod before turning to the men. "You heard him, fellas. Volunteers?"

A murmur went through the group as the men looked at each other with wide eyes. They'd already put in a long day, and the delicious smells from the mess tent beckoned.

As soon as Mutt stepped forward, Nate's blood pressure surged. The skunk only wanted to curry favor with the captain in order to step pretty into the dance on Saturday. Nate could care less about dancing, but that leadership post still dangled in front of him like a shiny red apple. What he wouldn't give to send home an extra five dollars a month. If it kept his mother out of the breadlines and his brother out of trouble, he'd endure blisters and aches any day. He stepped forward.

Val joined him. "Always volunteer, right? I told you what my father said."

"He sounds like a wise man," Nate said. "Better than mine, anyway. Sticking your neck out in my house just volunteered you for a slap about the ears."

Red grunted and sauntered forward to join the line. "You fellas are crazy, but I'm not staying here by myself Saturday night. I aim to dance with all the pretty girls."

As soon as they had a suitable group, the captain offered them a grim nod. "We haven't had time to school you in firefighting techniques. Webber, did you read that section of the manual?"

A flush prickled up Nate's neck. The book hung heavy in his shirt pocket. "No sir. I haven't gotten to that one . . . yet." He hadn't gotten to any of it.

Dahl gestured to a truck waiting near the camp gate, the same one that had returned them from fence removal earlier. "You fellows should have time to look it over on the way. And then keep your eyes on the rangers and follow their lead. No funny business. I want every man back safe in his bunk tomorrow—you hear?"

"Yes sir." Nate gulped. They scattered to retrieve tools and canteens before gathering beside the truck. Nate picked up his shovel, the wooden handle pressing into his blistered palm.

ate followed Red, Val, and the others as they tossed gear into the empty truck bed and then hauled themselves in. The rangers had promised a long bumpy ride, so Nate unfastened the blanket roll from his shoulder and used it as a cushion for his already sore back as he leaned against the wooden slats. He folded his arms and lowered his hat across his face, hoping to catch a little shut eye on the trip.

Red elbowed him. "Hey, what about that book Dahl was going on about? Ain't we supposed to read something before it gets too dark to see?"

"Right." Nate dug into his pocket, slid out the small green manual, flipped it open, and thumbed through the pages.

Mutt dropped onto the floor across from him, his legs jutting out toward Nate. "What's it say? Don't get burned?"

"It probably says fools and fire are a deadly combination." Nate skimmed the headings. Fire started with the letter *F*. He knew that much, anyway. He ran his thumb along the bold titles. The letters blurred as the vehicle jounced down the dirt road.

"So what's it got?" Val glanced over his shoulder, a bit like an overeager puppy.

Mutt leaned back and used his rucksack for a pillow. "Read us a bedtime story, Webber." He snorted. "Better you than me, though. I get motion sickness trying to read on the road."

Good thought. Nate shoved the open book toward Val. "Yeah, me too."

The kid took the manual and squinted at the small print. "I don't think a chapter on fishing is going to help, Nate." He thumbed through the pages before jabbing his finger at a different section. "Wildfires. Here it is."

"Checking to see if you were paying attention," Nate muttered, fixing his gaze on his boots.

The young man glanced up at him for a brief moment before returning to the words.

Nate leaned back and closed his eyes, listening as Val droned his way through the chapter. A few pages in, he stopped.

"What's wrong?" Nate opened his eyes.

Val flipped through a few more pages and frowned. "It only talks about why wildfires are bad and how much damage they do. It doesn't say how to fight them." He lifted his gaze. "In Brooklyn, there are fire wagons and pumper trucks. They got those here?"

Red shoved his hat back. "They got us. Bucket brigade, maybe?"

"I guess we'll find out when we get there." Nate pressed fingers against his weary eyes. "But with all those trees, it's going to take more than a few men with buckets."

Evening passed into night, a dark cloak spreading across the sky, speckled with stars. The truck's bouncing causing Nate's head to ricochet off the panel wall several times along the journey. Even so, he managed to grab a few snatches of sleep, his mind drifting from waking to dreaming and back again with little knowledge as to which was which. Eventually he'd gathered his pack onto his bent knees and laid his head against the rough canvas, like a schoolboy asleep at his desk.

After several hours the vehicle rumbled to a stop, throwing them all against each other like so many dominoes. The growling engine cut out, plunging them into silence. Val got to his feet and stared out the back. "Oy vey," he whispered under his breath, just loud enough for Nate to hear.

Every muscle in Nate's neck seemed to complain as he straightened and rolled to his knees. Hoisting himself higher, he peered between the truck's slats for a look. The glow of the burning trees sent a jolt through his system. It looked like the devil himself had taken up residency in the forest. The red and orange glow crept along the lower part of the forest, reaching into the tree's limbs in only a few places, but the searing light and heat kicked his heartbeat into a crazy rhythm. He grabbed his gear and shovel and clambered off the truck with the others.

The ranger met them around the side. "Leave your blankets and food here. Make sure your canteen is full. Grab a Pulaski from the crate in the back of my truck. We're going to clear a firebreak and see if we can cut this thing off here before it progresses farther into the park." He hurried off to where a couple of men and a team of horses busted a path through the vegetation.

"What in the world's a Pulaski?" Mutt strapped a canteen to his belt.

Nate strode over to the park truck and spotted a box of double-edged tools waiting for them. "I'm guessing he's talking about these." Turning the wooden handle over in his grip, he tested the weight of the ax-and-hoe combination.

Red retied his bandana so it blocked some of the smoke from his face. "You've got to be kidding me."

Val appeared at Nate's side. "What are we doing, exactly?" The younger man's face glowed in the firelight, fear hovering in his eyes. Several others gathered around Nate.

He ignored the terror brewing in his own gut. These fellows were looking to him for courage. "Remember that ditch we dug last week? Easy." He huffed out a breath. "Come on, boys. You want to make that dance on Saturday, don't you?"

Red smirked. "Think how we'll impress the girls with this story. Our first month on the job, and we save the park from burning down."

Mutt braced a Pulaski across his broad shoulders. "What I wouldn't give for a couple of hoses and a fireplug about now."

Nate started toward the firebreak where the men were working with the plow. "Keep each other in sight range. Don't wander off. Stay close to the line and keep an eye on the man ahead and behind you."

"Yes sir, boss." Mutt spit at the ground near Nate's feet.

Red prodded the man in the back with his ax handle. "You gonna keep yapping, or are you going to get to work? The sooner we bust this ground, the sooner we get back to camp."

Val lifted his canteen in the air. "Hotcakes for breakfast when we're done, fellas!"

Nate rubbed a blistered hand across the back of his stiff neck as he led the way. *Lord, just get us all home.*

Ten

Elsie loosened her scarf and lifted her face to soak in the spring sunshine. She'd always loved the view from this part of the Bunsen Peak trail, but today it seemed even more breathtaking than usual. Other than a few patches of snow, the path remained clear, and the strenuous walk got her blood pumping.

Graham's enthusiasm to see everything had put him in the lead, with Rose puppy dogging at his heels. She didn't seem to notice that he'd spent the day treating her like a sweet younger sister, doing everything short of pinching her cheek.

Mary and Hal dragged far behind. The poor fellow was more suited to life behind the hotel desk than out in the rugged wilderness.

And here she was stuck in between, like a spare tire.

Elsie paused at one of the hairpin turns in the trail and looked over the panoramic vista. She could see the hot springs and the red roofs of Fort Yellowstone a couple of miles away and a thousand feet below—like glimpsing a friend in the distance. She'd miss Mammoth when they left. The open spaces and wide skies were so different from the dense lodgepole forest of the Canyon area. The places even smelled different. Mammoth was sage with the occasional whiff of sulfur; Canyon was pine. *You could blindfold me, and I'd still recognize either place.* Elsie closed her eyes and drew in a deep breath of the mountain air.

Graham's laugh carried back to her on the wind. Just like the unique smells, that sound transported her back to her childhood in Washington, DC. She shook off the thought, forcing her eyes open to secure herself in the here and now before memories took her down twisty, unwanted paths. Graham had asked her for forgiveness, and the request hung heavy on her heart. Forgiveness was letting go, right? Why was she so unwilling to release her clenched grip on the past?

Mary came up beside her. "Has your father gotten back yet? Any word on the fire?"

The word jarred her as usual. *The forest fire.* Elsie lowered her hand from picking at her collar, the unconscious habit grating at her. "They returned late last night. Since things were still wet, it stayed fairly small. My father thinks it was probably started by some roadwork just outside the park. They took some of the CCC boys to help." In fact, he'd raved about the men's gumption. Untrained, unconditioned, but eager to give it their all.

"That's why they're here, isn't it?" Mary wove her arm through Hal's. "I wonder why you boys weren't asked to help?"

"I stay far away from fires." Hal sounded almost indignant. "My goal is to make it to manager and then someday own my own motel in Cody or Cooke City. I'm not looking for hero status."

"Own a motel?" Mary's eyes widened.

He puffed out his chest. "Sure. That's what Bernie and I decided this winter. Just think, if you and I get hitched someday, you could boss around all the pillow punchers."

Elsie watched Mary's face as she processed this tidbit of information. She'd had more than her fill of hotel work the past few summers—Hal must know that. Mary extricated her arm and walked over to study the view. "I wonder what the boys thought of their first forest fire."

Hal thrust his hands into his trouser pockets. "Dirty, hot work? Smoke-filled air? I imagine it wasn't too different from a smelly New York factory. Probably reminded them of home."

Elsie had never heard Hal say a negative word about anyone. Mary's constant chatter about the "new boys" must be getting on his nerves. She cleared her throat. "I imagine it was pretty fearsome."

Graham walked back toward them, Rose following a few steps after. "We didn't mean to leave you behind." He lifted his arms. "I can't believe this place. It's astounding."

"There's so much more to see, Graham." Rose took off her fuzzy beret and ran fingers through her curls. "How was your practice run with the bus? Did you drive very far?"

He smiled at her. "All the way past Madison to the West Yellowstone train depot and then back around to Old Faithful."

Elsie thought through his route. "The fire burned over near the western boundary. You must have been close to it at one point."

"I suppose I was, but I didn't see anything. Too busy grinding the gears." He grimaced. "Those things are a bear."

Rose brushed fingers against his arm. "I wish we could have gone with you. I could have shown you the sights."

He hooked a thumb through his suspenders. "We've got all summer. I can pick you girls up and take you anywhere you want to go."

Elsie thought she could probably warm her hands on the excited glow radiating from Rose's face.

Mary winked at the other girls. "Our own personal driver. This is going to be the best summer yet. Right, Rose?"

Hal folded his arms across his chest, scowling at Graham. "Those touring cars aren't your personal plaything."

"Who put lemons in your coffee, Hal?" Mary laid her hands on her hips. "You're not usually this much of a sourpuss."

The young man's eyes flashed. "I'm not the one who planned a big shindig on your last night here at Mammoth and then invited every eligible man in the park. I've been waiting all winter to see you, but all you can talk about is parading each muscle-bound Gus through the ballroom like so many cattle at the stock show."

Mary gasped. "Hal—"

"No." His face was a storm. "Mary Prosser, I won't be your chump or your fallback. If you're more interested in some gangster off the streets of Brooklyn or a reckless bus driver than a steady man from Wyoming, then so be it." He turned and trotted down the slope toward Mammoth.

Mary stood agape. "Well, I never."

Elsie could hardly believe it herself. Hal Henderson had hardly strung five words together at a time, too busy working like a mule in a harness or staring at Mary like she was a diamond in the window of the finest jewelry store. "Should we go after him?"

"Let him cool off," Graham said. "I don't know the fella well, but I'm guessing he might need a few minutes to put his heart back together before being expected to speak again."

Rose hurried over and slipped an arm around Mary's shoulders. "Don't worry, Mary. He's just feeling blue because he's stuck here managing the housekeeping cabins and you're heading off to Canyon. He'll calm down."

Elsie wrapped her arms around herself. Rose was the tender heart of their little threesome, and Mary was the laugh. So what did that make her?

The brain? What would they do without Rose's steady presence this summer? If only she'd decided to come to Canyon too.

Mary blinked rapidly and blew out a quick puff of air. "That was quite a little spectacle. It's not like we're exclusive." She tossed her head so that you could almost picture the blond curls bouncing even though she kept them firmly tucked under her pink cloche hat. "I hope he's not going to be such a bore at the party."

Elsie watched as a ground squirrel popped its head out around a nearby sagebrush, possibly eyeing them as a source of a handout. "Hal seems pretty steamed. I wonder if he'll even come?"

Rose cocked her head. "Of course he'll come. And Bernie too. They both agreed, and they've promised to bring their Victrola." She squeezed Mary's hand. "And then you two can kiss and forget this silliness."

Mary's lips pursed. "We'll see. He's right, you know. There are plenty of other men to choose from. Ones who wouldn't expect me to make beds and sweep floors for motel guests the rest of my life."

Graham grabbed the strap of his pack. "It's getting late. Perhaps we should get moving. I'm not sure about you ladies, but I have to work in the morning."

Rose moved closer to him. "We all do, I'm afraid. But the party will be here before you know it." She lowered her eyes. "You'll be there, won't you?"

He grinned at her. "I wouldn't miss it, kid."

Her own smile faded as Graham walked away. Glancing back at Elsie, she sighed. "Are you coming?"

"I'll be along in a minute. You and Mary go ahead." A few moments of peace and quiet without the drama of romance—or the lack thereof—sounded heavenly.

As her friends trotted after Graham, Elsie drew in a deep breath and turned toward the sweeping view of the valley below. This had been one of the first places her father had brought her after they moved to the park. She'd been as jumpy as a field mouse back then—afraid of her own shadow and embarrassed by her scars.

"Hello?" A male voice carried down the hill toward her, interrupting her thoughts.

Ranger Vaughn rode toward her on a tall chestnut mare. He removed the Stetson from his head, revealing his close-cropped brown hair. "I just passed your friends on their way up."

The new ranger's broad shoulders and winning smile never failed to turn Elsie's legs into pudding. "It's nice to see you again, Ranger Vaughn. How are you settling in?"

He pressed the hat to his chest and grinned. "Please—call me Teddy. I hate the whole 'Ranger' thing, myself."

"But isn't the title an honor?"

His eyes widened. "Oh . . . I know . . . I mean, I just didn't think you . . ." He swallowed, his Adam's apple bobbing. "*You* shouldn't have to call me that, considering who your father is and everything."

"I'm sorry, Teddy. I didn't mean to be rude. And please, call me Elsie."

He dismounted, laying a hand on the horse's neck. "And you're right. It is an honor. I'm thrilled to be working at Yellowstone."

"Really? That's nice." She fiddled with the button on her sleeve. Mary always said to ask a man questions about himself, but she'd have to come up with something better than 'really?'

"I spent two years at Rocky Mountain National Park, near where I grew up, but I've always longed to work here. Ever since I first put on the badge."

She couldn't resist darting a glance at his chest—just to see the badge, of course. "What made you want to be a ranger?"

"Well, it was my mama's dream, really. She was a supporter of Theodore Roosevelt. She got to shake his hand once." He rubbed his chin. "That's where I got my name, if you hadn't guessed."

"I hadn't." It seemed fitting for this handsome ranger to bear the name of a president who'd established five of the national parks.

"She suggested the profession to all four of us boys, but I was the only one who pursued it." He smiled. "I think she'd pretty much given up hope."

"Why Yellowstone? I've never been to Colorado, but I've seen photographs and stereoscopes of Rocky Mountain. It's beautiful."

"I figured at least some part of these ambitions should be my own." His mouth quirked upward. "No one wants to completely follow his mother's plans, does he? But it's worked out. I wanted to be a fireman, and guess what I spent the past two days doing?" He straightened his shoulders. "It's an honor to protect the park."

She steeled herself. Would fire haunt all her days? "You worked the fire last night, and you're out here patrolling so soon?"

"I'm low man on the pole, so they say. Plus, I'm happy to do it. I want to be familiar with all the corners of the park."

Rose, Mary, and Graham had been gone quite a while. Mary would tease her endlessly if she dallied too long with the ranger. "I should catch up to my friends. It was nice to talk with you."

He caught her arm as she passed him, and the gentle brush of his fingers made her pulse race. "I hear you're leaving soon. Your father says you're moving to Canyon?"

"Yes, after the big party." Had any of the rangers been invited? Her stomach quivered. "You're welcome to join us, Ranger . . . um, Teddy."

His mare nickered softly, and Teddy moved to stroke the horse's nose. "I wouldn't want to intrude. I don't really know many of the staff yet."

A breeze caught the end of Elsie's scarf and fluttered it about her face. If only she had an ounce of Mary's poise and confidence. "I could introduce you around, if you wanted."

He lifted his gaze to meet hers, his brown eyes intense. "I'd be honored, Elsie. Truly. Should I come by for you about eight?"

"I'll be going over early to help set up." She nodded toward the trail where her friends had disappeared. "We all are. I could meet you there."

He took a step closer, his long shadow falling over her. "Perfect. I'd love to help, and then I can get to know some of your friends before festivities begin. That will free us to focus on dancing."

Weakness spread through her limbs. How would she ever coordinate them enough to keep from trampling on the poor man's feet? "Six o'clock, then?"

He grinned. "I can't wait."

Nate squirted the last dropper of milk into the raccoon kit's mouth, not that the hungry little pig seemed the least bit grateful, its little handlike paws clutching the glass tube. This one and its sibling had scarfed down a tin cup of the stuff. How much could two raccoons eat, anyway?

The smaller of the two had already nestled into a corner of Nate's footlocker, cuddling with a rolled pair of socks.

In the next cot Moretti scowled. "Next time you go off somewhere, you better hire a babysitter. Those things mewled all night long. We finally put them back in the showers hoping their mama would come and claim them."

"I already tried that."

"Well, at least we got a few hours of shut-eye."

"You could have been out digging firebreaks with us, you know."

When Nate discovered the abandoned kits, the captain told him to walk them into the brush and leave them. Nate ran a finger over the little guy's ringed tail. Might as well hang a dinner bell around its neck while they were at it. He and Val had managed to take turns on feeding duty. Even Red had gotten in on the act after Mutt threatened to toss the scamps out to the bears.

Nate held the kit at eye level. "Looks like you and your brother might be our unofficial mascots. Question is—will you go with us to Canyon?"

"We're not keeping the fleabags here," Moretti said. "And don't expect me to watch 'em while you're making pretty at that dance. Not unless there's cash in it for me." Moretti leaned on his elbow.

"How about a canteen credit?"

The fellow lifted his eyebrows. "Hmm. I'll think about it. Or if you don't want that invite—"

"Captain said they weren't transferrable."

Moretti fell back on his bunk. "Only a loon would turn it down, anyway."

Get dressed up and hobnob with local girls? Most of the boys were beyond excited, but to Nate, it sounded like a recipe for trouble. He didn't want to spend the evening chaperoning a bunch of overexcited young men. Or chance running into that college girl again.

His folks could hardly afford to feed their whole brood, so sending them to college had never been a consideration. Only Charlie had the brains for it, and he seemed more determined to get himself sent up the river than off to university. How much must something like that cost, anyway? More than Nate would see in a lifetime, that was sure.

How could he, Red, and the others hold their heads up around these privileged girls? And likely as not, there'd be plenty of college men there too. Red already had the scoop—horse wranglers, desk clerks, dishwashers, porters, bus drivers—the place would be filled with respectable fellows with their polished wing-tip shoes. *Why are they inviting us? Are we the comedy act?*

The folded invitation rustled in his pocket. He hadn't needed to attempt reading it. All of the men who'd volunteered for the fire brigade had received one. It was clear from the excited talk what the typed words meant.

The kit had drifted off, so Nate placed it beside the other. The smaller of the two had grabbed hold of the sock ball and was chewing on it in his sleep. Nate worked it free of the raccoon's teeth and sighed. One more thing to mend before Saturday night.

Eleven

Mary unwound the curlers from Elsie's hair and smiled. "Perfect. Ranger Vaughn is going to fall over with glee. You've never looked so pretty."

Elsie pressed a hand against her trembling stomach. "I'm not sure what I was thinking, inviting him like I did."

"You were thinking he's a good-looking fellow who'd make a great dance partner." Her friend swept a perfume bottle into her hand and squeezed the bulb, dousing Elsie with thousands of fragrant droplets. "Give him a chance, Elsie. He's perfect for you. Rugged, strong, capable—he's basically a younger version of your father."

"He's nothing like my father. And what is that fragrance?" Elsie coughed, grabbing a tissue to wipe some of the perfume from her neck before it soaked in. "That's not Les Fleurs Favorite."

"You simply cannot continue using those plain old Colgate scents, Elsie. *Parfum* is the elixir of love. If you douse yourself in cheap American toilet water, you're going to attract cheap men." She waved the cut-crystal bottle under Elsie's nose. "This is the latest indulgence from Paris, Bellodgia by Caron. The perfumer in Missoula insisted it would make us smell like we'd basked in a field of Italian wildflowers flourishing in the Mediterranean sun."

"So are you trying to attract French or Italian men?"

She plopped onto the corner of the bed and sighed. "Honestly, I don't know what I want. I just know that I don't want to be stuck with some fellow who owns a seedy two-bit motel somewhere, where I'll be making beds for the rest of my life. Oh, Elsie, what am I going to do?" Her voice pitched upward.

Elsie turned, the intensity of her friend's plea jarring her from her own worries. "What do you mean? Is this about Hal?"

"He wants to get married." Mary's face crumpled.

"But that's wonderful." Elsie hopped up from her seat and sank onto the bed next to Mary. "Isn't it?"

"No. It's awful. I can't marry him. He's so . . . so . . ." She shook her head, tears springing to her eyes. "So Hal."

"Oh, honey." Elsie gathered Mary into her arms and squeezed her narrow shoulders. If only Rose were here. She was so much better at these sorts of things. Then again, she was still smarting over her last sweetheart. "You don't have to marry him. Not if you don't want to."

Mary coughed, then hiccupped against Elsie's shoulder. "What if he's my only chance? What if my darling Frenchman never comes along? Hal's a nice fella."

Elsie drew back, studying Mary's face. "Do you love him?"

Distress passed across her face. "I don't know."

The indecisiveness in her voice made Elsie pause. How could she not know what she wanted? Elsie had dreamed of teaching since she was twelve years old, sitting in the tiny classroom of Mammoth School. "Well, you don't have to answer him right now. Tell him you need some time to think."

"If only I were more like you." Mary ran a silk handkerchief under her eyes, managing to look elegant even in the middle of a crying jag. "You want an outdoorsy fella so you guys can play ranger for the rest of your life."

Elsie grasped the strings of compassion sliding from her fingertips. "I've told you before, I don't want to get married. I want to teach."

"Don't be ridiculous. You can do both. Or marry a ranger and you won't have to work. Teddy is perfect. That's why I told him to seek you out."

Elsie jumped to her feet. "Mary Prosser, you didn't!"

Her roommate sniffled, using the tip of her pinky finger to wipe the last tear from her lashes. "You'll thank me later. I'll be godmother to your brood of children." She pressed her hands over her eyes a second time. "I'll have plenty of time because I'll be an old maid, still mopping floors at Canyon Lodge."

A bitter taste rose to Elsie's mouth as her friend played games with her sentiments. "You never should have said anything to Teddy. Now he thinks I'm interested."

"You *are* interested. And Elsie, the man's been off fighting forest fires. He deserves to spin a pretty girl around the dance floor. You've already spurned Bernie. Hal says his brother is heartbroken."

"I doubt that." Elsie fingered the curls tickling her neck. Bernie had never been more than a convenient placeholder so Mary could invite Elsie along on dates.

"Please, be nice to Teddy tonight. For me?" Mary blinked her red-rimmed eyes. "I have to know someone is having fun at this party. I'll be spending the whole night ducking Hal. Hopefully some of the CCC boys will want to dance."

"Of course I'll be nice. But you must promise to stop talking about broods of children because that's never going to happen." Not for her.

Mary jumped up. "Deal." A smile crept to her face as she lifted two dresses from the bedside chair. "So which do you think I should wear—the blue or the red?"

Elsie leaned forward to study her chin in the mirror. Was that a blemish? She glanced at the reflection of the dresses. "The blue matches your eyes."

"But *red* makes a statement."

How quickly Mary had recovered from her distress. Elsie turned in her seat to stare at her friend. "What sort of message are you trying to send?"

The blonde held the red dress in front of her and swished it around. "It says, 'I like to have fun.'"

Poor Hal.

"I like the blue. It says, 'I am serene, like Yellowstone Lake on a sunny day.'"

Her roommate made a face before tossing the garment toward her. "Then you wear it. I'm never serene. I'm bubbly and feisty like your beloved geysers."

She had a point. Elsie draped the pale blue crepe over her lap, the smooth fabric teasing her skin. "Can I? You wouldn't mind?"

"You can keep it. It looked smart in the bright lights of the department store, but out here? Not so much." She unbuttoned the red dress and slipped it on over her chemise.

Her definition of *smart* needed some alterations, but Elsie wouldn't argue. The blue silk was much prettier than the flowered dress she'd ironed two nights ago. She hadn't considered that she might be stepping out with a ranger. The thought settled around her shoulders like an itchy wool sweater. How had she gotten herself into this?

She laid the dress on her bed and examined the buttons running up the front. If she adjusted a few, she should be able to alter the dress so it buttoned to her throat. Elsie glanced at Mary fussing with her face powder, adding some to the edges of her collarbone.

Elsie picked up her best sewing needle. Mary could show a little skin. It was fine—hers was a smooth, milky white. But not Elsie's. She guided thread through the needle's eye. *Frankenstein*. That's what the children had called her years ago, pointing and laughing. In time, she'd learned how to make the taunting stop. Buttons to her neck, and cuffs to her wrists. Out of sight, out of mind. What they couldn't see, they couldn't ridicule.

She tied off the last button. The silhouette of the dress wouldn't be as pleasing this way, but it drew attention to her most appealing feature. Men had often complimented her blue eyes and friendly smile. As long as she kept everyone's gaze focused above the collar, she'd be perfectly fine.

Nate ran a wet comb through his hair, trying in vain to get the cowlick near his brow to lie flat. If only he could keep his hat on all evening. All around him in the tent, men jostled and wisecracked—some getting dressed for the dance, others grousing about being left behind. Bribing the crew with party invitations had been a wise move. Next time such a sweet delight was offered, the men would be falling over each other to volunteer for anything the park service had in mind.

"You're going to be a lady killer tonight, my friend." Red slapped Nate on the shoulder. "We're going to romance those pretty girls right out of their dancing shoes."

"Val will, but I'm not so sure about you." Nate chuckled. "You still smell like soot. Did you wash?"

Red lifted hands to his face and took a deep whiff. "You're fooling me. I showered three times. It's probably because I was closer to the fire." He tugged up his sagging pants and cinched his belt. "You boys were all running scared, after all."

Nate hid a smile. The experience had strengthened the bond within their little group, and the good-hearted ribbing reminded him of spending time with Sherm and Charlie. So many things about his fellow workers brought up memories of his brothers. By the end of their stint here in Yellowstone, they were going to be like family.

Unfortunately, families didn't always get along. Mutt moved through the narrow aisle between the cots like a bull, bumping Red's shoulder just enough to send him stumbling.

Red sneered. "Hey, watch it."

The fellow grunted. "Didn't see you there. Maybe if you grew a few inches."

"Not all of us can be mountain-sized."

"Pah. You're not even a molehill, Irish."

Nate stood. "Come on, guys. No harm done." Emotions were already running high, and the last thing they needed was a fistfight. "We're going to have a good time tonight, remember?"

"Like anyone would take a second look at this runt." Mutt jutted his chin. "Ladies don't dance with men who are shorter than they are. You're going to be hugging the wall all night."

"For your information"—Red puffed out his chest—"I already made the acquaintance of the prettiest girl there tonight, and she promised to save me a dance. I don't wager she'll do the same for you, with those clunky feet of yours. You're liable to crush some dame's toes."

Nate couldn't resist glancing at Mutt's size twelve boots. They did look rather ridiculous, especially since the man's wrinkled trousers were a couple of inches too short.

They'd all put on civilian clothes for the evening, but that had only served to remind everyone of what ragged situations most of them came from. When they were sporting their new oversized CCC duds, it was less obvious who had made do—for a very long time, in some cases.

Mutt ran thumbs under his lapels, the plaid suit frayed around the hems. "Sure as sugar, the lady only fawned over you 'cause she hadn't met me yet. I bet you five clams she drops you like a hot potato to dance with me."

"You're on."

Nate's shoulders knotted. Neither man had five of anything to his name, except maybe fleas. They wouldn't get paid until the end of the month and a five-spot was all they got to keep out of their twenty-five dollar pay. Probably a good thing, too, or these fellas would be gambling away every cent.

Val stuck his head inside the tent. "Hey fellas, our ride is here. Wait until you see it."

Nate slipped the comb into his pocket and jammed a flat cap on his head. He followed Mutt and Red into the brisk evening air while several of the other men trailed after to see them off.

A smart yellow touring bus had pulled up in the yard, its canvas top rolled back. A dapper-looking fellow stood next to it, cap in hand. He shook hands with the captain before glancing around the camp with a grin. "I'm here to ferry the men to Mammoth for the dance."

Val, Red, Mutt, and the others piled into the vehicle with wide eyes as Dahl gave a last-minute lecture about behavior, decorum, and representing the camp.

Nate paused beside the driver. "We appreciate the lift, sir. We've spent the past week bouncing around in the back of an army truck. This is a nice change of pace."

The man tipped back his cap. "My pleasure. I'm still learning to handle this contraption, so I'm glad for the practice. Pretty soon I'll be hauling well-heeled visitors, so better I rehearse with you fellows." He stuck out his hand. "Graham Brookes, at your service. Fresh in from DC." The skin on the man's palms was twisted with scars.

Nate hesitated for a moment before clasping his hand. "Nate Webber—Brooklyn."

Brookes laughed. "You're as far from home as I am. You must feel like you've been dropped on the moon."

"You've no idea." Nate tipped his head, studying the driver's blue eyes. "Brookes? You related to Ranger Brookes?"

"My uncle, in fact."

"Nice man."

"He is, indeed. I wouldn't be here otherwise. I'd been out of work for almost a year. Didn't have two pennies to rub together. I had to beg, borrow, and practically steal to get out here."

Nate climbed inside, taking the seat next to the driver. You wouldn't have known the man had ever seen tough times from the look of his pressed uniform, but the scars on his hands said otherwise. Just went to show that you couldn't judge a book by its cover—or a man by his threads.

"So you work for the rangers?" Nate was still struggling to figure out the pecking order around here.

"No, I work for the Yellowstone Park Transportation Company. I'll be running tour groups all around Wonderland." He clamped a hand onto the gearshift and shoved as he jammed his foot on the clutch, the gears grinding. "Still can't quite get the hang of this motor." He cast a sideways glance at Nate. "You drive?"

"Nah, but I'd love to learn." Any skill he could master would be one more dime for his pocket when he got home. "Maybe you could show me sometime."

"Yeah, sure, if it's all right with my boss. Took me a couple of days to read the manual on the train. But once I got behind the wheel, it started to make sense."

"Would I have to read the instructions? Or could you just show me around the levers and pedals?"

Brookes chuckled. "I think it might actually be easier without being overloaded with the details. It was like trying to memorize a dictionary for a language I don't speak."

The bus bumped over the road until the driver guided it behind the Mammoth Hot Springs Hotel. The men in the rear grew quiet, as if the sight of the fancy hotel stole every word from their mouths.

After Brookes stopped the vehicle, he turned around to face the other men in the company. "I hope you fellas are ready to have a good time. I know several of the ladies have been planning and decorating to their heart's content. It might not be up to New York standards, but it's pretty fine for this part of the country."

Nate clambered out of the bus and ran a hand across his rumpled suit jacket. *The real question is, Are we up to their standards?*

Twelve

Elsie stood back and surveyed their work. The streamers twisted their way downward from the chandelier like waterfalls. The music of Duke Ellington's orchestra blared from Hal's tinny-sounding phonograph, sending her heart jouncing in her chest and her toes tapping.

As soon as he'd arrived, Teddy had jumped right in, slipping off his suit jacket and helping move tables and chairs. Now he'd gone to help Hal and Bernie set up a punch table in the rear of the room. It gave her a moment to steady her thoughts, because every time she looked at him, her nerves turned into a jangled mess.

Rose seemed quiet and withdrawn, her freckles standing out against her pale skin. The party preparation probably reminded her of the years she'd spent here with Pete. They'd been the reigning prince and princess of Mammoth, and to see her flitting around alone didn't seem right. But typical of Rose, she'd busied herself mixing up punch and snacks in the kitchen, a stained apron tied over her yellow-flowered dress.

Mary dashed over from the front windows. "They're here—the CCC boys. Elsie, I'm so nervous." She tugged at one of her black elbow-length gloves, then ran her fingers along the low neckline of her dress. "How will we welcome them?"

It wasn't like her friend to be anxious around men. Elsie straightened Mary's necklace. "How about, 'Welcome to Mammoth Hotel'?"

"We should have planned some grand gesture. Like singing. Or gifts."

"I think the grand gesture was inviting them in the first place."

The men sauntered in, their well-worn clothing instantly setting them apart. Most of the college boys sported stylish suits and two-tone oxford shoes.

Mary stepped forward to greet them. "Hello, boys. Welcome. We're just getting started. We're still waiting on some of the guests to arrive, so please feel free to mix and mingle."

Elsie searched their ranks, her gaze finally settling on Nate Webber and his friend, Red. Obviously Mary had spotted them too, from the nervous way her hands were twitching at her sides. She never behaved this way with Hal, but then she'd known him for years now.

Nate was clearly the best looking of the group, a fact that sent Elsie's heart rising to her throat. *Don't be ridiculous. You're here with Teddy.* Elsie glanced back at the ranger, who seemed to be doing his best to chat with Hal and his brother. Teddy looked distinctly uncomfortable. But then, he was the only ranger here, mixed in with all the pack rats and busboys. It must be awkward.

He turned and caught her eye, a smile brightening his face. He picked up two glasses of punch and headed her way. "You look like you could use this."

She took the glass from his hand. Good looking, helpful, and kind? "Thank you. Are you always so thoughtful?"

"I try." He gestured toward the group of men milling about in the entryway, still not comfortable enough to join the party. "I see the three-Cs are here. Shoddy-looking bunch, but they did good work on the fire. We'd still be out there if it weren't for them."

"Do you know their names?"

Teddy turned to her, his eyes crinkling around the corners as if he'd spent too many years in the bright sun. "No. I was driving a plow team, busting firebreak. The men followed behind with hand tools. We didn't get much time to gab."

"Of course." Just the word *firebreak* sent a shiver across her skin. It took a lot of nerve to face down a blaze and then turn around and attend a party a few days later.

Mary was already at Red's side, chattering a mile a minute, her eyes fixed on the redheaded worker. He gazed back at her with a lopsided grin as the other boys stood back and watched. A moment later, she'd claimed the man's arm and led the group through the room like a tour guide, pointing out the hotel's beautiful woodwork. The fellows seemed much more interested in her than the fine establishment. Mr. Webber hung back, staying near the door.

"Do you think we should go welcome them too?" Teddy offered his elbow.

Elsie patted his arm rather than taking it, not sure she could manage to put words together if they paraded around like a couple. "A fine idea." She stepped forward without waiting for him. "Hello, Mr. Webber. It's so good to see you again."

He glanced up, eyes wide. "Oh hello, Miss . . ."

"Brookes." She reminded him. Or had she ever bothered to introduce herself? "Elsie Brookes."

His mouth opened and closed. "Another one?"

Elsie paused. "I'm sorry?"

Mr. Webber shook his head. "No, I'm the one who should be sorry. It's just that our driver today was Brookes, and the ranger who supervises us—"

"Is my father." Even as she tried to keep her focus on Mr. Webber, she could sense Teddy coming up behind her.

The CCC man nodded. "Oh, I see."

"Your driver must have been my cousin, Graham. He arrived recently."

"Quite a family affair, this Yellowstone."

"Not really." She managed a smile. "I guess you've just been fortunate so far. And please, let me introduce you to another of our staff—Ranger Teddy Vaughn." She turned to the man behind her. "Teddy, this is Nate Webber from Brooklyn, New York."

Mr. Webber stuck out his hand. "Ranger Vaughn, I think we met at the fire."

Teddy shook his hand, snapping a quick nod. "I was just telling my date here what fine work you all did."

Elsie took another sip of punch. *His date.* This would take some getting used to.

Nate glanced toward her but turned his attention back to the ranger. "I appreciate that, sir."

"And I told Elsie's father as much." Teddy slid an arm around Elsie.

Elsie picked at her white gloves to distract herself from Teddy's hand on her waist. "I hope you and your friends have a good time tonight. We want you to feel at home with our little group."

"So I see." The man nodded. "I've heard a little about the staff. The savages, is it? It sounds like fun work."

"We're blessed to work in this beautiful place, and I've made some very dear friends here. Perhaps I can introduce you to some of them this evening."

Teddy squeezed her waist. "There might be time for that later, but if you'll excuse us, Webber, I'd like to spirit Elsie away to the dance floor." Without waiting for a reply, he tugged her toward the open hall.

She hesitated. "There are only a few couples out there. I don't want everyone watching us."

He stopped in the center of the floor and took her into his arms. "It's not often I get to dance with the prettiest girl in the room."

Her heart jumped, even as heat rushed to her cheeks. No one had ever said such things about her. A man like Teddy Vaughn could draw the eye of any woman in a fifty-mile radius. Why on earth had he latched on to her?

Elsie struggled to keep pace with Teddy's feet. One wrong step and she'd collide with his broad chest. The silky sleeves of her dress slid as they moved. She pressed her wrist hard against his shoulder, hoping to capture the smooth fabric before it exposed her forearm. She should have worn elbow-length gloves like Mary.

He grinned in response, taking the opportunity to move a step closer. "See, I knew you would love it."

Within moments, several other couples joined them—mostly fellow savages, though Mary had wasted no time enticing her CCC man out to the floor. Was she trying to make Hal jealous?

Teddy leaned his head close. "I appreciate you inviting me tonight, Elsie. It's tough being the new man on staff. I could use some friends."

"I'm happy to be your friend. I think you'll fit in fine once you get used to everyone."

He lifted his eyes and glanced about the room, quickly filling with dancing couples. "I'm surprised to see so many young women working in the park."

She tried to relax, but keeping her arm pinned to his shoulder made it a challenge. The scars on her arms were less gruesome than those just under her collar, but she didn't intend to show off any of them. "Most of us work for the hotels and restaurants."

He grinned. "So you ladies take care of the tourists while we men take care of the park. Is that it?"

"There are men working for the concessionaires too. The wranglers, busboys, gear jammers, pack rats, and so on. It takes a lot of people to make a summer run smoothly around here."

"I'm looking forward to this summer. And I hope I can see you when I'm in the Canyon area."

This was going so fast, Elsie couldn't keep up—with the steps or the sentiment. "Teddy, I think Mary gave you the wrong impression about me. I'm not looking for a summer romance."

He snugged his arm around her waist. "Neither am I."

She jerked her eyes up to meet his. "You're not?" A flush crept up her neckline.

A smile crept across his face. "No ma'am. I'm looking for a far more permanent situation. Not right off, mind you. But I don't believe in wasting precious time." He leaned his face close so his lips nearly brushed her ear. "I'm ready to settle down. And when I do, it would be good if the woman I choose understands what she's getting into."

Elsie's stomach performed a little flip. "Getting into?"

"The life of a park ranger isn't easy. It's not the picket-fence sort of existence a lot of girls are looking for. But you already know that; you were raised to it." His brows lifted. "So I think we might be a good match."

The song ended, and Elsie stepped free from his embrace, pulling the cuffs back over her wrists before Teddy could see. He might think they were suited, but one glance at the twisted, mottled skin on her arms, and he'd change his mind.

Nate eased his way around the crowded room, keeping Mutt and Red in view at all times. Red had already danced three times with the outspoken blonde. Nate had no desire to cross the dance floor with anyone, so it would be best to stay along the outer edges of the room. *Avoid the skirts; stick to the outskirts.* People watching was more his tune. He claimed a cup of coffee from the refreshments table and cradled it with both hands, chest level, as a barrier to any woman who might approach.

Mutt skulked in the shadows on the far side of the hall, his eyes fixed on Red and his partner.

Nate calculated the number of steps it would take to intercept the man if he decided to cause trouble. *He's smart enough not to make a scene, right?*

Elsie Brookes leaned against the far wall, the pale blue of her dress matching her eyes—not that he was noticing. The ranger had made it clear she was here on his arm. Then again, he was nowhere to be seen at the moment, and her lips had lost that upward curve they'd displayed earlier.

Why was he looking at her lips? Nate forced his attention away, gulping the hot coffee instead. The liquid scalded his throat, the pain an effective diversion. This was going to be a long night.

The college girl's face had remained etched in his mind since the moment he'd come upon her at Norris Geyser Basin. She wasn't a traditional knockout like Red's dance partner, but when Elsie had started in about Yellowstone's geysers, her eyes came alive. It reminded him of dawn creeping over the rooftops back home and spilling into the world at his feet. Nate hadn't been able to stop thinking about her ever since. Especially during the long night working on the firebreak.

Ranger Brookes's daughter. *Figures.* The man probably wouldn't look kindly on Nate mooning over her. If Nate had harbored any delusions about romance, he could put them out of his head now. He wanted to be on the forestry crew, and that decision was in Elsie's father's capable hands. He swigged a second gulp of the steaming brew.

"Why do you make that face? Is there something wrong with the coffee?"

Nate choked, his throat refusing to cooperate as Elsie Brookes appeared at his elbow. He managed to swallow without spitting on the lady. "Oh no. It's great. Just hotter than I expected."

She waved toward the table. "Make sure you and your friends eat some of these sandwiches. We made too many, I'm sure." Her smile was as wide and friendly as the Wyoming sky.

That smile could turn a man to butter. "It's nice of you, miss. You folks have been so kind."

"We're glad you're here. We have a few new faces joining our ranks as well. It seemed appropriate to start the summer off with a get-together." Her eyes flicked toward Red and Mary as Mary's boisterous laugh carried across the room. "Some of us seem to be enjoying it more than others, it appears."

Graham Brookes appeared at Nate's other shoulder, wiping engine grease from his fingers with a soiled handkerchief. "Hiya, Nate. I see you met my cousin."

Miss Brookes's lips pursed. "Do you like to dance, Mr. Webber?"

"Um, yes. Sure. Would you like to—"

"Great idea." She nabbed his elbow and stepped toward the floor without a backward glance toward her cousin.

Like a puppy on a string, Nate followed her to the dance floor as the music slowed. He'd never expected someone like Elsie Brookes would actually want to dance with him. What had come over her?

She stepped into his arms and smiled up at him, their height difference suddenly noticeable. "I hope I didn't put you on the spot there. It's really not like me to be so forward."

Her fingers fit perfectly in his hand, the touch of her skin sending an unexpected jolt up his arm. Then again, nothing about this evening was going as expected. He resisted the urge to count the steps out loud. "I don't mind. I'm honored."

Miss Brookes tipped her head, glancing back to where Graham stood talking to a pretty brunette. "I'm still getting accustomed to having my cousin here."

"Oh?"

"It's a long story." Her brow wrinkled.

"So where's your date?"

"Teddy? He's not my . . ." She paused, lowering her gaze. "Well, I guess he is. He stepped out to get something for the kitchen crew."

Was that a blush? Nate turned once more to glance at Mary and Red. The pair had moved closer together, Red's hands clasped around the blonde's waist. At least someone was seeing some romance tonight.

On the far side of the room, Mutt adjusted his ill-fitting jacket and moved forward. The burly fellow walked toward the dancing couple with a glint in his dark eyes.

Nate stepped the wrong direction, landing squarely on the girl's toe. "Sorry. Looks like I'm better with a shovel than the two-step."

Miss Brookes squeezed his hand. "I'm not the best dancer, myself."

"You're wonderful. I'm just trying to keep an eye on my friend there."

Her soft laugh tickled his ear. "I'm watching Mary too. I hate to think of her toying with his affections."

Nate steered her a few steps closer to Mary and Red. "Things are about to heat up. Do you see that fella heading our way?"

She turned to look just as Mutt tapped Red's shoulder. "Oh no. Will there be trouble?"

Red thrust Mary behind him, a blazing look in his eyes. The sharp voices carried across the room.

Nate bent closer to Miss Brookes. "Red and Mutt have been like two dogs circling each other since we arrived in the park. She's just an excuse for them to test each other's mettle."

She sighed. "I hate to say it, but Mary might be thrilled to have two men fight over her."

"A fight is what I'm hoping to avoid." He let go of his dance partner and moved toward them.

Miss Brookes grabbed his hand. "There's something else you should know." She pointed toward the far wall. "See that short fella to the right? Smart-looking suit. Glasses."

A grim-faced man stood beside the kitchen door, arms crossed.

She leaned close and spoke under her breath. "Mary's boyfriend."

Great. Nate kept a grip on Elsie's hand as he headed toward Red. "Red, Mutt, let's take this outside."

Mutt's lip curled. "This doesn't involve you, Webber. I want to teach this runt a lesson. It's time the little lady danced with a real man."

Red curled his fists. "I'd like to see you try, pig face."

Nate stepped in just as Red surged. The smaller man collided with Nate's shoulder, twisting as Nate grabbed onto his arm. "We're guests here. Do I need to remind you of that?"

Miss Brookes latched onto her friend's elbow and hauled her back a safe distance.

Mutt snorted, caught hold of Nate's sleeve, and swung him to the side. "Don't worry. I'll remind him."

The force sent Nate stumbling across the slick tile until he lost his balance and landed on the floor.

Red hoisted his fists in front of his face like the bare-knuckle boxers back home. "Let's see you try it. I'm all-around champion in my neighborhood. You ain't never fought until you've crossed paths with an Irish scrapper."

"I'm going to mop the floor with your ginger head."

Nate staggered to his feet as the crowd pressed in. "Mutt, Red! Take it outside. Now!"

Red didn't wait for Nate to get in the way this time but lunged toward Mutt with a guttural growl. "You've been asking for this, you slob." He got two good jabs in at Mutt's belly before the larger man sent him flying with a left hook.

Red slammed into the refreshment table, upending the punch bowl. Pink liquid cascaded across the table, orange slices spinning along in its wake.

"I told you, the lady wants a real man, not some little pip-squeak," Mutt said.

Nate needed to get these brawling bulls out of there before they got the whole crew shipped home. He grabbed Mutt, using the momentum to shove him against the wall. "You've made your point. Now let's leave."

Mutt shook him off and took several steps toward the two girls. "I still need to dance with the lady. She'd be disappointed if she only got to dance with little strawberry top."

Mary's eyes widened as she ducked behind the ranger's daughter. "You're not touching me."

Mutt frowned, his brow furrowing into a series of ridges. "Come on, doll. You can't be serious about that kid." He puffed up his chest, jerking his chin upward.

He couldn't be so dense as to think she'd actually be attracted to such a display, could he? Nate spread his hands in front of him, palms out. "Look, Mutt. You've scared the lady. Let's call it a night."

Ranger Vaughn finally showed up, taking up a position at Nate's side. "You'd better listen to him, fella. Or we'll take you out of here the hard way."

Red had managed to reclaim his feet by this time, his hand pressed to the side of his head. "I'm not done with him. He can't make a move on my girl and get away—"

The dark-haired man Elsie had pointed out to Nate earlier chose that moment to plow into Red from behind, pitching him onto his face. "She's not your girl. Not either of you."

The ranger grabbed the third man by the collar.

"Hal!" Mary burst into tears. "Don't make things worse." She rushed from the room.

The ranger and several other men escorted Mutt and the other brawler outside while Nate helped Red to his feet.

Red cupped a hand over his nose, blood trickling from between his fingers. "What happened? I didn't even see that guy coming."

Nate pressed his CCC bandanna into Red's hand. "The fellow who clobbered you from behind was Mary's boyfriend."

His eyes widened above the bloody handkerchief. "What? No."

Nate clapped him on the shoulder. "You know how to pick 'em, friend."

Miss Brookes reappeared with a towel filled with ice in her hand but a firestorm in her expression. "I think you boys had better go. The chief ranger will be here soon."

"I'm really sorry, Miss Brookes. These guys"—he dug his fingers into Red's shoulder—"will make it up to you, somehow." He gestured toward the smashed table, where some of the women were already in the process of mopping up the mess. "Compensation. Or something."

She shook her head. "I should have realized . . . with Mary . . ." she dropped her gaze. "This was our fault." She reached out and touched his wrist. "Thank you for helping to break it up."

The touch sent a surge of warmth through him. "Can I help you clean up?"

"I think you'd best get your friend out of here before there's more trouble."

Graham jangled his keys nearby. "I'll give you boys a ride back to camp. That big fella already started walking, after throwing a punch at the ranger.

He's lucky he's not in the jailhouse. As far as I'm concerned, he can hoof it all the way. Might cool him down."

"After the mess we just caused," Nate nudged Red toward the door, "I'm surprised you're taking pity on us."

The gear jammer shot Red a glance. "Just don't bleed on the upholstery."

Thirteen

Elsie swept shards of broken plates into the waiting dustpan, already imagining the hotel manager's lecture. He'd trusted them with the hall. She never should have let Mary talk her into inviting the CCC men. But then again, Mary was the heart of the problem—all her flirting with strangers and leading Hal on a merry chase. After the fight, she'd raced upstairs with Rose on her heels, leaving Elsie and the others to clean up the mess. Teddy was still outside talking to some of the other partygoers. Had Mutt really punched him?

"Elsie?" Her father strode into the hall, his brow furrowed. He wore plain clothes, his shift long since past. "What happened? I heard there was an altercation."

She emptied the pan into the wastebasket, the glass causing an oddly musical sound as it settled to the bottom. "Mary Prosser happened."

"Meaning?"

A wave of tiredness swept over Elsie, her arms suddenly feeling like lead weights. She hated feeling this way about her roommate. Mary might have her faults, but she was a good friend. "A few of the men were jealous for her attentions and started a dustup."

"Brawling. Figures." Father's eyes narrowed as he surveyed the room.

"I take it the men from the camp were involved?"

"Two from the CCC, one from our crew. Ranger Vaughn took care of it, and Graham drove the CCC men back to camp."

He shook his head. "I'm disappointed. This was supposed to be a reward for them. I didn't expect horseplay, though I suppose I should have. Do you think alcohol was involved?"

"Not that I'm aware of. They were acting pretty childish, if you ask me."

"Well, pretty girls can have that effect on a fellow. Especially in front of his buddies." He sighed. "I'll make sure they're reprimanded. Maybe if we work them until they drop, they'll be too exhausted to cause problems. Between their labors and their classes, they won't have much time for trouble. They're a little rough around the edges, but half of those boys are probably crying for their mamas at night when they think no one is watching."

She thought back to Nate Webber. He did seem a little downhearted, now that she thought about it. "I suppose it's difficult to be so far from home."

"Well, quite a few of them will be your students soon. Some might be ready for upper-level classes, but there are probably others who can barely sign their names."

"One fellow was a big help in calming everyone. The others seemed to listen to him. When they weren't throwing punches, anyway."

"Let me guess." Her father smiled, folding his arms. "Nate Webber."

Surprise trickled through her. "How did you know?"

"I've had my eye on him. Good man. A natural sense of command—though he doesn't recognize it in himself."

Her father liked to spot talent and encourage it. It's probably why the superintendent had chosen him for the CCC project. "Maybe he'll be one of the advanced pupils."

Papa gazed at her, his eyes warm. "Caught your fancy, did he?"

"Don't be silly. I just think he might be a good student."

"That's right. I heard you came with Ranger Vaughn."

Her breath caught. "How did you know that?"

"He came by to speak to me this morning. Said he should have asked my permission to take you out, but your invitation had taken him by surprise." He held his hands out. "You could do far worse. Teddy seems like a nice young man."

Hadn't he just said the same about Nate Webber? "Perhaps he is, but I'm far too busy to be stepping out with rangers."

"Of course you are." His face grew serious. "But when God drops the right man into your life, I'm sure you'll recognize him."

Shouts from the back hallway intruded on their discussion. *Not more fighting.* Father strode toward the ruckus, and Elsie hurried after. A cluster of the crew stood at the rear door, but they separated and made a path as Elsie's father broke through.

Smoke billowed from the massive trash bins behind the Mammoth Hotel, flames surging upward and casting an eerie glow on the side of the building.

Elsie froze, the sight and smell flashing her back to her childhood faster than she could grab hold of the memories.

"Don't play with those when Papa's not here!"

Graham lit a second firecracker and tossed it onto the rocks in front of the house. "They're harmless, Elsie."

"The window's open. You'll wake Dottie."

"Your sister could sleep through an elephant stampede."

A loud hiss jarred her back to the present. Teddy had a brass fire extinguisher in his hands, spraying the containers with a white foam, but his actions did little to quell the flames.

"Go for the hoses!" Elsie's father shouted to him. Turning back to her, he gestured toward the lobby. "Get everyone out. Now. Go!"

She hadn't seen such fear in his eyes for years. *Not since he and Mama came home that day.* A wave of heat from the blaze released the grip terror had on her muscles. She waved her arms at her coworkers. "Evacuate the building!"

Elsie raced down the hall and ducked her head into the kitchen, pantry, offices—anywhere people might be lingering. Most everyone had already hurried out to see the excitement. The front hall was empty, but the Victrola still played, Bing Crosby serenading the empty room with "Brother, can you spare a dime." The fire might be outside, but her arms and chest stung as if somehow reliving that day years earlier.

She opened the front door and darted into the fresh air. Turning to stare at the hotel, she placed a hand over her racing heart. The partygoers milled around, most heading back toward the rear of the building to watch the progress. The sound of spraying water cut through the night. Hopefully they'd gotten to it in time to save the building.

The park bus rolled to a stop and Graham jumped out, his mouth hanging open. "What's happening? Is that smoke?"

Why him, Lord? Elsie sank onto a nearby bench, her legs shaking so badly she didn't dare take another step. She should probably follow the others, but the last thing she wanted to see was flames. The acrid smell already burned her nostrils.

He hurried to her side. "Are you all right? Is everyone out?" He glanced up at the building.

"The main level is clear." Elsie forced the words out.

"Upstairs?"

"I didn't—I . . ." She got to her feet. "Rose took Mary upstairs."

"Stay here." He ducked past her and back into the hotel.

Elsie pressed both hands against her collar, feeling her pulse throb against her fingers. The minutes ticked by slowly until Graham reappeared with Mary and Rose in tow.

Elsie rushed forward to meet her friends. "Thank goodness!"

Mary frowned. "I don't see what all the fuss is. The fire must be nearly out. It doesn't look like it's touched the hotel."

Rose hung on the gear jammer's arm, resting her head on his shoulder. "Thank you for rescuing us, Graham. We might never have realized we were in danger until it was too late."

Graham slipped his gloves over his scarred palms, casting an uncertain glance at Elsie. "I'm no hero, Rose. I just wanted to make sure you were safe."

The sun was just climbing into the sky the next morning as Nate stared at the wet ruins of the trash bins behind the hotel, a sinking feeling in his stomach. Mutt, Red, Val, and the others stood nearby, their grim faces reflecting the magnitude of what had happened.

Three men glared back—Ranger Brookes, Captain Dahl, and that young ranger who'd been at Miss Brookes's side, Teddy Vaughn. Ranger Brookes folded his arms across his chest as he studied the assembled CCC crew. "I'm sure you boys thought this was a bit of harmless fun, but fire is the biggest danger out here. Grizzlies, hypothermia, falls, lightning strikes— they're nothing in comparison. Fire could have ripped through this building in minutes, and lives were put at risk, including the staff who so graciously hosted you last night. This is how you thank them?"

Red stuck his hands in his trouser pockets, rolling forward on his toes and back. "Excuse me, sir, but me and Nate were in the bus with that Graham fellow. We couldn't have done it. But Mutt was missing from camp until well after midnight."

Mutt sneered. "I didn't do it. Why would I?"

Nate swallowed. "Ranger Brookes, how did it start? Do we know?"

Brookes's eyes settled on him. "You tell me."

Why did these men assume they were the culprits? Nate walked to the garbage bins and studied the waterlogged contents before turning to survey the back lot. "They might have sat here and smoldered quite a while before bursting into flame."

Ranger Brookes came to stand beside him, staring at the bins for a long moment. "I suppose that's possible."

"Probably during the party. Any other time, someone would have seen it." He leaned closer. Brown banana peels and sodden potato skins rested beside several cigarette butts. "Maybe someone came out for a smoke and didn't extinguish it before tossing it in the bin. Eventually it caught fire and went up in smoke."

"You're claiming this was an accident?" Captain Dahl's brows drew together. "We had a brawl that caused significant property damage"—he eyed Mutt and Red—"and then a fire just happened to break out?"

Ranger Vaughn gestured at Mutt. "That one was furious, out of control, and he smelled of booze. He even threw a punch at me. No one can account for his whereabouts after."

Mutt spread his hands. "Yes, I was mad at Red—and at Webber for taking his side. If I was going to torch something, I'd start with their bunks. I got no gripe with the folks here."

Ranger Brookes studied each man in turn, his gaze settling on Red. "I hear you were angry at one of the hotel employees."

Red shuffled his feet. "Sure, I was. He jumped me from behind. But I didn't start no fire."

Nate cleared his throat. "Red never left my sight after the scuffle, sir. Not until we were back at camp."

Vaughn wiped a hand across his brow. "You could have come back here with him and helped him set the fire. I should have taken you all to the jail for the night. It might have saved us this trouble."

That man is pretty quick to point fingers. Nate studied the smoke damage on the side of the building. The rangers had been fortunate to get it out in time. Another few minutes and the evening could have had a very different ending. "Could it have been someone on your staff?"

Vaughn sputtered. "You're accusing us?"

"Not you." Nate corrected. "The savages. That fellow that jumped Red, maybe."

Ranger Brookes pressed a hand to his eyes. "We could do this all day. Vaughn, why don't you empty those bins and see if you find anything significant. Blind accusations will get us nowhere."

Dahl stepped closer to the men and jabbed a finger toward Mutt. "Be that as it may, I want you to pack your bags and be on the next train out of here. I won't stand for carousing and brawling in my company."

The big man's face fell. "Captain, I didn't—"

The stone-faced officer cut him off. "Even if you're not responsible for the fire, you still started a fight *and* punched a park service employee. I want you packed by lunch." He turned to Red. "We'll see if scrubbing the kitchen and latrines straightens you out. The company heads out for Canyon tomorrow; I want those areas gleaming before you pack up or you'll join Mutt. Lieutenant Stone at Canyon can decide if you need further disciplinary action." His eyes narrowed. "Webber, I expected better from you. I'll have to rethink that foreman post if you can't even control your men at a social function."

"Yes sir." Nate's stomach turned.

Ranger Brookes's face softened as he looked at the men. "I'm sorry this happened at all. I had high hopes for each of you."

Nate gazed at the ground. High hopes. That's all anyone ever had.

Fourteen

Nate tucked the raccoons in the box, then tied it closed with string. Tiny noses pressed against the air holes, followed by a paw. Since the mother had never returned for her young, the fellas had voted to take the two kits—Kit and Hutch, as they'd dubbed them—along as camp mascots. "Don't worry, guys. You're going to love Canyon camp. I hear there are plenty of trees to climb and creeks to splash in."

He shuffled the rest of his things into the footlocker, careful to remember his mess kit. Frankly, he was relieved to leave Mammoth behind. Evidently nothing else had come of the fire investigation. The rangers couldn't determine a cause, but all seemed to still blame the CCC crew.

He hoisted the crates into his arms before hurrying out to the truck.

Val helped stack the matching footlockers in the truck, grunting with each lift. "How many more we got?"

"Just mine, I think." Nate hoisted it up to the truck bed.

"Good, my back is aching. We've only been here a couple of weeks. What are these guys packing in these things? Rock collections?" He straightened and grimaced, pressing a hand against his lower spine. "I hear we'll be packing school books soon."

Nate held the raccoons' box to his chest. "I was a royal failure in the classroom."

"You? I had you pegged as a college man."

"You've got to be fooling me."

Val frowned. "It's the way you talk. You sound educated. I pictured you sitting at home with your nose in a book. Like me."

"I listen." Sherm had been good about sharing what he learned. Nate missed that.

The younger man nodded. "That's true. Remember when we were up on the mountain with Ranger Brookes? None of us were really paying attention—except you. You were able to tell the rest of us what was going on. Me, I need it written down. I read every chance I get."

Nate handed the boxed raccoons to Val. "Can you find a safe place to stow them? Someplace where Lieutenant Stone won't spot it? I'm not sure he'd approve."

"Approve? He'd have all our hides." Val took the box and peered in through one of the air holes. "Sure. I know just the spot." He disappeared behind the luggage.

Nate turned his back and leaned against the tailgate, surveying the camp. It had only been a few weeks, but this sagebrush studded landscape hemmed in by distant snow-covered peaks already felt like home. And now, here they were, heading off into the great unknown. Again.

Ranger Brookes's daughter had said she and Mary were moving to Canyon too. How far was the hotel from the CCC camp? Hopefully far enough to keep Red out of trouble. Red needed to steer clear of that blond bombshell, and the last thing Nate wanted was to be close to Elsie Brookes. He'd dreamed about the college girl last night. The pale blue dress had emphasized her startling eyes—the ones that smiled at him as he swept her around the floor at the Mammoth Hotel. Even just thinking of her sent a wave of heat across his skin. *Not good.*

Once the trucks were loaded with supplies, the men clambered aboard and headed out. Nate found an open spot between two supply boxes, thankful to stretch his legs in front of him. The crates blocked the view, but as sore as he was, the idea of sitting folded up like one of his mother's salted pretzels didn't appeal.

The thought of home sent a pang through his chest. The other men had spent much of their free time writing letters, but that avenue wasn't open to him. He could probably get Val or Red to help, but that would mean admitting his situation. He scrubbed open palms across his face, the truck's swaying motion hypnotic. His hand bumped against the hard cover of the manual, now a fixture in the breast pocket of his jacket. Why did he bother to carry it? He took it out, flipped through the pages, and watched the letters march by like perfect army ranks. Pictures sure would help.

He turned back to the first page and squinted. Sometimes, if he worked hard, he could read a few words. He pressed the heel of his hand against his left eye. His right seemed to be more cooperative when it came to deciphering the strange codes of the alphabet.

Val scooted off the crate he'd been sitting on and plunked himself next to Nate. "See, I knew you were the type to have your nose stuck in a book. You've been carrying that thing around for a week. What are you doing—memorizing it?"

"I like to learn." Nate shut the cover. "I just don't have a brain like you graduates."

Val drew up his knees like two mountain peaks in front of him. "I'm not a graduate. Still got two years to go." He glanced away, as if he'd somehow let something slip. "Hey, maybe the new teacher can help you with that. Get you caught up. I think that's what the government had in mind for the education program."

Red grunted from across the way, apparently still awake even though he was curled up in his bedroll. "I'm hoping for electronics classes. I want to build radios someday. Wouldn't that be swell?" He rolled over and put an arm over his ear.

Nate spent little time considering the future. He had enough trouble dealing with the here and now. "Somedays" were for fellows with time and money. He stuffed the book into his pocket. "What does your old man do?"

Val shifted, jerking one shoulder up toward his ear in a half shrug. "He's a . . . a . . ." The kid lowered his voice. "He's a rabbi."

A rabbi? Nate lifted his eyes, glancing around at the others. The camp was full of men from various backgrounds, and almost everyone had immigrant parents of some sort. "You went to Sunday service with us in Gardiner last week. Why didn't you mention you were Jewish?"

Val chewed his lower lip. "Not sure how the guys would take it. I figured it was better to keep my mouth shut. I'd just as soon you kept it under your hat."

"If that's what you want." Nate glanced up at Val's brown hair. "Speaking of hats, aren't you supposed to wear a cap or something?"

He leaned back against the crate. "Yeah, well, don't tell my father. I joined up without his permission, as is. He doesn't put much stock in government programs. Wouldn't like seeing me in a uniform."

Nate folded his arms across his knees, then rested his forehead on his wrists. "My father was a police officer. He's all about the uniform."

The two men lapsed into silence as the truck continued to jounce along. Nate had almost dozed off when a yelp jerked him awake.

Red was holding the side of his face. "Something jumped on me while

I was sleeping. I think it bit me." He leaned close to the man beside him, jerking a finger up toward his temple. "Moretti, what was it? Did anyone see? Tell me it wasn't a rat or something."

A shout from farther down the line sent all the men scrambling to their feet in the swaying vehicle. "Something's underneath there. Can anyone see it?" Bukowski bent to peer around the crates.

Val pulled a flashlight from one of the boxes. He aimed the flickering light between the stacks of supplies, the light swaying with the movement of the truck.

A pair of eyes gleamed from the gap.

He dropped to his knees. "What is that thing?"

Nate scooted closer. "It's one of the kits. Did you make sure the container was secure?" He held out a hand to the critter, hoping the animal wouldn't nip him out of fear.

Val frowned. "I opened it for a minute to get a look at them, but I closed it back up."

"Not well enough." Red snorted a laugh.

Moretti clambered over the boxes. "The other one's still in there."

Hutch poked his head out, the tiny mask surrounding the glittering black eyes. He crawled up into Nate's hand, then up his arm, burrowing into the area between his neck and shoulder.

Nate cradled the raccoon against his chest. "It's all right little fella. We'll be home soon."

The sight of Teddy striding up to her parent's house sent a flutter through Elsie's stomach. She'd finished packing an hour ago and was reading a book on the porch while she waited for Mary and their ride. She hadn't expected a visit from the good-looking ranger. In fact, she'd done a pretty good job of ducking him since the dance.

The fire had put her in such a state that she'd left the hotel without even saying good night to Teddy. And she couldn't get his comments about settling down out of her mind. Elsie had allowed herself a date or two in the past, but never let it go beyond that. She touched her collar, her thumb brushing the top button.

Teddy grinned as he climbed the three small steps to the front porch. "I was hoping I'd find you here." He pulled out a small gift box tied with a red ribbon, then passed it from hand to hand for a moment before holding it out to her. "I know you're leaving today. I got you a going-away present."

"I'm only going to Canyon."

"I know, but . . . just open the box. I think you'll like it." He sat beside her on the porch railing, a few inches closer than she'd like. "I'm excited for you to have this, Elsie."

His deep voice almost seemed to rumble in his chest as he said her name. She shivered slightly, squeezing the tiny box between her fingers. She barely knew the fellow and he was bringing her gifts? Hal bought Mary trinkets all the time—but they'd been together for two summers, off and on.

Elsie swallowed. "I'm going to miss Mammoth. I've lived here a long time. After this summer, I'll be heading off to Missoula for college."

"I've only been here a couple of weeks, but it already feels like Yellowstone is the best thing that's ever happened to me." His eyes caught hers.

"Wonderland has that effect on people."

He smiled and gestured toward the gift. "Please, open it."

Elsie untied the ribbon, slid a trembling finger under the top flap, and pulled it open. A glint of light sparkled off a small silver case. Drawing it out, Elsie turned it over in her hand. "How lovely." She traced a fingertip over the flower engraved on the shiny surface. "Is that an evening primrose?"

"Herma said you liked them."

"I do. They remind me of the sulfur spring with the same name. It's one of my favorite places."

"Maybe you can show it to me sometime." He leaned in close and pointed at the etching. "I engraved it myself. It seemed so functional and masculine without some kind of adornment. I'd hate for you to think I'd gotten you something practical without an ounce of sentiment."

Practical? Elsie turned the case over, the silver warming in her palm. On the opposite side he'd etched the word "Wonderland." Popping open the hinged lid at the top, a tiny gear and lever appeared.

Teddy placed his hand over hers. "Let me show you how it works." His touch was warm. He pushed on the lever, clicking it a few times. A tiny flame shot up from the front of the gadget.

Elsie gasped, shoving it toward him and scooting away. "A lighter! I haven't seen one like it before." She put her shaking hands behind her.

"Isn't it perfect?" He turned it over in his fingers. "You'll never need matches again. It's fueled by naphtha."

The strong odor of spirits accosted her, burning in her throat. Seeing that spark so close to her fingertips had turned her stomach. "Th-that's very generous of you, but I couldn't possibly accept this. It must have been very expensive."

"It will come in handy. Look, I purchased one for myself too." He straightened and drew a matching case from his trouser pocket. "Only, no flowers. I etched a pine cone on mine. And 'Wonderland,' for where we met." Teddy's brown eyes shone, like an overeager child. "Please, Elsie. I want you to have it."

His expression melted her resistance. She brought out her hand, opened her fingers, and let him set the dreaded thing on her damp palm. He had no idea of her fears, of her past. Why would he? Elsie snapped the lid shut and ran a thumb over the tiny flower. It truly was a thing of beauty. Horrible beauty. She swallowed, her mouth dry. "Thank you, Teddy. You're very kind."

He sneaked an arm behind her. "I hope it's not too presumptuous, but I'd like to think of this as a little piece of me going with you." He smiled, the dimple in his cheek catching her eye even while his touch sent her thoughts into disarray. "And I'd like your permission to visit you sometime." He slid his fingers up her wrist. "Would that be all right?"

"Y-yes. Of course." She pulled her hand away, lest he brush the scars on her inner arm.

Elsie pressed the silver case close to her heart. As long as she didn't think too much about what the object contained, she might be able to love it. Perhaps, in time, she could learn to appreciate the gadget's usefulness as well. "Thank you, Teddy." She lifted her head, not quite able to meet his eyes. Maybe she could learn to appreciate this tenderhearted ranger a little bit too. With his help, she might get past some of her fears. "I'm sure I'll treasure it."

Fifteen

The first few days in the new camp had been a wake-up call. If the CCC men thought Mammoth was rustic, the muddy clearing at Canyon was a shock. All that awaited them were stacks of supplies. No buildings, no latrines, no mess hall. Thankfully, some of the men had construction experience, and the rest were pretty motivated to learn. Hard work meant they'd at least have a decent place to shower and eat, so they were all willing to break their backs to make it happen.

As the main group worked on the mess hall and latrine, a smaller crew tackled the large army tents where they would be quartered for the summer. It took the men a few hours to arrange the tents into long lines. Nate plunked his footlocker at the end of one of the cots and straightened his aching back. "Be it ever so humble, there's no place like home."

Red grinned. "Or as my ma would say, 'May you always have walls for the wind and a roof for the rain.' It might be canvas, but it's still a roof." He spread the wool blanket across the mattress and tucked the corners.

Val sorted a stack of novels. "With how it's howling today, we'll be lucky not to blow away."

"Or have one of those pine trees land on us." Nate pulled the two folded letters from home out of his shirt pocket and ran his fingers across the lines of Eva's handwriting. Lucy had added her name in scrawling print at the bottom of the page. So far, he'd done a decent job of hiding his problem from his buddies. If he could just keep his head down, he might make it through the season without anyone knowing.

He tucked the letters into a small box he'd stashed in his footlocker. He could read a few short words. When things were quiet, maybe he'd try again. Eva was only seven, so she couldn't know that many.

Bukowski stuck his head through the tent flap. "Lieutenant Stone wants everyone in the mess hall, pronto. Captain Dahl is here for an inspection."

Nate snatched his jacket from the foot of his bed, then followed the men into the new building and fell in line with the others standing at attention. Pride surged through him as he watched Dahl tour the room. The crew had done a fantastic job under less than optimal conditions. This facility would serve the Corps for years, assuming the president decided to continue the program.

The hint of a smile softened Dahl's stern visage as he ran a hand across the smooth boards framing one of the small windows. "Fine work. And in record time too." He turned to face them. "There's still much to be done to finish the camp—shower buildings, storage facilities, and recreation hall." He folded his arms across his broad chest. "But those will come in time."

Dahl paced up the aisle, nodding to each man. He clapped Val on the arm as he passed, a twinkle in his eye. "Good work, son. I always meant to ask you when we were at Mammoth—how old are you, anyway?"

The younger man's eyes widened. "I'm eighteen, sir."

"Sure you are." He faced him, his gray eyes twinkling as he stared up at the gangly youth as if just seeing him for the first time.

Val swallowed hard. "Sir?"

Nate felt for his friend. He'd suspected the same. Many of the men were thin from months of lean living, but Val had the look of a spindly beanstalk that had grown faster than his ravenous appetite could maintain. He was seventeen, at most. But a confession like that could get him sent home to his mama's arms. Likely one who struggled to feed a growing boy. Nate had never seen such meals as they served here. Bacon, fruit, steak, cheese, bread, pie—and always enough for seconds, thirds, and beyond.

Dahl's shorter stature forced him to gaze up at Val. "I was *eighteen* when I signed up for the army, just before the Great War—or so I told them."

"I . . ." The rod in Val's spine seemed to loosen a notch and the tension in his shoulders eased. "Yes sir."

The captain moved down the row, pausing at Nate's side.

Nate straightened under the man's intense gaze. There was no questioning his age. Had the captain discovered something else about him?

Rather than addressing Nate, Dahl turned to face the room. "As I was saying, we still have work to do here. But our job is out in the park, not designing window dressings and planting flowers." He studied the group. "We'll leave a skeleton crew here to continue camp construction—those of you with experience in the building trades in particular. Lieutenant Stone has given me a list of names of the men who have been most useful to the process."

He shot a glance at Nate. "I'm placing Webber in charge of the forestry crew. He will serve as your area foreman and will liaise with the park rangers, Lieutenant Stone, and myself."

Nate locked his jaw to keep his mouth from dropping open. *Foreman?* A charge of electricity shot through his body.

"Webber, I expect you to handle any problems on the site—disputes, equipment, safety. Can you do that?"

Nate managed a nod. "Yes sir. I'm honored, sir." He'd failed in so many aspects of his life, but he'd always had the ability to make friends easily. Now to figure out how to work that skill into leadership.

The captain lowered his voice, injecting an unexpected note of warmth. "The boys will answer to you, but you answer to me. Understand?"

He sensed the double meaning in Dahl's words. There was a mild warning, but it was also a reminder of support. He wouldn't be flailing out there on his own. The thought went a long way to steady his racing heart. "Yes sir, I understand."

"Good." He turned to face the others. "And listen up, men. Webber will be writing me weekly reports. I expect good news on your progress."

Nate's stomach dropped, a cold sweat breaking out across his skin. Weekly reports? *Written?*

"The camp teacher also arrives in a few days. We'll hold the classes in the mess hall after supper three nights a week, for now." The captain lifted his brow. "We'd hoped to have a male teacher from one of the local universities, but that hasn't panned out. I have a couple of men coming in to teach some basic machine repair and other trades on the weekend. But for your three Rs, it will be a local gal who has assisted at the Gardiner school. I expect you to be on your best and most respectful behavior with this young lady. She's the daughter of one of the park's rangers, and any reports of disrespect or lewd behavior will be dealt with in a swift and severe manner. Savvy?"

A unanimous answer of assent filled the room.

Nate struggled to sort through the mixture of news that had been dumped at his feet in the past five minutes. Reports? Classes? Reading and writing?

Dahl headed for the door. "Then I'll let you get back to your evening. Welcome to Canyon." He paused at the door, one hand on the frame. "Miss Elsie Brookes will come in on Monday to teach the first class and get a sense of your educational needs. Don't miss this golden opportunity to better yourselves."

Elsie Brookes. Nate splayed fingers over his aching temples. Why was it that every golden opportunity came with a steep price tag?

❧

Elsie walked through the camp entrance, her shoes sinking into the two-inch deep mud. The clearing had once held a series of outbuildings that served those working on the construction of Canyon Lodge. Now the clearing was a gaping wound in the dense lodgepole forest, and the earth seemed to be trying to reclaim its ownership.

Her stomach churned. Nothing she'd learned working with children had prepared her for this. Teaching letters and numbers to a group of street-wise New Yorkers? They were going to laugh in her face.

The smell of fresh-cut wood tickled her nose as Elsie slogged her way toward the smaller building. Would that be an office? Where were all the men? The camp seemed quiet, except for a distant hammering coming from a skeletal building on the far side of the encampment.

Elsie paused at the steps leading up to the door. Her father had said that a Lieutenant Stone would be there to greet her. She checked the timepiece hanging from her pocket. She was almost twenty minutes early. She juggled a box of books and paper tablets, twisting to adjust the heavy bag dangling from her shoulder. She couldn't set them in the mud, but the strap dug against her tender skin.

Elsie lowered the box onto the bottom step and wrestled her way out of the shoulder strap. A teacher had to come prepared, and she'd done her best to think through every situation. She'd hardly slept the past few days as her mind played through every horrible scene she could imagine—the men erupting in laughter, throwing rotten fruit, drawing rude pictures on the blackboard, and starting fights. Or worse—they were better educated than she expected, expecting her to teach lessons on Latin and advanced geometry.

It would be somewhere in the middle. It had to be.

A door slammed on the larger building across the clearing. "Miss Brookes!" Red loped toward her, his unlaced boots slapping against the mucky ground. "Over here." He gestured toward the long, squat building, windows nothing but gaping holes in the side of the structure.

Of course it would be Red. Mary had spoken of no one else since the party. Elsie crouched to retrieve the crate, trying to hook the bag over her shoulder in the same motion. Her balance shifted under the uneven weight and the box slipped from her fingers, crashing back to the step.

"Let me get that for you." He grinned, bending to lift it.

She stepped out of his way. "Thank you. It's rather heavy, I'm afraid."

"No problem. After all the buckets of nails I've hauled this week, it feels like cotton candy." He gripped it against his chest and faced her. "I suppose I'm probably about the last person you want to see after what happened at the hotel. That was quite the rhubarb, wasn't it?" He hoisted the box up higher and started across the clearing toward the other building. "I shoulda realized that little gal was playing me." He shrugged one shoulder. "A looker like her would never settle for one of us. After all, what've I got to offer?"

"Mary wasn't . . ." Elsie paused. *Wasn't what?* Wasn't playing with Red's and Hal's feelings? She couldn't defend her roommate on that front. Elsie readjusted the bag, holding it in her hands rather than letting the strap dig into her neck. "Mary still speaks of you."

He stopped and turned, his eyes bright. "She does?"

"Yes." Endlessly. Every minute of the day and half the night. Elsie studied Red, his quirky grin causing her to smile in return. He wasn't the typical well-heeled man Mary chased after.

"Well, I'll be." He straightened, almost gaining another inch in the process. "Miracles do happen."

Some of her anxious thoughts about teaching this group faded. Red was just a fellow, like any other. Maybe if she could think of each pupil as an individual rather than as one of a pack of nameless men, she'd be able to face them.

"We're over here in the mess hall for now. Windows go in tomorrow, so that'll make things a little quieter."

"The mess hall?" She pointed at the other building. "What's that one?"

"Latrine."

Good thing she hadn't gone inside.

"We're building a recreation hall next. It'll have two classrooms in addition to a camp store and game room. Captain Dahl has promised us a Ping-Pong table. I'm thinking we can figure out how to make a pool table too. How hard can it be?"

She entered the wide space filled with long tables. No blackboard. Of course—why would there be? Elsie lowered her bag to a corner table. "The camp seems very quiet. Where is everyone?"

Red placed the box beside her other things. "They're out in the field with Webber, cutting beetle-infested trees. They should be back soon."

"Nate Webber?"

"Yeah, he's one of the foremen now. Most of the fellows are happy with that choice, though we'd all jump at the extra fiver that comes with the job."

"Will he be in the high school class? For those finishing their degree?"

"I don't think he signed up."

She reached into the box and drew out a handful of readers. *Levels one through three.* She'd hesitated before adding these to the stack. Chances were, most of the men could already read far above this level, but she wanted to be prepared for anything.

Red sat on the edge of the table. "So Mary . . . she's thinking about me, eh?"

"Some." She should have kept quiet. There was no need to set up this man for more heartbreak. Mary might be fascinated with him, but she had her heart set on a rich husband. Red didn't look like someone who'd ever had more than a dime in his pocket.

"And she's working at the Canyon Hotel?"

"We work long hours. There's not much time for socializing."

"So do we, Miss Brookes. But Yellowstone's moon seems particularly romantic, if you know what I mean." A dopey grin crossed his freckled face as he dug into her box and retrieved an old poetry collection, flipping through the yellowed pages.

She took the book from his hands. "Let's focus on reading and writing. Romance is outside the scope of the class."

"Since this is an all-male class, I imagine you're right about that. Plus, the captain read the riot act to the boys about keeping our eyes on the books and not on the teacher."

Her hand went to her throat out of habit. She hadn't even considered that any of the men would look at her in that way. "I'm not Mary, so I don't think it will be a problem."

He shrugged. "Not for me, but maybe for a few of the other fellows. It gets pretty lonely stuck here with a hundred other men. But I'll let you know if any of the fellas are going to be trouble, Miss Brookes." He finished unloading her box. "Since I got my cap set on another, you can trust me. I'll watch out for you."

She pulled her collar tight, suddenly keenly aware of her awkward status here. "Thank you, Mr.—" She hesitated.

"It's Walsh, ma'am. But everyone calls me Red. And I'm happy to look out for you. My mama would expect little else. I got sisters, you know." He brought up his hands and fisted them in front of his face. "I've done battle in the schoolyard plenty of times for their sakes."

The door slammed open and a dour-faced soldier stepped into the entrance, legs spread. "Walsh? Are you threatening our teacher?"

Red dropped his hands and jumped back. "No! No sir."

The instant change in his demeanor startled Elsie. "Mr. Walsh was simply demonstrating proper fighting technique. I had asked him a few questions."

The officer strode forward. "I'm Lieutenant Stone. You must be Ranger Brookes's little girl?"

Elsie steeled herself against his patronizing tone. She held out her hand to him. "Miss Elsie Brookes." She resisted adding, "At your service."

She'd expected a vise grip, but he barely put any pressure on her fingers at all. "Just so you're aware, the men are here to work. School is extraneous."

She pulled her hand back and pressed it to her ribs. "They'll be better workers if you exercise their minds in addition to their bodies."

His brows lifted a hair. "This whole program is an experiment. The president thinks he can shape this generation of loafers into a better class of Americans by giving them work, food, and schooling." He gave a scoffing laugh. "Discipline is what they really need."

Red remained silent, but his gaze faltered.

She hoped the military man would leave before her students assembled. He probably expected her to teach with a wooden rod in her hands at all times. "But these are not soldiers. They're good men looking to help their families. Education can only help them."

"Miss Brookes, we're feeding them, clothing them, putting roofs over their heads. In exchange, we expect hard work."

"Understood, *sir.*"

The snap in her voice might have been a little too strong. The lieutenant narrowed his eyes at her before striding out the door, his muscular frame evident in every step.

She blew out a long breath as he departed. "Well, isn't he a bundle of fun!"

Red chuckled. "I don't think you're going to need my protection, Miss Brookes. You seem perfectly capable of standing up for yourself."

As the others headed off to class, Nate took refuge in the new showers. The cold water cascaded over his aching spine like a waterfall. They'd visited the Tower Fall the previous week and seen the creek tumble free from its bed between giant stone spires jutting toward the sky and cascade into the forested ravine below. Nothing he'd experienced before could have prepared him for that sight. No one in Brooklyn had told him the country contained such magnificence. Apparently he had a lot to learn, and Yellowstone would be his teacher. A young woman armed with a handful of books couldn't hope to offer him that sort of education.

Nate tipped back his head and let the water cool his sunburned face. They'd spent today on the slopes of Mount Washburn. A lot of the snow had melted since they first visited, but there were still some lingering patches. Tasked with marking the dying trees, he'd tromped up and down the steep slopes with a paint can, scampering over rocks and fallen trunks while his crew practiced with the long two-man crosscut saws. It seemed a shame to fell the pines, but Ranger Brookes had assured him leaving the sick trees would endanger the whole forest. Best to cut out the weaklings and let the strong take their place.

Out in the forest, he finally felt like one of the strong. The men had listened, following his directions with hardly a word of opposition. They'd put in hours of good work. When one would falter, he'd throw out a few encouraging words and the man would double down on his efforts.

He turned the faucet, cutting the flow of icy water. A quiet evening stretched out ahead of him as most of the fellows hit the books. He'd spent a few pennies on a notepad and pencil at the Pryor Store over by the campground. He couldn't write his family, but he could draw them some cartoons detailing his existence here. The girls would love that. He wasn't a great artist, but he'd drawn caricatures since he was a boy. He'd already managed to capture Red, Val, Mutt, and Dahl.

He'd spotted Miss Brookes the moment he walked into camp tonight. She stood in the doorway to the mess hall, her green skirt fluttering in the evening breeze. The sight had stolen his breath. How would the men learn anything while looking at her? It almost made him want to join the class. *Almost.*

Maybe that's what he'd sketch tonight. A cartoon of Elsie Brookes with that notebook in her hand and the pencil tucked over her ear—like he'd seen her that first day at Norris Geyser Basin. His sisters might not recognize her as a teacher right off. He'd have to make her a little more stern. She was far too sweet to be a schoolmarm. Maybe he'd make the image a mixture of Elsie and some of the teachers from his past. That might be a little more believable.

He toweled off and pulled on his clean pair of dungarees. These CCC duds were finally starting to feel like a part of him. Maybe because he no longer had to cinch his belt to the very tightest notch in order to prevent them sliding off his hips. The combination of good food and hard work was throwing on muscle and weight at a rapid clip. Even Val was starting to fill out, looking less like a walking skeleton. Nate draped the towel over his bare shoulders and leaned into the mirror to study the red tinge in his cheeks. Shaving tomorrow would be a painful business.

Val appeared in the doorway, his hair slicked back as if he'd combed it special for the teacher. "The lieutenant told me to fetch you."

Nate reached for his shirt. "Did he say why?"

The young man bobbed his head. "He wants you to sit in on the class tonight. See if the teacher can hack it. You know, if she can keep control."

A wash of cold swept over Nate as if he still stood in the showers. "I didn't sign up."

Val shrugged. "I'm just the messenger."

Nate shoved his arms into the sleeves, his damp skin sticking to the fabric. "Captain Dahl told me to supervise the men on the jobsite. He didn't say anything about running roughshod over some schoolteacher."

"You want me to say that to the lieutenant?"

"Absolutely not." Nate chuckled.

"Good, because I value my life. And yours." He offered a mock salute before ducking out the doorway.

Nate gripped the sides of the porcelain sink and stared into the mirror, no longer focusing on his own reflection. Instead he saw all the teachers who'd scoffed at him over the years. He certainly wasn't going to give Elsie Brookes the chance to join their ranks.

Sixteen

Elsie fell onto her bed, her arms and legs weighing at least a million pounds each. The clear evening promised a brilliant sunset at Artist Point. Normally she loved watching the fading light paint the canyon in various shades of orange, pink, and purple as Lower Falls rumbled in the distance. But tonight? She had no energy left—not even enough to stop for dinner in the employee cafeteria. She curled on her side and closed her eyes. And tonight had just been a short class to meet her students. How tired would she be when she started teaching them for real?

How long had she dreamed of her own classroom?

Never once had she imagined it would be an unfinished mess hall filled with hulking men in folding chairs. She'd stared at them for several dizzying moments before gathering her thoughts enough to speak. Why did her father believe she could do this?

Rather than run screaming from the building, she'd reached a shaking hand into her book bag and drawn out a tablet of writing paper. Mrs. Williams from the Gardiner School had encouraged her to start the class by finding out where each student was academically. Elsie placed a sheet of paper in front of each man and asked him to write a little about himself. His name, birthplace, school experience—and just for fun—his long-term dreams and goals.

Some of the men had launched right in, but others stared at her with big eyes. Eventually they put pencils to paper. All but one. Nate Webber pushed the paper back at her. "I'm just here to observe."

"That doesn't mean you can't tell me a little about yourself."

He shook his head, eyes dark. "Reading my chicken scratch would be a waste of your time. I'm not one of your students."

Elsie had left the paper in front of him regardless, hoping he'd change his mind. She'd love to know a little more about the quiet, green-eyed man. Red said he led by example, but by refusing the assignment, he'd proven otherwise. Even if he'd already earned a diploma, it wouldn't hurt him to scribble a few lines to encourage the others.

She'd had trouble not being distracted by his sullen presence in the back of the room. He'd obviously made an effort to spiff himself up for class, but his demeanor screamed that he'd rather be anywhere else.

Most of the papers were a wild mixture of misspellings and half-finished compositions. A few stood out, like the eager, young fellow she remembered from Norris Geyser Basin—the one who'd answered her question about the boiling point for water.

Elsie sat up in her bed, reached for her bag, and pulled the papers out into her lap. Val Kaminski. His writing was smooth and well organized, and he said he hoped to write books like his heroes, Mark Twain, Henry James, and Upton Sinclair. This young man had read *The Jungle*? She'd have to be at the top of her game to stay ahead of him.

She walked over to her shelf and slid out Hemingway's *A Farewell to Arms* and added a few Jack London novels. Maybe she could make a separate class for a few students who showed promise and were interested in literature and creative writing. Mr. Kaminski would be an obvious choice. Maybe Nate Webber would even join. Obviously, she'd insulted him by asking him to write a simple theme about himself. Even if he'd already finished high school, it didn't mean she couldn't find a way to challenge him.

Elsie added *Moby Dick* to the stack. What red-blooded American male could resist an epic quest for a mythological whale? She'd get Nate Webber into her class if it took all summer. She tapped her fingers on the cover, her mind again drawn to the man who'd sat in the back of the room with his arms folded.

Mary opened the door, a plate of food balanced in her hands. "With an armload of books and that frown, you look like a teacher already." She laughed. "I brought you some dinner, since you missed it. Cook said you could return the dishes tomorrow."

Elsie stacked the novels on the floor by her bed. "I had too much on my mind."

Her roommate shoved the plate into her hands. The rich fragrance of chicken and potatoes made Elsie's stomach rumble. She carried it over to the small desk and sat down.

"Busy first day? Lots of eager pupils?" Mary plopped onto Elsie's bed and picked up the stack of papers. "Look at this atrocious handwriting. What is it with men and scrawl? Only a handful of the fellows I've dated could write a legible love letter. Not like your Teddy."

"He's not *my* Teddy." Though receiving two letters within a few days had been flattering. Teddy's notes weren't quite love letters, more like accountings of his daily responsibilities. Still, it was sweet of him to think of her. "I'm not sure a man's penmanship is an accurate indicator of his potential." Elsie took the silver lighter from the box on her desk and ran her finger across the engraved flower. She still hadn't had the courage to use the thing, but just holding it made her feel brave.

Mary fanned the papers across the bed. "Only a couple of good prospects among them. Oh, look . . ." She lifted one messy sheet. "Red is in your class?"

Elsie dropped the lighter into the box. "You probably shouldn't look at that." She stood and reached for the essay.

Mary scooted out of reach, reading as fast as she could. "He says he went to school through ninth grade. That's not so bad."

"Mary, give that to me." Elsie lunged forward. "It's private. I didn't assign this theme so you could spy on your boyfriend."

She smiled, never taking her eyes from the lined paper. "He's not my boyfriend—yet. Oh, he wants to build radios. My father says there's a lot of money in radio." Mary lowered it an inch, catching Elsie's eyes above the top margin. "Did he ask about me? He knows we're friends, right?"

Elsie snatched the sheet from her roommate's hand. "He's there to learn, not to make dates."

"Can't he do both?" Mary slid back to the edge of the bed and lowered her feet to the floor, leaving Elsie's quilt rumpled. "Besides, I'm a fast reader." She hopped up and snatched her pink sweater from the back of the chair. "Good night, Els. Don't wait up." She dashed out the door, slamming it behind her.

Elsie shook her head, her gaze dropping to the paper with Red Walsh's name scrawled in large letters at the top. She skimmed through the lines, settling on the last two sentences.

"My dream is to kiss a girl named Mary under the Yellowstone moon and then spend my life proving myself worthy of her. I'll be waiting outside the lodge tonight, if she feels the same."

The few bites of food settled into Elsie's gut. Passing notes in class was one thing—but passing notes through the teacher? She tossed the paper on top of the stack and reached for her cardigan. If she was somehow responsible for this Romeo and Juliet love affair, she'd better go make sure they didn't drink the poison.

⚜

Nate adjusted the pillow bunched behind his back as he sat cross-legged on the bunk, drawing tablet balanced on his lap. The stink of Red's aftershave made him choke. "Where are you going so late?"

Red drew a comb through his hair, studying his reflection in a small hand mirror. His lip quirked. "What makes you think I'm going anywhere?"

"Call it an educated guess."

"Well, a little education can take you far." He dropped the grooming tools back into the open footlocker and slammed the lid. "I intend to see if that's true."

"Red, if you're planning to do something foolish—"

"Foolish would be not chasing love when it knocks at your door." Red shrugged into his jacket.

Nate got up and reached for his own jacket. "You've already had your bell rung once over a girl. If you're heading off for another beating, I'm not letting you go alone."

Red scowled as Nate followed him outside. "Three's a crowd, you know."

"And 'A threefold cord is not quickly broken.'" Red seemed determined to look for trouble wherever he went. Nate was reminded of keeping an eye on Charlie. *Look how well that turned out.*

"Just so you know when to make yourself scarce. And if anyone asks, we're just taking a walk."

"Trust me, I have no desire to see you make a fool of yourself, but I also want to be sure you arrive back in camp in one piece. We've got a lot of work to do this summer."

Red punched Nate's arm. "I knew you cared."

"Hey, fellas!" A breathless voice came up behind them, accompanied by the thudding of boots. "Where are you going?" Val loped up to them, like an overgrown puppy on the loose.

Red groaned. "Go home, kid. It's past your bedtime."

"Let him come." Nate thrust his hands in the pockets of his jacket. "We're just taking a walk, right?"

Red shot him a pained look.

Val fell in beside Nate, his long-legged gait setting a good pace. "I like it here in the forest better than all that sagebrush in Mammoth. It feels friendlier somehow."

"Spookier, too." A bird shrieked in the distance, as if in answer to Nate's observation.

A sly grin spread across Red's face. "More places for bears to hide. Seen any yet, Val?"

The youth glanced around. "No. You?"

"Lots of times."

"I imagine we all will before the summer's out." Nate buttoned his jacket against the evening's chill. "Cookie said they come around to eat the garbage."

Red laughed. "Garbage—and people out walking in the woods."

Val halted. "You're joshing me."

"Red, leave him alone." Nate elbowed his friend.

Red continued walking, not waiting as the other two fell a few steps behind.

Nate turned to the younger man. "Dahl seemed to doubt your age. What's the true story?"

"What's it matter? I do the work of a man, don't I?"

"You did today, that's for sure."

"Thanks." The kid shrugged. "I'm sixteen."

The number tugged at Nate's heart. *Sixteen. He's just a child.*

"You going to rat on me?"

"'Course not." But from now on, he'd think twice about inviting him along on an evening rendezvous with Red. Who knew what the other man had planned? If it was that girl from Mammoth, he was playing with dynamite.

It only took about fifteen minutes to walk to the hotel. The parking area filled with fancy automobiles made Nate hesitate. Red didn't plan on going inside, did he?

He quickened his pace, catching his buddy. "What do you have in mind? We'll stand out like sore thumbs in there."

Red scanned the parking area. "I didn't think it out this far. Said I'd meet her here, but I'm not sure she'll show."

"Said you'd—how'd you do that? When did you even see the girl?"

"Red?" A feminine voice called from a nearby grove of trees. A moment later, the slender woman stepped into the open, her blond hair shimmering in the evening light.

"There you are." Red ducked forward, catching her hands in his. "I didn't think you'd come, doll."

A tentative smile spread across her face. "I wouldn't miss it." She glanced over his shoulder at Nate and Val. "You brought friends."

Red turned to face them. "Ah, yeah. Fellas, you can go now."

Nate shook his head. "Not a chance."

Mary giggled, weaving her hand through Red's arm. "It's all right. I'm pretty sure my roommate's just a few steps behind me. Want to walk to the dump?"

"The dump?" Red's brow furrowed. "Why would you want to go there?"

"You'll see." She grabbed Red's hand, tugging him after her. She lifted her voice. "Elsie, are you coming?"

Miss Brookes stepped from the shadows, her hands tucked into her sweater pockets. "Hello, everyone. Nice evening for a stroll."

A stitch of tension eased from Nate's muscles. "Sure is." With another young woman along, he'd feel less like a police detail and more part of a social group.

Val straightened. "Hey, Miss Brookes. I enjoyed your class today."

She smiled. "And I was impressed with your essay. Twain and Sinclair? Do you read a lot of novels?"

"Every chance I get. Though my father says novels are a waste of time."

Elsie frowned. "Jesus taught using stories. I think God designed us to love a good story."

A shadow passed over his face. "Yes ma'am. I think you're right."

Nate turned and followed Red and Mary, determined not to let the couple get too far ahead. Besides, he had little to offer in a conversation that revolved around reading.

Elsie fell in beside them. "I have some other books I can bring for you to read. Maybe you can pass them around—give the others a chance with them when you're done, Mr. Kaminski."

The kid blushed. "No one calls me by my last name."

"I'm sorry, I don't remember your given name."

"It's Valentine, but I don't like getting ribbed about it. So Val is easier."

Valentine? What else hadn't Val told them? A sixteen-year-old Jewish boy who loved to read—he must be feeling pretty lonely in this pack. Nate rubbed his ear. "Val, how did you read so many books if your father doesn't approve?"

"He goes to bed early."

Elsie turned to Nate. "What do you like to read, Mr. Webber?"

"Please, call me Nate." He jammed his hands deeper into his pockets. "So, Val, what do you want to do when you're done here at Yellowstone? Go into a trade?"

The young woman frowned at the abrupt subject change, but it drew her attention back to their companion.

Val chattered the rest of the walk, talking about odd jobs he'd worked and his dreams of going to college and becoming a novelist. It figured the kid was smart. Nate hadn't put that together before tonight, but the young man's awkward ways had suggested he wasn't suited to a life of hard labor. Maybe sitting in front of a typewriter would be more his speed.

Elsie smiled at the younger man. "I'm starting college in September. I've been working for years as a maid to afford it."

"You haven't started yet?" Nate asked. "I thought you said all of the savages were college students."

Her expression faltered. "Most are. But I started working at the hotels while I was still in high school. And since my parents couldn't afford university, I'm still here."

"But you're a teacher?"

Her lips drew into a line. "I help at the local school. I'll be studying education."

"You should take the men to see the geysers." Now there was a classroom experience he could get behind. "You could teach them right there in the field."

She hesitated. "Well, we have rangers for that. I could ask one of them—"

"But we like you, Miss Brookes." Val frowned.

Looked like the kid had a crush on the teacher already, not that Nate could blame him. "Val is right. You're building a rapport with the men."

Elsie's face brightened. "I suppose I could arrange something. We could read some papers about the geysers—study the science behind it. And then go and see them firsthand."

"What better classroom is there?" Nate could barely keep his eyes away from the young woman's face whenever she smiled. "I'm sure they'd enjoy that."

"What about you?" She cocked her head. "You'd come along, wouldn't you? Even if you already have a high school diploma, you could still learn something new."

Val bumped Nate's arm. "Nate will come. He's been talking about the geysers ever since that day you saved Mutt from falling in."

Only it hadn't been Mutt's close call that fascinated him. It was the way Elsie had lit up as she talked about the geysers and hot springs. As if the knowledge inside her couldn't help but bubble to the surface, because she knew he'd love it too. *And she was right.* Is that what made a great teacher?

Noises up ahead drew Nate's attention. The road had opened out into a large meadow, and a crowd of tourists sat on log benches watching something at the bottom of the hill. A tall metal fence separated them from the action. The guttural snarls in the distance sent shivers down his spine. "What is this place?"

Elsie sighed. "It's the bear feeding ground. The rangers dump scraps from the restaurants and hotels out here so folks can see the bears close up."

"No fooling?" Val hurried forward, moving through the crowd until he found a seat near the front. Mary and Red had already claimed a bench in the far back.

Elsie glanced at Nate. "Do you ever feel like the nanny?"

He chuckled. "For Val or the two lovebirds over there?"

"Both."

"They're adults, right? Well, Red and Mary are, anyway." He led the way along the row of benches, choosing one at the midway point with a good view of the bears. A ranger near the front narrated the animals' actions for the gathered visitors.

Over a dozen of the lumbering brutes were digging through a pile laid out on a platform in the middle of the field, while at least that many seagulls wheeled about overhead.

A massive bruin bellowed, charging at one of the smaller bears and running it off. The youngster splashed through a tiny brook that meandered through the meadow as the crowd responded with mingled sounds of shock and admiration. A second ranger on horseback sat nearby, a high-powered rifle balanced across his lap.

Nate shook his head. "I can't believe what I'm seeing. How many bears come here to eat?"

"Sometimes there are twenty or more. It can get pretty loud when they're battling for spots to feed."

Like the breadlines on a bad day. He'd once seen a woman throw a young boy out of her way in a frenzy to fill her food basket. The child lay bleeding on the pavement, a gash in his arm from where he'd fallen against a fireplug. The memory crowded through him, gnawing at his insides. He'd skipped countless meals to make sure his mother and sisters ate. Were things easier now he was gone? His monthly check from the government should provide food for the table. A lump rose in his throat.

Another fight broke out, the large animals bellowing and chasing each other, only to have an opportunistic neighbor rush in and fill the vacated spot. The ranger paused his lecture to let the crowd watch.

Nate jumped to his feet and headed to the back, needing to get away from the sounds. How many families could eat on the scraps being thrown out there for the wild animals?

"Nate?" Elsie followed, catching him just past the final row of benches. "What's wrong?"

He continued walking a few more feet, wanting to be clear of the jeering crowd. "Not my sort of entertainment, I suppose." He rubbed his arms, trying to perk up his circulation. "Aren't you cold?"

Elsie stood there with just a thin sweater over her dress. She drew her arms around her middle. "A little. I'm used to it, though." The setting sun did little to warm the meadow.

Nate shrugged off his heavy twill jacket. "Here. It's our fault you're out here tonight. We can't have you catching a chill." He glanced around. "What about your friend?"

"Oh, I think she's warm enough." Elsie nodded toward the couple on the rear bench. Red had his arm wrapped around Mary's waist.

Seventeen

Elsie packed a bundle of laundry into the molly cart and rolled it through the hall toward the last room. The hotel was only half-full, the rooms a luxury few visitors could afford right now.

She knocked on the door before letting herself in, calculating how many hours it would take to pay one semester's tuition. The teaching position at the CCC camp helped, but it was still going to be close. She'd need a job on campus as well.

The last room tidied up quickly. She stripped the bed, laid out new towels, and swept the floor. At this rate, she'd be done early. Maybe she could put in a shift at the laundry room. She didn't like bending over the steaming vats with the other bubble queens, but the extra hours would help.

A knock on the doorframe made Elsie jump. She glanced up in time to see Graham stick his head inside. "There you are."

Rose peeped out from behind him, then rushed forward and grabbed Elsie in a hug. "Elsie, I've been looking everywhere for you."

"What's wrong?" Elsie stepped out of her friend's embrace. "Why are you here?"

Rose smiled. "Nothing's wrong, silly. I have two days off, so I thought I'd come spend them with you and Mary." She glanced at Graham, her eyes shining. "Graham was sweet enough to drive me. He's a good driver too."

Graham tipped his hat. "It was my pleasure, believe me. You're much better company than the dudes and dudettes I usually haul around." Her cousin had picked up the savage lingo quickly, already employing the silly western nicknames park staff used—"dudes" for yellow bus tourists, "sagebrushers" for those who stayed in the auto camps.

Rose squeezed Elsie's hand. "Graham let me sit up front next to him since there weren't any tourists on this trip. And it was such a beautiful day we kept the canvas rolled back. I'm glad I remembered to tie a scarf around my hair, or I'd be a mess."

Elsie finished loading the cart. "You are always pretty as a picture, Rose, even with your hair mussed." It was true. Between Mary's Hollywood-style glamor and Rose's girl-next-door sweetness, Elsie felt like the ugly stepsister. Especially with her long sleeves and buttoned-up collar. "And you're just in time. I arranged for a showing of *Highlights of Yellowstone's Geysers* in the community center tonight. A bunch of the CCC men are coming."

Rose helped Elsie make the bed. "I'm sure Mary's happy about that. Can you stay, Graham?"

"I'd like to, but I've got to get the bus back to Mammoth." Graham leaned against the doorframe. "But before I go, could I treat you two ladies to lunch at the café?"

Rose beamed. "Say yes, Elsie. Please?"

Elsie's stomach turned. Forgiveness didn't mean she had to socialize with him, did it? Since moving to Canyon, she'd managed to avoid her cousin. "I have lessons to plan. But you two go ahead." Obviously, Rose's crush had expanded into full-blown puppy love. She just couldn't tell if Graham felt the same.

Rose smoothed the bedspread. "I can't wait to hear all about your experiences with the CCC men."

Graham's eyes narrowed. "Are they behaving themselves? No more fist-fights or garbage can fires?"

Elsie wiped the small table. "They've been perfect gentlemen."

"Graham, I can go to the café with you, if you'd like." Rose moved toward him.

His gaze flicked to Elsie. "I probably should be getting back, come to think of it. I've got half a sandwich in my bag. It will hold me over."

Rose's smile faded. "All right."

Elsie followed him out the door, wrangling the cart behind her. "Graham, how are my parents? My mother?"

His hesitation spoke volumes. "Auntie says to tell you she's fine and she hopes you're having a good time."

"She *says*?" Her heart plummeted. "What's the truth, then?"

He removed his cap, leaving his hair ruffled. "That's the message she entrusted me with."

Elsie rounded on her friend. "Rose?"

"I spoke to her three days ago, and she seemed tired. But that's been normal lately, right?"

"What are the two of you not telling me?" Elsie struggled to keep the bite out of her voice. "Is it her heart? Has she been overdoing it?"

Graham reached for the cart handles and helped her maneuver it toward the laundry room. "You didn't hear this from me, but she took a tumble on the back stairs."

"She fell?" Elsie's breath caught in her chest.

"She's not hurt." Rose added. "But your father . . . he thinks she may have fainted."

Elsie leaned against the wall, suddenly feeling a little dizzy as well. "I shouldn't have moved to Canyon. I need to be there."

Graham gripped her shoulder. "And that's why she told me not to say anything, Elsie. She doesn't want you to worry."

She recoiled from his touch. "I want to see her. Can I come back with you?"

Rose gasped. "But you have to work."

Her friend's words barely penetrated the chaos in her thoughts. "They won't mind. We've got too many pillow punchers right now and not enough visitors. Mary can run the film tonight." She glanced up at Graham. "But I do have to teach on Monday. Can you bring me back before then?"

"I'm returning to Canyon late tomorrow evening. You can tag along." Graham's voice was low. "But your mother wouldn't want you to rush home on her account. You know that."

"I need to see her."

Graham lifted his gloved hands. "Let's go."

❧

Nate clutched the roll of papers as he strode off into the woods, desperate for a breath of air. Several of the guys had started a baseball game in the yard, but the last thing Nate needed was to swing a bat right now. That wouldn't fix anything.

He sank onto a fallen log and dropped his head into his hands. The papers rustled against his cheek. *How did I get myself into this mess?* Lowering the documents, he unrolled them and stared at the typeface plastered across the top and the series of blank lines that followed.

"Reports." That's what Dahl had said when he tossed the packet onto Nate's bunk. Reports by Monday. Nate mulled over the information he could

include: acres cleared, top workers, difficulties encountered, equipment needed. He knew what needed to be reported. Why couldn't he just tell Dahl and Ranger Brookes directly? What was it about the government that they had to have everything on crisp white sheets to stick into a folder somewhere?

He glared at the papers, then rolled them up and jammed them into his shirt pocket. Hopeless. He couldn't write any better than he could sprout wings and fly. Nate got up and started walking. If he just kept going, eventually he'd make it back to civilization. He could get himself a job of some sort that didn't require reading and paperwork. Factory work or cleaning fish in a cannery. He could push a broom or a plow—whatever. Jobs were scarce, but there had to be something that didn't involve reports.

Nate continued on, stumbling over logs and shoving through brush. He had no idea how far he'd gone when he slowed, the roar of a river echoing through his chest. He'd made it to the edge of the canyon, the Yellowstone River far below. Nate scrambled to an overlook where he could gaze over the thundering falls. How much of that water came from the snow melting off the highlands where he and his team had been working on beetle-damaged trees?

His attention wandered to the steep canyon walls opposite him, the colors so varied that they could have been painted by a divine hand. Elsie could probably name each different type of stone in that canyon.

This place could really get to a man.

If he walked away from this opportunity, he'd not only lose the steady paycheck, he'd miss experiencing all this. Mist rose from the canyon, a peaceful response to the bellowing waterfall. If only he could find solace here too.

As much as he wanted to keep the foreman job, the CCC needed a man who could keep a foot in both worlds—the administration and the day-to-day work. Clearly, that wasn't him. The truth of the matter splintered his soul. No matter the humiliation, he owed Lieutenant Stone the truth.

By the time he got back to camp, the game had gone into extra innings. Nate walked past the yard and the new boxing ring Red had built. There would be time to talk to Stone later in the evening, perhaps after supper. Some of the men were going to the hotel for a movie night, but Nate doubted the lieutenant would be among them.

A loud tapping sound caught his attention as he ducked through the tent flap. "What is that? Sounds like a woodpecker."

Val sat cross-legged on the ground, a typewriter balanced on his foot-locker. "Hey, Nate. Isn't this amazing?"

"Where did you get that?" Nate walked to the kid's side and crouched beside him.

Each time Val pressed a key, a silver lever flew up and struck a letter against the white paper. "Captain Dahl sent it over from Mammoth. We're starting a camp paper. How does this sound, 'Camp Baseball Game Gets Blood Flowing'?"

"Pretty good. You might have a knack for this."

Val grinned. "Especially since Nowak got a baseball to the face and broke his nose. You should have seen it. That's when I decided to run back and get a start on the story. Nobody's going to scoop me."

Nate glanced around the tent with mock horror. "You mean spies from a rival paper?"

"Nah, but some of the other fellas want to write too. I want to make sure I get this story. Hey, Nate"—his eyes lit up—"could you do some of those cartoons? You could illustrate the story."

Nate retreated to his cot. "How'd you know about that?"

"I noticed you working on some last night. They're good."

Nate dropped onto the bed, weariness from the day settling over him. "Thanks." At least he could manage *something* with a pencil.

"So will you?"

Nate laid back and dropped an arm across his face. "I don't know. I only draw them for my sisters. I've never drawn for anyone else."

"But the boys would get a hoot out of it. You could draw Nowak with the ball bouncing right off his schnoz."

Nate chuckled. "How long are you going to be tapping away on that thing?"

"Just a few minutes. I wanted to write up the details before I forget them."

Write up the details. Nate rolled to his side and propped himself up on one elbow. "You know what—I might be interested in doing those drawings. But I'd need something from you in return."

Val's hands stilled. He glanced up with wide eyes. "Name it."

"Help me with my weekly reports." The lieutenant wanted paperwork. He didn't say how it had to be done.

"What did you have in mind?"

"I'll dictate them to you. You"—he gestured to the typewriter—"do your thing, there." Nate slid the rolled-up papers from his pocket and flattened them against his knee. "Could you type right onto these forms?"

"Sure." Val held out his hand. "Give 'em here."

Nate sprang up from the bed and thrust the cursed things into his friend's hand.

Val squinted at the top page. "Doesn't say it needs to be typed. You could probably just handwrite it."

"Don't you think Dahl would be more impressed if it were typed? Besides, my handwriting . . ." Nate shook his head. "Nobody wants to read that."

The kid chuckled. "Yeah, lots of folks have that trouble. My teacher was pretty quick with the ruler across the knuckles if you didn't write neatly. Worked for me, not that I'd recommend that to Miss Brookes."

"She doesn't seem the type to use the ruler."

A dopey smile crossed Val's face. "Nah, she doesn't. Pretty little thing, don't you think?"

"Sure. I suppose." Nate cleared his throat. "Do we have a deal?"

"You bet. Want to start now?"

Nate glanced out the door, checking that the game was still going. He grabbed his notepad and pencil. "You type; I'll draw. We'll be done before the game ends."

Elsie's mother shifted on the small sofa. "I told that boy not to say anything." Her hair was pulled into a knot at the nape of her neck, a few thin locks loose around her face.

"I didn't give him much choice." Elsie adjusted the pillows to support her mother's back. "He winced when I asked how you were doing. Just like you're doing now."

"It's nothing—a few bumps and bruises."

"You fell down the stairs." Elsie dragged a chair close. "Did you lose your balance?"

"I was feeling woozy. It happens."

Elsie's father walked through the room on his way to the kitchen. "More often all the time. I'm going to speak to Roger about a leave of absence. I want you to see a better doctor. We can go to Billings or Salt Lake, even."

Elsie twisted in her chair, her eyes following her father. Had things gotten that bad? "How long would you be gone?"

"Teddy can oversee the CCC crews for a week or two. They've gotten pretty self-sufficient." He finished knotting his tie and leaned over to place a kiss on his wife's forehead. "I have to go over to the campground."

Mama's brow furrowed. "Don't bother Superintendent Toll yet, Harold."

She turned to Elsie to explain. "We're still discussing it."

When Papa left, Elsie pressed herself into the chair to keep from running after him. She waited until his truck disappeared down the lane before she spoke to her mother. "What's there to discuss?"

"Your father worries. He can't be here all the time. I can't seem to convince him that I don't need that sort of hovering."

It had only been a few weeks since Elsie had moved, but her mother was noticeably weaker. "Maybe if I came back to Mammoth—"

"Absolutely not." Mama's blue eyes flashed. "We're so proud of what you're doing at Canyon. And you need the money for school. Herma comes over and stays with me when she's not on duty. And Graham stays here on the evenings he's in Mammoth. This house is full of people most of the time."

"Just as you like it."

"Just as I like it." Mama waved a hand in the direction of the stairs. "I made a mistake, and I paid for it. You know what they say about pride and falls."

Elsie generally found strength in her mother's words. Not tonight. "I suppose."

"Now tell me all about Canyon. How are you and Mary settling in?"

Elsie tried to focus on the past weeks, even though her heart wanted nothing more than to cling to the here and now. She recounted several stories to appease her mother, lingering on the story of taking the fellows to see the bears.

Mama frowned. "I wish they wouldn't feed them like that. It makes them look like trained circus animals. They should be wild, foraging in the mountains for food, not begging for scraps."

"So grizzlies should have pride too?"

"I suppose." Mama laughed lightly. "I'm glad you're making new friends. You've always held yourself apart."

Elsie ran her fingers along the arm of the chair. "I'm not as sociable as you, Mama."

"You keep a wall between yourself and others . . . even with those you love."

"What do you mean?"

Mama waited a moment, as if choosing her words. "Ever since the fire, you've kept everything locked inside. Your father and I let it happen, because we thought you needed time to heal." She rested her hand on Elsie's wrist. "I think that was a mistake. It's time to open up a little."

A lump grew in Elsie's throat. The truth of her mother's words rattled around in her soul.

"When you hold yourself separate from the world, you cheat others of the light God has placed inside you. There is no love without risk, without hurt."

Elsie touched her collar. "I have reasons to stay closed off."

"Fiddlesticks. You've turned your scars into a shield, an excuse to keep others away. We all have things about ourselves we'd like to hide, but it doesn't mean we should give in to that desire." She took Elsie's hand and tugged it away from her neckline. "I'm glad you're at Canyon this summer. It's a chance for you to spread your wings a little. I don't want you to find yourself alone one day."

"I'm not alone. I have friends."

"And how much do they know about what's going on inside you?" Mother sat back and winced again. "You're just like Wonderland, Elsie. Beautiful on the outside, a mystery within."

A laugh bubbled up in Elsie's chest. "Are you saying I'm a volcano waiting to erupt?"

"I'm saying"—she leaned forward and touched Elsie's cheek—"you are filled with wonders yet to be discovered."

Eighteen

Elsie followed Teddy along the Upper Terrace path, the sunshine brightening her day. The tight blue weave of Teddy's shirt clung to his shoulders, drawing her eyes even when she should be watching her footing. She couldn't seem to resist staring at his back and the muscles rippling beneath his shirt. Her mother had said pride went before a fall. Maybe attraction did too?

She had a few hours before she'd meet Graham back at her parents' house for the return journey to Canyon. Even though her mother was sleeping, a romantic walk had been the last thing Elsie had imagined herself doing today.

Teddy glanced over his shoulder. "Almost there."

She didn't bother reminding him that she had walked this trail since she was ten years old and knew every spring and pool along the path.

Angel Spring had been active this month, and water trickled from one terrace to another, the sounds providing a cheerful backdrop for their stroll. Elsie could never quite decide whether the chalky-white travertine layers reminded her more of Mayan pyramids or multitiered wedding cakes. *Hmm. Perhaps it's best to avoid any wedding analogies.*

The farther they got from the hotel, the fewer people they saw. Most visitors were returning to the cabins and campground for the evening to partake of a late meal or enjoy campfire stories from the ranger on duty. "I can't believe you're off today," Elsie said. "How did you manage that?"

"I worked early this morning." He blew out a long breath as they reached the top of the steep hill. "Your father told me you were here, so I hoped I could steal you away for a few minutes."

"And so you have." She couldn't hide the tremble in her voice. No man had ever sought her out the way Teddy had. The very thought made her head spin.

The valley spread before them, the familiar view a comfort. Elsie sighed. "I've only been gone a few weeks, but I've missed this place."

He eased up behind her, placing a hand on each of her arms. "And I believe it's missed you too. It's not the same, you know."

Elsie suppressed a shiver. She should be marveling at his touch, but every time he got close to her, she struggled against an overwhelming urge to step away. Was that normal for first love?

His palms slid to her wrists as he stepped closer, pulling her into an embrace from behind and resting his cheek against hers. "And I've missed you too."

She swallowed, willing herself to remain stationary. Why was her heart racing so? "You barely know me, Teddy." His touch seemed too fast. Too familiar.

His thumb rubbed against her sleeve, the sensation muted by her scars.

She tucked her hands beneath her elbows. The last thing she wanted this man doing was feeling her puckered skin. If she continued seeing him, he'd find out eventually. But for the moment, she just wanted to pretend she was like every other girl. Was that wrong?

Her motion didn't seem to alarm him, in fact he looped his arms under hers, clasping his hands in front of her.

Elsie tried to relax a little, leaning back against his strong frame. It was a beautiful view, and the setting sun cast a rusty-orange glow across the evening sky. She released the breath she'd been holding and tried to focus on preserving this moment, shooing away fear and uncertainty. The scene would make a lovely postcard.

"I know more than you think." His voice was a mere whisper, inches from her ear.

Elsie tensed.

He lifted one hand and tugged off her knitted cloche hat, allowing the wind to tickle the strands of her hair.

Unwanted chills ran up her spine. Was he getting ready to kiss her? She hadn't anticipated anything going that far. Not this soon, especially. Thankfully he couldn't see her expression because she was sure terror was written across her face. Did she even *want* to kiss this man? He was attractive, sure, and that drew her, but there had to be more to a romance than that. What had her mother said? *"It was his servant's heart."*

He nuzzled her hair, brushing his nose against her ear and inhaling deeply. "You smell amazing, you know that? What is that fragrance?"

"Something Mary bought. I-I don't remember the name." She could barely remember her own name, for that matter.

"Remind me to compliment her on it when I come see you this weekend."

"This weekend?" The statement stopped her. Wasn't he supposed to ask for another date? Or was presumption another thing about romance that she didn't understand? "I will," she said, not knowing how to interpret the clashing emotions inside her.

And with that, his lips brushed her ear, sending a shockwave through her. She couldn't hold still any longer, twisting in his arms in an attempt to put some distance between them. *I'm not ready for this.* Not now. Maybe not ever.

He loosened his grip enough for her to turn and face him, but kept his hands firmly planted on her forearms. "Elsie, it's all right."

She might not understand her inner turmoil, but she couldn't let this continue. It wasn't right to let him hope for a future together, not when she couldn't even imagine such a thing. He knew so little about her. "No, it's not. I'm not . . . I'm really not looking for this sort of—"

"Graham told me."

Elsie's heart jumped. "Graham told you what?"

His focus drifted south along her chin and neck before settling somewhere near her collarbone. He paused, as if to consider his words, before lifting his eyes to hers once more.

In that instant, she knew. "He told you about the fire."

"About what happened to the two of you. About . . . your injuries."

If she could have disappeared into the ground at that moment, she would have done so. A churning geyser seemed to have taken up residence in her stomach. "He had no right."

"I'm glad he did, Elsie. But don't worry, it won't change how I feel about you."

Elsie's mouth went dry. "And how's that?" Her voice cracked.

One corner of his mouth hitched upward, and he lifted a hand to her shoulder, trailing his fingers along her collarbone. "I think you're beautiful."

"You're . . . you're wrong." She steeled herself.

"How about you let me decide that?"

She froze as his fingers traveled along her blouse, then settled on the button at her throat. She grabbed his wrist. "No."

"It's all right, Elsie. I want to see. Let me prove it to you."

She jerked back, brushing away his arm.

"Don't be afraid. I just want to show you that it won't make any difference to me." He stepped closer again, a move she mirrored in the opposite direction.

Hot tears stung her eyes. "'Show me your scars,' is that what you're saying?" Her chest ached as if an expanding pocket of steam was demanding release. If she'd been in Geyser Basin, she would have noted the time in her logbook. "I'm not some sideshow oddity to be ogled at your whim."

His brow crumpled. "Of course not. I never said—"

"You never asked, either. I'm not showing you anything. Not today. Not ever. Put it out of your mind right now."

Teddy held his palms out in a gesture of surrender. "All right, all right. I'm sorry. I just thought it might set your mind at ease. I didn't mean to come on so strong." He turned away and stared out over the view. "I didn't anticipate you misconstruing my intentions."

Is that what she was doing? Elsie closed her hand around her collar, keeping it close to her neck. She might as well be standing there naked. How dare he even consider such a thing?

"So that's the sort of man you think I am." Teddy walked a few steps and turned away from her, his head lowered.

Her shoulders sank. Every time someone got close, her thoughts and feelings jumbled together like a knotted skein of yarn. Teddy must think her rude, presuming the worst about him—and maybe she was. He only wanted to find a way to break through her defenses. Was that so bad?

Her fingers hovered at her throat. She'd hidden her scars for years, unwilling to endure the pain in people's eyes when they saw her. Was this the time and place to let go of that? Is this what her mother had meant when she encouraged her to open herself up to others?

"I think you're beautiful." Teddy's words soaked deep into her heart. She wanted to wrap them around her shoulders like a silk shawl and just hide there. She'd hardly dared dream of a real relationship—a future—a

man capable of seeing beyond her scars. But could she let him? She touched the buttons at her neckline.

Teddy turned and met her eyes. "Elsie?"

He had no idea what he asked of her at this moment. If his face filled with revulsion or pity, this mirage would vanish in a heartbeat.

"I . . . I'm sorry, Teddy." She dropped her arm. "I can't."

Teddy stared at her in silence before finally offering a nod. "You'll trust me—in time." He held out a hand to her. "Come on. I'll walk you home."

Trust him. After a long, shaky breath, she let his fingers close around hers. If she couldn't get past this fear, there would be no future for them.

Then again, she hadn't expected one.

❧

Mary's eyes narrowed. "He asked to see your scars? That's . . . that's an odd request." She wrinkled her nose. "Did you show him?"

"No, because no matter what he says, I know they *will* matter." Elsie didn't like the childish tremor in her voice.

"Oh, honey." Her friend reached over and took her hand. "I know how you feel, but you do make too much of it. Sure, kids laughed once upon a time. But they were kids. I'm sure Teddy's not like that."

"I hardly know what Teddy's like." Elsie pulled her hand away. "I'm not ready to share that part of me yet—to see pity in his eyes." The evening was etched in her memory, but her brain spun the images around and around, still trying to make sense of them.

Mary sighed. "When is he coming to see you again?"

"Friday." Maybe she shouldn't have said anything. Once her friend caught a whiff of romance, she could be like an electrical storm in search of a mountaintop.

"So soon? We have preparations to discuss. You're not going to be alone with him this time. Not until we know what he's really after."

Relief washed through Elsie. Having someone who understood made all the difference.

"And," Mary's eyes took on a familiar glint. "You'll need something new to wear."

"Mary, every penny I make is going toward school. I don't have extra to spend on dresses."

"You can borrow something of mine, then." She rose and opened the wardrobe they shared, flicking through her dresses. "And I'll invite Red so we can all go out together. We can't have you off rotten logging with a park ranger."

"This might all come to naught."

She swung around and fixed her gaze on Elsie. "Did he kiss you?"

"No!" Elsie's heart lodged in her throat. She wasn't so naive that she hadn't sensed the desire in him. Thankfully he'd not pressed the matter, because she'd have fainted right there, and he'd have been forced to carry her home like a sack of potatoes. Wouldn't that be romantic?

"You didn't tell Rose before me, did you? Since she's gotten so close with Graham, she seems to hear everything first." Mary made a face.

"That's because my cousin has a big mouth." Elsie pressed fingers against her temples, a headache building behind her eyes. "I wonder who else he's talked to about me."

Mary chose a flowered dress and a pink sweater and laid them across Elsie's lap. "What does it matter? You'll be leaving for school in late September, anyway."

"That doesn't leave much time for romance." But Teddy knew her plans. He wouldn't expect her to stay in Yellowstone just for him. Would he?

"You can't worry about such things. You'll be diving headfirst into studies once you get to campus. Enjoy the summer while it lasts, that's my philosophy." Mary added a silk scarf to the ensemble she'd picked out for Elsie.

Elsie slid her hand across the feather-soft sweater. Mary flitted through love like a bluebird in a sun-kissed meadow. If only it could be that easy. Elsie had watched many savages fire up summer romances only to have them wither away months later. She'd just never expected to count herself among them.

"When God drops the right man into your life, I'm sure you'll recognize him." Her father's words trailed through her mind. Teddy had certainly popped into her life when she was least expecting it, but how was she to know if that was God's doing? It sure would be nice if He could be a little clearer about these things.

Nineteen

Nate mopped his face with a bandanna as the sun beat on his shoulders. The view from this side of Mount Washburn stole the breath from his chest—or would if he had any left over. He'd spent the last three hours helping Red, Bukowski, Moretti, and Nowak drag limbs into a slash pile. For as far as he could see, hillsides of green trees rose to meet the brilliant blue of the sky.

Had colors ever been this bright in Brooklyn? When O'Sullivan convinced him to sign up for the CCC, all Nate thought about was protecting his little brother and sending a few dollars home each month. He hadn't expected to enjoy the work.

Some of the men were singing "The Sidewalks of New York" as they swung axes and pulled crosscut saws through the beetle-damaged trees. The nostalgic waltz tune about the city seemed out of place in the forests of Yellowstone—just like them, really. Nate shook his head. Plucked from so many isolated immigrant neighborhoods throughout Brooklyn and the Bronx, the men had seen their share of scraps in the past month. He'd never heard so many ethnic jokes. It seemed just a matter of time before one of these petty squabbles erupted into a full-out brawl.

"Hey boss, what's next?" Red hollered at him. "You want us to haul more to this pile or start another farther down?"

Nate studied the slope. They'd made a good dent in this patch. He gestured to where the second group was busy felling another whitebark pine. "Let's make another pile over in that area."

Ranger Brookes was due this afternoon to inspect their work. They'd cut several trees today, and Nate hoped for more by nightfall. The park superintendent had already confronted Lieutenant Stone about the crew's snail-like pace. The fact that none of the men had timber experience, added to the travel time to and from Canyon Camp, meant the job was taking longer than anticipated. Evidently, the superintendent had hoped to clear the whole hillside of diseased trees in the first month, but the heavy layer of snow hung on too long for them to get to the upper stretches of the mountain. Sadly, the more acres Nate walked, the more diseased trees he spotted. This beetle infestation was on a larger scale than they'd feared.

What seemed to burn the superintendent the most was the schedule. CCC regulations limited them to forty hours a week, plus no work on Saturdays, Sundays, or holidays. The boys had been delighted to learn that, but the rangers groused about it. They weren't accustomed to such rules regarding their paid laborers.

Nate set his jaw. It just meant they'd have to work faster and smarter to make up the difference. He was determined to be a good leader, and that meant impressing Ranger Brookes. "Hey, Red—" He pointed at the dying trees to Red's left. "Do you think we could finish those two in the next hour?"

Red nodded. "I'll get Moretti and Nowak and their guys on it. They were bragging about their speed with a saw just last night."

"Tell them they can have my canteen scrip if they get them on the ground by three."

Red grinned. "I'll let 'em know."

Nate clambered farther up the hill, craning his neck to see into the treetops.

A squirrel hopped from a nearby trunk, jumped across the fallen limbs scattered across the ground, and scurried up another tree. If only Nate could climb like that, he could examine each tree in detail.

Nate took a swig of water from the canteen, then splashed a little into his hand and ran it across the back of his neck. The sun was blinding today. Not hot, exactly, but the intensity seemed to parch his skin like desert winds. Several of the fellows were sporting sunburns on their necks and chests, especially those who'd stripped off their shirts as they worked. By the end of the summer, their families wouldn't recognize them—bronzed, muscled, and healthy. It was a transformation, indeed.

The sight of a man hiking toward them drew his attention. A park ranger was winding his way up through the forest toward the crew. Nate retied his bandanna and loped over to the group. "Look smart, men. Ranger coming."

One of the fellows groaned. "It's not like we're lollygagging here, Webber."

"You're right. Sorry. He's going to be pleased." *I hope.*

But the man walking toward them wasn't Brookes. Nate bit back a groan as he recognized Ranger Vaughn striding up the steep slope, stepping over fallen trunks. Nate lifted a hand in greeting.

Vaughn came up beside him, barely winded from the climb. "Webber, I hear you're in charge."

"Of this team, yes sir." Nate shielded his eyes from the glare. "We were expecting Ranger Brookes. I hope nothing's wrong."

The man shrugged. "His wife isn't well, so I came to do the inspection for him."

Nate chewed on this bit of information. Elsie's mother? "Nothing serious, I hope."

Vaughn slid the straps of his pack off his shoulders and let it fall to the ground. "Do you know her?"

"Not personally."

Vaughn unhooked his canteen and twisted the cap off. "Elsie and I are quite concerned, of course."

He'd nearly forgotten the two were an item. Elsie hadn't mentioned Vaughn when they went to see the bears two weeks ago. But then again, why should she? It's not like that had been a date.

Vaughn slugged down some water and wiped his mouth with the back of his wrist. "I'm taking Elsie out to dinner tonight. Maybe for a nice moonlit walk. Should cheer her up."

Why was the man telling him this? "She seems like a nice girl. Smart. The men like her."

The ranger's brows pinched together, a scowl brewing behind his eyes. "The men—"

"—as a teacher." Nate hurried to correct his words. He needed a distraction. Anything to get this conversation away from Vaughn's love life. The picture of this stuffed shirt with the sweet Elsie Brookes turned his stomach. "You can see how much they're getting done here. We've nearly cleared this whole stand of sick trees." Nate gave the man a sideways glance. Sure, Vaughn was probably born with a hatchet in his hand, but in a Brooklyn alley he'd lose his wallet in ten seconds flat.

Vaughn scanned the hillside. "How many trees have you dropped this week? Twenty?"

"Closer to thirty. It should be thirty-three by the end of the day."

The ranger nodded before pointing to an outcropping just west of them. "What about over on the northern face? Do you have anyone working over that way?"

"I've scouted the area with a few men, but I didn't see much."

Vaughn's eyes narrowed. "Take a second look. That's prime territory for the pine beetles."

"It's also still buried in snowdrifts."

"That a problem?"

Nate swallowed a retort. "Ranger Brookes told us to focus on the lower reaches until things melt out rather than slogging around in the ice."

"We want those trees cleared out before the larvae wake up and start spreading. If we wait, we'll be doing this all over again next year."

A loud crack followed by a frenzy of shouts caught Nate's attention.

"Watch out—she's going down! Tim-ber!" Men's voices rang out through the forest as the pine crashed through its neighbors, twisting and snapping limbs as it fell. Men scrambled out of the way.

The messy drop set Nate's heart pounding. He set off at a run, shoving through the brush. "What happened? Is anyone hurt?"

Red appeared out of the stand, panting. "It twisted sideways—didn't land where they aimed. Nearly took out one of our brush crews."

Vaughn came up beside him, scowling. "Your tree fellers need to be better trained. You should be able to land the timber right on a dime, otherwise everyone's at risk."

As if we don't know that. Nate didn't bother to respond, keeping his focus on Red. "Is anyone hurt?"

Red glanced around, eyes wild. "I don't know. I think everyone's fine. I didn't see Bukowski after the log fell."

Nate hurried toward the fallen tree, pushing through the broken limbs. "Bukowski? Nowak? Is everyone accounted for?"

Maguire's voice came from the far side of the stump. "Over here! Bukowski's hurt. We need help!"

Nate and Red scrambled toward Maguire.

Shorty and Maguire crouched over Bukowski, who sat upright with his chest heaving and one hand pressed to the side of his head.

Nate dropped to his knee, scanning the wounded man. "What happened?"

Maguire answered him. "Clipped him on the way down. Just caught him in the ear and shoulder. Another few inches, and he'd have been flat as a trash-can lid."

Nate pulled Bukowski's hand away, wincing at the bloody gash above the fellow's ear.

Red pulled off the shirt he had tied around his waist and tossed it to Nate.

Nate rolled it and pressed it to the side of the man's head, easing him back onto the ground. The manual in his pocket had a chapter on first aid, for all the good it had done him. But growing up with four siblings and a drunken father had taught him a thing or two.

Bukowski moaned, squinting against the pain. "It was just a limb. Clocked me good, though. Thought I was in the clear."

Red crouched on the man's far side. "It changed directions in the air. We weren't expecting that."

Nate kept the shirt pressed to Bukowski's wound and glanced over his shoulder to where Ranger Vaughn lingered. "You got a doctor here?"

"In Mammoth."

Red chewed his lip. "Think it's that bad?"

Nate chose his words carefully. "He's going to need some stitching. My sewing skills are lacking. How are yours?"

"Ain't got any."

Bukowski's eyes had glazed a bit, sinking to half mast. He probably had a concussion too. Hopefully not a cracked skull. Nate studied him. The man's shoulder was bloody and twisted slightly. Might be broken as well. This was definitely more than they could handle on their own.

"Red, can you take hold of this? Don't let up on the pressure." Nate slid out of the way as Red took his place. He wiped his hands on his dungarees and took a few steps away to get some air. He'd pushed the men hard in order to impress Brookes. Now Bukowski had paid the price for his haste.

He bent forward, bracing his hands against his knees and willing his stomach to steady. He'd seen blood before, but never because of his own stupidity. After a few deep breaths, Nate stood and faced the crew. "Maguire, Ricci, Shorty—can you guys set to making a litter? We need to get Bukowski to the truck. The rest of you, get this tree cleaned up and the piles set. We'll call it a day." His hands were trembling as he gestured to the work site. Nate pulled them close to his ribs, tucking them under his elbows. *And not the kind of day I ever want to repeat.*

The ranger came up beside him. Nate braced himself for a chewing out. Vaughn shook his head. "I know what you're thinking, Webber. It's written all over your face." He watched the crew, climbing across the hillside like so many ants. "It happens. Don't be too hard on yourself."

The unexpected sympathy sent a second wave of guilt through Nate. He so wanted to dislike the man who'd earned Elsie Brookes's devotion.

"Have a couple guys haul your injured man to the medical clinic in Mammoth. We can stay here and get the slash burn going." The ranger drew a silver lighter from his shirt pocket. "It's critical to torch the debris so the beetles don't spread."

"I just told them they could knock off early."

"We don't need the whole crew. You and me—and one or two others, just to keep an eye on things. We'll have ourselves a late afternoon bonfire." He tossed the gadget to Nate. "Should have brought some hot dogs."

"I thought you were only here for an inspection." Nate caught the lighter, warm to the touch as if Vaughn had kept it clamped in his palm for quite some time.

"Don't mind staying to help out for a few hours, seeing as you're short a man. I just need to get back in time for a late supper. Wouldn't want to disappoint my girl."

Nate turned the object over in his hand, the shiny case seeming a mite fancy for a simple park ranger. "Nope. Couldn't have that."

Twenty

Elsie took Teddy's hand as he helped her from the front seat of his car at Yellowstone Lake, and her friends climbed out of the back. The sun sparkled across the immense lake, the weather seeming to bless this little outing the girls had planned for the first day of July. A breeze riffled the surface, kicking up tiny wavelets that caught the light and made it dance across the water.

Teddy had been the perfect gentleman at the dinner they'd shared with Mary at the Canyon Lodge last night, and the experience had scattered her misgivings to the wind. She'd relived the incident at Mammoth hundreds of times now, certain she'd misread his intentions. It's a wonder he wasn't regretting ever asking her out.

On the ride to the lake, Mary's and Rose's laughter from the back seat had set her heart at ease. With business at the campground being slow, Rose was having trouble getting enough work hours at Mammoth. But for Elsie, having her best friends along, plus Red and Nate, meant she wouldn't have to awkwardly entertain Teddy alone. The last thing she needed was to embarrass herself again.

As Nate stepped out of the automobile and gazed out over the lake, the pleasure in those green eyes was clear. He and Rose strolled toward the lakeshore, together with Red and Mary. Elsie typically didn't like to play matchmaker, but she hoped he'd lure Rose's attention away from Graham.

Elsie retrieved the supplies from the car. "It's a beautiful day."

Teddy took the picnic basket and hung it over his arm before claiming her hand. "It doesn't get much better. I'm glad we could do this, Elsie. We haven't had much time together."

She scolded the butterflies gathering in her stomach. "Me too."

"We could have come on our own, though." He glanced unhappily toward the rest of their party. "And I wish I didn't have to head back tomorrow. You really should move back to Mammoth." He lowered the basket to one of the tables and pulled her into his arms.

Elsie put a firm hand against his chest. She needed time to get comfortable with his affection. And she also didn't want everyone seeing. "I'd like to be there to keep an eye on my mother, but I need the extra teaching money for college."

He frowned. "I can't believe we just got together and you're already talking of leaving me."

"I . . . I'm not. Not exactly." Elsie fumbled through her words. "I've never kept my plans secret from you."

"Yes, but I thought . . ." He released her, dropping his hands to his sides. "Just tell me one thing. If things work out between us—what then? You don't need some fancy degree to be a park ranger's wife."

A wash of cold swept over her, as if she'd stepped into the frigid waters of Yellowstone Lake. "Teddy, I want more than that. I've always dreamed of being a teacher."

He cleared his throat. "There's a school here at Yellowstone, but not at most parks. What if I'm reassigned to Alaska? Or someplace else?"

She focused on the basket, flipping open its lid with trembling fingers. "Is that your dream? To work in Alaska?"

"Not exactly. But my job would have to come first—for both of us. You understand that, don't you?"

Do I? She'd never really considered marriage a viable option before, so she hadn't really thought through the issue.

"You could always school our children, but you don't need a degree for that." His frown deepened. "I don't like the idea of waiting years for you to finish at university."

Her stomach twisted. "I think it's a little early to be worrying about this."

He glanced away, his lips pressed tight for a moment. "We'll discuss it later. Today we're here to have a good time, and that's what I intend to do."

Elsie dug into the basket and started removing the supplies. Anything to break the tension stirring between them. "I brought hot dogs for us to cook. We should get things ready."

"How about a walk by the lakeshore, first?" He reached for her hand again. "Then I'll come back and get the fire going. Did you bring the lighter I gave you?"

"I brought matches."

"You shouldn't need matches. That's why I bought you the lighter." His brow furrowed. "You aren't afraid to use it, are you?"

"No, not exactly." Elsie sorted through the salads and condiments, hesitant to speak poorly of the man's thoughtful gift. It did feel a bit unusual to carry a vial of flammable liquid around in her pocket. What if it ignited accidentally? "I don't want the case to get scratched. I keep it on my desk at home." She lifted her eyes to meet his. "Where I can see it every day."

A smile crinkled across his face, and he stepped closer. "That's sweet, Elsie. Like you. But the lighter's a tool. It should be used. Otherwise, what's the point?"

"I will use it. I promise."

He reached into his shirt pocket. "I keep mine right here by my heart."

She couldn't resist placing her hand over his, against his chest. "Well, then, *you* can start the campfire. We can take that walk after we eat."

He chuckled. "You drive a hard bargain. I'll grab some wood. But first . . ." Before she knew what he was doing, he leaned in and brushed a gentle kiss against her lips. He drew back with a smile. "I've been wanting to do that for weeks."

Her heart had landed somewhere in her throat. As he walked off to get the wood, she reached her fingers up to her mouth, still feeling the touch of his lips on hers. Things were moving so fast with Teddy. Marriage? Children? She knew from watching her friends that she should be twirling in circles about now—at least on the inside. She sank onto the bench. No one had ever said she'd feel queasy.

Nate turned back to look at the view, the sight of the kissing couple sending a kink into his day. He needed to keep his eyes on his own date. Red had twisted his arm into coming on this outing at the last minute in order to keep the numbers balanced, and to be honest, it hadn't been that difficult. He'd jumped at the opportunity to see more of this park, even if it meant being matched up with a girl he didn't know.

Red and Mary continued walking along the lakeshore, the gravel crunching under their feet. Rose stood next to him, her hands firmly planted behind her back.

He cast one last glance over his shoulder before turning to Rose. "I'm glad Red invited me along. I hope you don't mind being saddled with me."

She smiled, the breeze lifting the curls from around her pretty face. "I was just thinking the same thing."

"You must have been to Yellowstone Lake hundreds of times."

She sighed. "A few, yes. Pete and I used to come here and rent a boat to go fishing. He loves fishing."

The wistful tone in her voice tugged at him. "Does he work for the park?"

"Yes, though not this summer." She glanced out over the water as if imagining days gone by. "He was a pack rat—a porter—at Old Faithful Inn. We dated for three summers. He even transferred to the University of Wyoming so we could be at the same school. He was my gallant knight, and he treated me like a princess." Her voice trembled. "But now he's got someone else."

Losing someone you loved hurt, but having them walk away was a double blow. "I'm sorry. That must have been rough."

Her brown eyes glazed with tears. "What's been hard is being back here and facing all the people who knew us as a couple."

Nate couldn't resist brushing his hand against her arm. "Well, I didn't know you as a couple. I'm hardly a knight, but maybe we can be friends?"

"I'd like that." She smiled and nudged him back. "Listen to me. We're out here for five minutes, and I'm already spilling about my old loves. You're easy to talk to, Nate Webber. Elsie was right about that."

His heart leapt. "She said that?"

"Mm-hmm. When she invited me to come today. I actually thought her cousin might be along. You know Graham?"

"The fellow who drives the buses, right? Is he a friend of yours too?" Suddenly he sensed where Rose was going with this. First Pete's name and then Graham's. That bumped Nate pretty far down the list.

"Yes, but Elsie doesn't approve. So here we are."

She sure knew how to make a man feel good. Nate took a deep breath and blew it out between his teeth. "Would you like to take a stroll, maybe?"

"You go ahead. I should probably help Elsie get the food ready." She walked toward the picnic tables.

Nate fixed his attention on the lake and watched the gulls skim over the rippling surface. No matter. He wasn't here to meet women and didn't need the distraction. The sight of Red and Mary walking arm in arm in the distance sent a quiver through his gut. It would be a nice distraction, regardless.

He turned to follow Rose. Maybe he could help too. It looked like Vaughn had the fire going already, but an extra hand was surely welcome.

Within thirty minutes, three of them were cooking hot dogs over the fire, the juices dripping onto the rocks and sizzling. Mary and Red hadn't returned, but Vaughn, Nate, and Rose held sticks over the open flames. Elsie stayed off to the side and fussed over salads and drinks on the table instead.

Nate propped his hot dog skewer between two stones and wandered over to join her. "Aren't you cooking one for yourself?"

She cast a quick glance at the leaping flames. "I'm not a big fan. I'll stick with the fruit salad and cheeses."

"It looks like you brought plenty. I wish Red and I could have contributed."

"I'm just glad you could join us." Elsie lowered her voice so only Nate could hear. "Rose is a sweet girl. I'm sure you two will get along marvelously."

He matched her volume. "I think she has her sights set elsewhere."

Elsie rolled her eyes. "Yes, my cousin. I'm doing my best to dissuade her."

Nate propped his foot up on the bench. "He seems like a nice fellow."

"I suppose." Her nose wrinkled. "But we have history, Graham and me. She's already had a rough go of it with Pete. I don't want to see her hurt again."

And yet she trusted him—a near stranger? Nate wasn't sure what to make of that. "One can't argue with the heart."

"I suppose. But you can't blame me for trying." She glanced back at Vaughn, laughing beside her friend. A wariness crept through her gaze.

With a sigh, she returned her attention to the food, adding cheese and crackers to her plate. "I've been thinking about your idea of taking the men to see the geysers. How would I go about arranging such an outing?"

"We don't work on the weekends. Could you go next Saturday?" He walked back to retrieve his hot dog before it scorched. After plunking it in a bun, he claimed the seat across from Elsie. "I'm sure Lieutenant Stone would approve use of one of the trucks. The cooks could pack some lunches."

Vaughn finally wandered over and sat beside her. "Lunches for what?"

She smiled at the ranger. "I'm going to take my class on a field trip to see Old Faithful next Saturday."

"Just you and a bunch of men? I'm not sure I like the sound of that."

Nate added some potato salad to his plate. "It's not like that. It's a class trip. She's been teaching about the geology of the park."

Vaughn seemed to catch himself. "Of course. I didn't mean anything by it."

Yeah, right. This guy was as possessive as a kid with a handful of penny candy. Nate glanced at Elsie to gauge her reaction.

Her attention had dropped to her plate as she placed another slice of cheese on a cracker. "You could always come with us, Teddy."

"I have to work. I don't get every weekend off like these . . . these fellows." Teddy leaned forward and grasped her hand. "I wish I could join you. I don't like the idea of you going alone."

"She won't be alone," Nate bristled. "We're not a bunch of thugs, Ranger Vaughn. I'll be there and so will Red."

Elsie brightened. "You will? I mean—you're more than welcome to join us. I'd be delighted to have you there."

Vaughn shifted on the wooden bench, his pinched expression not a challenge for Nate to read.

Nate wiped his mouth with the napkin before speaking. "I'm one of the foremen. It makes sense for me to be there to keep an eye on things." He glanced over at her boyfriend. "And it might put Ranger Vaughn's mind at ease." *Or not.*

The ranger's fingers drummed against the table. "I suppose."

"It's settled then." Elsie added another scoop of fruit salad to her plate. "Saturday it is."

The rest of the meal was uneventful as talk shifted to park activities and favorite hikes. Mary and Red finally appeared and joined them, filling their plates and jumping into the conversation.

Red was quick to nab a piece of the apple pie. "So what's this talent show I keep hearing about?"

Mary slipped her arm through his. "We do it every year, though it moves around between the hotels. This year it'll be at the Old Faithful Inn, so we're calling it the Old Faithful Follies. There are singing and dancing acts, comedy, magic—a little of everything. A lot of the staff participate and even some of the visitors. There's a competition between the different crews too."

Red swiveled around to face Nate. "We should do something like that in our camp."

"Why not?" He might be pretty low on the talent scale, but some of the others might contribute. "I've heard Val sing in the shower."

"And Enzo can juggle. I saw him doing it with mess kits the other night, though he boasted he can juggle axes."

"Just what we need. A second trip to see the doc in Mammoth."

Elsie held out a basket of crackers to Rose. "Maybe the CCC boys could join our show? We could make them part of the competition. CCC against savages."

Red chuckled. "You'd win, easy. You've got more pretty girls. We've just got a bunch of ugly mugs."

"Oh, I don't know about that." Mary kissed his cheek.

Rose took a last bite. "I think it's a brilliant idea. And we've got all summer to put together acts."

Vaughn shifted closer to her. "No reason you couldn't team up across lines, is there? If, say, Rose and Nate wanted to put together something?"

Nate wished he knew the man well enough to kick him under the table. Anyone paying attention could see Rose wasn't interested in him. "I'm afraid I got the short straw when it came to talents. Can't dance, can't sing. Rose would be better off finding another savage to team up with her."

She shot him a wide smile, the kind that sent a wave of warmth through a man. "I'm sure you're too humble, Nate. But I do have someone in mind."

Of course she did. Nate broke off another piece of bread and popped it into his mouth. Turnabout was fair play. "What about Ranger Vaughn? He might have a song or two in him."

The ranger straightened. "I'm happy to watch and enjoy. Elsie? Are you in the show?"

She shook her head. "I don't perform. I prefer to help behind the scenes."

Too bad. At this moment in time, there was no one Nate would rather see on stage.

aturday arrived quickly, complete with sunshine and blue skies. Elsie grasped Nate's hand as he helped her down from the cab of the CCC truck in the busy parking area at Old Faithful. Men were jumping out of the back even before Red got the engine shut off. The delight of being on a sightseeing trip had managed to transform the group into a passel of school-boys on an outing. Elsie had never had such fun. They'd already stopped at Midway Geyser Basin to see the giant hot spring called Prismatic Lake, and the men's delight was contagious. It was difficult to merely scratch the sur-face of things to see in each location, but she promised herself that they'd find time for more trips before the end of the summer. She desperately wanted to see their reactions to the mud pots at Lower Geyser Basin.

Elsie balanced a clipboard and a couple of books against her hip. "We'll start here at Old Faithful, and then make our way around the trail to see the other geysers." She checked the timepiece dangling from a pin on her sweater. "We still have plenty of time before sunset."

Nate pointed at the building to their left, its high sloping roof topped with a series of flags. "Is that the Inn where you'll be having the end-of-the-summer talent show?" Several of the yellow buses were parked out front, wedged in between the hordes of family automobiles and flashy coupes.

"Yes. And we'll have to go inside so you can see it. The building is simply magnificent."

"Better than the Canyon Hotel?"

"Not grander, maybe, but more interesting. You'll like it." She couldn't wait to witness their reactions. "Trust me."

Seeing Nate among her pupils had brought an unexpected surge of joy. Val had informed her that the foreman didn't actually have a high school diploma, and yet for some reason he'd avoided signing up for her class. It didn't make sense. He seemed plenty bright, and his presence clearly encouraged the others.

He'd stayed at the rear of the group at their last stop, as if determined to maintain his image of being a chaperone rather than a pupil. It was too bad, really. She found him the easiest of the men to talk to, perhaps because they'd spent time together outside the classroom. Something about Nate just seemed safe and relaxed, as if he had no expectations or demands of her. His eyes radiated a gentle kindness. To tell the truth, she felt far more at ease around him than she did with Teddy. Though maybe you weren't supposed to feel relaxed around someone you loved.

Do I love Teddy?

A question for another time. Elsie slowed her steps as they approached the railing surrounding Old Faithful, the men clustering in one area to stay out of the way of the many tourists. The rocky mound might be somewhat nondescript if it weren't for the constant plumes of steam rising from the cone. Val followed in her footsteps, his lanky frame casting a shadow wherever she went. "Can I carry those books for you, Miss Brookes?"

"That's very kind of you, Val." She gladly released the geology texts into his arms.

"Careful, kid," Red grunted. "If you're too much of an apple polisher, her ranger boyfriend might decide to rearrange your face."

A jab of irritation cut through Elsie. "Val is just being a gentleman, Mr. Walsh. The rest of you could take a few lessons."

"Sure, he is." Shorty smirked. "I know his kind in Brooklyn. They practically own the place. Am I right, kid? You Jewish?"

Val's face flushed.

Jewish? Elsie paused. Why would that matter? But she couldn't miss the uneasy glances that were traded by some of the men.

"Val's a Canyonite, like me and the rest of the fellas here." Nate moved up to stand beside the kid. "If you'd rather be something else, Shorty, there's a truck rolling out of camp at dusk. You can be on it." He clamped a hand on Val's shoulder. "But I thought you needed the dough, like the rest of us."

Shorty hunched his shoulders. "Yeah, I do."

"Then nothing more needs to be said, does it?"

"I reckon not." The fellow gave Val a quick nod before he wandered toward the rear of the group.

It didn't take long for the men's focus to return. Old Faithful's steam vent was puffing like a locomotive. Elsie knew they probably still had a little time before the show really got rolling.

One of the fellows piped up from her left. "It's almost ten o'clock. Does it go off on the hour, like folks say?"

"Not on the hour, no. But it does go off fairly regularly. That's what makes this geyser unique from the others you've seen." She spent the next ten minutes reviewing with the group how the geology of Yellowstone worked. They'd gone over it in class, read articles, and even written a short paper on hydrothermal features, but there was something special about seeing them in person.

Nate stepped forward, leaning against the railing. "What's it doing now? Is that the eruption?"

Water had begun burbling from the cone, jumping and falling in rapid surges. Elsie turned to watch. "It's just warming up. It can do this for a long period before the true eruption." She never got tired of the building anticipation that occurred as a crowd watched one of her favorite geysers. She lifted a hand to shield her eyes and gestured them forward.

The men gathered along the wooden rail separating the tourists from the fragile ground around the feature.

Nate, like most of the men, kept his gaze locked on the action, his smile widening a little more each time the water danced higher, teasing them in preparation for the main event. After about ten minutes, the spout rocketed upward, clearing the cone by a good twenty feet, spraying and steaming into the blue sky. The men applauded, hooting and hollering their appreciation for this fantastic natural spectacle.

Their reaction sent a ripple of pleasure through her. After years of watching Old Faithful, she'd never grown bored with its performance. It was mind-boggling to think that Wonderland's hot springs were completely natural features, intricate combinations of water, gas, and pressure—but not formed by the hands of man. *God, You have filled our world with wonders.*

As the stream slowed, she couldn't help noticing Nate's countenance dropping along with the water. As his gaze lowered, emotion splayed over his face.

She edged up close to the man. "What's wrong?"

"I . . . nothing." He shook his head, as if shaking off his odd reaction. He lifted his attention back to the fading geyser. "I was just thinking about my family. My older brother. He would have loved this. Used to talk about seeing the world."

"Used to?"

Nate swallowed. "Lost him a couple of years ago."

A wound in Elsie's heart opened wide. "I'm sorry." She touched his elbow. "I lost a sister. Many years back, but it still hurts to think of her."

He blew out a long breath, the animated conversations going on nearby seeming to nudge him back to the moment at hand. "Who'd have thought a geyser could make me melancholy?"

"You'd be surprised how often Yellowstone's features seem to trigger powerful feelings among onlookers. I think they reflect all the emotions we keep bottled up inside. And then, after a time—" She lifted her hands. *"Whoosh."*

Nate chuckled. *"Whoosh?"*

She loved the sound of his laugh. It's a shame Rose hadn't fallen for the man. "What would you call it?"

"I really couldn't say."

The men had started moving along the boardwalk toward Upper Geyser Basin. She should be leading the way, but after Nate's confession, she had no desire to hurry off. Instead, she and Nate walked side by side in the group's wake. She pointed out some of the wildflower signs along the way. "Herma Baggley put those in. She's the ranger who designed the trail."

Nate's brows shot upward. "A woman ranger, huh?"

"And a good friend. She has a master's degree in botany, and she's writing a book about the plants of Yellowstone."

"Sounds like a smart lady." Nate stopped to study a bubbling pool. "Like you, I suppose. Have you thought of becoming a ranger—like your father?"

Elsie paused beside him. She had, at one time, before the park service placed a moratorium on hiring women. "I've always felt God nudging me toward education. A good teacher can change lives."

"You're already doing that, with these fellows."

His words warmed her heart. "But for some reason, you haven't joined my class. Why is that?"

His posture went stiff as he turned away to take in the view rather than answering her question.

"Nate, I'd assumed you'd already earned a high school diploma, but Mr. Kaminski assured me that wasn't the case."

"Remind me to talk to Val about minding his own business."

Obviously, she'd touched a nerve. But she couldn't let this slide. She needed to know why Nate was avoiding her. She circled around to his other side to look him in the face. "Is it me? You don't want to take classes from me?"

His green eyes widened. "No, of course not. Why would you think that?"

"What am I supposed to think?" She gestured to the bubbling springs around them, the group continuing on without them. "You obviously have interest in the subject matter. You're intelligent—I can tell from your questions. So it must be me."

"It's not you." His voice caught and a strange look fell across his face.

Val hollered to them from up ahead, encouraging them to catch up. The group had gathered around the Giantess Geyser. Elsie needed to take control of the class again before they swept past some of the best springs without stopping to study them. She wanted to give them time to experience Jewel Geyser in Biscuit Basin. She knew they'd enjoy one of the rangers' favorite crowd-pleasing tricks—tossing sweat-stained bandannas in the pool and watching them get sucked under the surface. The neckerchiefs would return a few minutes later fresh and clean, courtesy of the geyser's spray. *Whoosh.*

Elsie shot Nate a look she hoped said, *"We're not done here,"* before walking off to join the milling collection of men. It was nice to have at least a few eager students.

Twenty-Two

As rain pattered on the roof, Elsie sat at the small desk in her room and flipped through the papers. She'd given the men a week to write their observations from the trip. Their descriptions of the geysers were both illuminating and, at times, humorous. Most of them had come a long way in their ability to express themselves in writing, but their grasp of geology was still lacking.

Mary sat cross-legged on her bed, reading a romance novel one of the girls had loaned her. She'd sighed twice in five minutes, so it must be good.

A sudden pounding on the door made them both jump. Mary hopped up with a giggle. "Red or Teddy?"

"I doubt it. We didn't hear 'man on the floor!'" Elsie capped her fountain pen just as Mary flung open the door, revealing Rose standing in the hall, tears dripping as fast as the raindrops trickled off her coat.

Elsie stood. "Rose, what's wrong? What are you doing here?"

"I didn't know where else to go." She dragged her overnight case through the door. "I quit my job at Mammoth."

"What?" Mary's mouth dropped open. "Why on earth—"

"I can't stand it. Without the two of you, and without Pete . . ." Rose covered her face with her fingers, stifling a sob.

Elsie grabbed her other hand and tugged her inside while Mary collected her case. "Let's get you dried off and warmed up."

Mary pulled off their friend's coat and then wrapped a terry robe around Rose's shoulders. "How did you get here? Did Graham bring you?"

Rose crumpled onto Mary's bed, hiding her face in the pillow.

Mary glanced over her shoulder at Elsie. "Is that a no or a yes?"

Elsie sat beside Rose and rubbed her back. "I thought you were over Pete. You've barely said a word about him since the day you arrived."

The girl rolled to her side and curled her knees up to her chest. "I-I didn't want to seem like a crybaby." She sniffled and pulled a handkerchief from her pocket. "But look at me now."

Elsie remembered her conversation with Nate about bottled up feelings. *Whoosh.* "We can only keep these things inside so long."

Mary sat on the foot of the bed. "I thought you were carrying a torch for Graham now."

"Graham said . . . He called me a little sister." She let out another wail. "A *sister*—can you believe that?"

The weight of her friend's grief fell over Elsie. "So is this about Pete or Graham?"

"Both. Neither. I don't know."

Elsie glanced at Mary, at a loss for how to help.

"You both have someone." Rose mopped her splotchy face. "You can't understand."

Elsie fought back a laugh. "I've gone my entire life without 'having someone,' and I'm not entirely certain I do now."

Her friend struggled to sit up. "But what about Teddy? He's so sweet, Elsie. You two are perfect."

Mary smiled. "Yes, Elsie finally landed her ranger. Now she can stay in Yellowstone forever."

"You know I want more than that," Elsie said.

Mary shrugged. "So get married and go to school. Who says you can't do both?"

"But Teddy doesn't want me to. He keeps talking about me staying here with him, or moving to a different park. How can I give up everything I've dreamed of?"

Rose's teary eyes widened. "How could you *not*? I would give up all my dreams to marry a good-looking man."

The words twisted in Elsie's gut. Trade her dreams for love? Most women would choose like Rose, especially for someone as dashing as Teddy. But she'd worked hard to make college—and teaching—a reality. God had given her this dream, hadn't He? Would He want her to give it up for marriage?

"He said that?" Mary raised a brow. "He sounds like a man in love."

In love? An ache grew behind Elsie's temples. How had this discussion gotten sidetracked with her problems? She turned back to Rose. "Why did you quit your job? What are you going to do now?"

Rose folded her arms around her waist. "I talked to Mrs. Harris. She said there are a few workers who would rather be in Mammoth, so she'd see about making a trade. I couldn't stand the thought of seeing Graham all the time, knowing he doesn't care a lick about me. He passes through Canyon often, but at least he's not based here."

"I know he's fond of you, Rose. He just doesn't . . ." Elsie scrambled for words.

"He doesn't love me. No one does. No one but you two, anyway." She got up and wandered over to Elsie's desk. "Where'd you get this?" She picked up the silver lighter and opened the lid.

Elsie jumped up and moved toward her friend. "It's a silly thing Teddy gave me when I left Mammoth. He must not have known I was deathly afraid of fire."

"It's beautiful." Rose flicked her thumb over the lever, a single flame popping out the vent at the top.

Elsie took a step back. "Please, don't do that in here."

"Well, he must have known," Rose said. "Graham told me Teddy has asked him about the fire multiple times since seeing Graham's scarred hands. In fact, Graham's so worked up about it, he's been ducking the man."

A shudder coursed through Elsie. Why was Teddy so interested? "What did Graham tell you?"

"He says all he wants to do is forget it. Like you, he doesn't talk about it much."

"But Teddy asked him, anyway?"

"More than once." She turned the silver case over in her fingers before lighting it a second time. "But I don't want to think about Graham. Not anymore."

The flame sent a fresh tremor through Elsie. It made her queasy to see Rose playing with the gadget as if it were a children's toy. "Can you put it back, please?"

Rose met her gaze. "Certainly." She closed the lid. "First, can I ask you something?"

"Of course."

She held up the lighter. "When you were a child, Graham lit the fire that burned you both so badly. Is that the only reason you didn't want me seeing him?"

This was her not thinking about him? "He didn't light the fire, exactly." Elsie swallowed. "He was playing with firecrackers and one . . ." She struggled to finish the sentence as the memory's cold fingers clamped around her. "One got away from him."

"So if it was an accident, why did you tell him to stay away from me?"

Mary finally joined the conversation. It had been unlike her to stay quiet so long. "You told Graham to stay away from Rose?"

Elsie touched her throat, a fluttering sensation in her stomach. "I never said that."

Rose's eyes narrowed. "He said you blamed him for your sister's death."

That was harder to argue with. "Yes. I hold him responsible."

She tapped the lighter on her palm. "But he saved you that day. Just like he rescued Mary and me when the fire broke out at the Mammoth Hotel."

Mary frowned. "He hardly *saved* us, Rose. The fire was in a garbage bin. It never reached the hotel."

"It could have," she shot back.

"It didn't," Elsie said. "And the thanks should go to Teddy, for spotting it in time." She snatched the lighter from Rose's fingers. She couldn't stand seeing someone fiddle with the item as if it didn't hold the power to change all their lives with one careless slip of the hand. Gift or not, she'd just as soon get rid of it.

"Teddy." Rose's face flushed. "Graham's far more courageous, Elsie. You just can't see it. He's walked into a fire—twice." She shook off the robe and grabbed her dripping coat. "He's much more of a hero than your Teddy will ever be." She practically spit the words and stormed out the door.

Mary shook her head. "What's gotten into her? Melodrama is usually my game, not hers."

"Too much time spent mooning over my cousin." Elsie dropped the lighter into the desk drawer and slammed it shut. "Graham has convinced her he's a knight who can slay fire-breathing dragons. One of these days she'll learn life isn't a fairy tale."

Mary sighed. "Too bad. It would certainly be simpler."

Elsie collected the day's essay papers, exhaustion draping over her as the men filed out of the room, still debating today's history lesson on the Constitution. The fragrance of baking bread made her stomach growl—just one of the distractions of studying in the mess hall. It was little wonder they'd been plagued with black bears breaking into the kitchen when the place always smelled so good.

She sank into one of the chairs and lowered her head into her hands for a moment, her mind buzzing from all the activity of the day. It was odd how teaching both energized her and sapped her at the same time. During class, she flitted from one student to another, each one's progress sending a wave of satisfaction through her chest. But when the room emptied, her strength seemed to go with them.

Now to gather her things and trek back to her dormitory. An evening of grading and then up early in the morning to tidy the hotel rooms for the next day. The summer was flying past, what with working two jobs and keeping up with Mary and Rose. It was hard to believe that the season was half-gone already.

And then there was Teddy.

She stacked the books and papers. If there was one thing she didn't want to think about, it was the brown-eyed ranger who now wrote her daily and had driven to Canyon to see her three weeks in a row—including today, when he'd stopped by during her lunch break, unannounced. Although his attention was nice, she never felt completely at ease around him. And every time he visited, he made some comment about her staying in Yellowstone. Every day the hollow in her stomach grew deeper. *Lord, I don't know what to do.*

The door opened and Val appeared, Nate on his heels. She hadn't seen Nate Webber since the day at Old Faithful, but she'd thought about him all too often. His refusal to join the class other than for field trips troubled her. But what bothered her more was that she couldn't seem to overlook it. Why should she care if one of the CCC men didn't want schooling? She had more students than she knew what to do with as it was.

Seeing him walk through the door stirred her troubling thoughts once again. A flush crept to her cheeks. She stood, lifting the stack of books like a shield.

"Excuse us, Miss Brookes." Young Val touched the brim of his slouchy hat. "We were just going to move the tables. We're having a little entertainment tonight."

"And to think I wasn't invited." Elsie smiled as she headed for the door.

His mouth dropped. "Would . . . would you come? I mean, we should have invited you!" He spun around to face Nate. "Nate, she should come. Why didn't we invite some folks?"

Nate laughed, placing his hand on the younger man's shoulder. "Because they don't need to see us embarrass ourselves."

"I was only teasing." Elsie paused in the doorway. She should know by now not to bait the fellow. "You enjoy your evening."

Val rushed to her side. "No . . . please. I'd love it if you came."

"Val," Nate's voice lifted. "Let the lady go. She's already had a long day, I expect."

Elsie glanced toward him. "So have you. Teddy told me you were up on Mount Washburn today."

Nate's eyes darkened. "That's right. And every day, pretty much. It was so *kind* of him to stop by."

The look on his face sent a tremor through her. Had something happened during today's inspection? Her father had been careful to maintain good relations between the conservation workers and ranger staff. Hopefully having Teddy fill in for him hadn't undone that rapport. She scrambled for a change of subject and focused on the leaflet of papers in Nate's hand. "Are those programs for this evening's performance?"

Val grabbed one from Nate and shoved it at Elsie. "I typed them, and Nate did the illustrations. He does the best cartoons. Have you seen them?"

She opened the half-page program and scanned the artwork. She couldn't resist smiling at the humorous big-headed caricatures. "Is this Red?" She pointed to one. "And Maguire?" Her gaze settled on a grim-faced man in a flat hat in the bottom corner. *Teddy.* She slapped it closed and handed it back to Nate. "Very nice. I can see the resemblance."

His Adam's apple bounced in his throat as he slid the bundle of papers behind his back. "I . . . I'm sorry, Miss Brookes. I didn't intend—"

"No, please don't apologize." She forced a smile to her face. "You fellows need to let off steam. I understand." She shifted the books to her hip. "I'm just glad there's not one of the sourpuss teacher."

Val lifted his hands. "Oh, we'd never—"

"Elsie, I *am* sorry." Nate repeated. "And if you'd like to come tonight, we'll make it up to you."

"Oh, I don't know. I don't want to be the only woman."

Those heart-stopping green eyes locked on her. "Bring Mary and Rose and any of the other girls you want. Red's doing an Irish ballad. He'd love to have his favorite blonde there."

She resisted touching a hand to her own mousy-brown hair.

"And I'm reading Shakespeare's Sonnet 18. 'Shall I compare thee to a summer's day?'" Val offered. "If I knew you were in the audience, it'd be . . . it'd be . . ." Red splotches mottled his cheeks. "It'd be swell."

She reached out and touched his sleeve, his embarrassment melting her resistance. "I'd be honored to attend."

A grin spread across his angular face.

She turned to Nate, who was already sliding tables across the tile floor. "What about you—are you reading too?"

Nate straightened, releasing his grip on the wooden table. "I . . . uh . . . no—"

"Nate's not much for books, Miss Brookes." Val left the programs by the door and hurried over to grab the other side of the long table.

"You don't like to read, Mr. Webber?" Elsie shifted her books to the opposite hip. How could a man so intelligent and witty not also be well read?

"I . . ." His attention shot around the room before focusing back on Val. "I should get these moved."

Perhaps it wasn't that Nate didn't *like* to read. She rifled through the facts. He avoided her classes, even though he was interested in the subject matter. He asked intelligent questions. He had all the hallmarks of an excellent student, yet he treated books like they were something that could turn around and bite him.

Maybe . . . She spent a long moment observing the fellow shifting chairs from one side of the room to the other. Was it possible that Nate—sweet, kind, bright man that he was—*couldn't* read? The idea rippled through her thoughts like a stone tossed into a quiet pond.

"You'd best set up plenty of chairs, then," Elsie called out. "I'll go round up a fan club."

Twenty-Three

Nate stood in the back of the room, leaning against the wall rather than taking a seat anywhere in the audience. As exhausted as he was, if he sat down, he'd be dozing in minutes. And to be honest, he wanted to be as far from Elsie Brookes as possible.

He'd seen the realization flash across her face like the theater lights on Fulton and Flatbush back home. So far, he'd succeeded in hiding his problem, even from Val, who'd typed five of his reports. Were women more perceptive? He'd never been able to hide anything from his mother, either.

Nate leaned his head back against the wall as he shut his eyes. He'd been up since dawn, cutting trees, hauling brush, scouting forest, dealing with Vaughn. Now this?

Elsie and her friends probably had a good laugh about his situation. She'd returned for the show less than an hour after leaving and had brought Rose, Mary, and four other young ladies with her, plus a handful of male employees from the hotel. Even Graham Brookes had shown up, taking a seat next to Rose.

His crew could probably care less about the extra men, but they were delighted to see a handful of pretty girls in the audience.

Nate studied the backs of the audience's heads. A group from the Bronx performed a comedy routine sparring with jokes about camp life. The two Polish and two Irish boys were trading ethnic digs so fast, the audience barely had time to catch their breath because they were laughing so hard. The tensions in camp between the different nationalities seemed to be dissolving day by day and had now apparently become a source of comedic pride between the guys.

He craned his neck, trying to catch a glimpse of Elsie. What if she told her father or that ranger boyfriend of hers about his little problem? There were no stipulations in the CCCs that you had to be able to read. They were grunt laborers, nothing more. Nate ran a hand across the back of his neck. *Except the foremen.* He never should have let Lieutenant Stone and the others believe he could read orders and write reports.

Fifteen minutes later, after three songs and one humiliating Shakespeare recitation, Nate saw Graham whisper something to Rose before rising from his seat and sneaking out the side door.

The gear jammer has the right idea. If Nate escaped before the show finished, he could avoid the conversations and mingling. He could avoid certain females as well. Nate slipped out into the yard, shutting the door slowly so as not to make a sound.

Graham had walked to the far corner of the building and lit a cigarette, standing with his back to Nate. If Nate was careful, he could hoof it across the yard toward his tent without being forced to chat with the driver.

He was halfway there when Hutch bumbled out of the darkness and made a beeline for his leg. Nate grabbed the growing coon, grunting as he lifted the round bundle to his chest. "Hey fella, how are you doing? I haven't seen you or your sister in days. Been keeping yourselves out of trouble?" He kept his voice low.

"Nate?" A woman's voice called out in the darkness.

Collared. Nate turned, tucking a squirming Hutch under his elbow.

Elsie walked toward him, a troubled expression on her face. "I saw you leave, and I was worried."

Hutch's paws were scrabbling against Nate's side, untucking his shirt and digging at his ribs. Graham had disappeared from sight. Was he avoiding Elsie too?

Nate juggled the animal and jammed his shirt tail back into place. "No need. I just have an early morning tomorrow. I need to help load the equipment into the truck before the men assemble."

"Equipment?" She tipped her head as she studied him. "I thought you had Saturdays off work."

"Oh yes—hey!—stop that!" Nate removed the raccoon from his shirt a second time and placed it on the ground at his feet. "You're right. I guess I don't know whether I'm coming or going anymore."

"Who's this?" A smile spread across Elsie's face as she kneeled on the ground in front of him.

Hutch was already clambering up Nate's leg as if it was another sapling in the woods. Nate unhooked the critter's claws from his dungarees. "Hutch, you're being rude. Say hello to my friend Elsie." He managed to free Hutch's grip and turn him around to face Elsie, his rear paws scrabbling at the air as if he was still climbing.

She bent closer to examine him. "Looks like a youngster. How did you end up with a raccoon in camp?"

"We have two, actually. Their mother met with misfortune, I'm afraid." Nate lifted Hutch to perch on his shoulder. "Back at Mammoth. We brought the kits with us."

She reached up and stroked the animal's back, Hutch's mottled gray fur ruffling with her touch. "Raccoons can be a handful. I hope they don't make trouble for you."

"Oh, they're plenty of trouble. Just ask Cook, or any of the guys for that matter."

Raucous laughter from the hall spilled into the night, and she smiled. "Nate, I wanted to speak with you."

"I really should get this little fella tucked in." For all the good it would do, nocturnal creature and all.

A touch to his arm stopped him in his tracks. "Nate. Please." She narrowed her eyes. "I think I know why you're not taking my class."

"I told you, school and me—we don't mix."

"Because you can't read. Am I right?"

Hutch took that as his cue to leave. Scrambling down Nate's back, he hopped to the ground and bumbled off toward the tents. *Lucky guy.*

Elsie didn't wait for an answer, her fingers gripping his wrist. "I can help you, if you'll let me."

He lowered his eyes, trying to think of anything other than the touch of her hand. "No. You can't."

"Why do you say that?"

He glanced past her at the mess hall to make sure no one had followed her out. He took a step closer and lowered his voice. "I'm not smart like the others, Elsie. I can't read. I've tried over and over, trust me. For some reason, God decided to make me dumb."

"Nate Webber." She frowned. "You are not dumb. I lectured the class on the geology of Yellowstone's geysers. You grasped in five minutes what I spent days trying to teach them."

"I'm a good listener, college girl. You should have figured that out by now."

She dropped her hand to her side. "You're a smart man."

Nate finally met her gaze, suddenly aware of how close she stood. "I really have you snowed, don't I?"

"I mean it. I can help. Does anyone else know? Red? Val?"

"I think Val suspects."

She nodded. "What if I talk to Lieutenant Stone? I've already added some creative writing courses for Val and a few others. The lieutenant doesn't seem to mind as long as I don't charge the government extra for my time. I could arrange for us to do some one-on-one classes. In fact, there are probably others—"

"No." Nate jerked his head up. Why wouldn't she listen? "No thank you, Elsie. I don't want to study with you."

Her brow wrinkled. "With *me*?"

The hurt look in her eyes cut into him. "That's not what I meant." For some reason his thoughts always turned into a scrambled mess whenever she got too close. He'd been around women plenty of times, but no one had ever had this effect on him. "Elsie, I don't want anyone to know."

Applause and shouts caught their attention. The show must be coming to a close.

"I'm sure you're not the only one," she repeated.

"It doesn't matter." He didn't like the bitterness in his voice, but she had to understand. "They *can't* know. My job—I have to write these blasted reports every week. Val has been helping me, but if Dahl finds out, he'll demote me. My family needs that money, Elsie."

"All right. I won't tell anyone—if you let me try to help. We can meet outside camp."

Men were starting to trickle out of the mess hall. Best to agree and deal with this later. "Fine. Tomorrow evening?"

"Seven o'clock, by the camp store."

"I'll be there." His heart pounded as he backed away from her. "But you're wasting your time."

"We'll see."

Determination flooded Elsie. She had to help Nate learn to read. It was a crime to think of a man like him not being able to enjoy novels and newspapers or to write reports about the good work his crew had been doing.

A man like him. Her heart skipped. She needed to stop thinking about him so much. It couldn't be right for someone who was seeing one fellow to be—

A familiar smell sent her pulse racing. She jerked her head up. A wisp of smoke appeared behind the hall. Filled with dread, she whirled toward the tents. "Nate?"

He was only halfway across the yard. Glancing over his shoulder, he paused.

She scurried toward him. "Are you fellows burning trash behind the kitchen?"

"No." Nate's attention turned to where she'd been staring. "Is that—"

"Smoke."

He jolted forward and sprinted past her, disappearing around the side of the building.

For a moment she stood frozen, then she took off after him. The wispy plume had thickened, curling up into the night sky. As she rounded the corner, she spotted Nate, his shape silhouetted by the flames leaping from the two trash bins just outside the mess hall. He raced over to the structure and pounded on the rear windows, shouting the alarm.

Within minutes the yard filled with men. The hall sat on the edge of the clearing, only thirty feet from the forest, the trees illuminated by the glare of the blaze.

Elsie backed away, wrapping her arms around herself to stop the tremors coursing through her body. Nate and two others had grabbed fire buckets kept in the kitchen and were smothering the small blaze with sand before it had time to crawl up the side of the building and onto the roof. How many people had still been inside the hall when this started? She shuddered at the thought.

Graham was among the men spooling a hose out of the back of the latrine area.

Mary came running over and swept Elsie into a tight hug. "Oh, Elsie. I can't believe this. What happened?"

"I . . . I don't know. Where's Rose?"

"I saw her come out of the hall. She was one of the last. Came out with Graham, of course. She's besotted with that man, no matter what he says or does." Mary searched the milling crowd. "She's over on the other side with some of the other girls. Do you suppose the cook dumped something hot into the garbage bins? Grease? Ashes from the stove?"

Elsie ran a hand down her throat. "Someone probably tossed a cigarette butt into it."

The flames were hissing out, a putrid smoke rolling up into the night sky. Elsie turned away, the sight more than she could handle. "We should go."

Her friend tightened her grip on Elsie's arm. "I want to wait and make sure Red's all right. I know it's nothing, but I want to see him. He'll walk us home."

"I can make it back on my own—it's not far."

Mary's lips pursed. "You will not. There have been plenty of bears around lately. At least have one of the men escort you. I'm sure any of your students would be willing. How about that nice Nate fellow?" She lifted her penciled brows. "I saw you talking to him out in the yard. Is there something I should know? Or should I say, is there something *Teddy* should know?"

"What? No." Irritation prickled across her skin. "We were talking about books."

"Books?" She rolled her eyes. "Of course. I forgot who I was speaking to. Hey"—her face lit up—"speak of the devil. There's Teddy now." Mary waved at him and bumped Elsie's arm. "You didn't tell me he was spending the night at Canyon."

"I didn't know he was." Didn't he spend time in Mammoth anymore? She rubbed a hand across her stiff neck muscles.

Teddy hurried up and stopped next to them, face grim. "I was driving past, and I smelled smoke."

"It was a rubbish fire, but I think they've got it under control. I thought you'd left for Mammoth already."

He wasted no time draping an arm around her shoulder and squeezing it. "I got caught at the ranger station. I went looking for you this evening but couldn't find any of you. I was worried."

"The men invited us to a talent show."

"I'm surprised you didn't tell me about it at lunch." His brows knit together, but he glanced toward the activity. "I should go see if they need help." He rushed to join the milling group.

Mary giggled. "As if a hundred fellows couldn't take care of a small garbage can fire. Just like a man to want to be the center of things."

"I didn't tell him because I didn't know about it." Elsie clenched her fists. "He makes it sound like I purposely hid it from him."

Lines formed in Mary's brow. "Are you sure you didn't? Red told me about it two nights ago, and I mentioned it to you. Only we didn't get an invitation until you batted your eyelashes at your teacher's pet."

She turned and stared at her friend. "You mentioned it to me?"

"You don't remember? Well, you have been distracted lately." Mary shrugged. "Or maybe you wanted to come without Teddy in tow."

The truth in her second statement rattled Elsie. She *had* been relieved to come to an event without Teddy hanging on her arm. What did that say about her?

Elsie turned and watched the mop-up, her pulse slowing now as the danger passed. Nate and Teddy stood to one side, Teddy gesturing toward the bins, evidently angry about the evening's events. Nate kept his shoulders stiff, listening to the man's lecture without responding. What could Teddy be upset about? It's not as if any of this was Nate's fault.

A wave of exhaustion draped over Elsie, turning her knees to rubber. Teddy, Nate, Graham, Rose—when had her life grown so complicated? Mama had said to let her walls down a little. She failed to mention how troubling it could be.

Twenty-Four

Nate hoisted Elsie's bag of books higher on his shoulder and continued walking along the creek, the teacher following a few steps behind. As long as they hiked, he didn't have to face her expectations. Why did she even want to bother with him? His schoolteachers had given up on him years ago.

"Hey, slow down," she called out. "We're at least two miles from camp. No one's going to see us."

"What about your ranger friend?" The words slipped out before he could button his lip.

"Teddy?" She stepped over a tree root. "I'm pretty sure he's back in Mammoth by now."

Nate waited for her to catch up. "He was pretty steamed last night. Called us *'careless bums'.*" The memory rankled. Just because the man had a hat and a badge didn't make him any better than Nate's crew. In fact, Nate would take Red and Val over Vaughn any day. Elsie's father, Ranger Brookes, had worked beside them rather than shouting orders like a prison warden working a chain gang.

"He shouldn't have said that, but he was upset." Elsie pushed away a limb leaning over the trail. "It would be easy for a little incident like that to turn into a major forest fire. And so close to the hotel? That would be a disaster."

She was right, of course. The sight had shaken him too. If the fire had broken out an hour earlier while the show was getting started, they'd never have spotted it. And with nearly the entire crew crammed into the hall, plus their guests? His stomach churned at the thought. Or if it had started later, after everyone was in bed—then what?

The fire had left everyone on edge. Before the men turned in for the night, there had been two separate fistfights. Ricci had repeated a Polish joke from the show to a buddy in the latrine, only to have Bukowski and Nowak jump him on his way out the door. Then Moretti pinned Nowak an hour later. *Just as everyone was starting to get along.* As a result, most of the crew found themselves with extra duties today.

"Did you figure out the cause?" Elsie asked.

Nate shook his head. "No one saw anything, and Cook said he hadn't been out there since supper and he'd only dumped food scraps. Nothing that would explain the flare up." He rubbed the back of his neck. "It acted more like a fuel fire. Blazed up hot and fast. Like someone had filled the bin with oily rags and dropped in a match."

"Why would anyone do that?"

"Don't think they would." He led her to a log overlooking the creek and waited as she found a place to sit. "We all worked hard on that building. The crew was proud of it. I can't see anyone wanting to endanger it. Not anyone from our camp, anyway."

She shielded her eyes as she looked up at him. "Are you suggesting someone from outside the camp might have done it?"

"I'm not suggesting anything." He sat next to her, keeping a safe distance between them.

She took her bag from his hand, opened it, and removed a small book. "It was probably just an accident."

The sight of the reader made him break out in a sweat. Nate covered his eyes for a moment before dragging his fingers through his hair. "I wish you'd let this go."

"You said yourself that your job is dependent on reading."

He could use a raccoon distraction about now. "It's not like I haven't tried."

She laid a hand on his leg. "I know. I understand. Just humor me."

He looked at her slender fingers resting on his knee. Elsie had no clue what she did to him. If she did, she wouldn't be alone with him out here, and she certainly wouldn't be touching him. "I appreciate your help, Elsie. But it's a waste of your time."

She smiled and opened the book. "It's my time to do with as I choose, right?" She held it out to him, open to the first page. "Do you know any words?"

"Not very many."

"Show me which ones."

He sighed, leaning close to peer at the page. Squinting, he pressed his fingers against the paper, tracing the line. "The ca—cat . . ." he trailed off as the letters swarmed like a kicked-over anthill. Nate rubbed his eyes. Repeating the first two words, he paused. The next word had an "s" and a "t." "Stood?"

"Sits."

He bit his lip, shifting away from her. "I can't."

She pointed to the next line. "Try this."

He set his jaw. Again, he got the first word or two, but he couldn't make it through the sentence. She had him try another.

"Is that how it always is?"

"What?"

"You start slow with some hesitation, but eventually you get the word right. After that, though, you're guessing based on the first letter."

"I can get some short words. But I can't get the longer ones at all."

She took her hand and covered most of the page. "Try reading just the first words of each line."

He mangled his way through the list, getting some of them and trying not to be distracted by how her pale skin stood out next to his tanned arm.

She sat up, looking at him. "Nate, you *can* read."

He grunted. "A word here and there, sure."

"What goes wrong after the first couple of words?"

"They move."

The frown that spread across Elsie's features took him back to his grade school classroom. The teacher who accused him of lying. His throat tightened. *Here we go.*

"They move?"

Nate stood, his leg muscles stiff from sitting on the low log. He turned and faced her. Best to get this over with. "The words are like train cars on a track." He shoved his hands in his pockets. "When I first glance at the page, I see the order to it. But then," he glanced up at the tree branches blocking the sky. "Everything derails. The letters jumble around and squeeze together, looking more like a flock of sheep milling around a pen." He squeezed his fingers into a fist. "Just when I figure out where one is, its neighbor has wandered off somewhere. If I focus on that one, I lose the ones I've already corralled."

She tapped her pencil against the book, studying his face as if she was piecing together what he meant. "So it's not the words that are the problem."

"I didn't say that. Longer ones start shifting before I've even gotten started."

She nodded, closing the book. "I see."

Finally. Nate relaxed, the tension gripping his spine releasing. Now she could go back to teaching Shakespeare and geology to the students who mattered. He wandered over to the creek. It cut a path through the meadow, the sunlight sparkling off the water like so many jewels. A bulky brown shape downstream caught his eye. "Is that . . ." his voice choked off. He remembered watching the grizzlies wrestling each other for the scraps of food at the feeding station back at Canyon. But there they'd had a heavy fence and an armed ranger standing between the bruin and the crowd.

Elsie jumped up, tucking the book into her bag. "What?" She hurried to his side.

As he watched, the creature lifted its massive head, water dripping from its shaggy coat.

Not a bear, he could see that now. "Buffalo . . ." The word slipped out with a long breath—probably the one he'd been holding.

She slid in beside him, leaning against his arm as she stared upstream. "Big fellow."

"What's it doing out here? I thought they all lived at the Lamar Buffalo Ranch." The animal stood in the water, midstream, water nearly touching its belly and dripping from its brushy beard. Nate's heart beat against his ribs, his terror from the moment before transforming into wonder.

"It must be part of the wild herd. The bison bulls sometimes wander off on their own if they're not strong enough to claim the females. I've never seen one in this area, though."

"He must be lonely." Nate couldn't help but feel sorry for the lone male. "It's sure an incredible sight."

"It makes the trip worthwhile, doesn't it?"

"I'm glad it wasn't a complete waste of your time. Thanks for trying to help me with the reading, but it's good that you're giving up on the idea."

"Giving up? Not a chance. But we should give that big fella some space.

They don't look kindly on being interrupted." She swung the bag over her shoulder. "Can you meet tomorrow evening after supper?"

She couldn't be this stubborn. "I'm sure you really don't want to do that."

"Why not?"

"Because I'm hopeless. You shouldn't bother."

She quirked a brow as though daring him to say more. After a moment, Elsie's smile melted his resistance.

He folded his arms. "If you're willing to put up with me, college girl, why not?"

"I think we should meet outside again. Can you think of a lovelier classroom?"

"No ma'am." He couldn't.

And certainly not a lovelier teacher.

❧

The yellow tour bus rolled to a stop in front of the Canyon Hotel, the open windows and rolled-back canvas top allowing the conversations of the excited visitors to pour into the warm afternoon air.

Elsie gripped the strap of her bag as she strode past, the heavy books swinging against her back. She couldn't get over Nate's description of lines of words. No wonder he struggled to read. But why did he see them that way? She'd spent enough time gazing at those green eyes—far more than she should—but couldn't see anything unusual about them, aside from their fascinating color.

As Graham finished unloading his passengers' luggage and handing it over to the pack rats, he stopped to wave at Elsie. Jogging her direction, he caught up. "Elsie, I'm glad I ran into you."

She batted away her instinctive negative feelings toward her cousin. Her mother had asked her to forgive him, after all. "It looks like you've settled in well as a gear jammer. My father must be pleased that he recommended you."

Graham doffed his cap and tucked it under his arm. "I hope so. It's been a dream job. I thought I would be happy just to have a paycheck, but this is incredible. I meet the best people. One of those fellows is a banker with Wells Fargo in San Francisco. Can you imagine? After all the bank failures a few years ago, I never expected to meet one."

She hugged the bag to her side. "Maybe he can get you a job when you're done here."

"I hope so. He seemed impressed with my driving skills. Said the hills and curves reminded him of home."

"I was surprised to see you at the CCC talent show last night."

"Rose invited me. That fire was pretty crazy, though." He ran a gloved hand across his face. "Brought back unpleasant memories."

Ones she didn't want to discuss—especially with him. "Graham, I'm a little worried about Rose."

Graham met her gaze with a slow shake of the head. "Poor kid has been through a lot, it sounds like."

"And you're not helping."

"I—what?" His brow furrowed. "What are you talking about?"

Elsie stepped aside to let a handful of tourists go by. "You must know how she feels about you."

He covered his eyes. "Elsie—"

"She's my friend, Graham."

"Which is exactly why I put her off the idea." A black-billed magpie sailed past and landed on the top of the bus, flashing its iridescent tail feathers. "She's a lovely girl, and kind too. She deserves a handsome young guy, not . . ." He turned his hands outward for a moment before stuffing them in his pockets. "Not someone like me. I want to spend time with lots of different girls, not be someone's steady fella. Even without these paws, I've got enough problems to fill an entire steamer trunk. I told her, I'm not just a stumbling block; I'm the whole Continental Divide."

"And I understand how you feel—trust me, I do." She tried not to think about her own scars. "Why do you think I've tried to keep you apart?"

"Then we're in agreement."

"But you do have feelings for her?"

He closed his eyes. "That's beside the point."

"I don't think so." Elsie leaned against the yellow bus. "If you didn't care for her, you wouldn't still be hanging about. You'd have let her down and then made yourself scarce. But you're still here. Still trying to be her friend."

"The only reason I've been hanging about is because she needs a friend."

The sentiment echoed though her heart. He was close but hadn't gotten it exactly right. "No, Graham. *You* need a friend."

"Yeah, well, that's not your problem, is it?"

Elsie dug through her pain, searching for a seed of forgiveness lodged somewhere in her heart. *Lord, please help me find it.* "It's been hard for me, seeing you here. And then, the fires." She paused, searching for the right words. "Graham, I know you didn't mean to start the fire that killed Dottie."

"But I didn't just start it, did I?" His eyes filled with tears, and he turned away. "If I hadn't panicked and run when it first started, you wouldn't . . . you wouldn't . . ."

I wouldn't have gone in after my baby sister.

"I was so scared. But fear didn't stop you. I had to drag you out kicking and screaming, even after the burning timber knocked you down. You didn't even realize . . ." Graham's voice cracked. He closed his eyes. "You were the hero. I was nothing but a coward."

Her cousin's admission tore through her, erasing something dark and ugly. She wrapped her fingers around his arm, pulling his gloved hands into hers. "You carried me out and put out the flames on my dress with these hands. Those aren't the actions of a coward. And as for the rest . . ." *My home. My life. My sister.* "Graham, I forgive you."

Twenty-Five

What is this gizmo?" Nate perched on the log and frowned at the strip of paperboard with a small rectangle cut from the center. He and Elsie had met four more times without much progress. Both of them had been frustrated. Then today, she showed up with this thing.

"It's an idea I had. I thought it might help you focus on one word at a time." Elsie demonstrated, sliding the ruler over the page. A single word showed in the gap, while everything else remained hidden. "It won't fix everything, but I hope it will help you practice without getting overwhelmed."

"I don't know about this, college girl." She'd actually fashioned it from two strips nested together. The smaller one slid along inside, increasing the size of the opening. "Hey, you can make it wider."

"For longer words. Or you can work up to a few words at a time." She pressed it back to the page. "Let's keep it small for now."

"How did you think of this?"

"I was grading arithmetic assignments using a slide rule. Have you operated one before?"

"Once or twice. For some reason, I can do figures, just not words."

"With a slide rule, the window draws your eyes to the answer. This should work the same way. You don't need all the rest of the words confusing your vision." She scooted closer. Her leg brushed against his. "Try it. It's just an experiment."

A single word stared up at him. *Dog.* Nate slid the gadget over, pausing on each complete word. *Runs. To. The. Woods.* "The dog runs to the woods."

Elsie grabbed his arm, her fingers pressing into his bicep. "Yes!"

Energy shot through his chest and shoulders, and he moved the ruler and ran a finger over the words. He'd read a whole sentence! Setting it back on the page, Nate centered the window over another word and stumbled through another line. Elsie helped him to sound out each word until his cadence eased to a halting rhythm.

She grabbed his wrist, jostling the book. "Nate, you're doing it." She slid her grip up to his elbow, the warmth of her hand against his skin sending a new shockwave through his system. "You're reading!"

The ruler had slid askew with the jarring motion, so he straightened it, and the next word fell into the window on cue. *Went. Over.* "The fish went over the falls." He whispered the line a second time. "That's incredible." He pushed his way through two whole paragraphs just to prove it wasn't a fluke. His eyes ached with the effort, but the words made sense for the first time in his life.

The pressure of Elsie's touch anchored him with the courage to keep at it, though a large part of him wanted to stop and pull her into his arms. She'd cracked open a door he'd thought was forever closed to him. Is it possible that reading would get easier for him? Could he someday join the classes the other fellas were taking? His heart lodged in his throat. At the end of the page, he stopped and caught his breath.

"You read the entire page." She laid her cheek against his shoulder. "Yesterday you couldn't get through a single line. I'm so proud of you."

"Proud of you." How long had he waited to hear those words? Every bit of tension washed out of him, as if draining from his feet. What would his

father say at this moment? Would he echo Elsie's sentiment or insist it was too little, too late? "I'm . . ." Nate shook his head, a surge of emotion climbing his throat. He turned to face her, his heart pounding as if he'd just run five miles. "Thank you. Thank you for sticking with me."

She grinned, her face aglow. "You did this. It was all you, Nate Webber. I told you—you're brilliant."

If only his childhood teachers could hear her words. "I wouldn't go that far. I think I finally found a teacher who understands me." *A woman who understands me.* The thought swept over him like the wind through the branches above their heads. *Lord, this woman understands me. How is that possible?*

In that moment, he reached for her face, unable to resist the energy coming from her smile. He ran a finger along her cheekbone. "Elsie, you're the first person who's ever cared enough to make an effort to understand me."

Her smile softened, her lips parting slightly. "I do care, Nate. More than you know."

Nate wanted nothing more than to lean in and kiss her, but he pulled himself up short. He wasn't the type to kiss another man's girl. However, he couldn't resist glancing at her lips and imagining their softness against his own. Was she thinking the same?

He dropped his hand back to the book, tearing his gaze away from hers. If he looked into her eyes one moment longer, he'd lose all control. This day was about reading, not stealing kisses in the woods. Especially not from someone who was already taken.

Her grip on his arm lessened, and her hand fell away. "I am excited for you. If you keep working, this could open so many doors for your future."

He nodded, not trusting his voice. Nate ran his hand over the page as the words jumbled together. But he'd sorted them out once, and he could do it again. "I'll be able to read my sisters' letters."

Her quick intake of breath drew him back. "You have letters from home that you haven't read? Why didn't you ask someone to help you?"

He scrubbed a hand across his weary eyes. "I hate that I'm so prideful, but . . ." He shrugged. "People here don't know what I am. I'd like to keep it that way."

"What you are? I don't understand."

He managed to keep his hands in his lap. "A fool. A failure."

She frowned. "You're not serious."

"I've heard it my whole life."

Elsie reached over and took his hand. "Then let me set you straight." She stood without releasing his fingers, brushing the pine needles off the seat of her trousers with her free hand. She turned to face him and squeezed his fingers. "If you met someone who was polite, chivalrous, a natural leader, and a hard worker; someone who saw the potential in other men and helped them to reach it—would you call him a failure?"

He tried not to think about her palm pressed against his. "Well, no, but—"

"How about if he worked hard to teach himself new skills? Or made friends wherever he went?"

"Elsie, I—"

She put her fingers against his lips, stopping his words and sending a jolt of electricity through him at the same time. "I won't have you insulting my friend. He's kind, generous, and yes—smart." She drew both hands away. "Nate, I don't know who has filled your head with these misconceptions, but you're about as far from a failure as I can imagine."

The lump in his throat grew. "I don't know what to say."

"Don't say anything. Just stop repeating those lies and insults. God stitched us all together differently. Your brain is as good as mine or Val's or anyone else's; it just views things differently. And if you don't believe in yourself, who will?"

Believe in himself? The concept was so foreign—it was laughable. He believed in his brothers. In his crew. He believed in God.

And now he believed in Elsie Brookes.

⁂

Elsie juggled the books in her arms as she walked the road to her dormitory. Nate had offered to escort her back from the junction, but she'd needed the time to clear her head—and her heart. He probably did too. She'd seen the look on his face after he'd finished reading through the page. At first it was just excitement, but then the intensity in his eyes had been like a single spark bursting into a flame. A shiver coursed through her. For a moment, she thought he was going to kiss her. And it terrified her how desperately she'd wanted him to.

Her mind tiptoed through what might have happened. He'd have leaned in, she'd close her eyes, and then she'd feel the touch of his lips on hers, first petal soft . . . and then what? She had no frame of reference. She'd never allowed herself to get this close to anyone except Teddy. And he'd never kindled these sorts of thoughts in her.

What was she thinking? She couldn't entertain such romantic notions. Her feelings had become a firestorm, whipping through her life. Every possible outcome was bad. Teddy. Nate. School.

She'd always thought herself a faithful person—to her family, her friends, her dreams. How had she ended up in this place, where she was stepping out with one man, yet imagining herself with another?

With school rushing toward her, her emotions were multiplying like the pine beetles Nate's crew was fighting to control. Teddy was offering her a place at his side. As he said, she didn't need a degree to be a ranger's wife. He was prepared to hand her everything else she'd believed out of her reach: love, family, a home in Yellowstone. Exactly the life her parents enjoyed. So why did her heart yearn for more?

An automobile roared past, breaking the relentless cycle of her churning thoughts. This summer was proving eventful, and it was still only July. She needed to focus her attention on getting through the last month and then packing for college. She might learn techniques at the University of Montana that could help Nate—and others like him. She sighed. By that time, he'd be long gone from her life. She needed some way to help him more now.

Kissing not included.

Meeting in the woods had been a bad idea. Suddenly the savages' jokes about couples going "rotten logging" made far too much sense. She'd wanted to allow him privacy to study without being embarrassed, but obviously being alone was a bit of a distraction as well. The touch of his arm against hers, the light in his eyes when he made his first breakthrough—they'd sent her heart pounding double time.

She'd been so focused on going through the motions with Teddy that she hadn't realized how much she'd come to care for the gentle CCC man. And in a moment, her feelings had fanned from a gentle crush to a full-blown inferno in her chest. *Lord, what should I do? What do You want for me?*

Elsie shifted the pile of books so she could reach into her pocket where she'd stashed Teddy's last letter, unopened. She didn't need to read it to know what it would say. More professions of his love and requests that she stay—requests that weighed on her like the sandbags used to prevent dirigibles from taking flight before their time.

But this was her time to fly.

And with that, her path became clear. She wasn't being fair to Teddy.

Pain settled in the back of her throat as she thought of him and all his grand hopes for the future. A future, she realized for certain, that would not include her.

Reaching the dormitory, she hurried to her room and let herself in. A peaceful silence descended as she shut the door behind her. She stashed the letter in the dresser drawer on top of a stack of identical envelopes. *"One can't argue with the heart."* Isn't that what Nate had said to her about Rose?

But she couldn't rush into Nate's arms either. She hadn't dreamed of college for years just to have the dream waylaid by her fickle yearnings. It was time to be practical and think of her future. To be faithful to the dream God had placed in her heart.

From now on, she'd only see Nate Webber in the classroom.

❧

Nate wielded the saw with both hands, dragging it through the whitebark pine in a steady rhythm with Val manning the other side. The harder he worked, the less time he had to think about a certain girl. He could still hear her words ringing in his ears, with every pull of the blade. *"If you don't be-lieve in yourself, who will?"*

No one had ever accepted him with such open arms until Elsie Brookes came along. How would he get such a woman out of his thoughts—and his heart?

"Nate," Val panted, "slow down." His grip loosened from the handle as Nate yanked it back. "What's gotten into you?"

Nate stopped and wiped sweat from his forehead. It had been dripping into his eyes, but he'd barely noticed. "Just trying to get this one finished before lunch."

"At this rate, we'll have the whole grove felled before the next meal. You're supposed to be the slow old man of the group, remember?" Val squatted on his heels, unbuttoning his shirt and flapping it.

"And you're the energetic kid." Nate picked up the canteen and tossed it at him. "Maybe I'm just trying to show off."

"Well, your showing off is going to put me in the infirmary." He stripped off his shirt and mopped his face with it. "Besides, who're you grandstanding for? It's not like that pretty teacher is here."

Nate stiffened. "I don't know what you mean."

A grin crossed the younger man's face. "The whole camp's buzzing with it, Nate. Red saw you head off into the woods with Miss Brookes. After the razzing you gave him for rotten logging with that blonde, he was quick to spread the word about you two."

Heat washed over Nate. "I wasn't . . . we weren't—" He bit off his words. He let go of the saw and walked several steps away from the tree. "Is that what people are saying?"

"What are they supposed to say? If she weren't the ranger's daughter or the other ranger's girl, half the men in camp would be dogging her door. You've got guts, man."

"That's not how it is."

"So you expect me to swallow that you two were just taking a walk in the woods?"

"We're friends. We were talking about class stuff. Book learning."

Val laughed. "Sure. All right. If you say so."

Nate jerked his head up. "It's true. You're not the only one who wants to better himself while he's here."

The young man spread his arms in surrender. "Fine. You were talking about books. Only," he folded his wiry arms across his bare chest, "you're not a reader. I've kept that quiet, but you can't lie to me."

Nate felt like his legs had been kicked from under him. "How long have you known?"

"A while. So is Miss Brookes really teaching you to read? Or are you just hoping to make her your gal?"

Nate wrestled with the question. He'd gone into the woods with Elsie to work on reading, but he'd nearly kissed her in the process. Were the men's assumptions so far off base? He took the canteen and slugged back a swallow of the tepid water. "Like you said. She's with that ranger fellow."

Val returned to his end of the saw. "You say she's with him, but face it—he's not here. You are." The kid wiped the sweat off his brow with his wrist. "And the whole camp is rooting for you."

Twenty-Six

E lsie's stomach churned as she and Teddy walked to Artist Point. When she'd suggested the romantic spot, his smile had been so intense that pain jolted through her system. But after spending a couple of sleepless nights wrangling with her heart, she knew she'd made the right decision. Teddy wasn't the man God had chosen for her—if He had a man for her at all.

"I couldn't believe those guys were so careless as to let a fire break out in the middle of their camp." He took her hand as he talked. "It's already setting up to be the worst fire year on record, and they're part of the problem."

"It was an accident. And not unlike the one we had at Mammoth at the beginning of June." She didn't like hearing him run down the CCC boys. Her father was back on the job coordinating with Lieutenant Stone and Captain Dahl, a fact that probably made Nate breathe easier. And learning her mother was doing better was a bright spot in Elsie's week.

"You're right about the Mammoth fire. That's part of what makes me jumpy. The men were present at that incident too. If they've got a firebug in their midst, we need to root him out."

The thought sent a chill through Elsie. "A firebug? You think the fires were set intentionally?"

"There wasn't enough evidence left at this one, but the fire at Mammoth was definitely arson. Didn't your father tell you that?"

She fingered the collar of her blouse. "No, he didn't."

He gave her a sideways glance before reaching over and claiming that hand in his large palm. "Why do you do that?"

"Just a habit."

Teddy tugged her to the side of the trail and pulled her into his arms. "Elsie, you don't need to be afraid. I'd never let anything happen to you."

She laid her hands against his shirtfront to keep him from moving any closer. "Teddy, I appreciate that, but I think we need to talk."

He lowered his head to the nape of her neck and breathed deeply in her hair. "Isn't that what we're doing?" Teddy slid his hands up her back.

A squirrel raced past on a nearby limb, chattering. The sound gave Elsie something to grab onto before she lost her nerve. "Listen, please. Teddy, it's not working."

He brushed a kiss along her jaw. "What's not?"

She pushed against his chest. "No, stop. Listen to me."

Teddy drew back, a stitch forming between his brows. "What is it?"

A deep breath somehow got stuck midway in her lungs. She cleared her throat, thankful for the space he'd opened between them. "I'm leaving for college at the end of the summer."

His expression relaxed. "We've discussed this before. You don't need to. Put the money away for a rainy day." A smile toyed at the corners of his mouth. "Or our honeymoon, though I should probably pay for that."

"I am *going* to school." She repeated the words. "I've dreamed of this for too long for you to just cast it aside."

He blew out a long breath and shoved his hands into his trouser pockets. "Fine. I'm not happy about it, of course. But I can wait." He started down the path again, resuming their walk as if nothing had just transpired.

She trotted after him. "Teddy, I don't want you to wait. Four years—that's nonsense."

"We'll take it one year at a time. I don't think you'll really finish. You'll get homesick and be back in a few months."

She stopped in her tracks. "No. I won't."

"You've never been away from home, Elsie. You've grown up here." He turned to face her, his eyes wandering to her neckline. "You'll get away from your parents and your friends, then what? Classes and homework—you think those will sustain you?" He reached for her hand. "You'll miss me. You'll miss Yellowstone."

Tears stung her eyes, and she knocked his arm away. "Teddy, you need to hear me. I'm not just talking about school. I'm trying to tell you that I'm not marrying you. Not this year, not next year. We're not right for each other. I'm sorry."

They'd stopped just short of the viewpoint, and the sound of the waterfall roared from the yellow-rocked canyon. Teddy stared straight at Elsie, his face stricken. After a few minutes, he finally spoke. "You're making a mistake." He shook his head slowly, shadows forming around his eyes. "I hope you understand what you're giving up."

She folded her arms, pressing them hard against her ribs. "Yes, I'm pretty sure I do."

❧

Nate sat on his bunk, trying to maneuver the paperboard device over his baby sister's letter. Unfortunately, her lines were a wavy mess, so he still struggled to track the words. Something about Mama, work, and Charlie. He'd gotten that much. He frowned, splaying his hand across his eyes. Would it always be so hard?

The jaunty sound of whistling outside the tent flap warned him Red was approaching. Nate hid Elsie's reading tool beneath his pillow, folded the letter, and tucked it back in the envelope.

"Hey, did the post arrive already?" His short frame darkened the door. "I'm expecting a letter from my father. He wants me to see a man at his old factory about a job." He chuckled. "I don't think he has a clue how far away Wyoming is."

"Nah, this letter's an old one."

Red came in and plunked onto his own bunk, his booted feet kicked out in front of him. "All this sunshine makes me sleepy. I've been out walking with Mary, but she had to get back to her pillow punching. I can't believe folks shell out to have pretty girls come in and make their beds for them." He glanced at his messy cot. "Then again . . ."

"It's a shame she doesn't get Saturday and Sunday off like we do."

"You're dead-on about that. But I'll see her at the pictures tonight. They're showing a filmstrip at the hotel. You coming?"

"I don't know." Nate tapped the envelope against his knee, not quite ready to return the link to his family back to his footlocker.

Red sat forward. "Lots of skirts, Webber. I know you've got your eye on one in particular."

"Val said you've been telling tales on me."

"Ain't no tales. It's the God's honest truth. I've seen you and her out walking in the woods over near the bear feeding grounds. The canyon and the waterfalls are the opposite direction. There ain't nothing out the route you two were going. Trust me, Mary took me out there once too." He lifted his brows.

Nate's stomach tightened. "It's not like that. She's tutoring me is all."

The laugh that burst from Red nearly shook the tent. "Is that what you call it?"

"Red." Nate's voice came out in a near growl. "I won't have you spoiling that girl's reputation. She's got herself a steady guy, and even if she didn't—she's not likely to be seen with the likes of me."

"She could do a lot worse, Nate. And that ranger fellow is nothing but a wet sock. Him on his high horse coming over and telling us how to do our work."

"That's because he's got the big hat and we don't."

"You'd be a better ranger any day." Red scoffed. "That Ranger Brookes—Elsie's father? He's the real McCoy. In fact, all of them but Vaughn. Something's not right with that man."

Nate sat back, letting his friend's words wash over him. Why was he arguing? He felt the same, and it was good to hear the sentiment come out of someone else's mouth. "I don't know what she sees in him," he confessed.

Red sat forward, jutting his finger toward Nate. "Now we're talking. Knew you'd taken a shine to the lady."

"What of it? It's not like I can do anything about it. She's spoken for."

"So what are you doing out in the woods, if you two aren't an item?"

Nate slipped the letter back out of the envelope. "She's teaching me to read."

Red went silent, a rare occurrence. After a few heartbeats, he spoke. "You're pulling my leg. I've seen you reading that CCC manual for hours."

"Not reading. Gleaning a word here and there, but not reading."

Red sank back on the bed. "I never would have guessed. Has she been able to help?"

"Some, but . . ." Nate tapped two fingers against his temple. "This is a pretty hard nut to crack."

"So you're going out with her every day to get some private schoolin', and she doesn't know how you feel? That's got to be rough."

"If she found out, she wouldn't come anywhere near me."

"Did you cook this up as an excuse to spend time with her?"

"No." Nate sat up. "Not at all. This was her idea. At least at first." But now, she'd invaded his thoughts so completely, all he could think about was their next lesson. Sitting side by side, talking, laughing, reading. The smell of her hair, the touch of her hand. Nate let his head fall forward into his hands. "I don't know anymore."

His friend was silent for a long time. Finally, he reached over and took the letter from Nate's lap. "How's about I read this for you?"

Nate lifted his head. "I'd appreciate that."

Elsie whomped the pillow onto the bed with a little more force than was necessary, the action releasing a smidgen of the tension in her arms.

"I know they *call* us pillow punchers, but let's not send any feathers flying." Mary rescued the rest of the linens. "I don't want to be stitching seams tonight when I could be out with Red."

Elsie ran a hand across the coverlet, smoothing any wrinkles she'd just caused. "Red again? I didn't think he'd end up as your steady date. Other than Hal, you haven't stayed with one man this long."

A smile darted across Mary's face. "I've never liked one as much."

Elsie straightened. "Why'd you choose him over Hal? He's not better looking. He's got no prospects to speak of." The sour words spilled from her lips before she could stop herself. But maybe if she could figure out why Mary chose Red, her longing for Nate would make some sense.

Her friend's smile vanished as quickly as it had arrived. "Elsie, I know you're in a mood today, but don't take it out on me and Red. You're the one who keeps insisting the CCC men aren't a bunch of street thugs."

Elsie sat on the corner of the bed, hot tears taking her by surprise.

Mary froze. "What . . . what's wrong? Is it your mother?"

Elsie covered her face with her hands. "No. Mother's doing much better ever since they returned from Billings."

Her friend crouched in front of her. "What, then? Is it Teddy?"

After a quick swallow, Elsie nodded. "I . . . I turned him down."

Mary closed her eyes for a moment. "I thought this might be coming."

A sob trapped in Elsie's throat forced its way out as a pathetic hiccup. "He kept saying he wanted me to stay. But I can't give up college." Elsie sent her friend a look, pleading for her to understand. "And then there's Nate."

"Nate Webber?" Mary bit her lip, then pulled Elsie to her feet. She made quick work of the room, straightened the coverlet, and grabbed their mop bucket and laundry pile. "Come with me. We'll take our lunch break. I'm getting you out of here before you get tears on the fresh linens."

Elsie set the towels back in the cart, fighting the urge to bury her face in their softness and never emerge.

Mary walked her out into the yard. "Let's head to the café. My treat. We'll have a strong cup of coffee and a piece of cake. Tears deserve cake."

"Then we better get a few platefuls." Elsie dabbed a handkerchief against her eyes. "Because I've made mistakes in my life, but this one? Marrying Teddy would have been an Old Faithful–sized mistake. But I still feel awful—like it's somehow my fault.

The two women made their way across the road to the café in silence. As they maneuvered through the crowded eatery, Elsie focused on keeping her tears at bay. She didn't want to look mournful among all the happy tourists celebrating their day in Wonderland.

When they were seated with coffee and dessert, Elsie forced out the story, including the bits about Nate.

Mary sighed. "I knew something seemed off between you and Teddy. I shouldn't have pushed him at you." She guided a forkful of cake to her mouth, then chewed slowly as if taking time to consider her words. "I think he's your Hal."

Elsie sat back in her seat, studying her friend's face. "My Hal?"

"He *thought* he knew exactly what you wanted, but that's because he didn't bother to really get to know you."

The fragrant smell of the hot coffee overwhelmed Elsie's senses. She cradled the cup in her palms, the warmth of the porcelain soothing. "I want to teach. I can help students learn about all the wonders in the world. It's what I've worked toward for years, but he thought I'd toss it aside as if my plans meant nothing."

Mary leaned forward, pinning Elsie with her gaze. "He was in love, but not with *you*."

"He said he was. He wanted to marry me."

"He just thought he was in love with you. But any man who cares about you will care about your dreams too. Your dreams are a part of who you are. A big piece. If he wouldn't take time to see that, then he was in love with some girl he cooked up in his own imagination."

Elsie considered her words. "He wanted a woman who would be content living out *his* dreams."

"Yes! Elsie, you need a man who truly loves all of you, including the hopes God has given you. A man doesn't get to pick and choose certain pieces of you so you fit the mold he has for a perfect mate." Mary ran a hand over her hair, the strands picking up the sunlight filtering through the front window. "Hal thought I wanted a clean-cut, wealthy guy who owned a hotel."

"That's what you said you wanted."

"True." She laughed. "But I was wrong. It took me a while to realize my true dreams were for someone who would laugh with me. Crack silly jokes. Treat me like a million bucks instead of trying to make a million of his own." She made a face. "I got a letter from Hal yesterday. He's got a new girl, some pearl diver at the lodge. Even when he's boasting, he's as dry as paper."

Elsie ran her fingers around the edge of her plate. "I feel badly for hurting Teddy."

"So apologize to him and let it be water under the bridge." Mary leaned forward. "But here's a question for you. What will you do next—about Nate?"

That thought had kept her tossing and turning late into the night. "Nothing. I made one enormous mistake by allowing a romance to usurp my dreams. I'm not doing it again. I'm just going to concentrate on getting ready for school."

Her friend took a sip of her coffee and made a face. "Why do I always think I'm going to like this stuff? I want to be all modern and sophisticated with my black coffee, but I still prefer iced tea." She tapped her fingernails against the table. "How can men hope to understand us? We don't even understand ourselves."

A warmth settled in Elsie's chest. She sat back in her seat. "Isn't that the truth."

Mary grinned. "Now that you have everything figured out, can I stir the pot a little?"

"What do you mean?"

"If you believe God gave you the dream to go to college and become a teacher—to help kids learn more about this big, beautiful world—is there a chance He put Nate here to play a part in it?"

Elsie set her cup on the table. "You're always the romantic, aren't you?"

"You know it, sweetie."

Twenty-Seven

Nate followed a large group of the men down the road to the Canyon Hotel for a history lecture, only half-aware of their joking and laughter drowning out the evening birdsong. His thoughts were elsewhere. Even Red and Val seemed to recognize his mood and steered clear.

Nate couldn't figure it out. In the past two weeks, his lessons with Elsie had gone from encouraging and friendly to encouraging but distant. She'd asked him to move their lessons to the classroom, but after much discussion he'd convinced her to meet in a meadow just out of sight of the camp.

She paced around the clearing while he stumbled through the words. He still made progress, but at a crawl. Was she tiring of the extra work?

He supposed it had something to do with what Red had told him— that Elsie had finally dumped the arrogant ranger. Nate was proud of the college girl. She deserved someone who could see her talents and encourage her to use them, the way she did for everyone else. Red's second piece of news had been less heartening. Mary wanted him to know her roommate wasn't interested in having a beau. She had her sights set on college, and nothing would change that.

Nate had tried to cast off his infatuation like the bark and debris they tossed on the burn piles. But like everything else in nature, his feelings were persistent. The more he uprooted them, the faster they seemed to grow.

He followed Val into the elegant hotel, the open windows capturing the cool breeze sweeping up from the rim of the canyon. Chairs were spread out in rows facing a small screen. Guests, savages, and CCCs mingled, eager voices talking about the upcoming program. Small children darted around the aisle, their excitement at staying up beyond their bedtime creating an air of silliness and wild abandon.

The smell of popcorn took him back to the days when he and Sherm would sneak into Ebbets Field to watch the Dodgers. They never had money for seats, much less popcorn, but the scent triggered a wave of memories, regardless.

Red elbowed him. "There's my girl over there. You two be all right on your own?"

"I'm not sure, Red. We might get lost." Nate dug for his sense of humor. "Or maybe the kid here will get his pocket picked by one of these gentlemen."

Val straightened his tie. "More likely, they're going to think I'm a grifter. What are we doing here?"

"We were invited, remember? The hotel invited the whole crew." Nate glanced around. Most everyone had taken them up on the offer too. The CCCs outnumbered the hotel guests two-to-one.

One of the rangers stood at the front and gestured for folks to take their seats.

Nate found a place for him and Val near the door. As the man spoke, Nate tried to focus on the lantern slides and retelling of Yellowstone's history, but instead he found himself gazing at the back of Elsie's head. She shifted about in her seat, as if to scan the room. Was she looking for him? He brushed away the thought. Just as likely, she was checking on her students. Or maybe her cousin.

He settled back in the chair, giving himself over to the stories of Indian wars and army rule. His sisters would eat this stuff up. He'd need to remember the tall tales for when he got home. *Home.* His sisters' letters had been filled with stories too. Apparently Charlie had another brush with the law, but their father had gotten hold of him and straightened him out. The thought had sent Nate's mood into a tailspin. He should be there looking out for the boy. Their father's methods were little better than those of the soldiers who pursued the Nez Perce through Yellowstone.

Nate closed his eyes, letting the story wash over him. He was busy imagining himself on the run with Chief Joseph, when Val bumped his leg with the side of his fist and jarred him back to reality.

Val hooked his thumb toward the aisle, shooting Nate a pointed look.

Nate turned his head in time to see Elsie disappear out the side door. What did Val expect him to do, chase her down?

The kid leaned close and whispered out of the corner of his mouth. "Go after her."

"And do what?" What did a sixteen-year-old know about women? Nate shifted against the stiff back of the wooden chair. Then again, did he have any better understanding at twenty-four?

Apparently his legs agreed with Val, because within five minutes every muscle was twitching. There was no way he could sit still to the end of the lecture with this much energy coursing through his system. "I'm going out for some air," he whispered to Val.

The youngster's grin held a little too much enthusiasm for Nate's tastes.

Nate eased his way down the aisle and then stepped through the doors and into the cool, dark night. Elsie was nowhere to be seen. Just as well. He wasn't sure he trusted himself not to say something stupid. He walked a circuit around the parking area in a vain attempt to burn off his jitters.

He was sure he'd seen desire in Elsie's eyes a couple of weeks ago, the day he'd nearly kissed her in the woods, and that image had burned itself into his memory. But she was right to focus on school. She didn't need Vaughn or him—or anyone else—messing up things for her. He needed to honor her decision, even if it left a gaping hole in his heart.

Nate stopped by one of the yellow buses parked near the hotel for the night. Leaning against it, he stared up at the stars, the display of lights draping him with a newfound sense of peace. He and Elsie could still be friends, right? In reality, they'd never been anything more than that. If she were here right now, they'd talk about geology, teaching, and Yellowstone. *And then I'd kiss her.*

He pressed fingers against his brow. *Don't be an idiot.* It might take more than one lap around the lot to clear his head.

"Nate?" Elsie's voice carried down the sidewalk.

He swiveled, the clear-headed words he'd thought just moments ago now jumbling in his mind like they often did on the page.

"Are you leaving?" She walked toward him, then stopped a few paces short.

"No. Just needed some air."

"Me too."

How was it he could still see the blue of her eyes here in the dark? Nate locked his knees to prevent himself from walking over and taking her into his arms. It didn't help matters when she stared at him like that.

"Nate, I feel like our lessons have been a little . . . stiff lately." She hesitated. "Like you're ill at ease with me."

He swallowed the urge to laugh. "Funny, I thought the same about you." Oh, how he missed her. The way she smiled and laughed at things he said. The way her eyes lit up when he learned a new word. Could he tell her that? He swallowed. "Red told me about you and Vaughn."

Her gaze lowered. "We weren't a good match."

"No." The reply slipped too quickly.

The briefest of smiles touched her lips when she looked up again, meeting his eyes. "He cared nothing about learning who I am and what is important to me. I intend to go to college and become a teacher. He only wants a sweet little wife."

"You have to become a teacher. Look what you've done for the men. For me." He stopped himself from reaching for her hand. No matter how badly he wanted to touch her, he missed her friendship more. "How about we walk for a while? Unless you wanted to hear the rest of the talk?"

"I know how it ends."

As they walked, her silence provided plenty of time for his thoughts to run rampant. He reminded himself to give her space. Give himself space. She was his teacher, after all. *I have a crush on the teacher.* He almost chuckled. *I guess there's a first time for everything.*

After several minutes Elsie spoke. "I told Mary I should concentrate on college."

"I think that's wise."

"Only, I'm having trouble with that."

"With college?"

"With concentrating." She slipped her hand under his arm.

The touch sent a rush of heat surging through him.

How had he already fallen behind in this short conversation?

"You've been on my mind, Nate Webber."

He stopped in his tracks. "Are you saying—"

"But the summer is nearly over. You'll go home to Brooklyn, and I'll be heading to Missoula." She tipped her head, a question shining in her eyes.

"I see." Only, he didn't. Was she talking about friendship?

"It would be a little crazy, wouldn't it—us?"

Us. Nate reached down to cover her fingers with his own. Her skin was cool to the touch. "Definitely crazy."

She bit her lip, her gaze not breaking from his.

He stepped closer and cupped her jaw with his hand. What had he just been thinking about friendship? "You know what would be even more nutty? A college girl stepping out with an illiterate laborer."

Instead of backing away, as he'd feared she would, she tightened her grip on his arm. "Or a well-respected foreman with a lowly pillow puncher."

Nate couldn't resist her any longer. He drew her completely into his arms, lowering his face to the top of her head. Her hair smelled like lavender and . . . and something else. Popcorn from the hotel?

She slid her arms around his waist, her body surrendering to his embrace even as she nestled her cheek against his shoulder.

He could feel her breath against his neck, the sensation driving any sensible thought from his mind. "I'm not sure this will help your concentration," he murmured into her hair.

"I'm concentrating better than I have in weeks." She lifted her head and smiled, looking straight into his eyes.

The sight of her smile weakened any resolve he had left. He bent down and pressed his lips to hers, as he'd dreamed of doing since that first day at Norris Basin. Soft at first, he didn't dare move away for fear that she'd come to her senses. Her lips tasted of popcorn too. He was pretty sure that smell and taste would never make him think of baseball again.

She leaned into his kiss, and by the time they drew apart, he'd forgotten how to breathe. Elsie kept her palm against his cheek. "This is crazy." Her words barely stirred the air.

Nate rested his forehead against hers. "If this is crazy, college girl, I'm not sure I want to be sane."

Elsie tapped a pencil on her knee as she graded papers at the small desk she shared with Mary. A lot could happen in twenty-four hours. She'd learned that lesson at a young age, but it still surprised her every time.

I kissed Nate Webber.

The delicious memory sent a shiver across her skin, just as it had all day while she scrubbed toilets, changed sheets, and helped tourists find their rooms. She'd decided not to date, and then two weeks later she was kissing the man. This was so unlike her. But evidently her sensible side had checked out some time ago. She swept a hand through her hair, the stuffy air in the room making it difficult to think. Elsie went to the window and propped it open.

Returning to her desk, she retrieved the book she'd set aside for Nate. The thought of meeting him for another reading session sent her heart dancing in giddy circles. Focusing on their task at hand would be challenging now that she knew the touch of his lips.

Nate thought of himself as a failure, and she was determined to prove him wrong. Reading was just the first step. Writing would be the next hurdle to address. She pulled open the desk drawer and dug around for a notepad, tipping her head to search through the layers of school papers. Her fingers brushed against the lighter, still hidden there. Her chest tightened as she drew it out, the metal cold to the touch. She'd need to find a way to return it to Teddy. She hadn't wanted the extravagant gift in the first place, but now it mocked her decision.

"If they've got a firebug in their midst, we need to root him out." His words were like a scratchy record on a Victrola. The idea that someone would start fires on purpose sent an icy feeling across her skin. Elsie stared at the silver case nestled in her palm. She'd never had the courage to try the ridiculous gadget. No wonder Teddy thought she'd wash out of college— she didn't even have the nerve to work a lighter.

Elsie sank onto the desk chair, placing the bag in her lap. It was a ridiculous fear that needed to be addressed. After a deep breath, she opened the top and flicked the lever, the tiny gear kicking out a spark. It took two more tries before the flame appeared, a miniature orange flag waving in the draft from the open window. Taking her thumb off the button, the light extinguished, leaving behind an acrid scent of phosphorus.

The firecracker sailed through the open window and landed on mother's lace curtains fluttering in the summer breeze.

How easily a single spark could lead to disaster.

She snapped the lid shut and slammed the lighter back into the drawer, her palms damp. That's where it would stay until she figured out how to get it back to Teddy. Perhaps her father or Graham would return it for her. Either way, she didn't want the dreadful thing here a moment longer than it needed to be.

Jumping up, she hurried out of the dormitory and into the fresh air. She had thirty minutes to walk the short distance to the CCC camp for evening classes, and the late-day sunshine calmed her ruffled spirits. The record-breaking temperatures and clear days had made for a gorgeous summer. If this was to be one of her last summers in Yellowstone, at least it was shaping up to be the best yet. Teaching the CCC men was much better than making beds all day, though finding the time to do both jobs had been a challenge. She hadn't been to Geyser Basin since the trip to Old Faithful. Her plans for detailed records of geyser eruptions had gone astray.

Maybe she could invite Nate to accompany her there this weekend. She'd managed to claim a rare Saturday off, and she certainly wasn't going to waste it.

Rose was walking toward her, looking happier than she had all summer. "Elsie, what did you say to him?"

Elsie paused. "To whom?"

"To Graham, silly." Rose's pink dress matched the blush in her cheeks. She caught up to Elsie just as she was passing Pryor General Store. "He's been much more attentive of late. I think he might be coming around. Did you give him your blessing?"

"He doesn't need my blessing. I'm sorry that I made you both feel like you did." Her unforgiveness had driven a wedge not just between her and Graham, but also between her and Rose. "But I do worry, Rose. Graham"— she scrambled to put voice to her concerns without deepening the rift— "The fire was long ago, Rose, but it affected us both deeply."

"I know that." Rose touched Elsie's wrist, a smile warming her heart-shaped face. "It shaped you into the friend I love today."

Elsie blinked against the tears that collected in her eyes. She didn't deserve the good friends God had gifted her with. She pulled Rose into a quick hug. "I love you too. That's why I want you to be careful. He told me he wasn't looking for a steady girlfriend. But if you've somehow changed his mind, then I hope he can grow into the kind of hero you've always dreamed of."

"I think he's pretty heroic already, though he doesn't see it. I'll always be grateful that he saved you as a child. Plus, he's helped with both fires here at the park."

Both fires. Rose's words sent a chill through her. Graham had been at both the Mammoth Hotel fire and the recent one at Canyon. "You invited him to the talent show at the CCC camp, right?"

She nodded. "He was staying over at Canyon and taking the tour bus group to Old Faithful the next morning. I thought he'd enjoy visiting with the men. He's talked about them a few times since meeting them at the dance. He'd planned to borrow Charlie's coupe and drive over to Lake to see a friend, but he decided to come with me instead." Another smile teased at her lips. "I'm so glad he was there that night."

Elsie tried to recall the event. She'd seen Graham at the show, but had she seen him leave? "Were you with him all evening?"

Rose frowned. "What are you implying? We weren't out necking in the woods or anything."

"No, I didn't mean . . . Did he stay for the whole show?"

"People were milling around, you know that. They had refreshments set up in the back plus some of the guys talked him into helping with the backdrops and scenery, so he was up and down all evening." Rose folded her arms and grinned. "I saw you sneak out too. That explains what I hear about you and Nate Webber."

Heat rushed to Elsie's face. "News spreads fast."

"I remember him from the Lake trip. He seemed like a good egg. Easy to talk to and not bad looking, either."

"And yet he couldn't tempt you away from my cousin."

"Not a chance." She turned to face Elsie. "I'm so thankful Graham has earned your forgiveness."

"He didn't have to earn it. God just had to work on my heart." Elsie smiled as her mother's words echoed through her memory. *Forgiveness isn't earned, Elsie. It's bestowed.*

Nate studied the gurgling, belching mud pot in the Lower Geyser Basin, but it did little to distract him from the feeling of Elsie's hand in his. He leaned closer to her. "It reminds me of some of the guys after Cook serves his famous pork and bean stew."

She laughed, a more pleasant sound than the glugging puddle at their feet. "Just think, those gasses come from deep under the earth and erupt out here, like a shaken-up bottle of soda pop. The mud isn't boiling; it's just bubbling up with gasses."

"As I said—bean stew." He squeezed her hand. "But I think I prefer this."

As they moved away to let a group of eager tourists view the mud pots, Elsie checked her watch. "We should head back if we want to catch Graham's bus on its way to Old Faithful."

"You've spoiled me today with the private tour. A fellow could get used to this." He tucked her hand in the crook of his arm.

She adjusted her hat against the hot summer sun. "I wanted to show you some of my favorite spots. Next time we'll bring the crew."

Her smile could melt him in two seconds flat. Thankfully the path heading back to the parking area took longer than that. He'd stretch the whole day if he could. "Now as my way of thanking my beautiful tour guide, I'd like to buy her dinner at the Inn." Unlike many of the other fellows, Nate had squirreled away the spending money the CCC had allotted him since joining up. He couldn't think of a better way to spend it than romancing his girl. *My girl.* That had a nice ring to it.

"That sounds lovely."

A ranger walked toward them, leading a group of visitors. Elsie pulled her hand free as the man tipped his flat hat in greeting.

Once the trail cleared, she glanced at Nate with a sigh. "I'm sorry."

"I understand." He did. Most of the park probably thought of her as Vaughn's girl or Ranger Brookes's daughter. What would they think to see her with a lowly CCC recruit?

"It's a little awkward. Teddy is still new to the ranger staff, but he is one of their own." She gripped his arm and stepped close. "But I don't regret my decision. Not for an instant."

"So kissing you right here, right now, would be a bad choice, right?" He settled for rubbing his thumb along her knuckles and moving up toward her wrist. "It will be hard to keep this secret. Red's probably already spreading the word."

"So is Mary." She slipped her wrist back from his grip, tugging at her cuff. "There are no secrets in Yellowstone. At least, not for long."

"I'm getting that idea."

As they reached the parking area, two of the yellow buses sat empty near the trailhead. "Is that Graham over there?" He gestured toward a cluster of picnic tables on the far side of the road.

Elsie stood on tiptoes for a better look. "It looks like it." She frowned. "Who's he with?"

As they watched, Elsie's cousin leaned over and planted a kiss on the petite blonde by his side. His hand circled around her back as he pulled her close.

Elsie gasped, clutching at Nate's arm. "It's not Rose—I can tell you that much."

"It looks like Graham's found romance elsewhere."

The second driver leaned against his vehicle, likely waiting for the tour group's return. "Are you talking about Graham Brookes?"

Elsie looked at him warily. "Yes, he's my cousin."

"Well, Graham's leading the gear jammer tourney this year." The fellow chuckled. "I've given up trying to catch him in points. Got me a regular girl, and she frowns on the whole game."

"What's involved in the tourney?" Nate asked.

A pained expression crossed Elsie's face. "It means a different girl at every stop. I should have realized that silly wager had been resurrected. I've been so busy teaching at the CCC camp; I haven't been paying attention to the savage scuttlebutt."

"So you haven't heard, then? They upped the stakes this year." The gear jammer leaned forward. "It's how many girls you can kiss on a *single circuit* of the park. Brookes has pushed the total to four, just this week."

"Four?" Elsie's mouth dropped open. "Graham? Are you sure?"

Nate raised his brows. Of course he felt bad for Rose, but when this story got back to the CCC camp, the jammer would be a hero among the fellas.

The driver opened the door and snatched a cigarette from a box on the seat. "It's all in good fun. The girls are in on it. They like being the one to push a gear jammer to a new record."

"Rose isn't one of those girls. She thinks she's in love with him." Elsie frowned.

Nate took her arm. "I don't think it will do any good to confront him now. Let's walk. It looks like we still have some time left." Graham certainly didn't appear to be in a hurry.

She followed him back down the trail toward the geyser basin, plumes of steam rising from the springs. "I can't believe my cousin. Kissing four girls in one day? He told me he wasn't interested in settling down—with Rose or anyone else. But I had no idea he had something like this in mind."

"I guess you were wise to warn Rose to steer clear."

"But I didn't. We just talked, and she was excited because he'd been paying her more attention. I told her I'd forgiven him." Her forehead crumpled.

"Have you?"

"Yes." She paused. "But now this? She's going to be heartbroken. After losing Pete this year, she'd sunk all her hopes into Graham." A gust of wind swept through the basin, carrying a whiff of rotten egg. "You don't suppose she's one of the four, do you?"

"You said there are no secrets in Yellowstone. Wouldn't someone have told you?"

"I hadn't heard of Graham's exploits, either. I don't know how he's keeping it quiet around Canyon."

He squeezed her hand. "Are you going to tell Rose?"

"I suppose I'll have to. Though I hate to do it. Graham has already been a strain on our friendship. We used to be so close."

"Better she hears it from you."

Elsie sighed, her countenance falling a bit more. "Yes, I agree. But it's going to be difficult."

Today wasn't shaping up to be the romantic outing he'd planned. "We could skip dinner and head back, if you'd prefer."

Elsie's eyes widened, a smile softening her face for the first time since they'd arrived at the parking area. "Not a chance. Just because my cousin is being a skunk doesn't mean he should ruin our evening. This summer is more than half over; I'm not missing anything else."

He couldn't resist the grin sweeping over his face. "That's the spirit, college girl."

Twenty-Eight

Elsie dropped her things in her room before setting off in search of Rose. Nate had offered to join her for moral support, but the truth would come more easily without an audience.

Even with what they'd witnessed, the day had been nearly perfect. They'd put aside the incident with Graham and enjoyed a delicious meal at the Inn. On the ride home—with a different driver—she'd snuggled into Nate's shoulder for the duration. The proud smile he wore nearly made her heart burst.

For now, she'd tuck that joy away for safekeeping.

It seemed funny that they'd gone from friends to inseparable in a few short days. The summer was passing at such a quick clip. Soon she'd head off to college and Nate's six-month stint would be nearly finished. They'd just have to enjoy this month and let the future take care of itself.

As she walked, her fingers traveled up to her collar, a habit she'd been fighting since Teddy pointed it out to her. Nate didn't know about her scars. When he'd called her beautiful earlier today, the word had echoed through her soul. Why must men be so focused on looks?

Rose and the other bubble queens were hard at work in the laundry room, the steam billowing from the machines like the mist back at Upper Geyser

Basin. The huge smile Rose cast her direction sent Elsie's heart spinning downward. Best get the news over with—like ripping off a bandage.

Minutes later, Rose was crumpled in a sobbing heap on the steps. "It can't be true. You must have seen someone else." The tears she shoved aside with the side of her fist said otherwise.

"I'm so sorry, Rose. Didn't he say anything to you? You've spent a lot of time together."

"Do you mean, how could I be so foolish?"

Elsie sank beside her. "Of course not. Rose, sweetie, I'd never think that of you."

She shot Elsie a dirty look. "But you'll think it of Graham in a heart-beat. And you'll assume that some horrible story told to you by another gear jammer is true? Have you talked to Graham? He might be able to explain this."

"Rose, I saw him." Elsie scooted closer, rubbing her friend's arm. "How in the world could he explain this away?"

"Just because he was kissing one girl doesn't mean he's been spooning with girls all over Yellowstone." She wiped away another tear.

Something in her tone gave Elsie pause. "Have *you* kissed him?"

Rose's tirade stopped in an instant. Hurt pooled in her eyes. "How long have we been friends, Elsie? Do you actually think I'd choose to be part of his record-breaking day? Or are you saying he wouldn't be interested in doing that with me?" She pushed up to her feet with a storm cloud brewing on her face. "I'm done talking about this."

Leaving Elsie alone on the step, she went back inside and slammed the door.

Elsie rested her head on her knees. She'd expected tears and anger. But Rose defending Graham? That had been the furthest thing from her mind.

Mammoth had never looked so heavenly, the sun illuminating the billows of steam rising from the hot springs. Elsie let herself into the house, dropping her bag by the door. She'd stopped by the ranger station to see her father, but he'd been out on patrol. Walking back to the kitchen, she stopped in her tracks.

Her mother sat at the little breakfast table with a cup of tea and a book. She set down the cup and beamed at Elsie. "I didn't know you were coming home. You should have sent a message. I'd have made something special."

"I . . . I can't believe you're out of bed. That's special enough."

Mama rose to her feet, spreading her arms to embrace her daughter. "Oh, you know me. Good days and not so good days. But it's been a great week overall, so that's encouraging."

"You look well." Elsie pulled out a chair for herself.

"It's all this glorious sunshine. I've been outside as much as I can, soaking up the light. I think God put healing power in the sun's rays, don't you?" She took a sip of tea. "Your father's all worried about fire danger, of course. He has the tendency to see a tarnished lining in every silver cloud."

Elsie retrieved a cup for herself. "It's been a beautiful summer in Canyon too. Not as warm as here, but very dry." She stopped. She hadn't come to talk about the weather.

Mama's eyes were shining. "I can see you have news. Do I get to hear it now, or do I have to wait until your father gets home?"

"I'd rather tell you first." A ripple of uncertainty shot through Elsie, and she suddenly felt like a little girl searching for her mother's approval. Best to get it over with. "I know you encouraged me to open myself up to Teddy."

Mother tapped the table with her fingertips. "That's not exactly what I said."

"Well, it hasn't worked out, anyway. I liked the idea of perhaps someday marrying a ranger, but Teddy wasn't the right man for me."

Her mother popped a quick nod. "I agree."

"You do?"

"Of course. When I said you should open up to people, I didn't mean Teddy Vaughn. That fellow is nothing more than an insecure boy." She lifted her eyebrows. "He was over here so many nights in a row—I had your father ask him to leave."

"But you love having people over."

"Not one who's determined to keep my daughter from her dreams. He kept speaking about the two of you as if everything was decided." She lifted her cup and gestured toward Elsie with it. "I figured if that were the case, you would have come and told me yourself. And frankly, I didn't believe you'd stand for it."

"He did seem a little concerned with getting things settled quickly."

"Then he stopped coming by altogether a couple weeks back, so I guessed you'd set him straight." Mama leaned forward, touching Elsie's knee. "Elsie, when I said you should open yourself up, I meant to life, dear. Not to some man. I wanted you to live without your past dogging every step, making every decision for you. See what God has planned for you. Though personally, I'd be delighted if you did find love one day."

Her mother went to the cupboard and brought out a box of cookies purchased from the bakery in Gardiner. "I've always liked to do my own baking, but in recent months I've learned to appreciate these as well." She put some on a plate and brought them to the table. "I have a hunch that's not all your news."

Elsie sighed. "Is it that obvious?"

"I haven't seen you smile this much in a while. Now who is it?"

The back door swung open, and Elsie's father walked in. "Both my girls are here? What a treat."

Mama stood on her tiptoes to place a kiss on his cheek. "You must be ready for lunch. There are sandwiches in the icebox. We're having a cookie appetizer." She turned to wink at their daughter. "Elsie was just telling me about the new man in her life."

"I could have told you that." Her father chuckled as he retrieved the food. "He works for the Canyon CCC crew, am I right?"

Elsie sat back, stunned. "How did you find out?"

"The fellow was so jumpy last time I saw him that I cornered one of his buddies until he spilled the beans. Apparently dating the boss's daughter makes a man jittery."

Mama had walked to the cupboard, getting plates for their meal. "You could have said something."

"Wasn't sure it was true until just now." He bent over and placed a kiss on the top of Elsie's head. "Nate Webber. Good man, strong leader. Time will tell if he's good enough for my little girl, but"—he shrugged—"it's not my decision, is it?"

The bands of tension that had gripped her heart since she'd gotten up this morning eased.

"Just remember," her mother said, as she laid three dishes on the table. "The key to a love that lasts is Matthew 7:12."

"The Golden Rule, I know." She filed that away to consider on the long bus ride back to Canyon. Her parents had long modeled the philosophy of working side by side to provide for the other's happiness. Could she have a relationship like that with Nate?

Nate read through the last two lines on the page, pushing through each word with the same effort he'd used on the crosscut saw earlier in the day.

Elsie walked a circle around the log that had become their favorite classroom, pausing to gaze at the burbling creek.

"You're not hovering over my shoulder. Are you afraid to sit next to me?" Setting down the book, he got up and stood behind her. "What's wrong?"

Her shoulders bounced in a halfhearted laugh. "I'm a little distracted."

"Distracting you is my job." He turned her around to face him. "But I must be losing my touch. I messed up at least four lines on purpose, and you didn't even notice."

"You did?"

"I don't think bears actually have a diet of fish, berries, and cheesecake."

"I think they'd accept cheesecake if it were offered. They'd be silly to pass it up." She pulled Nate close, wrapping her arms around his back.

Her touch sent a jolt through his system. No man should be expected to read when a beautiful woman stood nearby. Nate kissed her, first with a gentle touch and then more urgently as the fire kindled between them. When she slid her hand along the front of his shirt, it fanned the flames.

Maybe he should have stayed with the book. He lifted his face skyward for a moment to catch his breath. "You didn't answer my question."

"Whatever the question was, the answer is yes."

He chuckled. "Then I should have asked something more important." *Like, will you spend your life with me?* "I asked what was wrong."

She sighed and opened her eyes. "I'm worried about Rose. She didn't take the news about Graham well."

"I can't imagine she would. He should watch his back."

"No, it's worse. She defended him." Elsie wrinkled her brow.

"Love can be blind sometimes."

"I've known Rose for years, and she tends to see the best in people. She also loves with her whole heart."

Nate brushed a curl from her face. "She loves her friends too. Maybe she just needs time."

"I'm not sure if I have the patience."

"You have it in spades. Look how far you've brought me with my studies—all of us, really. Having someone believe in me?" A lump formed in his throat. "No one has ever done that for me before."

She touched the button on her collar, a motion he'd seen her repeat countless times since the first day they'd met. He intercepted her hand and brought it to his lips for a kiss.

"Nate." Her voice sounded shaky. "I want to tell you something."

"Anything."

She wove her fingers through his and drew them close to her heart. "You've seen the scars my cousin has on his hands?"

Nate remembered the day the gear jammer had driven him and the guys to the dance at the Mammoth Hotel. "He told me he was in a house fire as a child."

"I was there too." She took a shaky breath. "My baby sister died in that fire."

The statement shook him. His heart stilled for a moment until he could think of something to say. "How awful, Elsie. Then witnessing the fire at the camp must have brought back horrible memories." He recalled how she had stayed on the far side of the yard the whole time they were struggling to put out the small blaze, not even approaching after they'd doused the flames. Now it made sense.

"Nothing scares me more. I freeze at the sight of flames, even now."

"I can understand that."

"And Nate—" She glanced up at him, her eyes wary. "As a child . . . If Graham hadn't pulled me out, I would have died too."

Lost her sister. Nearly died. That was a lot to endure as a child—at any age, really. He tightened his grip on her hands. "Were you injured?"

She pulled her fingers free and stepped back. Unbuttoning the cuff of her sleeve, she drew it up to her elbow.

The sight of her twisted scars sent a jab of pain through his body. "Oh, Elsie." He turned her hand palm up and slid his fingers along the puckered skin, breathing out a long exhale. "It doesn't hurt, does it?"

"Sometimes. Especially when I get too warm." She undid the other sleeve and pulled it up to match. "It's one of the reasons I don't often work in the laundry or kitchen. I overheat easily."

The scars on her left arm weren't quite as bad, but they still made him ache. He drew her close, cradling her arms between them. "I'm sorry. I didn't know."

"There's more, Nate." She looked up at him, tears shining in her eyes. "I don't want to show you, but there's more."

His throat tightened. "More?"

"It runs up both arms and along my neck and upper chest. I ran inside the house after my sister, and I was knocked down when part of the ceiling collapsed. The fire caught my dress—the lace collar and sleeves. Graham put it out with his hands."

Nate closed his eyes for a moment in order to resist glancing at the areas mentioned, his mind trying to accept what she'd just told him. "I'll have to remember to thank him."

"He started the fire, and then he panicked. If he'd gone in and gotten Dottie right away . . ." She shook her head as if scattering the rest of the story. "But it's in the past, and I've forgiven him." She grasped his hand and touched it to her forearm again. "I needed you to know the truth about me."

"I want to know everything about you."

"Before I let myself fall in love with you." She blinked away the tears. "They say beauty is only skin deep, but in my case—it's not even that."

He felt the air rush from his lungs. Is that what was frightening her? "College girl, I fell in love with you ages ago." He lifted her arm and kissed the inside of her wrist. "And it wasn't for your skin. It was your heart—how you care for your students, for your friends, your mother. You even reached out to me, refusing to let me give up on myself. Your beauty isn't skin deep, Elsie. It goes so much further than that."

Twenty-Nine

With a sigh, Elsie pulled the sheet up over the mattress. "I can't believe the summer's almost gone."

"You say that every year." Mary wiped the mirror. "But at least you're coming to school with me this time. I've always hated leaving you behind."

"Not as much as I despised being left." Elsie tucked in the corners. The excitement of the upcoming school year bristled around the edges of her thoughts, but it was tempered with the reality of leaving Nate.

"Red says that a lot of the CCC men are heading home in September—the ones who didn't sign on for the second six-month stint."

Elsie didn't respond. She'd already heard as much from her father and from Nate. The Yellowstone camps would officially close in early October, depending on snowfall, and the men who stayed on would be reassigned. The idea of the camp being emptied left her hollow. But then again, she wouldn't be here to see it.

She laid the pillow on the top of the mattress. "Is Red going home or staying on?"

"He's committed to another six months. He's hoping they send the company to California."

"Nate too." A lump settled in her throat. "So far away."

"It might as well be the moon," Mary agreed. "But we can write. I love receiving letters at college. It's almost more romantic than dating, in some ways. It's a sweet, sweet longing."

Elsie could write letters. But Nate? Dare she hope he could overcome his pride and ask someone for help? Perhaps she could pre-address some envelopes for him. He could at least send her cartoons. He'd been entertaining his sisters with caricatures of his camp mates for months. Elsie had started adding a few lines here and there for him, explaining some of the drawings to the girls. Three of his pictures hung from the edges of her mirror: him running from a black bear, her cuddling Hutch and Kit, and Red and Val boxing.

Mary sashayed across the floor performing a waltz turn with the wicker broom. "We still have the end-of-the-year follies at Old Faithful Inn. It will be fun seeing some of the Mammoth folks again."

"Like Hal and Bernie?"

Mary shrugged one shoulder with a smile. "I wouldn't mind showing off Red to some of the Mammoth girls. They'll be green with envy."

"I suppose." Elsie placed a stack of folded towels on the end of the bed, all ready for tonight's guests. "But don't forget, the party at Mammoth ended up in a brawl and a fire. I'd really prefer that disaster not be repeated."

❧

Nate handed the last of the saws up to Val as the kid stood in the bed of the CCC truck. After the long night of thunder rolling over the park, reveille felt like it arrived hours earlier than normal. Unfortunately, the lightning had been nothing but empty promises. The fire danger had steadily worsened over the past several weeks. Ranger Brookes had told Nate and the other foremen to warn the men not to smoke while they were in the woods. If the lightning had started any blazes, they'd be hearing about it soon.

The men wandered from the mess hall, laughing and talking as they clambered into trucks. They had been diverted twice to work on highway landscaping projects, so they were excited to get back to Mount Washburn. It had become their second home.

Red jumped into the cab, taking his place behind the wheel. A toothpick dangled from the corner of his mouth. "Nate, did those rumblers keep you awake like they did me? I swear, I would start dozing and the thunder would start boomin' again."

"I dreamt we had a grizzly nearby." Nate climbed in beside Red and slammed the door shut.

"I don't know if I'm going to be able to keep my eyes open during class tonight. You're lucky to be getting private lessons. When she starts in about nouns and adverbs, my eyelids start drooping." He put the truck in gear and rolled onto the highway.

Nate turned to look out the back window at the crew. Some fellows had taken to standing during the trip, hanging on to the wooden slats as they bounced down the road. As the wind ruffled their hair and shirts, they usually wore big grins. There was something about this place that inspired joy, no matter how tough the work. Homesickness was a thing of the past for most of them, and Nate heard more talk of the future than reminiscences of home. This experience had given them much more than what they'd signed up for. When he got home to Brooklyn, he'd have to pay O'Sullivan a visit and thank the man for giving him the push. Nate had thought he was saving Charlie. He never dreamed he was saving himself.

Maybe he'd write the police chief a letter. Wouldn't that be a shocker?

He owed Elsie so much as well. They'd spent as many stolen hours together as they could, in between their long work shifts and her classes. If only it could be more. Soon she'd be leaving for school. The thought made him about bust with pride. His girl, at a university. Every time he called her "college girl," he was sure his smile grew an inch wider. He might not be worth standing on the same ground she walked on, but at least he could bask in her glow.

As Red parked at the trailhead, another truck was waiting. Ranger Vaughn leaned against the driver-side door. "About time you fellas got here."

Nate ran a hand over the back of his neck, the muscles tightening already. Since Brookes had returned, they hadn't seen the younger ranger, and that had suited Nate just fine. Vaughn had every reason not to like him, but hopefully he wouldn't take that out on the crew. "It's good to see you again, Ranger." He managed to greet the man without speaking through gritted teeth. "Ranger Brookes was here for an inspection just last week. Is there something we can help you with?"

"We had lightning strikes overnight and smoke was spotted over on the east side." The man's eyes practically gleamed. "Your crew is trained and ready, right?"

Nate ignored the sharp tone. "Happy to help, sir."

"Then follow me. We're driving north, then hiking in."

"Yes sir." He turned to the men. "You heard the ranger. Looks like the beetles get the day off."

Red grunted. "I hope fire duty earns *us* an extra day off. I wouldn't mind spending some more time with Mary. I like working in the woods, but I'd rather it not be the kind that involves smoke and flame."

Nate climbed back into the truck, wishing they'd known about this before leaving camp. He'd have packed a few more canteens of water. Hopefully there'd be a creek somewhere along the trail.

The heat of the day showed them little mercy. They'd hiked for miles, searching for the lightning strikes. Thankfully, none of them were more than a smoldering tree or two.

Each time they found one, his crew set to work, laboring side by side to smother the blaze before it could spread to nearby trees. Nate took great pride watching his crew work like a well-oiled machine.

The men had come a long way since their first trips up Mount Washburn. Just a few months ago he could never have imagined a day when he'd see Poles, Irish, and Italians laboring side by side, sharing canteens like brothers. Out here in the pine forests, it didn't matter if you grew up on pierogi or chicken tetrazzini—if you had a meal at all. When you got back to camp, Cook was going to feed you giant platters of meatloaf, green beans, sliced bread, and apple pie.

Vaughn grew more surly as the day went by. He'd started out at an impossible pace, but now that they'd squelched three fires with just a couple of saws and shovels, the man appeared deflated and angry. Would he prefer a blazing inferno?

Nate risked approaching him. "So what do you think? We going to make it home tonight?"

The ranger removed his hat and wiped his forehead, leaving a smear of soot. "Thought we'd see more than this. The woods are as crispy as old toast."

"That's good news, right?"

"Of course." His growl suggested anything but. "The rate we're going, we'll get your little boys all tucked in their beds before dark."

"A few of them were pretty worried about an English test this evening, so if you want to stall, I doubt they'd protest."

Vaughn's eyes narrowed. "I can't believe you guys. You don't work weekends or holidays. You get free classes, food, clothing, beds. This program is less like work and more like nursery school."

Nate bit his tongue. The park didn't pay a cent of their wages and purchased few of their supplies. It was a plum deal for the park service, but Vaughn wasn't likely to see it that way. Especially after a long, hot day. "My crew works hard. Ranger Brookes has been pleased with the progress."

"I can't believe Elsie's over there teaching scrubs like you to read and write."

The man was baiting him, and unfortunately, he was doing a great job. Nate set his jaw. "She's a great teacher."

"Too good for a bunch of bottom feeders." Vaughn stepped forward, going toe to toe with Nate. "I don't know what she sees in you."

Was he talking about the crew—or him, personally? Nate curled his fingers into a fist, but he kept it locked at his side. "Frankly, I don't understand it myself." He started to turn away, but the heat and the tiring day had loosened his tongue. "But I'm starting to figure out why she was too good for you."

Vaughn lunged, catching Nate square in the chest and barreling him to the ground, shoulder first. The heavier man landed on top of him.

Nate twisted, ducking Vaughn's fist as it drove toward his face. The ranger crushed his knuckles into the dirt, giving Nate the chance to unseat him and scramble to his knees. Before he could restrain himself, he landed a blow of his own, busting the man's lip.

The sight of blood sent regret swelling through Nate like one of Elsie's geysers. He scooted back and clambered to his feet. "I don't want to fight you."

Vaughn sat up, swiping a palm across his mouth and spitting on the ground near Nate's boots. "You're not worth it, anyway." He pushed to his feet and stomped off toward the trucks.

Nate rolled his shoulders to release some of the pent-up tension. He'd gotten a sudden flashback of ducking his father's blows, and the memory made him sick to his stomach. He'd wanted nothing more than to grab Vaughn around the throat and make him eat his words. It was one thing to insult him, but his crew? He turned around to see where they'd all gotten off to.

Evidently a large group of them had circled behind him, waiting. Red slapped his hand onto Nate's shoulder. "I knew I'd make a bare-knuckle boxer out of you, yet."

Nate winced as he pried Red's fingers from his raw skin. "I shouldn't have let him get to me."

Val grinned. "Miss Brookes would be proud."

Probably not. "Come on; let's head home. You've got a test on *Othello* to ace, am I right?" It was pretty clear that if any of them were ever going to join Elsie at university, it would be Val.

"C'mon, Nate." Red socked his arm. "Sign up for some time in the ring at camp. I could make a fortune off that right hook."

"I'm keeping my hands in my pockets where they belong. Mutt punched a ranger and got put on the first train back to Brooklyn."

Red ran two fingers over his chin. "That's why you don't row with the bosses, Nate. Stick to brawling with us. Though with a little coaching, you could wipe the floor with Vaughn's face right before we leave this fall—it might just be worth it."

Elsie leaned against Nate's shoulder as they sat by the stream, a pile of papers in her lap. The cottonwood tree overlooking the creek had become a favorite spot for them, safely away from the prying eyes of fellow savages and CCC men.

After they'd finished their lesson, Nate had spent the last hour telling her stories about Brooklyn. Her mind spun as she thought about all the shops, theaters, restaurants, and a brick library not far from his family's apartment. As much as she loved Yellowstone, his descriptions of New York made her want to see the place for herself.

While he talked, she flipped through his sketchbook, admiring his work. She paused on one showing his family, the pictures of his sisters and brothers bringing a lump to her throat. "You must miss them."

He didn't answer, just tapped the drawing on the opposite page—a good-looking fellow wearing a police uniform. "My brother Sherm."

"I wish I could have met him."

"He'd have loved you." There was a catch in Nate's voice as he spoke. He cleared his throat and flipped through a couple of pages in rapid succession.

"Wait, what's this?" Elsie stopped him, turning the page back and studying a drawing of Nate gripping the top of a spindly pine tree as it bent over precariously. The two raccoons clung to his coat tails.

"Val wanted a self-portrait for the next issue of the *Camp Canyon Crier*."

"I should frame a copy of that one to take with me to college." She couldn't resist touching Nate's pen-and-ink grin. The last August days were slipping away, signs of fall already taking hold at Yellowstone. "I counted my savings last night. I should have just enough for school—thanks to my second job."

"Counted it?" He lifted a brow. "You keep it with you?"

"Just this season's wages. I've got a big mason jar wedged in my bottom drawer. My parents have the rest in their bank."

"But what if someone steals it?"

She laughed. "This is Yellowstone, not New York, Nate. No one is digging through my room looking for cash."

"I suppose. It just seems like a lot of money to have hidden in your room. That's your future."

Your future. He said it so casually, as if it didn't matter to him that they'd be apart for so long. Maybe forever. "I'm going to miss you, Nate."

A smile spread across his features. "I'll miss you, too, college girl. I'll be slaving away God-knows-where, while you're feeding that incredible brain of yours."

She scooted closer, every inch of separation a reminder of the loneliness to come. "You'll miss this?" She nuzzled his ear, brushing her lips against his cheek.

He groaned, softly. "You're killing me, Elsie. You don't want to know how much I'll miss touching you, holding you. But I can't take your dreams from you. I won't."

"I wish you were coming with me."

"Nate Webber on a college campus? They'd run me out with torches and pitchforks."

"You don't give yourself enough credit. You're every bit as smart as me; it just takes you longer to put words on paper."

"Nobody has ever believed in me the way you do. But I'd say that words are pretty important, overall."

"Not when it comes to caring for trees."

"Trees aren't hard to figure out." Nate lowered his eyes. "Besides, I'm the one with everything to lose."

"Why is that?"

"You're going to be surrounded by smart men with bright futures. You're going to look back on your time with me and wonder what you were thinking."

"Never."

His face turned plaintive. "Don't say that. You deserve the best. I won't have you feeling obligated to me."

A hole opened inside her. "It's not like I'm biding my time with you until something better comes along. I . . . I think God has matched us together, Nate."

"I'd like to believe that." A stitch formed between his eyes. "But why would He put us together?"

"My parents say God brings people together to serve one another. To look to each other's needs more than their own."

"Like you teaching me to read."

"And you giving me the courage to follow my dreams."

He smiled and shook his head. "I can't take credit for that. You were set on this course before I showed up."

"Nate, I knew what I wanted, but I was terrified." She leaned against his shoulder. "Working with you helped me see exactly how God might use me. That I could make a real difference in people's lives."

"You certainly have in mine." He fell silent, his arm warm around her.

The gurgle of the water rushing past made her drowsy. She closed her eyes, allowing the gentle sound to carry away her thoughts of the future. She wanted to stay in this moment forever.

Nate's breath stirred her hair as he lowered his cheek against her head. "I wish I had more to offer."

She squeezed his hand. "You have more than you realize."

Thirty

On Saturday, Nate strode toward Canyon Hotel, hoping to catch Elsie during her lunch break. It would be nice if she had weekends off like he did, but it made sense that the pillow punchers worked their hardest on days when more tourists crowded into the park.

Small groups of hotel guests wandered the grounds, and children were running and playing in the bright sunshine. Nate unfastened the top button on his shirt, wishing for a breath of cool air. The days had been getting warmer and warmer. It was still cool by New York standards, but he must have gotten acclimated to living in the mountains. You could almost smell the sap cooking as the trees dried out, needle by needle.

A couple stood on the front steps of the savage dormitory, tight and cozy as if they hadn't even noticed the heat. Nate veered left toward the hotel. The last thing he wanted to do was get in the way of someone else's romantic moment. After all, he was hoping to steal a kiss or two from his own girl. That seemed unlikely with so many onlookers, not that this particular couple seemed to care.

Nate did a double take as he recognized Graham and Rose. Had she decided to overlook Graham's little smooching games? He couldn't imagine a girl putting up with that sort of carrying on. At least not from a man she wanted to be serious about.

Nate slowed his steps, trying not to watch as Rose treated the bus driver to a goodbye kiss—a long one. Nate jammed his hands in his pockets and averted his eyes.

By the time he glanced back, Graham was alone, sliding a cigarette from a cellophane pack. A smile crossed his face as he stepped off the porch and headed down the walkway. The gear jammer raised a hand in greeting. "Hey, Webber, you got a light?" He dug through his own pockets.

"No, sorry." Nate was thankful he'd never picked up the stupid habit. Red and plenty of the other men wasted a lot of their spending money on cigarettes.

"Oh, wait, I found it." Graham pulled out a box of matches from his back pocket. He stopped and lit the cigarette, pulling in a long drag. "Man, I needed that."

"Your girl doesn't like you to smoke?"

"Most of 'em don't." He shrugged, glancing over his shoulder. "So you saw that, did you?"

"I think the whole community saw it." Nate kept his voice steady. "Seems like you two have been off and on all summer."

"I thought staying away from Rose would keep my cousin happy." A crooked smile crossed his face. "But Rose is pretty persistent. She's a great girl."

Nate fell into step beside him, even though Brookes was heading away from the hotel. "I know Elsie is fond of her."

"Speaking of Elsie . . ." Graham tapped off ashes, crushing them under his shoe. "I'm actually sort of curious—and please don't take any offense at this—but I was surprised she broke things off with that ranger for you."

"That's not exactly what happened."

"Nah, I don't suppose it was." He shrugged. "That Vaughn fellow is an odd duck. I'm rather glad she gave him the heave-ho. I couldn't imagine having him as part of the family."

Family? Nate hadn't even let his mind wander that far ahead. Would his family approve of Elsie? *They'd probably love her more than me.* "She'd been helping me study. And over time, we became friends."

"And more, it seems." As Graham fiddled with the lit cigarette, Nate studied the puckered skin on the man's palms. Usually he wore driving gloves, but at the moment they were tucked into his breast pocket. Nate couldn't help thinking about the similar scars on Elsie's arms.

"I heard about your success with the tourney."

Graham shot him a wary glance. "News gets around."

"I think we'd all hate to see Rose get hurt."

"It's just a game, Nate. Simple summer fun." The gear jammer sighed. "Frankly, she's better than I deserve, but I'm not looking to settle down. What's a fellow to do?"

"Withdraw from the competition. Or cut her loose. At least be honest with her."

He turned and gestured back at the dormitory. "What you just saw there? That was me being honest. I explained to her about the tournament. To her credit, she says she's willing to fight for my attention." Graham shrugged. "And after a kiss like that, I'm inclined to let her try. I mean, I've kissed a few girls in the park, but—"

"You'd play that sweet girl off against someone else? She doesn't deserve that. She's still hurting from her last relationship."

"I'm not looking to hurt her. I've told her I'm not the man she thinks I am." Graham lifted his hands in surrender. "The problem is, she can't really win. There's a girl over at Madison with fewer inhibitions, if you know what I mean."

For the second time in a week, Red's offer of bare-knuckle boxing lessons sounded appealing. Or his father's false bravado. "Graham, I think the problem is, you're afraid to be the sort of man she needs."

The gear jammer took a final drag on his smoke, the burning embers glowing. "Well, we're all afraid of something, aren't we?" He dropped the cigarette to the ground and crushed it under his heel.

❦

Elsie stifled a sneeze in the dormitory's dank basement, but the large open room was perfect for rehearsals. Spending part of her day off helping the girls get ready for the show was a small price to pay for not acting or singing in it herself. Mary had her Marie Antoinette wig pinned in place, just to give her a sense of the height and weight as she walked. Thankfully, she'd saved the face powder for another day.

Right now, a line of girls were gathered around the piano, belting out the Canyon Camp anthem. One of the best things about the end-of-season show was hearing each of the groups perform their camp song. The savages would all line up and compete against each other for the best—and loudest—rendition. Typically, no one could beat the group from Old Faithful, but the competition for second place was fierce. Canyon had a good chance of besting Mammoth this year since the hotel had stayed closed, but it still depended on each group's talent.

Mary kept one hand on her towering wig as Elsie pinned the sides of Mary's gown. She was such a slim thing; it was hard to make the flowing gown fit her tiny hips.

"You need to hold still, or I'm going to accidentally jab you," Elsie murmured around the pins clamped in her teeth.

"I bet Jean Harlow never has this problem." Mary sniffed. "I read in a magazine that I should drink a milkshake every day to help me develop more curves. Isn't that ridiculous? I'm not sure those are the sort of curves I'm looking for."

"Man on the floor." A booming voice rang out, accompanied by squeals and giggles.

"Lucky you're decent." Elsie stood, patting the back of the dress. "I think that will hold, but I don't recommend sitting or you might find a pin in your derriere."

Mary turned in front of the long mirror. "It's perfect. You're a godsend, Elsie."

"We've always thought so." Elsie's father's voice carried from the doorway.

"Papa!" Elsie turned, her breath catching. "What are you doing here? Is Mama all right?"

He chuckled, coming up to give Elsie a kiss on her cheek. "Can't a father come visit his daughter without there being an emergency?"

"Of course you can." She threw her arms around him, breathing in his usual smell of peppermint and pine trees. "I'm so glad to see you."

"Your mother sends her love. And her brownies. She's been baking. I've got them out in the truck."

"Baking?" Mary spun around, her wig slipping sideways. "She must be feeling better."

"You know my girls. They thrive in the summer sun." He tweaked Elsie's cheek. "It's good to see you both doing so well." He eyed Mary. "Even if your fashion choices are a little unusual."

"It's for the follies." Elsie picked up her sewing basket. "Mary and some of the other girls are acting out a skit based on French history."

His brow creased. "No guillotines, I hope."

Mary gave a coy smile. "You'll have to come to find out."

"Well, right now I'm headed up to visit the CCC crew on Washburn. I thought I'd ask my girl if she would like to take a ride." He winked at Elsie. "You can be my assistant, like old times."

Elsie's heart lifted. "I'd love to. But I promised to help—"

"Oh, go ahead." Mary waved a hand. "We'll finish the costumes tonight. We need to focus on the song and dance bits anyway. I wish I could come with you. I'd love to see Red and the boys at work."

Elsie closed her sewing box. "Then I guess I'm free after all." It had been ages since she'd been anywhere with her father, and seeing her students—and Nate, of course—at work would be a thrill. "Are you sure they won't mind my intrusion?"

"Mind? I'd say they'd probably welcome it. There's nothing like having a pretty gal to show off for. We'll probably get twice as much work out of them."

"Well, I don't know about that, but I'm happy to go along. I've heard so much about what they're doing; it will be nice to see their progress in person."

Elsie hurried upstairs to change into sturdy walking boots and grab a canteen, then met her father in front of the dormitory. Minutes later they were in the truck headed north on the Grand Loop Road.

She leaned against the door so she could study her father's profile. He looked younger and happier than he had in years. Mother's recovery must have taken a weight off his shoulders. "I'm so glad you came. Don't let me forget, before you leave tonight, I'd like to give you my savings. Could you put it in the bank for me?"

"Got enough for school now?"

She couldn't resist the smile that surged up from inside. "Thanks to your encouragement, yes."

"Your mother and I are so proud. You know that, right?" He reached over and patted her leg. "God hasn't given you an easy path to walk, but you've taken every step with your head held high."

"There may still be twists and turns ahead, I imagine."

He chuckled. "You can count on it."

They pulled up to the trailhead and parked next to the two CCC vehicles. The yellow trucks with the letters on the side brought back memories of her trip to Old Faithful with the boys. She needed to arrange another outing before summer was out. It would be tough to get an additional Saturday off, but maybe they could do an evening jaunt to the Firehole River.

She climbed out and waited as her father got his pack settled over his shoulders. In the distance, an automobile sat beside the highway, parked in the shade of the trees. Two figures were inside. "Do you think they have a flat tire?"

Her father came up beside her. "I noticed the car on the way in. A young couple . . ." He cleared his throat. "Probably doing what couples do—canoodling or spooning, or whatever you young folks call it these days. They're not waving to us, so I don't expect they're looking for company."

"Papa!" Elsie laughed. "Canoodling? Honestly." She glanced back toward the vehicle. It did seem familiar. Was it the little Buick coupe that belonged to Charlie, the desk clerk at Canyon? He sometimes loaned it to the other boys for dates. Perhaps her father was right.

"If it's still there when we're done, I'll go talk to them."

They turned toward the mountain trail and followed the tracks of the men deep into the forest. Even in the cool shade of the trees, a sweat broke out across Elsie's forehead within minutes. She pulled off her beret to fan herself and touched her other hand to her neck. The pain always crept in as the weather grew warmer. The doctor didn't seem to believe that her scars could still ache after more than ten years, but then, he didn't have to live with them.

Up ahead, the sounds of axes and saws rang out between the trees, giving them a location to shoot for.

He looked over his shoulder at her. "I had my doubts about this crew when they first arrived, but they've made good progress. Do you remember how skinny and scared they all looked when they arrived in Gardiner?"

She did remember. Their clothes had been so loose, the men looked like scarecrows without stuffing.

As she and Papa crested the rise, she spotted small groups of workers clustered around trees in the distance. The fellows looked as strong and rugged as any ranger crew. She hadn't really noticed the progression, but her father was right. They'd filled out, their muscled arms and backs bronzed by the Wyoming sunshine. In fact, muscled arms and backs was all she could see right now. Most of the men worked bare chested, sweat making their tanned skin gleam as they wielded crosscuts and axes.

Several of the crew waved when they spotted her father, their big smiles welcoming. Would Teddy have received such a greeting? Red trotted over. "Ranger Brookes, good to see you." He nodded to Elsie. "Miss Brookes."

Her father tipped back his hat, his attention roaming the nearby forest. "You men are doing great work. It won't be long until this area starts seeing snow, then we'll have to button it up for the year."

"Snow?" Red pulled off his hat and ran an arm across his forehead. "It's sure not feeling like winter now."

"It will; you watch. One day will be hot, and then the next—snowflakes. Winter seems to come out of nowhere sometimes."

Elsie fingered her collar, wishing she could unbutton it a notch and let in a little air. "Snow sounds pretty good about now."

"Where's your foreman?" her father asked.

Red turned and pointed up the steep bank. "Nate's scouting up the slope a ways. He found a new stand of beetle-infested trees last week, so he's up there marking them."

"That boy has the best eye for spotting diseased trees I've seen in a decade." Father hooked his thumbs in his belt loops. "I wish we could keep him on. He's a natural forester. If he had some schooling, he'd make a fine entomologist."

Elsie stepped into the shade and lifted a hand to shield her eyes as she searched the woods for Nate's form.

Red gestured to a group of men working on a tree just beyond them. "Ranger Brookes, would you mind taking a look at one of the saws? I think it might need a new handle."

Her father followed him, but Elsie wandered off in the direction Red had pointed earlier. Maybe she could catch a glimpse of her fella at work. She hadn't gone far before she spotted Nate scribbling on a clipboard. He tipped his head back and pressed field glasses to his eyes. Her father was right, Nate looked every bit the forester.

"Who would have thought some guy from Brooklyn would look so at home in the woods?" she called out to him.

He grinned, then clamped the clipboard under his elbow and made his way over to her. "What in the world are you doing here?"

"I'm here with my father. We're checking up on you, you know."

Nate darted a glance around the forest, then reached for Elsie and pulled her in for a quick kiss. "I'm a sweaty mess—I hope you don't mind."

"You smell like sawdust and pinesap." She kissed him a second time, lingering for a moment. Good thing he'd kept on his uniform shirt, because standing this close with him bare chested might have been more than she could handle. "Like sawdust and hard work." She stepped back, swaying a little as he released his grip on her waist.

He squinted at her. "You okay?"

"Yeah, it's just so warm." She fanned her face with her hands. He probably thought she was swooning after the kiss. Maybe she was.

Nate took her hand, stretching out her arm. "You're wearing long sleeves. Can't you roll them up?"

"I don't like anyone to see, you know that." She tugged her hand away.

"They're trees, Elsie. And me. Your secret's safe."

A fluttering sensation took up residence in her stomach. "I'll be fine. It's better if I don't get sunshine on my skin, anyway."

"Here." He fanned the clipboard near her face.

"Ah, that's nice." After a moment she said, "What's this?" She took the clipboard and studied the tablet covered with rough maps and sketches of trees.

"I'm mapping the stand of trees, marking the sick ones. I blaze them with a hatchet, then next year's crew will come finish what we've started. They're going to bring in twice as many CCCs, plus a big group of local men—see if they can't get the upper hand in this battle."

"Next year's crew," she repeated the hopeful words. "Will you be back?"

His gaze faltered. "I'm only signed on for the one year. I'm not sure how it works, but I suspect that's all we get."

She latched onto his arm, pulling him close to her side. "Don't say that." She'd known this all along, but with each day her heart's cry grew stronger. "If you can't come back as a CCC, we'll have to get you hired on as a savage."

Nate made a face. "Can you really see me as a waiter or a busboy? Carrying luggage for the dudes? Besides, they're all college students, except for Graham."

"It just feels so wrong." She hated the sudden whine in her voice. Whenever the physical pain kicked in, her emotions seemed to tumble into disarray as well. *God, surely You brought us together.* "It can't be the Father's plan for us to just go our separate ways."

"I don't know about God, but that seems to be Uncle Sam's plan." He lowered his face to the top of her head. "But maybe it doesn't have to be."

"What do you mean?"

He breathed out a long exhale, ruffling her hair with his breath. "I don't know, but I'll think of something. I'm not ready to lose you yet."

❦

Nate squeezed Elsie tight for a quick moment, then released her. Her skin felt too warm. "Let's get you into the shade." He led her a few steps to the trunk of a pine tree. After their brief conversation, she was fighting tears. The sight tore at him.

"The Father's plan?" He'd believed in an all-powerful God, but he struggled to trust quite the way Elsie seemed to. A loving father wouldn't leave capable men to beg for a dime on the street in order to feed their children. He wouldn't let a family's hope be gunned down in a dark alley. Or burden Elsie with the scars of the past.

But somehow, in spite of heartache, she clung to faith. Nate glanced up toward the treetops, the blue sky showing in cracks between the greenery. Could he find that strength? *Help us out here, Lord. Help me find some way to stay in her life.*

He reached into his pocket for a distraction. "I . . . I got another letter from home. Do you mind . . . ?" But it wasn't there. He patted his other pockets.

"I'd be honored, Nate."

"I must have left it in my bag in the truck." He grabbed one of her hands. "Can you wait? I'll run."

"It took us forty minutes to climb up here."

"I know a shortcut. Trust me. I practically know each of these trees by name now. Wait here—or better yet, go back to the main work site. It's shadier there. I'll come find you."

She smiled. "All right. But then we'll just have to sneak off again."

He couldn't fight the grin. She was so beautiful—it bowled him over. "I'll sneak off with you anytime." He planted a kiss on her cheek.

He jogged toward the highway, hopping logs and pushing through brush like a squirrel. Maybe it was the need for action in the face of their mutual sadness, but the run made his heart lighter. The clearing he saw ahead must be the roadway, so he veered left to cut over to where the trucks were parked.

The thicket in front of him exploded into motion, a deer launching outward and bolting away.

Nate slid on one heel, landing in the dirt with a thud, his heart hammering in his chest. He stayed still as the animal crashed through the woods, springing on all four legs at once, like a kid on a pogo stick. In a flash, it was down the slope and across the highway.

That could have been a bear. He pushed up on one rubbery knee, smears of dirt caking the side of his work jeans. A mistake like that could get him sent home in pieces. A couple of the guys had surprised a bear in the woods near camp and thankfully lived to tell the tale. In another instance, Moretti had nearly stumbled into a hidden hot spring while hiking around Yellowstone Lake. This place deserved a little more caution than he was giving it.

He untied his bandanna and mopped his face, the heat adding to his shakiness. It's little wonder Elsie was feeling woozy, what with her shirt buttoned clear to her wrists and throat. He'd rolled his up past his elbows, while the men wielding the tools had stripped their shirts clean off. He'd been told

Yellowstone's temperatures never rose above eighty degrees, but someone had forgotten to inform the sun of that fact.

The wind was picking up, so hopefully that would bring some cooler temperatures. Maybe it would blow in another storm. *One with rain this time.*

An odd smell wafted in on the breeze, and Nate lifted his head. It smelled like fuel . . . and smoke.

All thoughts of bears fled his mind as he once again raced toward the highway. He'd be able to see the trucks in a few more—

Whoosh. The sound cut through the quiet afternoon, and Nate stumbled to a stop, struggling against his forward momentum. A curtain of fire covered the small parking area ahead, the side of the truck barely visible through the flames. Blazing tongues whipped upward, the nearby brush igniting within seconds. *The trucks.*

He moved two steps forward before realizing the wind was driving the flame his direction. Nate lifted a hand to shield his face as the heat and smoke reached him. His thoughts traveled back to that first wildfire he'd faced back in May. Vaughn had warned them fire could rip through a forest faster than a man could escape—especially when it moved uphill. And right now, the forest was drier than the bottom of a cracker barrel.

Nate jerked around and surged up the mountainside at a dead run. Elsie was up there—his crew, and Ranger Brookes too. The blaze was not going to beat him there.

Thirty-One

Elsie followed the sounds of chopping and sawing back to the work site. Her father was standing in a small circle of men, turning over a cross-cut saw in his hands and pointing at something along the toothed edge. The crew's respect for him was obvious in each of the men's faces.

A wisp of gray rose from the slope below, climbing into the air like a finger pointing at the cloudless sky. Even in the warm air, a chill seeped through her. The thin column floated on the breeze, growing larger by the second.

Elsie turned toward the men. "Is that smoke?"

Heads jerked up, including her father's. He stepped out of the circle, lifting a hand to shade his eyes.

Nate came loping up the hill, his chest heaving. "One of the trucks—on fire!" His voice hitched, the effort it had taken to run up the steep side of Washburn evident in every word.

The crew swarmed toward him, but Nate waved his arms. "No, don't. It's coming this way." He stopped and bent over, trying to catch his breath. After a moment, he straightened. "The flames have caught the underbrush; it's heading uphill."

Elsie's knees grew weak. More fire. Would she ever escape it?

Her father reached Nate in a few strides. "The trucks—were they engulfed? Were all the vehicles burning?"

"I couldn't tell, sir. I saw the one go up, though. It was a fireball. You could feel it." He ran an arm across his face, his glance darting up toward Elsie. "If the others aren't burning, they will be within minutes."

Elsie wrapped her arms around herself. She'd heard stories of Yellowstone fires—even seen them from a distance. But she'd never been face to face with one before.

The smoke thickened with each passing moment, billowing into the sky and curling around itself. She couldn't see the flames, hidden below in the tree cover. But how long would it take for the fire to reach them? With the speed Nate had apparently run, he must have sensed hellfire nipping his heels.

She wanted to rush over and throw herself into his arms, but she couldn't move. Her legs were locked in place.

Her father turned and surveyed the surrounding landscape. He took off his hat and ran a quick hand through his graying hair. "All right, men. We're going to fall back—or rather *along*—the mountain. Fire surges uphill, blown by updrafts and embers. We can't outclimb it, so resist the urge to go up. We'll head south, toward Sulphur Creek, and try to make it around the worst of it."

Elsie stood in place, a tremor taking up residence deep within. Would the fire overtake them? Many of the trees were already dying from beetle damage, and even the healthy ones were dry from a summer with less than normal rain. She rubbed her arms, trying to chase away the prickly fingers of dread creeping over her.

Her father reached her first, laying a hand on her shoulder. "It's all right, Elsie. We're just going to swing wide around it. I don't want to take any chances."

She nodded, her throat as dry as the ground at her feet. "I know. I'll keep up."

"I have no doubt." He winked. "You're a ranger's daughter. This land is part of you."

Nate eased in beside her, his breathing still ragged. "Should we take the equipment?"

Her father glanced over at the tools. "Grab your canteens and any small hand tools but leave the saws. We can pick them up and refit them later. We need to be able to move fast."

The men scattered to retrieve what they could, and Nate turned to Elsie. "I'm sorry. This must be about your worst nightmare."

She straightened. "I can make it." She fell in beside him as the men began the scramble south. "Your letters from home?"

He shook his head. "I guess I'll never know."

"Why would the truck catch fire? It doesn't make sense."

Nate shoved some tree branches out of the way, letting her go ahead of him. "I don't know. I feel like flames have been chasing us all summer. This can't be normal."

"Lightning strikes are common in this region. But trash cans and trucks?" She shook her head. "No. I've thought . . ." Her throat clenched, not liking where her mind was traveling.

"What?"

She ran her hands down her sleeves, trying to ignore that the aches in her arms had built into jabs of pain. "At first I thought maybe Graham was involved."

Nate frowned. "Graham? Why?"

"Well, he was at Mammoth that night. And at the Canyon Camp for the talent show." She bit her lip. "And I guess I just associate him with fire, after what happened when we were kids." The words sounded foolish as soon as they left her mouth. "But why would he do that? Why would anyone?"

He slowed his steps for a moment, then pushed forward, hooking his arm under hers and tugging her along. "I spoke with Graham yesterday."

The low tone in his voice sent a quiver through her. "And?"

"He says he explained the game to Rose, and she wants to keep seeing him."

A band tightened around her chest. Rose had been weighed down with sadness since Pete abandoned her. It was like a cloud she couldn't shake off. She seemed to be grasping at Graham's affections without realizing the dead end he represented.

Nate grabbed a branch and pushed it out of her way. "But there's a big difference between being a worm and starting fires."

Elsie tugged at her collar, wooziness creeping over her like a fog. "That's true."

"The fire when you were kids—that was an accident, right?"

She studied his face, particularly the worry lines scoring his forehead. "I was next door when it started. But Graham had been playing with fire-crackers, and he said one went in the window. And when the house caught on fire, he ran."

"Maybe . . ." Nate frowned again. "Maybe seeing you again triggered memories. Something he wanted to relive—or set right—in some twisted way?"

The idea seared through her. "Why would anyone want to relive such a horror?"

The trail had gotten steeper. He jostled his way past a few large rocks, then reached back for her. She took his hand, although she really didn't need to, allowing him to help her over the steep scramble.

The men had gathered up ahead and were staring back the way they'd come. Elsie turned to look and immediately wished she hadn't.

The forest edge was ablaze, flames climbing high into the treetops, sending lodgepole pines up like Roman candles. Usually a fire burned slowly through the undergrowth until it was hot enough to take full trees. This monster seemed to defy the rules. The massive curtain of smoke roiled into the sky. She looked away and tried to quell the panic that rose from deep within her.

Val placed both hands on top of his head. *"Oy vey iz mir."*

Red looked like he was about to be sick. "You can say that again, kid—whatever it means."

Nate gripped a canteen, his knuckles white. "The rangers at Canyon will see the smoke, right?"

Teddy. Her father had said Teddy was coming to Canyon today. A district meeting. "Yes, I imagine so." But what could they do? They'd start fighting it along the highway, but it wouldn't help them here near the ridge-line. The only way out was to hike.

Her father set his jaw. "I thought we could cut around it, but it's spreading fast. We'll have to head over the ridge and meet up with the spur trail. That'll take us back toward Canyon. It's a longer route, but it should be safer. And mostly downhill."

Downhill sounded good about now. Elsie pulled at her collar. She couldn't seem to catch her breath.

"Here." Nate tipped some water from the canteen over his bandanna and handed it to her. "You need to cool yourself off. Your face is beet red."

She pressed it to her cheeks and neck. Her knees wobbled. *Lord, don't let me faint. Not in front of Nate and everyone.* She staggered to a nearby log and sat, lowering her head to her knees.

Nate followed. "Elsie?"

"I'll be all right. Just . . . just need a minute." Spots danced in front of her eyes. Was it fear or the heat? Or some dreadful combination of the two?

Val joined them. "Anything I can do?"

"I think we're going to need to give Elsie a hand." Nate crouched beside her. "We can't stay, Elsie. We have to keep moving."

Didn't he know if she kept moving, everything was going to go black? She hid her face in the wet folds of the bandanna and nodded, hoping to buy herself a minute.

It didn't work. Nate hooked an arm under her elbow and lifted her to her feet. Val grabbed the other arm.

Her father's voice cut through the smoke clouding her thoughts. "Elsie? What's wrong?"

She dropped her hands and forced her eyes open. Father's face seemed fuzzy in her vision, until she managed to blink a few times. When had her ears started buzzing? "I'm all right. Just . . . overly warm."

Nate fiddled with the buttons on her cuffs, freeing her wrists and pushing the sleeves up above her elbows. He poured water into his hands and splashed it onto her arms and neck.

Val uncorked his canteen and pressed it to her lips. "Drink." His young voice trembled. He said nothing about the scars, but his eyes had darted to them and then away.

Her spirits shrank from the men's attention. She swallowed a couple of mouthfuls of water then pushed away the canteen. "Just let me get a breath of air."

Her father and Val eased back out of her circle of vision, but she could still feel Nate's steady arm under hers.

"We need to move, college girl," he murmured low, into her ear. "Maybe not so fast, but we've got to keep going."

She nodded and yanked at her collar, unfastening the snaps that held it closed. What did it matter now? She already looked a fool.

"Here." He tucked the wet cloth in around her neck, the coolness seeping into her skin like a gentle kiss.

"That's good. Thanks."

She followed the group through the woods, Val and Nate supporting some of her weight as she kept her feet moving forward.

After another twenty minutes of walking, they started descending the hill at an angle, cutting over into the Sulphur Creek drainage. With the easier path, she released Val's arm and waved him away. Leaning on Nate, however, was as much by choice as by necessity. As her mind cleared, the touch of his hand became a lifeline out of the clutching fear that seemed to dog her steps. "Are we keeping away from it?" Her mouth tasted like ash.

Nate checked over his shoulder. "Yes. It's still climbing the hill, but it's mostly staying to the north. I think we'll meet up with the road soon. Then we can hoof it back to camp." A frown flitted across his already grim face. "Or flag down a vehicle."

"I can't believe your trucks are gone."

"And your father's too, I imagine."

She hadn't thought about that, but he was right. "And he drove his own today. Not a park truck."

The crew walked in relative silence, without their usual joking and banter. Were they thinking of the stand of trees they'd been working so hard to save? Or were they still picturing what would happen if the fire caught them?

A sudden thought washed over her, and she couldn't help but tighten her grip on Nate's arm. "This fire is heading toward Canyon, isn't it?"

He nodded. "It is."

Nate never thought he'd be so glad to see Ranger Vaughn. But as the CCC crew straggled into the Canyon area, the sight of several rangers jogging toward them brought him a rush of relief.

Vaughn's face was grim as he approached Elsie's father. "Thank goodness. We didn't know what had happened to you. Did you get everyone?" His eyes widened. "Elsie, I didn't even know you were out there."

She maintained her grip on Nate's arm. "I'm fine, Teddy. We all are."

"The whole crew is accounted for," Ranger Brookes answered. "What's the situation?"

Vaughn's eyes stayed on Elsie for a long moment before refocusing on Brookes. "It looks like it started at the highway and spread from there."

Nate cleared his throat. "It started with one of our trucks, from what I saw."

"*Your* truck?"

"Vaughn." Elsie's father cut him off. "What's the situation here at Canyon? Are the facilities evacuated?"

"Mostly, yes. We're getting the last of the visitors loaded onto buses and taken out to either Norris or Lake. The savages are saving what they can, but we'll get them out next."

"And fire crews?"

He glanced over Ranger Brooke's shoulder, his focus once again zeroing in on Nate. "We've called in the CCC crew from Old Faithful. The men from Mammoth are heading south. I'd like to put this group in service too."

Nate's stomach dropped. Go back up there? It was about the last thing any of his men would want to do right now. "Sir—"

Ranger Brookes lifted a hand. "In a moment." He turned back to Vaughn. "We'll take volunteers. These men have already been out all day, and the fire's bearing down on their camp as well." He turned to Nate. "How many men did you leave in camp this morning?"

"Thirty or so."

Vaughn nodded. "I already have them assisting with the evacuation."

"Good." Brookes gestured to the men. "You fellows go back to camp and load up everything you can—tools and supplies. Leave the tents. Grab your personal belongings and those of the other men. Haul everything to the Old Faithful camp for now, then report back. We might need you."

Nate turned to the crew. "We've got two trucks left. Let's load 'em up."

Vaughn cleared his throat. "This group trained for fire duty, Ranger Brookes, and they know this area."

Nate set his jaw. "I volunteer."

Elsie's hand touched his back, but he kept his eyes fixed on the rangers. He couldn't bear to look in her eyes right now, but this time Vaughn was right.

Red stepped forward. "Same here. And some of the other fellows will too, I'm sure. You don't need us all to clear the camp."

Nate turned to his friend. "We need you driving one of those trucks, Red. We've only got a couple of men who know how to handle them."

The smaller man hesitated, then nodded. "All right. I'll get Moretti in the other one. He's a bit of a lead foot, but that might be useful today." He shot a glance at Elsie. "You want to come with us, Miss Brookes?"

Ranger Vaughn gestured to a yellow bus pulling up. "Graham's here now. She can ride with the other savages."

"What about my things?" Elsie's voice sounded softly behind Nate. "I've got some items in my room I don't want to lose."

Her tuition money. The thought settled in Nate's gut. "I'll go."

Vaughn pushed his hat back. "Wouldn't Mary have packed for you?"

"I need to be sure."

Nate caught her hand and squeezed it. "I can double-check for you, but you should leave with Graham." He wanted her safe. Nothing else mattered.

Vaughn grunted. "I'll go. I know which room is hers."

"Stop it, both of you. I won't be five minutes." She scowled at them.

Despite her show of confidence, Nate could feel her fingers tremble in his grip.

She turned to face Red. "You can wait for me?"

"Sure. It'll take time to load up the trucks, anyway."

Nate released her hand. "Elsie, hurry. Please. I need to know you're away from here."

Her eyes locked on his, as intense as he'd ever seen them. "I hate the idea of you going back up there; I hope you know that."

"I do. But I'll be careful. I promise."

"Elsie." Graham jumped out of the bus, leaving the engine running. "Have you seen Rose?"

"No. Why? Isn't she with Mary?"

He darted a glance around the parking area. "I haven't seen her since we went for a drive earlier today."

"I'll check the dormitory. She probably went out on one of the other buses."

He ran a hand along his shirt front. "You're probably right. If you see her, tell her . . . tell Rose I'm sorry."

Thirty-Two

Elsie had arrived at her room to find it emptied. Mary had been thorough about going through every drawer and bookshelf, even rescuing the men's compositions. The only item left behind was a note saying that she and Rose were evacuating.

It had been difficult to leave Canyon knowing that Nate and her father—and Teddy, too—would still be in harm's way.

Graham's message about Rose had set the hair prickling on her scalp, and she couldn't help wondering about it on the long truck ride to Old Faithful Inn.

Entering the timbered lobby was like stepping into a friend's embrace, but Elsie didn't have time to linger and appreciate its warmth. Instead she scanned the milling crowd of concerned tourists and staff for familiar faces.

Rose had worked her first summer as an ice-cream girl at the Inn, so maybe she'd taken advantage of the strange turn of events to stop in and say hello to old friends.

Elsie tipped her head back as she walked to the center of the massive lobby. As always, her eyes were drawn to the remarkable open space extending up to the rafters. The architect had designed it to resemble an indoor lodgepole forest, but Elsie always felt more like she'd stepped inside the belly of a whale and was somehow gazing at its massive rib cage all about her. From her vantage point she could see level after level of pine stairways, connected by balconies and guarded by twisted railings. Visitors peered down from the upper levels with as much curiosity as those who gazed up. Even the windows were scattered in odd places, without the typical symmetry one expected in a building of this caliber. The Inn, crowded with evacuees, felt like a living, breathing creature.

Elsie didn't find Rose in the ice cream shop or the restaurant. She scaled the stairs and catwalks, searching every alcove until she finally reached the landing below the tree house. The quirky little structure perched near the rafters must have been the fulfillment of one of the architect's childhood fantasies.

She gripped the burled limb railing as she climbed the last flights of steps and tried to ignore the stitch in her side. Her legs trembled after the long day of hiking. When she reached the top, she found Rose sitting on the floor of the framed-in platform, her back pressed against the side, legs tucked under her. She barely glanced at Elsie, her attention sagging back to the floorboards.

Elsie didn't allow herself to look over the side. She couldn't bear to think about all the empty space below them. She kneeled beside her friend, thankful the short wall blocked the dizzying view. "Rose, what are you doing?"

Her friend lowered her head to her knees. "I just needed to get my thoughts together."

"I saw Graham."

Rose turned away. "We're finished. I suppose you're glad to hear that."

Graham's words echoed in her mind. *"Tell Rose I'm sorry"*

Elsie scooted closer to Rose and wove a hand around her arm. "It doesn't matter what I think."

"It does." Rose's face crumpled. "But I wouldn't listen to you. I wasted the whole summer chasing a man who didn't care a thing about me. What's wrong with me? Why do I keep thinking I can live the fairy tale?"

"Nothing's wrong. You've been sad, and you were looking for something—or someone—to ease the sorrow. That's not unusual."

"But I just bought myself more pain. And I've ruined everything, Elsie."

Elsie brushed the hair from Rose's eyes, tucking a limp curl behind her ear. "I think Graham has to take some of the blame here too."

Tears slid down Rose's face, and she wiped at them with the heel of her hand. "Today is all on me. *All* of it, Elsie." She squeezed the sides of her head with her hands and moaned. "My head hurts from so much crying. I feel like that's all I've done this summer."

"Let's go find Mary and get some cake." Elsie helped Rose to her feet. "That will help."

"Will it?" Rose sighed, brushing off the back of her skirt. "Because I'm not sure anything can help at this point."

"Mary says cake always helps. Cake and friends."

"I suppose." Rose's voice had never sounded so empty.

Elsie gripped her friend's arm as they descended the winding staircases. As distraught as Rose was, leaving her to cry up here alone like a princess in her tower was not an option.

Nate walked along the deserted roadway near Mount Washburn, the smell of soggy ashes overwhelming his senses. Somewhere up ahead were the burned-out trucks. Wiping his face with a damp neckerchief, he tried not to think of how just eight days ago he'd pressed it to Elsie's flushed cheeks. He'd like to think it still smelled of her, but in reality, it reeked of smoke, sweat, and dirt. Just like the rest of him.

It had taken a week to squelch the fire, but most of the thanks went to the weather rather than Nate's crew. The light snow they'd received the past two nights had saved them. Even though the morning sun melted it away in short order, the cooler temperatures and moisture had sapped the fire's strength enough for them to gain the upper hand. Remarkably, no damage was done to the Canyon Hotel or any of the surrounding structures. Even the camp was untouched, except for the fact that it remained a half-dismantled mess.

Part of his company was bunking at Old Faithful, but the fire crew was lodged in a temporary camp at Roosevelt. With the hours they'd been keeping, he hadn't been able to see Elsie since the fire broke out. That probably explained the hollow ache in the center of his chest. In another week, his college girl would slip out of his life for good.

"I'll think of something." His words to her seemed no better than an empty promise, but one he'd repeated to himself every day they'd been apart.

The trouble was, he hadn't come up with any answers. For a brief moment he'd considered getting down on one knee and begging her to come back to Brooklyn as his wife. The daydream only lasted a minute or two before reality crashed in.

Elsie *had* to follow her dream to university. He refused to stand in the way of everything she could accomplish. Just because he wasn't school material didn't mean he would ever consider taking it from her. If anything, it made her goals all the more precious to him. In some small way, it was as if a part of him were going too.

They still hadn't heard where the remaining CCC men would be restationed for the next six months. They were taking bets on locations, with the top two choices being Arizona and California. At least they'd be someplace warm. As much as he missed his family, he wouldn't mind skipping out on a gray New York winter.

Nate shifted the Pulaski ax to his other shoulder and continued down the road. Most of the crew had returned to camp for the night, but a small group of them had decided to mop up along the highway. The rangers hoped to open the route in the morning, and they wanted to make sure everything was safe.

Nate picked up his pace as he spotted the burned-out hulks in the distance. The blackened metal frames of the two CCC trucks sent a tremor through his gut. Seeing that first truck erupt into flames would be seared into his memory for life, complete with the knowledge that he was the only thing that stood between that fire and his crew—plus the woman he loved. His pulse quickened at the reminder.

The dirt road crunched under his feet, pretty much the only sound in the bare, blackened forest. The sight nearly brought Nate to his knees. He'd spent most of the summer walking these woods with an eye toward protecting these trees and restoring the health of Yellowstone's forest. All that work, gone.

But it would recover. Just yesterday, Ranger Brookes had handed him a charred pine cone.

Nate had turned it over in his hand, the soot leaving stains on his already dirty skin. "What's this?"

"Those pines you've been working to save. They're all in there." The man had tapped the cone in his hand. "Normally that cone is so gummed up with resin and sap that the seeds sit dormant. Nothing happens. But see how it's opened up?"

Nate rolled it between his fingers. "The fire doesn't kill the seeds?"

"It sets them free," the ranger said. "Most of us ask God for an easy life. We even ask for it for our children. But sometimes it takes a little heat to break loose the seeds He's planted deep inside us. Seeds we probably didn't even know were there."

The heat of this fire had been incredible. Nate stopped in front of the remains of the two CCC trucks, their frames covered in soot and ash. Ranger Brookes's vehicle sat just to the right of them.

Not seeing Elsie this week had left a hole in his life, but as he stared at the devastation, he was glad she'd stayed well out of harm's way. Her father said she'd found a room in one of the dormitories at Old Faithful for the time being, but would return to Mammoth before leaving for school. Hopefully he would get a chance to say goodbye.

The thought of a goodbye left him as dry and lonely as the charred forest.

His foot brushed against something solid in the ash beside the first truck. He kicked it loose. A piece of metal from the vehicle? It tumbled through the dirt, its oblong form too neat for scrap. Nate bent down and picked it up.

He turned it over. It looked like a lighter. Using the tail of his shirt, he wiped it off, the grime settling into the letters formed by an engraver's tool. *Wonderland*.

Recognition sent a sour taste clambering into the back of Nate's throat, choking him. Three ruined vehicles, acres of blackened forest, the danger to Canyon and those he loved—could it all come to this? He'd held this very lighter in his hands before. Teddy Vaughn had placed it there. The same man who had tried to pound him into the ground.

A truck rolled to a stop on the road behind him. "Hey, Nate. You ready to head back?"

Nate ran his thumb over the filthy object. "Red, you good with making a stop first? We need to talk to a ranger."

Nate tossed the lighter across the map-strewn table at Roosevelt Lodge, and it slid to a stop in front of Teddy Vaughn. "Care to explain this?"

Vaughn glanced up, dark circles under his eyes. He'd put in as much work as any of them, maybe more. And he looked it. He reached over and picked up the object. He frowned. "Where did you find this?"

Nate claimed a chair across from him. "I think you know the answer to that."

Red perched on the edge of the tabletop. "Summer a little too slow for you? Maybe you needed some excitement?" He folded both arms across his chest. "Or were you trying to get back at Webber for stealing your girl?"

The ranger leaned forward and looked each of them in the eye, first Nate, then Red. "I could have had Webber sent home after our fistfight in the woods. I kept my mouth shut about that, didn't I?"

Nate matched his posture. "This lighter was beside our burned-out trucks. I just picked it up."

Vaughn glanced down, rubbing his thumb over the silver case. He didn't respond.

The silence didn't sit well with Nate. "I saw the truck go up, Vaughn. I thought maybe something was wrong with the engine, but it had been sitting for hours. It should have been good and cold." He gripped the table. "Somebody lit that fire on purpose. Apparently they used *your* lighter. The same one you used when we did the slash burn last month."

The ranger locked onto him with his deep-set eyes. "You're suggesting I did this? I've been working the fire for the past week. You've seen me out there cutting firebreaks and setting backfires. If I wanted the park to burn, why wouldn't I just sit back and let it happen?"

"Elsie told me you wanted to be a firefighter but became a ranger instead. Maybe you wanted the thrill of saving the park."

He tapped the lighter against the table. "She told you that? I'm surprised she talks about me at all. She didn't seem to care much."

Nate paused. The man's mournful expression took him off guard. He'd expected anger, not resignation and regret. "So you thought you'd trap her in a burning forest and then—what? Rush in to the rescue?"

He locked gazes with Nate. "I didn't even know she was out there. What was she doing up there, anyway? Kissing more CCC men?"

Nate stood sharply, sending his chair skidding back.

Red grabbed his wrist. "Take it easy."

Vaughn got to his feet slowly, as if the weight of the past eight days hung on his shoulders. "There's one big hole in your theory, Webber."

Nate unclenched his jaw long enough to respond. "What's that?"

The ranger dug into his pocket and pulled something out. With a grimace, he dropped the shiny object onto the table. "My lighter's right here."

Thirty-Three

Elsie sorted through her box of belongings wedged in the corner of their cramped dormitory room. Those intermediate readers had to be in there somewhere, and searching for them was better than sitting here feeling anxious about the start of college rushing toward her. She'd eagerly anticipated this for most of her life, and now that the opportunity was about to become reality, she wasn't sure how to feel. She seemed to be alternating between fear, excitement, sadness, and uncertainty—with a few other emotions thrown in for good measure.

Mary turned from the window, and she glanced at Rose, curled up on the nearby cot. "Her sleeping pattern has been so odd since we arrived," she whispered. "She's restless—up multiple times during the night—then naps for hours during the day. It's not healthy."

Elsie pulled out a handful of books and stacked them on the low table. She wanted to leave those readers for Nate. "She's sad. It's eating away at her."

"It's been a week—well, most of the summer, if you think about it. How long will she mope?"

"As long as she needs to, I guess." Elsie kept her voice low and glanced over at their friend. Rose had one more year of college, but she attended a different school. At least Elsie would have Mary for company.

Mary set her teacup on the table, picked up one of the books, and thumbed through it. "Speaking of sadness, do you think we'll get to say goodbye to the boys?"

"It sounds like we might be doing the follies after all, even with everything that's happened. They'd come for that, wouldn't they?"

"I hope so. Red was going to sing. I suppose that might be the best way to wrap up the summer. All of us together in one place."

The thought sent a rush of warmth through Elsie. On impulse, she grabbed her friend's hand and squeezed it. "Even with the fire and how it will be hard to say goodbye to them—it's been a good summer, hasn't it?"

Mary returned the squeeze, eyes shining. "The best."

Nate sank into the chair, staring at the two lighters sitting side by side—one shiny and one blackened. "But it's engraved. I saw it." He picked up the gleaming one.

"They're both engraved." Vaughn laid his hands on the table. "I purchased them both."

Red frowned. "So it *is* yours, you're saying?"

"It was a gift."

Nate turned the charred one over for comparison. They matched on the front, but the opposite side held a slightly different design. The silver one had a pine cone. The dirty one, a flower. He ran his fingertip over the dainty design. Feminine. "You bought it for Elsie."

"Back when I was certain she would return my affections."

Red took the shiny one from Nate's hand. "What was it doing in the road?"

"Did she return it to you?" Nate studied the man's face.

Vaughn shook his head, not meeting Nate's eyes.

Why would Elsie carry a lighter? She was deathly afraid of flame. Nate rolled it between his fingers, searching his mind for answers, but coming up empty.

"I don't get it." Red frowned. "If it was hers, what was it doing out there on Mount Washburn?"

Nate ran his hand over the back of his neck, his skin prickling. He could feel the tension rolling off Vaughn.

"I hate to point this out." The ranger folded his arms. "But she was at Mammoth when that fire broke out."

Red jerked his head up.

The room seemed to still around them. Nate could almost hear his heartbeat in his ears. "I don't like what you're implying."

"She was at the mess hall too," Red said.

Nate sat completely still, staring at the table. Elsie, the firebug? It wasn't possible. She could hardly look at a campfire, much less start one. And why would she put herself at risk that way, especially considering what she'd endured in her childhood? "What about the one in May, over by Madison? She wasn't anywhere near there."

Vaughn shook his head. "That was caused by a road crew working nearby. It wasn't arson."

Arson. Such a harsh word. It couldn't apply to Elsie, his college girl. The one already marked by flames, with her whole life ahead of her. What would happen if the park service investigated her for this? What would happen to her father?

Nate couldn't bear to think about it.

Vaughn let out a long breath. "Maybe we should talk to her cousin.

She claimed he started the fire they survived as kids. Maybe she was more involved than she lets on. She's always seemed strangely reclusive about those scars of hers. That could be guilt."

"No." Nate slapped the lighter on the table. "No, she didn't start that one. Or any of the others, for that matter. It's not possible. She was up in the woods with us when the last one flared up."

"We should still look into it. If she's lighting fires, she's putting everyone at risk."

Nate pushed back the chair and stood. "She's not responsible."

"How can you be sure?"

"Because I know her heart," Nate said, as he strode from the room.

He scrambled into the truck. He needed to talk to Elsie before Vaughn got the chance.

Nate struggled with the shift lever, shoving it into position like Red had showed him a few weeks ago. He hadn't asked permission to take the CCC truck, but in the heat of the moment, he didn't much care either. Whatever the consequences, he had to speak to Elsie.

He kept replaying the conversation in his mind. If the lighter was Elsie's, why was it sitting by the burned-out truck? Had she dropped it?

She and her father had arrived not long before Nate discovered the fire. He tried to picture a situation where she could have lit the fire, then calmly hiked up the mountainside. The idea was laughable.

Now Vaughn as the arsonist—*that* he could picture. But was it simply because Nate didn't like the man? Because he'd given Elsie expensive gifts? A lighter—what sort of man gave a woman a gift like that?

The truck jerked with Nate's inexperience.

Why hadn't she returned the blamed thing?

He chewed through and disposed of one scenario after another as he bumped down the road toward Old Faithful. He couldn't completely rule her out in either the Mammoth or Canyon Camp fires either. But his heart refused to accept the possibility that she was involved.

Nate slammed his palm against the steering wheel. This was all going so wrong. They'd had a blissful couple of weeks trying to ignore the fact their time together was short, but he hadn't anticipated losing eight precious days to this blasted fire. And now he had to face her with an accusation? It's not how this summer was supposed to end.

He'd dreamed of stolen moments, walks through the woods, evening filmstrips, and that one last talent show. A few more weeks—that's all it would take.

Take for what?

He hadn't really thought it through, but somewhere in his heart he'd already begun making plans. Two weeks to solidify their love. To win her so completely that she'd promise herself to him, even though she'd be away at school. Or to convince himself to quit the 3Cs and follow her to that campus. He couldn't attend, but surely he could find some kind of work. Or maybe the chief ranger would hire him on here, and he could wait. Wait for what? For her to return?

An ache burrowed through his chest. There had to be a way to make this work. Because he'd changed. This place had changed him. And Elsie? She'd transformed him.

Nate Webber from Brooklyn was a miserable failure who couldn't read, couldn't hold a job, and couldn't even protect his younger brother from falling into a life of crime.

But Nate Webber of Yellowstone? He was a man with a future, and it included Elsie Brookes.

Nate took a long breath, the pine-scented mountain air mixing with the odor of lingering smoke. How quickly this place had become a part of him and how much he would miss it. He could almost feel Elsie's arms slipping around his waist, tugging him close. No matter what happened, no one could take these memories from him.

God, if You're listening—I need a miracle.

He stretched, the muscles in his back aching after driving for an hour. Spindly pines lined the road. This stand looked healthy. At least they hadn't all succumbed to the fire. Nate reached into his pocket and pulled out the pine cone he'd picked up at Roosevelt and squeezed it in his fist. The scales were closed, glued shut by sap. According to Ranger Brookes, without fire it wouldn't open to disperse the seeds hidden within. God could bring good out of disaster. Could something good happen for him and Elsie?

Nate tucked the cone in his pocket and gripped the steering wheel with both hands. Whatever God had planned for the two of them, Nate still needed answers.

Elsie hurried toward Old Faithful, trying to ignore the silly flutters in her stomach. When Mary had poked her head into the room to tell her Nate was waiting to see her, Elsie's heart had leapt into her throat. She hadn't seen him—or any of the fire crew—since the first day of the fire, and it had taken everything she had not to go chasing after him.

When she spotted him pacing over by the geyser viewing area, she couldn't resist bursting into a run. Nate turned just in time to open his arms before she slammed into him.

He picked her up a few inches off the ground and swung her around. "Oh, college girl, how I've missed you."

She wrapped her arms around him, burying her face in his neck. He still smelled of smoke and pines. "I can't believe you came. And you're safe. And you got the fire out." Could anything be more glorious?

He pressed his lips to her temple as he lowered her feet back to the ground. "Unfortunately, I've got to turn around and go straight back. There's still a lot to do. I didn't tell anyone I was leaving."

Elsie ran her hands along his arms, trying to reacquaint herself with his touch. "I was afraid the fire would keep you busy through the end of the month, and I wouldn't get to see you."

"You know me better than that." He smiled at her. "I would have found some way to get here, even if I had to walk."

She stood on her tiptoes and kissed him, not caring who was around to see.

He pulled her in, returning her kiss and adding one of his own.

She sighed. "If it's this hard to be apart for a little over a week, I don't want to think of what's ahead."

"Neither do I."

She led him to the boardwalk, away from clusters of visitors waiting for the famous geyser's next eruption. "Where are you staying right now? Is Red with you? Mary's been beside herself with worry."

"We've got temporary digs at Roosevelt, but they're moving us back to Canyon for the last few weeks before we close camp. Red is fine. Trust me, I hear him moaning about Mary all the time. We make a miserable pair. Val deserted us for Bukowski and Maguire because he couldn't handle all the whining."

Elsie laughed, the thought of the two men commiserating bringing an odd sense of relief. At least it wasn't just her. "How long can you stay? You're not really driving back tonight, are you? It's getting dark."

"I know. But I have to. I'm absent without leave, and I took a truck."

She backed a step. "You what?"

"Red will cover for me." He paused, then took a breath before speaking. "Elsie, I need to ask you something."

A shiver raced across her skin. He wasn't preparing to propose, was he? She glanced around, the vent at the Old Faithful geyser wafting steam up into the evening sky as the first stars appeared. Did she want him to?

She forced her attention back to his face, his moss-green eyes melting any initial resistance. *Go ahead. Ask.*

He squeezed her hands in his, taking a step back as if to give her breathing space. "I found something at the burn site."

"You did?"

"It was a silver lighter with a flower engraved on the side."

Cold fingers crept down her spine. The lighter. *Her* lighter. She hadn't seen it since before the fire. In fact, it had been hiding in her drawer for weeks.

His gaze grew more intense. "Elsie, someone set the Mount Washburn fire. I saw it flash up around our truck, but it could potentially have been burning for a short time before that. Did you see anything when you and your father parked? Was there anyone else around?"

"We couldn't have missed a fire, Nate. Are you sure it wasn't some malfunction with the truck? Or with my father's truck?"

He went silent, a twitch forming in the side of his jaw.

The lighter was hers. How had it ended up there? The look in his eyes sent a tremor through her. "What are you thinking?"

His grip grew stronger. "Elsie, tell me about the lighter."

Elsie. Not "college girl." She slipped her hands free and stepped back. The crowd over by the geyser started chattering with excitement as the puffs of steam intensified, teasing an eruption. "Nate . . ."

He closed his eyes for a moment as if in pain. It was the same look he'd given her when he'd told her he couldn't read. Resignation. Defeat.

"Nate, I didn't do this." Her voice sounded tinny and far away. "I didn't. How could you . . . How could you even think such a thing?"

He opened his eyes, but he looked toward the geyser, now rising in the distance. "It wasn't your lighter? Teddy Vaughn didn't give it to you as a gift?"

"He did."

"Elsie, tell me you weren't responsible for this fire. Or any of the others."

"I just did. Nate, I don't know how it ended up out there."

"Was it in your pocket? Did you drop it?"

"I could hardly bear to touch the thing. I kept it hidden in my desk drawer so I didn't have to look at it. I intended to return it to Teddy, but I hadn't had a chance."

"How did it get from your desk to the scene of a crime?"

A crime. The words clanged inside her. If they thought she caused this—what would happen to her? She lifted her hands to her cheeks. What about her father? How could he continue to work for the park service if his daughter was accused of trying to burn down Yellowstone? Her stomach lurched. "Is that why you're here?" Tears sprang to her eyes. "I thought maybe you were here to propose, but that's not what you had in mind at all."

His mouth dropped open. "I . . . Elsie—"

A surge of heat pooled in her middle, like the magma that fueled the park's springs and geysers. "I can't believe you would think that of me. I love Wonderland more than anyone. I'd never hurt this place. You should know that."

He pressed a hand against his chest. "Elsie, I'm sorry."

Elsie turned toward the deepening sunset. The red and purple sky did little to ease the turmoil in her heart. There was no way she could face him. If he believed her capable of setting fires, then she might lose this amazing man, the one who continually put the needs of others—his crew, his family, his friends—before his own. The man who put her dreams ahead of his own desires.

She could stand here and try to convince him of her innocence, but that would mean looking into those green eyes and seeing pain and accusation instead of love.

There was only one choice she could bear at that moment. She walked away.

Thirty-Four

She won't speak to me. What am I supposed to do?" Nate dropped the footlocker lid into place after retrieving his guidebook. He was determined to make it through another chapter before leaving Yellowstone, even if it took him ages to slog through each paragraph. It felt right to be back at Canyon Camp, even though the hotel remained closed and empty. Most of the savages had stayed on at Old Faithful. Canyon was like a ghost town.

Red sprawled across his bunk and groaned. They'd spent all day moving equipment. He pressed his fingers to his forehead. "You've got to make it up to her somehow, Nate. Flowers. Candy. Her own volume of Wordsworth poetry. I don't know."

That type of antic might work on some girls, but Red hadn't seen Elsie's face when Nate all but accused her of being an arsonist. He'd replayed the conversation countless times in his mind, trying to figure out how he could have said things differently.

Of course she hadn't set the fire. He knew that. It was ridiculous to even entertain the thought for a moment. But she wouldn't even talk to him about it. How could he help her if she wouldn't discuss it? The thought of Vaughn opening a formal investigation sent a chill through him.

The lighter didn't grow wings and fly out of her room. Then again, in Yellowstone, you never knew. Hutch and Kit had dragged several strange items into the tent while they were gone. Nate had found a fountain pen under his bed. He was still trying to figure out who it belonged to. Hopefully not Lieutenant Stone.

"She doesn't seem the type to like elaborate gifts."

"All dames like gifts, Nate. And she accepted that silver lighter from Vaughn, didn't she?"

"There's a difference between *accepted* and *appreciates.*" It rankled him that Elsie had kept that token from Vaughn. Nate had no right to be jealous, but it didn't stop him.

Red rolled to his side and pushed up to his elbow. "Then something personal. A love letter, a poem, a song."

"How many women have you wooed? You come up with these lists awfully quick." Nate flipped open the cover to the book and sat on the edge of the bed, careful not to jostle the raccoon sleeping at the far end of the mattress. Kit only showed up occasionally to beg for snacks, but Hutch seemed to appreciate human companionship.

"These are important life skills, Nate. You go ahead and laugh, but when I'm happily married to the love of my life and you're still muddling through by yourself, you're going to wish you'd listened to me."

Nate focused on the page, fiddling with the ruler device Elsie had made for him. He'd gotten to where he could read two or three words at a time before sliding it along the line to the next section. But right now, his eyes refused to focus. He ran his hand across the page. She'd given him so much. And how had he repaid her? With doubts and questions.

"Use that brain of yours, boy. That's why God put it in your skull, you know." His father's words had faded in the past few months, but this week they'd roared back with a vengeance.

God had given Nate a brain, and thanks to Elsie, he'd finally started to unlock it. If he lost her, how long would it take for him to return to the life he'd had before? Nate Webber, failure. "I don't have much to offer her."

"Got that right." Red grunted.

"But I'd give anything to keep her." Nate let the book close. "How do I show her that? I don't have the first clue how to start."

Red sat up. "You could figure out who really started the fires." The bed frame rattled with his motion. "What's Vaughn going to do? You dropped that lighter in his lap, so he thinks it's her. What's going to happen now?"

Nate jumped to his feet and walked to the tent flap, staring out at the cool evening. "He can't prove anything. Just because the lighter was there doesn't mean she started the fire."

"The lighter was there, and *she* was there."

Nate rounded on his friend. "Now you think she did it too?"

Red spread his hands in front of him. "No way. I'm just trying to point out what Vaughn must be thinking."

"Someone could have stolen it from her room."

"Who even knew she had the thing?"

Nate folded his arms. "Vaughn."

"He looked pretty shell-shocked when you tossed it at him. I don't think he's that good an actor." Red rubbed his chin. "Plus, he has his own. Why steal hers just to start a fire?"

"Revenge?"

Red's eyes locked on Nate's. "She threw him over for you, remember? Unless he's got a screw loose, you'd be the target of his wrath, not Elsie. And it would have been a heckuva lot easier to frame you. People will have a hard time believing that the sweet little daughter of a park ranger could be a firebug. But some poor sap from Brooklyn? I'd almost believe it myself."

Nate sank back onto the mattress. Red was right. Vaughn hadn't shown any anger toward Elsie, just sadness. But toward him? "So who else has access to her room?"

"My girl, but I'd really like to rule her out too." Red ran a hand through his hair.

Nate thought about Mary but discarded the idea. She just didn't seem the type. Of course neither did Elsie, for that matter. Was there even a "type" when it came to arson? He lowered his head into his hands. "I don't know. Maybe some other savage went into her room when they were gone. One of the porters or busboys." A thought slithered through his gut. He lifted his head. "She mentioned something to me about Graham. He was at all the fires too."

Red narrowed his eyes. "But not this last one."

"No one was at this one, except for us and our crew. And Ranger Brookes. But anyone could have driven along that road and stopped there."

"And the gear jammer has transportation, which you can't say for all the savages and *C*s."

Nate ran a hand across the back of his neck. "Maybe we should go have a talk with him. Trouble is, he's always on the move. He could be here in Canyon or clear up in Gardiner. How are we supposed to find him?"

"We could put the bug in Vaughn's ear. Let him handle it."

"No, you were right. The best gift I can give Elsie right now is to figure out who's behind this."

His friend chuckled. "And you don't want the good ranger taking credit for it."

Nate set his jaw. "No, I don't."

Elsie folded the red sweater and added it to her bag. She wouldn't be sorry to say goodbye to this cramped room at Old Faithful. The crew here had been wonderful about letting them squeeze in after the fire threatened Canyon, doubling up in rooms so that they could make space for everyone.

Tonight was the Old Faithful Follies, and then tomorrow Graham would come pick her up for the drive back to Mammoth. She'd have one night with her folks, and then she and Mary would take the train to Missoula.

College. She'd dreamed of going for years, but now her heart felt empty, as if her fight with Nate had drained every emotion from her system. All that remained was a tiny bubbling mud pot of anger and regret, but even that seemed to be losing its steam. She sank onto the bed and pulled the bag into her lap.

Mary loaded bottles into her cosmetics case, sending a worried glance across the tiny room. "You're being quiet."

Elsie squeezed the bag against her stomach, hoping the pressure would make her feel alive. "I feel as if I'm walking around in a fog."

Her roommate walked over and sat beside her. "You need to talk to him, Elsie. Don't leave like this."

"What's the point? Even if we patch things up, I'm still leaving. Maybe"—she swallowed, her throat closing—"maybe it's easier this way."

"You know that's not true. There's nothing easy about this. You love the man. You can't just switch it off."

"Can't I?" Elsie rubbed her arms. Maybe she'd been wrong about the lack of emotions. Talking stirred up everything again.

"If you could figure out how to do that, you could write a book." Mary sighed. "I'm going to miss Red too, but I'm not going to look for some worthless excuse to call it quits."

"That's not what I'm doing."

"It is." Mary touched her shoulder. "He was right to ask you about the lighter. What was he supposed to do—ignore it? Hide it?"

"No, but he acted like I was responsible somehow. As if my life wasn't at stake, just like his and the rest of the crew's. And my father's too."

"I'm not sure there's anything sensible about starting fires. We had a boy who did that in my school back home. He said he liked the excitement. People rushed to put it out; firemen came. He liked to watch people scurry, I guess."

"Do you think that's what's going on here?"

"I don't know. But hopefully whoever is pulling these pranks is done."

The thought wove its way around Elsie's heart and squeezed. "It could happen again." Seeing flames climbing the trees on Mount Washburn had reawakened the old panic in her heart. Would she never be free of this? "It's like fire follows me around. First my childhood, now here."

"This is not your fault, Elsie."

She thought of the lighter. "No wonder he thought it might be me. I'm a magnet for this, somehow."

Mary frowned. "Now you're being ridiculous."

"Am I?" Elsie thought a moment. "When did you last see that lighter?"

"It wasn't there when I packed up." Mary stood up. "You had kept it on top of the desk. I don't think I've seen it since that night you argued with Rose."

"I took it from her and put it in the drawer."

"It wasn't there. I made sure to empty your drawers because I knew you were hiding your college money in there. I couldn't bear the thought of you losing your tuition money after working so hard this summer."

"So someone stole the lighter, but not the money?" Elsie frowned. "That doesn't make sense."

"Thank goodness they didn't. I don't want to leave you behind again. I've been looking forward to having you at college with me. It almost makes saying goodbye to the boys bearable."

Elsie pushed away the fresh jab of pain. "There will be other men on campus—that's what you've always told me."

"They're not as fun." Mary pouted. "College boys are much too serious. I'm done with them."

"Mary Prosser is done with men?"

"Not men. Just any man who's not Red Walsh."

Elsie went to the window and leaned against it. She stared at the view, an ache pooling inside of her. "But how do you know it will work out with Red?"

"I don't, silly. But I'm willing to give it everything I can. And that means kissing him goodbye with every intention of kissing him hello again."

Kissing him hello. Elsie closed her eyes for a long moment, the words almost too sweet to bear.

Mary sighed. "Let's finish packing so we can get over to the Inn. One last talent show. We'll make it the best."

Thirty-Five

Nate eased into Old Faithful Inn, careful to keep to the shadows. Somehow he doubted Elsie would welcome seeing him at the Follies.

The lobby was packed, extra chairs set up all across the cavernous room. On one of the balconies above their heads, a string quartet played, the music wafting down to the people milling below. College kids ran about in silly costumes and wore big smiles, men toting guitars and women with bouquets of flowers. All season they'd cared for the hotel guests, plumping pillows, hauling luggage, and delivering dishes of food. Tonight was all about fun. Even the hotel guests seemed to be getting into the spirit, slipping envelopes with tips to their favorite staff members and wishing them luck in their studies.

The sight sent a jab through Nate's heart. Somewhere in this mix, his college girl was getting ready for her first year away at school. Even though she was older than most first-years, she must be nervous. His arms ached to hold her. This was the first step toward her dream, and he couldn't even share it with her.

"Nate?" A soft voice called to him.

He spun around, his heart jumping. It fell just as fast. "Rose—hello!"

The young woman's eyes were shadowed, as if she hadn't slept in a week. "Nate, I'm so glad you're safe. I heard about what happened. Thank you for taking care of Elsie. I . . . I never dreamed . . ." She placed a hand against her mouth.

"Everyone is fine." Nate chose his words with care. Elsie had told him her friend was sensitive. "The fire is out."

"I know." She nodded, her lower lip between her teeth. "We're leaving Old Faithful tonight. Did Elsie tell you?"

She hadn't, but he'd heard it from Red. A lump settled in his throat. "I hope you have a great year. You deserve it."

The young woman's eyes filled. "I suppose. I'm not looking forward to going back. I thought this summer would fix everything, but . . ." Her focus darted away. "I guess nothing has changed."

"Maybe this year will be better for you."

She managed a weak smile. "I hope you're right."

"Are you in the show tonight?" Nate scanned the room, searching for Elsie.

"Only in the group number. Each of the areas compete, and we're all expected to participate. But I only joined Canyon a month ago, so I don't really feel a part of the group."

"And what about Graham?" As soon as the question slipped from his mouth, he realized his gaffe.

"I wouldn't know." Rose blinked several times, as if fighting tears. "I suppose he put his cap in with Mammoth, since he's based there. But he seems to have *friends* all over."

"I'm sorry. I shouldn't have mentioned him."

A blush spread across her cheeks. She looked away.

He needed to learn to keep his mouth shut. Excusing himself, Nate made his way to the far side of the room. It was probably best he stay clear of all the girls tonight. He seemed to have a gift for making them cry.

Red and Val had claimed seats on benches near the front of the dining room. If he could navigate the crowd, it looked as if they had a spot saved for him.

Graham Brookes appeared by the door, not far from where Rose was standing. His eyes were wide, his hat clutched in his hand. He made a bee-line for Rose and whispered in her ear. She nodded and trailed after him into the lobby.

Not again. Nate reversed directions and followed them. He didn't like the stiff expression on Graham's face. The usually calm gear jammer looked decidedly rattled, as if he'd driven Dunraven Pass with no brakes. If Nate had managed to make Rose cry, there was no telling what Graham could accomplish.

Nate stayed just inside the doorway to the dining room and watched as the pair argued. Graham's voice lifted, carrying across the room as he clamped a hand onto the young woman's arm. "You can't say anything, Rose. You can't."

She flung off his grip, covering her face with her fingers.

Graham stepped in close, his voice lowered so Nate couldn't make out their conversation.

Rose turned so her back was toward Nate, but he couldn't miss the tremors in the girl's slumped shoulders as she listened to the man's words. Whatever story the bus driver was feeding Rose, it certainly wasn't something she wanted to hear.

Nate edged closer.

"I don't know what you were thinking. It's not what I wanted. Not any of it." Graham's voice pitched upward.

"I just wanted you to really *see* me."

He gripped her arms, giving her a quick shake. "I have. I do, Rose. But this has to stop. It won't work. You've got to understand that."

Hadn't they already busted up? Nate eased back into the shadows.

"Look, Rose. I've got to go. Everyone's going to think it's my fault."

"It is your fault." Her words were filled with strain. "If you'd only—"

"No. It's done. I'm leaving."

"But what about your aunt and uncle—and Elsie?"

"It's better this way. I can't face them." He dropped his hand from her arm. "I've got to go. But promise me you won't say anything."

"What would I say? Graham, I don't want you to go."

He shook his head, turning to leave. "It doesn't matter. Too much has happened."

As he pushed out the door toward the parking area, Rose darted down the opposite hall.

Inside the dining room behind Nate, the program kicked off with singing. The lobby had emptied as guests claimed their seats. Nate dashed for the front door. He wasn't letting Graham Brookes vanish on him. If Graham was responsible for the fires, he wasn't going to leave Elsie to take the heat. She'd been through enough. Nate's heart hammered in his chest as he hurried out the door. "Graham, wait!"

The man glanced back over his shoulder, his face turning ashen. "I don't have time for another of your lectures, Webber."

"No, look—" Nate jogged to catch up. "I just want to talk."

"I'm done with talk." Graham shook his head. "I've been the source of gossip this entire summer, and I'm not putting up with any more. I know what you're all thinking."

"And what would that be?"

"I overheard Vaughn comparing notes with another ranger. They're saying the fire on Washburn was arson."

Nate grabbed his elbow and dragged him to a stop. "So you're running? Just like Elsie and I and the rest of the crew had to run from the fire *you* started?"

Graham jerked his arm free, beads of sweat appearing on his temples. He held up his palms, his hands trembling. "You think, because of *this,* I've got some perverse fascination with fire?"

"Do you?"

"I would never hurt my cousin, Nate. The fire when we were kids—that was an accident. A horrific accident that will haunt me for the rest of my life."

"So where were you when the Washburn fire started?"

Graham grimaced, his eyes growing damp around the edges. "I was with Rose."

"That's convenient. The woman I just heard you swearing to secrecy?"

"That's why I was leaving. I know how it looks."

Nate ground knuckles against his leg. "Look, I have my own opinions, but Vaughn—what you overheard—he doesn't think it's you."

The driver paused, his brow furrowed. "But he was talking about the house fire back in DC. He mentioned me by name."

"A silver lighter was found at the fire scene."

"I don't understand."

"It belonged to Elsie. Vaughn gave it to her months ago." Nate cleared his throat. "Vaughn thinks she's involved."

"Elsie? You've got to be kidding me." Graham collapsed back against the side of the bus. "This just keeps getting worse. No one would believe that, would they?"

"I certainly don't." Nate stepped closer. "Because I think you went into her room and stole that lighter. Am I right?"

A long second passed before Graham's eyes locked onto Nate's. "No."

"Don't lie to me." Nate took hold of Graham's arm.

Graham leaned his head back against the bus and gazed up toward the sky, not fighting Nate's grip on him. "I wish it was a lie, Nate. That would be so much easier."

"What do you mean?"

"I didn't steal the lighter." Graham's voice lowered. "Rose did."

"You expect me to believe that?"

He shook his head, still not meeting Nate's gaze. "Not really. That's why I'm leaving. No one will believe me." Graham unbuttoned his collar as if needing a breath of air. "She showed it to me that day. Said Elsie didn't want it and gave it to her."

Nate let his hand drop and waited for the man to continue, trying to make sense of what he was saying.

"I took her out for a drive that day, to talk. I told her I was spending more time with Gloria over in Madison."

"She must not have taken that well."

"She was fiddling with the lighter while I was driving. I asked her to put it away." He glanced at Nate. "It scared the pants off me. I'd never seen her so quiet and calm. I'd expected tears, not eerie silence."

"What happened?"

"I parked on the side of the road so we could talk." Graham lifted his hands. "That's when she told me she'd started the fires at Mammoth and Canyon."

Nate's stomach turned. Was this another clever lie, or was this man telling the truth? "She said that?"

"I didn't believe her either." He dropped his arms to his side. "She got angry and got out of the car."

"What did you do?"

"I begged her to get back into the car, but she refused and started walking. I couldn't think of what else to do." Graham shook his head. "She was acting so nuts, and I got scared. She knows the park well, so I thought she'd be safe if I left her there while I went to get Elsie or Mary. I figured maybe one of them could talk some sense into her. But I couldn't find anyone. And then, the evacuations started."

Nate stepped closer. "Where did you leave her?"

Graham hung his head. "By Mount Washburn."

Thirty-Six

E lsie edged around to the outside of the rows of tables and caught Mary as she came down from the platform. "Where's Rose? It's almost time for the final songs, and I haven't seen her the whole time."

Mary balanced her tall wig with one hand. "I saw her out front talking to Graham earlier. She disappeared down the hall toward the kitchen."

"The kitchen? Whatever for? She's not on refreshment crew tonight. The Old Faithful savages are taking care of everything."

"You know Rose—she has to be in the middle of things." Mary waved her hand. "I think she's just trying to get out of singing. She's never made peace with the Canyon Camp song. You'd better go find her."

Something's wrong. After discovering Rose crying in the Old Faithful tree house at the top of the three-story lobby, she'd been afraid to leave her friend alone. Rose seemed to have fallen into despair this summer, and no amount of silly savage events could lift her from the doldrums. Hopefully getting back to school would help.

Nate apparently had skipped the show as well, a fact that gnawed at Elsie's heart. Mary's words about kisses goodbye leading to kisses hello had given her a new hope that maybe she and Nate could survive this separation.

Most of the CCC men were in attendance. It seemed strange to see his crew without Nate at the lead.

Had he given up on her?

She walked through the room, edging around the back tables to get to the kitchen. Two of the Old Faithful girls were there, loading trays with slices of cake to serve after the show. Unfortunately, neither had seen Rose. Elsie made her way outside. Rose wouldn't leave, would she?

The sidewalk outside the Inn was quiet, as most of the guests had come in to watch the show, with just a small group of tourists left sitting on the benches near the geyser. It had only been a few days since her argument with Nate out here, but she couldn't see the spot without thinking of the tortured expression on his face. He'd not wanted to accuse her; she realized that now. She still didn't know how her lighter ended up at the fire scene. Only she and Mary knew it was in her desk drawer. No one else spent time in her room.

No one except . . .

"I've ruined everything, Elsie." Rose's words came piling back through Elsie's memory. She'd assumed her friend was talking about Graham, but what if she was referring to something else entirely?

She could still see Rose flicking the lever on the silver lighter, fascinated with its mechanics. *"He saved you that day. Just like he rescued me and Mary when the fire broke out at the Mammoth Hotel."*

Elsie's knees weakened, and she sank onto a bench. It couldn't be Rose. Her mind raced. It made no sense. But when did arson ever make sense? Elsie dug her fingers through her hair, trying to force an explanation.

Nate came bursting out the door, his chest rising and falling like he'd been running at full tilt. "Elsie!"

She jumped to her feet. "You're here."

He hurried to her. "I'm sorry. I never should have—"

"No, please don't apologize. I'm sorry I wouldn't listen."

He took her hand and squeezed it, his eyes intense. "I just spoke with Graham. He said Rose had your lighter."

Her skin went cold. "I was just thinking about it. Rose hasn't been herself all summer . . . and even more so since the Canyon fire."

"Where is she?"

"I don't know. I was just looking for her."

"She'd quarreled with Graham just before I spoke to him. She left crying. Is there someplace she would go if she were upset?"

Her throat tightened. "I found her in the tree house the day of the fire."

Nate stepped back and glanced around. "Where is there a tree house around here?"

"In the lobby." She grabbed his hand, the warmth of his skin against hers providing the rush of confidence she needed. "Come with me." She hurried back toward the building, Nate on her heels.

Skirting around to the lobby entrance, she ducked inside and stopped to gaze up toward the ceiling. "See? Up there." She pointed at the strange square structure above the third level of balconies, nearly brushing the rafters. Music flowed from the dining room, the sound of singing and laughing making the room seem merry even in light of their fears.

Nate tilted his head back, gazing upward. "Elsie, tell me that's not smoke up there."

A thin haze clung to the wooden beams of the high ceiling, barely visible in the evening light. Elsie's heart slowed. *Lord, please. Please, no.*

❧

Nate's leg muscles were trembling by the time he rounded the last flight of winding staircases leading to the tree house and the crow's nest above. Hiking up and down the slopes of Mount Washburn had strengthened his legs to the point where he could cover the distance in record time, but the fear simmering in his gut made it feel like he was slogging through deep snow to get there. If a fire had been set up here, it would be to the roof in seconds. And then what?

A railing blocked the last short flight, but Nate didn't pause. He vaulted over it, then pushed his way up the last few steps.

Rose lay curled on her side, staring at a crumpled pile of papers smoldering in the corner.

"What are you doing?" Nate hurried over and stomped on the papers, grinding the flames into the floorboards. A box of wooden matches sat nearby. He scooped them up and shoved them into his pocket.

The girl sighed and pushed up to a sitting position, her hair askew. "They're letters. Ones from Pete, a few from Graham." Her eyes remained glazed, unfocused.

Elsie appeared at the top of the steps, her face flushed from the climb. "Rose, honey . . ."

Nate spread the papers and made sure every ember was out. His heart was pounding so hard—they could probably hear it in the lobby. He looked over the wooden railing at the people milling below. No one had any idea how close they had just come to disaster. A thin veil of smoke drifted around the beams, the smell of burning paper hanging in the air.

He turned to face the two women. "Elsie?"

She sat on the floor, her arms wrapped around her friend. "Nate, my father is downstairs watching the show. Why don't you go let him know what's happened? Ask him to come."

"You'll be all right?"

She looked up at him, eyes glistening. "We're not going anywhere."

Thirty-Seven

Elsie's stomach churned as she placed the last suitcase in the back of the truck. "Mary, we need to hurry." Wisps of steam rose from the Mammoth Hot Springs, drifting across the distant terraces. She'd miss that view.

"I'm coming." Her friend's voice trailed out to her. "I'm going to change my dress."

"Again?" Elsie turned and surveyed the little red-roofed house she'd lived in for the past decade, the sight sending a wave of homesickness through her before she'd even left the yard.

Mother stepped onto the stoop, a bag clutched in her hands. "You almost forgot these. I baked yesterday so you and Mary would have treats for the train. It's been a while since I felt well enough to do that." She gently shook the bag. "I went ahead and included the snickerdoodles I'd made for Rose. Maybe you can find someone to share them with on the journey."

Elsie took the sack from her mother and pulled her into a long embrace. "It's sad to think of her not going back to the University of Wyoming."

Mother rubbed circles on Elsie's back. "Doctor Murphy is looking into programs at the state hospital. Hopefully they'll be able to help her."

It made Elsie queasy to think of her friend facing federal court. Her father had promised to help out in whatever way he could. "She didn't mean to hurt anyone."

"We know, sweetheart. But laws were broken, and we need to be sure she doesn't resort to this behavior again."

Mary came out onto the step, her flowered dress just barely covering her knees, makeup bag in one hand. "She'd always been sensitive, but I never dreamed her capable of anything like this. Rose told me the first fire was to get Graham's attention, but she hadn't expected it to make her feel good too." She wrinkled her nose. "How can a fire make you feel good?"

Mother wrapped an arm around Mary's waist and squeezed. "The mind is a funny thing. Sometimes wires get crossed. We'll be praying for her." She looked over at Elsie. "I'm thankful you and Nate caught her before anyone was hurt."

Even just hearing Nate's name brought tears to her eyes. Saying good-bye to him last night at Old Faithful was about the hardest thing she'd ever done. She couldn't bear the thought of not seeing him for months. She and Mary had already promised each other that if the men were stationed any-where in the West, they'd find some way to visit.

His final kisses had melted her all the way to her toes. The summer had been far too short. But then again, how much time would have been enough? Elsie pushed away the dismal thoughts. She could mope all the way to Missoula if necessary, but for now she needed to focus on getting herself there.

Her father jogged over from the museum. "Are we ready? We'd best get you girls to the station or you're going to miss your train. Unless you've decided to put off college for another year?"

"I've waited long enough." Elsie wiped her eyes and did her best to smile. This was a happy occasion, a dream come true. So why did she feel like bawling like an orphaned bison calf?

The strength in her mother's hugs brought a fresh wave of tears from both Elsie and Mary. "Mama, I'm going to miss you so much. Please follow the doctor's orders and get plenty of rest."

The two girls piled into the park truck that her father had been using since the fire. It was a short ride from Mammoth to the train station in Gardiner, but Elsie was determined to soak in every moment. The mountains stood like sentinels as they drove down the road and out the stone arch that marked the park's north entrance.

At the station, Elsie kissed her father on the cheek. "Be sure to save up the good stories from the fall and winter. I'll want to hear them all."

"You know I will." Her father smiled, handing the girls' cases to the railway porter. "You make us proud, Elsie. Remember that. Now, give me a quick hug, because I see someone else waiting to say goodbye."

"What?" Elsie turned, her heart leaping to her throat as she spotted Nate and Red waiting on the platform.

Mary had already dashed across the platform and thrown herself into Red's arms.

After embracing her father, Elsie hurried over and grabbed Nate's hands. "What are you doing here? I thought we said goodbye already."

Nate smiled. "Old Lieutenant Stone has a softer heart than we gave him credit for. When he found out you were leaving, he gave us passes."

Red grinned. "And a truck. And a list of supplies to pick up in Gardiner."

She slid her arms around Nate's waist, burying her face in his chest. "I'm so glad."

"I hope you don't mind the surprise." He whispered the words into her hair.

"Are you kidding? Another chance to kiss you goodbye? Why would I mind?"

Red swung Mary around and grinned like a schoolboy. "It's not our only surprise either."

Mary giggled. "You're getting on the train with us? Because that would be over the moon."

Nate squeezed Elsie's waist. "Not quite. But Lieutenant Stone received word on where we'd be sent for our next six-month hitch."

Elsie stared up at Nate's eyes, wishing she could memorize the exact shade. She was going to miss him so much. "So where are you headed? Nevada? Texas?"

A grin spread across his face. "Guess again, college girl."

Mary squeezed Red's hands. "Oh, it's California, isn't it? Or Oregon?"

He tipped his head toward Nate. "I think we'd better out and tell them. Otherwise they'll miss their train trying to guess it."

The train whistle sounded.

Elsie looked up at Nate, hating the idea that they would be forced apart. Again.

He grinned and leaned in close, lowering his voice so only she and Mary could hear. "We're going to Fort Missoula."

"What?" Mary screeched, bouncing on her toes. "Missoula? That's only about five miles from campus."

All the breath left Elsie's lungs for a moment. "For the whole winter?"

Nate grinned, then leaned in and kissed her, lingering, with total disregard for anyone who might be watching. He released her and looked into her eyes. "You said God had a plan in mind for us."

Warmth flooded through her. "I never realized how perfect it would be."

"They've got a sign shop and a machine shop—even some electronics classes. Red might learn to build radios after all. We'll be producing signs for parks and recreation sites. So I hope you don't mind continuing our lessons for a few more months. If I misspell some of those words, there's going to be a high price to pay."

She locked her hands around the back of his neck and kissed him again. "There's your answer."

"Don't miss your train, college girl. I'll be seeing you in a few weeks after we get Canyon Camp buttoned up for winter."

Mary was clinging to Red with happy tears streaming down her cheeks. "I can't believe it."

He laughed. "Yeah, well, I'll miss that lovely California sunshine, but I wouldn't trade this for the world."

Elsie grabbed Mary's hand and they ran for the train, climbing aboard just before it started easing out of the station. Waving to the two men, they slipped down the aisle to some open seats.

Nate and Red waved from the platform, the sight sending a surge of joy through Elsie. *Missoula*. She waved back, blowing a kiss.

As Mary had said, a kiss goodbye was just one step away from a kiss hello.

Epilogue

June 1, 1937

There they are." Nate leaned forward, his pulse speeding up. Even though it was June, tiny flakes of snow drifted through the afternoon air, and the wind remained unseasonably cold. The parking area near Artist Point was mostly empty, only a few brave souls venturing down to look at Lower Yellowstone Falls as the clouds spit moisture at them. In contrast, a large group of young men plodded up the trail toward them, heading for two large trucks.

Elsie squeezed next to him for warmth. "They look so young."

"They *are* young."

The line of men in dirt-stained dungarees and shirts hiked slowly, shovels and picks in their hands. Floppy hats covered their heads, but most had slung their coats over a shoulder as they walked—evidence of a hard afternoon's work.

Nate shook his head. "I was never that young."

"You were the old man of the group, remember?" She shivered with the memory and the cold. "That day you arrived at the Gardiner station four years ago, I remember thinking you all looked half-starved and homesick."

"We were." Nate chuckled. "I put on twenty pounds in the first two months." He scanned the line, studying each face as they passed.

"Twenty pounds of muscle." She squeezed his arm. "Why do you think all us pillow punchers were suddenly chasing after you boys?"

He couldn't resist the smile, leaning down to press a kiss to his wife's forehead. "I was doing all the chasing, or have you forgotten that, college girl?"

"You're going to have to stop calling me that, you know. You're the college student now."

"I'm not sure taking two forestry classes a year qualifies. It'll take me a long time to catch up to you. Maybe when I'm about eighty?"

"Those classes will help you this summer when you're supervising the crews. The park service is thrilled to have you. They don't have nearly enough experienced men to guide these city boys."

"I think it stretches the boundaries of the LEM program to hire me."

"Local experienced men—who could be more qualified than you?"

Nate shook his head. "As soon as they hear my Brooklyn accent, they're going to know I'm not Wyoming born and bred."

Elsie settled a hand on his shoulder, the simple gold band on her finger reflecting a glint of sunlight. "It's funny; I don't even notice it anymore."

He couldn't resist claiming that hand and placing a kiss on top of her knuckles. His mother had been saving his grandmother's ring for Sherm but was delighted to pass it along to Nate when the time came. He squeezed Elsie's fingers, never feeling more whole than when he had her hand in his.

"I'm glad Red and Mary are coming out for a few weeks. I'm sure the boys will prefer his electronics classes to my boring old arithmetic and history."

"It was generous of him to volunteer. I never thought he'd actually build those radios like he wanted."

Elsie tightened the belt on her coat. "I think it was Mary who volunteered him. She liked the idea of coming back to Yellowstone and not having to make anyone's bed but her own." The flakes of snow were falling faster now, gathering on the edges of Elsie's hat. "And I can't wait to meet their little boys."

It wasn't until the last few men emerged from the trailhead that he spotted the familiar features.

He'd only seen his little brother twice since leaving Brooklyn, and the last time had been two years ago. Charlie must know that Nate had pulled strings to get him stationed here. Hopefully that hadn't angered the boy. Nate just couldn't resist the opportunity to have him close.

Elsie sighed. "He looks like Val. All knees and elbows."

Charlie had grown several more inches in the past two years, now towering over the rest of his crew, his angular features even more pronounced than they had been as a child.

"He looks like Sherm." Nate stepped forward, leaving Elsie by the car. "Charlie."

His brother glanced up, a moment passing before recognition spread across his face. "Nate?" He dropped the shovel to the dirt and jogged over, throwing his arms around his older brother. "Am I glad to see you."

"You are a sight." He hugged Charlie hard, smacking his shoulders before releasing him and stepping back to look him over again. "I can't believe you're taller than me."

Charlie straightened to his full height. "Six foot two, according to the doctor at Camp Dix."

Nate couldn't resist giving him a gentle punch in the stomach. "And what—about 130 at the most?" He'd sent money home every chance he got, but his mother said feeding growing boys was like bailing a leaky boat. You couldn't keep up.

"Not for long. Every time we turn around, they're putting more food in front of us. If I'd known you ate this well, I'd have run away and joined you years ago." He glanced around. "Did you bring Elsie?"

Nate turned and waved her closer. She stepped away from their Buick and hurried over to join them. "Charlie, I'm so happy to see you again."

"Hey, sis." Charlie bent down to give her a peck on the cheek. "Keeping this guy in line?"

"I try." She glanced between the two brothers. "I can't get over the resemblance between you two. How are Eva and Lucy?"

Charlie rolled his eyes. "Boy crazy."

"What?" Nate gasped. "Since when?"

Elsie laughed, looping her hand under his arm. "A brother's work is never done. Or so I hear. Maybe we'll have to lure them out to Yellowstone next. Do you think they'd rather wash dishes or plump pillows?"

"Maybe we should keep them far away from this place. Remember that romantic Yellowstone moon?"

The other men had piled into the waiting trucks, and several of them shouted to Charlie.

He waved, then turned back to Nate and Elsie. "I've got to go."

"That's all right." Nate blinked several times, surprised to feel the emotion surge through him. "You'll actually be seeing me this summer. I'm going to be supervising some of the crews." He cleared his throat. "Yours, if you'll have me. Or if that's too much big brother for you, I'll trade for one of the other camps. I'm just glad to know you'll be nearby."

A grin spread across Charlie's face. "You're pulling my leg. How did you manage that?"

Elsie laughed. "My father made a few telephone calls. It didn't take much convincing. Your brother is quite in demand out here."

"Someone's got to show you kids the difference between a whitebark pine and a lodgepole pine." Nate tipped his head toward Elsie. "And Mrs. Webber here will be schooling you on the three *R*s."

"With a good amount of geology thrown in." She smiled. "As a bonus."

The men hollered again from the truck. Charlie grimaced and gave them each a bear hug. "I guess I'll see you soon, then. This is going to be the best summer ever." He jogged over to his crew, and one of the other boys reached out a hand to haul him into the truck bed.

"*Best summer ever.*' Did you hear that?" Nate waved. "He may change his tune when he figures out exactly how hard we're going to work him. He may decide he doesn't like having his older brother for a boss."

She reached up and cupped a hand under Nate's chin. "A little hard work never hurt anybody. Look what it did for you."

He pulled Elsie into his arms, lifting her toes off the ground in his enthusiasm. "It got me the love of my life."

"And this summer we're going to work on the next chapter, right?"

He lowered her back onto her feet and kissed her lips. Tiny flakes of snow were clinging to the knitted red cap covering her hair. "Tell me you're not talking about a geology book."

She smiled, turning her face in toward his palm. "I was thinking more about our family's next chapter."

He circled his arm behind her back, using his free hand to brush a stray snowflake from her nose. "I can't wait."

AUTHOR'S NOTE

Dear Reader,

I hope you enjoyed this 1930s tour through Yellowstone National Park. With a landscape that is overflowing with remarkable geothermal features, wildlife, history, and people, it was a challenge to pick and choose what aspects of the park to feature in *Ever Faithful*. I feel like I barely scratched the surface of all Yellowstone has to offer. Is it any surprise that early visitors nicknamed it Wonderland?

For the sake of story flow, I did stretch the summer season by a few weeks. I hope you'll forgive me for that. I'm sure the characters appreciated having a little more time to enjoy this incredible place—and each other.

For those of you who enjoy learning a little more about the history that goes into a novel, here is a little background to some of the history featured in the story.

- **The Civilian Conservation Corps.** As described in *Ever Faithful,* the CCC was one of President Franklin Delano Roosevelt's most successful New Deal programs. From 1933 until 1942, the CCC employed more than 2.5 million men, mostly between the ages of eighteen to twenty-five, to work various conservation projects on public lands. Not only did these men do backbreaking work, they also *learned.* It's said that as many as forty thousand illiterate men may have learned to read during their time in the camps. Others finished high school or took trade classes—and a few even earned college scholarships (I'd like to think Val Kaminski was one of these).

Some of the enrollees had experienced little outside their own urban neighborhoods, but through participation in the CCC, they were given the opportunity not only to see the country, but to mix with men from a wide variety of backgrounds. By the time America went to war, a generation of men had already experienced camp life and were ready for the next chapter in their lives.

- **The Yellowstone "savages."** Starting in the late 1800s and lasting into the present day, the seasonal staff who work for the concessionaires at Yellowstone National Park have been referred to as savages. No one is entirely sure how the nickname originated, but generations of summer staff remember the term with fondness. I know the word can be a sensitive one to certain audiences, and I truly hope it didn't offend. The other lingo—*pillow punchers, gear jammers, pack rats,* and the rest—also comes from park history.

- **The Yellow Buses.** Don't you just love the vintage yellow bus on the front cover? Did you know you can still tour the park in one? The vintage buses began making a comeback in 2009, when Yellowstone's concessionaire purchased eight of the vehicles from Skagway Streetcar Co. They spent $1.9 million refurbishing these buses to bring them up to today's safety standards and put them back on the road. So now, like the "dudes" of Graham's era, you can have a Yellowstone gear jammer show you the sights of the park. The legend of "a girl at every stop" came straight from a camp songbook published in the 1920s, but the tourney was my own addition. From the tone of some of the lyrics, I don't think it was much of a stretch.

- **The Park Hotels.** It's true that many of the park's hotels did not open for the 1933 season. Affected by the Great Depression, tourists were choosing less expensive accommodations like housekeeping cabins and tents or simply staying home. The Mammoth and Canyon Hotels have both been replaced by newer structures, but the Lake Hotel (1891) and the Old Faithful Inn (1904) still look much as they did in Elsie's era.
- **Yellowstone's Wildlife.** In the 1930s, bison were still recovering from near extinction. By 1902, there were only around two dozen wild bison in the park. The government brought twenty-one more from private herds and managed them as a captive herd. As their numbers increased, they began releasing animals to mix with the remains of the wild herd, and the bison you see in Yellowstone today (now numbering between two and five thousand) are their descendants. The bison are only one of the park's conservation success stories. Wolves are not mentioned in *Ever Faithful* because they were extinct in the park at the time. It's only in the past few decades that this incredible predator has been reintroduced. Both of these species are important pieces of Yellowstone history.

    Bears, on the other hand, were much easier to see in Nate and Elsie's era. Official feeding stations, as described in *Ever Faithful,* existed for visitor entertainment until World War II. In 1970, the park banned visitors from feeding the bears and began installing bear-proof garbage cans. Much has changed!

There's so much more I'd like to add, such as the changing wildfire policies in our national parks, mountain pine beetle ecology, mental health in the 1930s, learning disabilities and illiteracy, and great things to see in Yellowstone. You can learn more about *Ever Faithful* and Yellowstone at www.KarenBarnettBooks.com. Sign up for my newsletter while you're there, and you'll receive updates on future books and more behind-the-scenes information.

I hope that *Ever Faithful* and the other titles in the Vintage National Parks collection have inspired you to get out and enjoy these national treasures for yourself. I believe God delights in His intricate and ever-changing creation . . . and that includes you!

Blessings!
Karen Barnett

READERS GUIDE

1. Have you had the joy of visiting Yellowstone National Park? What were some of your favorite "wonders" you saw while there? If you haven't visited yet, what would you most like to see?

2. Elsie has dreamed of being a teacher since she was little—a desire she feels God planted in her heart. Is there a dream you've held close for many years?

3. Even though Nate is grown, he still hears his father's harsh words telling him that he's dumb and a failure. In the story, what helps him move past them? Are there hurtful words from your past that you've internalized? What are some ways you can put these voices to rest?

4. Early in the story Mary says to Elsie, "I'm never serene. I'm bubbly and feisty like your beloved geysers." If you were to describe yourself in Yellowstone terms, which would you choose?
   a. Bubbly and feisty like a geyser
   b. Calm and serene like Yellowstone Lake on a sunny day
   c. Strong and stubborn like a bison
   d. Playful and mischievous like a raccoon kit
   e. Temperamental and explosive like a mud pot
   f. Loving and fiercely protective like a mama grizzly
   g. _____ and _____ like a _____ (fill in your own).

5. Elsie's parents believe that the key to love and happiness is found in Matthew 7:12 which says, "Therefore, whatever you want men to do to you, do also to them, for this is the Law and the Prophets (NKJV)." Do you believe this command can be applied to marriage? What does that look like?

6. Early on, Mary and Rose seemed to think that Teddy was Elsie's perfect match. Why didn't things work out between them? Do you think her parents' teaching played into her decision? What was it about Nate that Elsie preferred?

7. Were you surprised to discover the arsonist's identity? When you first started reading, who did you think it was going to be and why?

8. Throughout the story, Rose is showing symptoms of depression, but her friends don't take it seriously. Mary even says, "How long will she mope?" Do you have a close friend or family member who struggles with depression or anxiety? Have you dealt with these issues in your own life? Were you able to get help? How has our understanding of depression changed since Rose's time?

9. Elsie's relationship with her cousin Graham is tenuous at best. Her mother tells her, "Forgiveness isn't earned. It's bestowed." Is there someone in your life you've struggled to forgive? How did you get to the point where you could "bestow" forgiveness on that person? Or have you?

10. It's not until after Elsie has granted forgiveness that she learns about Graham's kissing adventures. Do you think she was wrong in

forgiving him? What do you do when someone you've forgiven stumbles again?

11. The cones of the lodgepole pine are *serotinous,* a scientific term meaning they don't open unless conditions are right. For this species, they only release their seeds after fire melts their thick coat of pitch. Ranger Brookes compares the cone to our lives as Christians. There are many references to fire in Scripture, but these are some of my favorites. Can you think of how the story of the lodgepole pine is similar? How is it different?

a. Beloved, do not think it strange concerning the fiery trial which is to try you, as though some strange thing happened to you; but rejoice to the extent that you partake of Christ's sufferings, that when His glory is revealed, you may also be glad with exceeding joy. (1 Peter 4:12–13, NKJV)

b. I will bring the one-third through the fire,
Will refine them as silver is refined,
And test them as gold is tested.
They will call on My name,
And I will answer them.
I will say, "This is My people";
And each one will say, "The LORD is my God." (Zechariah 13:9, NKJV)

c. When you pass through the waters, I will be with you;
And through the rivers, they shall not overflow you.
When you walk through the fire, you shall not be burned,
Nor shall the flame scorch you. (Isaiah 43:2, NKJV)

ACKNOWLEDGMENTS

It's said that writing a novel is a bit like eating an elephant—you take it one bite at a time. Just like any other feast, I think a meal is best when shared. Here are a few folks who helped me get this task done.

Thank you to the amazing folks at Yellowstone National Park for assisting me with research. Archivist Anne Foster and librarian Jackie Jerla patiently guided me through their massive collection and managed not to laugh when I acted like a kid at the world's biggest candy store. Thank you also to Alicia Murphy, Yellowstone National Park historian, for answering questions and reading scenes.

Thanks also to the following individuals:

- KyLee Woodley for sharing her expertise—and her heart—regarding dyslexia, reading, and education.
- Kate Yakis, who served on a helitack crew during the devastating 1988 Yellowstone fires, for sharing her experiences and knowledge.
- To my brother and sister-in-law Mark Dunmire and Helen Cohen for advice on all things Brooklyn.
- My incredible critique group, Heidi Gaul, Marilyn Rhoads, and Christian Suzann Nelson.
- My agent, Rachel Kent, who loves Yellowstone with a passion.
- And, of course, all the great folks at WaterBrook for helping me to spin stories set in these fantastic places: Shannon Marchese, Lissa Halls Johnson, Jamie Lapeyrolerie, Chelsea Woodward, Mark Ford, Pamela Shoup, and so many others. You're the best!

And as always, I couldn't do this without my ever-patient family who puts up with late nights, missed meals, research trips, and all sorts of nonsense so I can pursue this writing dream. Steve, Andrew, Bethany—I love you more than words can express.

Ready for more adventures through National Parks?

Travel to Mount Rainier and Yosemite!

Find out more at www.waterbrookmultnomah.com